This Land,
This Love

This Land, This Love

Linda Sole

St. Martin's Press ❧ New York

FIC
SOLE
L

Library of Congress Cataloging-in-Publication Data

Sole, Linda.
    This land, this love / Linda Sole.
      p.   cm.
    ISBN 0-312-18195-7
    I. Title.
    PR6069.038T48   1998
    823'.914—dc21   97-51166
                                         CIP

First published in Great Britain by Judy Piatkus (Publishers) Ltd

First U.S. Edition: April 1998

10 9 8 7 6 5 4 3 2 1

For my husband, with love

A Message for my Readers

Over the years I heard so many stories about Grandfather Sole that he became a giant of a man in my mind and I was inspired to create the character of Aden Sawle. Aden is not Grandfather Sole of course and the story is a complete fiction – except for one incident. Grandfather Sole did fight and beat the gipsies singlehanded, but his reason for doing so and whether there were three or thirty of them has been lost in the mists of time and legend.

I hope you will enjoy reading this story as much as I enjoyed creating it.

This Land,
This Love

Part One
A Girl's Dreams

1

Dusk was falling fast, enveloping the land, shrouding it in a blanket of velvet darkness, gradually taking it from her sight, piece by piece. She strained to see across the low-lying fields, seeking out the familiar places she knew so well, but tears misted her eyes and she knew that she was remembering rather than seeing. The words he had spoken all those years ago kept running through her mind, over and over again until she thought she would go mad or die of grief.

'This land ... this land is ours. Never forget that. It may break our hearts and our bodies at times but always, always, we hold to the land ...'

It wasn't the land that had broken their hearts, though, it was other things: pain and grief ... and betrayal.

She raised her head proudly, dashing away the stupid tears. She had brought them to ruin with her pride and her dreams ... dreams she now saw as the foolish yearnings of a lonely, naive girl.

Well, she had reaped a bitter harvest. Much of the land was gone, as were the riches he had heaped at her feet in the days when he had loved her. She had killed that love, little by little, drop by drop – and now there was nothing left.

It had all gone: money, love, laughter – and the man she needed, needed so much that her body ached for the loss of him.

All gone. All but these few acres. Somehow – no matter what it cost her – she would save at least this land for her children then perhaps ... but there was no hope of more. It was over, finished. She had driven him away with her coldness and her silence, – and the pain was almost more than she could bear.

Pain and regret for what might have been if only ... but tears would not help her now, nor would memories. She had to be strong, she had to hold on to what was left, but just this once she would let herself remember the way it had been at the beginning. So many years had passed but she could remember that morning as if it were only yesterday; it was vivid and real in her mind ... as if it were happening now.

The rooms above The Cottrel Arms were low-ceilinged and rather dark. Rebecca walked into the parlour and frowned as she saw her father was not there. She'd thought she'd heard him come up earlier, but he must have gone back to the taproom almost at once; they'd be busy downstairs.

Jack Cottrel was the landlord of the popular inn, which was why he seldom had time to spend with his daughter – why she sometimes felt as if she hardly knew him. She sighed and was about to turn away when she heard the sound of laughter in the yard below and went to look out of the window. What was going on down there?

Market day had brought the sleepy little town to life. Nestling at the edge of low-lying fenland, Chatteris shimmered that morning in a haze of warm sunlight. It was one of those wonderful spring days when the air is filled with the scents of blossom and petals drift sweetly on the breeze, skipping and dancing along the pavements. There was a buzz of excitement in the yard, which was bustling with people dressed in their second-best clothes (the best were of course kept for Sundays and church). On market days, everyone who could came swarming in from the surrounding villages and isolated farms, eager to spend their money at the market stalls, and for a break from the routine of their lives.

A man had just brought in a waggon drawn by a team of two perfectly matched horses. Their grey coats shone as though they had been thoroughly groomed that morning, their tails hanging in bunches of burnished silk strands; they were good horses, strong and powerful – like the man who drove them. Something about this particular man made Rebecca look more closely at him.

He stood talking for a moment after he had handed the waggon over to a groom, his black hair glinting in the sunlight with the sheen of a bird's wing. He was tall and his laughter had a warm, infectious quality as it floated up to her through the open window. Then he glanced up and she saw the weathered complexion of a man used to spending his life outdoors. He seemed to sense her watching him and grinned at her, obviously finding her curiosity amusing.

She drew back from the window as if she had been stung, her heart pounding. What did he find so funny? His laughter rang out again several times, then became lost in the general cacophony from the streets and the cattle market pens beyond: grunting, blaring and cackling blended with the rattle of wheels on cobblestones. She could no longer pick out the sound of his laughter. How ridiculous! For a moment his smile had disturbed her, rousing her from her reverie, but it was forgotten as her father came into the room and began to speak.

'So there you are. Finished your unpacking then?'

'No, not yet.' She smiled at him. 'I was just getting used to things again.'

'It will be strange for a start. Bound to be.' His thick brows met in the middle. 'You could always ask your friend to stay if you're afraid of being lonely.'

She had returned to her home that spring morning of 1890 after spending a year at a finishing school in Switzerland with her friend Celia – the pretty, charming but sometimes spoiled daughter of Lord Charles Braithewaite. It was Celia's father who had persuaded Rebecca's to let her have that last, very expensive year of schooling and she should have been grateful, but was not, because it had only made her more aware of the differences between her prospects and those of her friend.

She blinked hard, fighting the surge of emotion her father's thoughtfulness had evoked. 'Celia will be too busy to come. Besides ...' Lord Braithewaite would not consider their home a suitable place for his daughter to stay, but she could not hurt her father's feelings by saying so openly. 'I'm sure I shall find enough to ...'

The words died on her lips as she turned to see the figure standing in the doorway behind her. It was the man from the yard, and close to he was even more disturbing than he had seemed from a distance.

'Father,' her heart jerked oddly, 'someone has come to see you.'

He had left instructions that no one was to come up but the barmaid must have let this man through, which was a little surprising considering Dotty Prentice's sharp tongue. She usually had no difficulty in keeping customers in their place, even when they had had a few drinks too many.

'Oh, it's you, Aden,' Jack said, and his frown eased as he swung round. 'I told Dotty we weren't to be disturbed. Rebecca has just come home from school.' His gaze rested on her. 'This is Aden Sawle – a farmer from Mepal. His mother and yours were friends years ago.'

She sensed a reluctance in him; he seemed to welcome the man and yet be wary of him at the same time.

Aden Sawle studied her in silence for a moment, bringing a faint flush to her cheeks. 'Pleased to meet you, Miss Cottrel,' he said at last. 'You'll be glad to be home, I dare say?'

'Mr Sawle.'

Rebecca inclined her head. She wasn't sure that she was pleased to meet him. His dark eyes seemed to intrude into her thoughts and he was clearly amused by what he read – or sensed – about her feelings towards him.

'You may as well stop now you're here, Aden. Rebecca has some unpacking to finish.' Her father spoke as the silence became awkward.

She had been given her cue and took it thankfully. This farmer was altogether too sure of himself! As she passed him she caught a sharp woody smell mixed with body musk. Her stomach tightened and she drew her skirt away, giving him a look she had learned from a rather haughty mistress at the school in Switzerland. It was meant to put him firmly in his place but his mouth quirked at the corners and laughter lurked deep in those velvet dark eyes.

Then the door closed behind her, muffling the sound of the men's voices as she walked along the gloomy passage to her own room. Her pulses were racing and she was annoyed. How dared Aden Sawle come up uninvited – and what right had he to look at her in that way? He was passably good-looking, she supposed, but arrogant and conceited – a most unpleasant creature!

Safe in her own room, Rebecca closed the door and leaned against it to catch her breath. Her heart was still beating much too fast and her skin felt hot.

She moved away from the door, glancing without enthusiasm at the trunks waiting to be unpacked. Now that she was back in the private rooms above her father's inn in the small, sleepy Cambridgeshire town, she had begun to miss her friends and to realize that it was unlikely she would see much of them in future.

From now on Celia's life would be full of society dinners, dances and handsome men, while hers would be – what?

When they had first met at their boarding school both girls had been feeling lonely, away from home for the first time and floundering like fish in shallow water as they attempted to settle in. Because they were both newcomers, and because Celia had been a shy, vulnerable girl in need of someone to lean on, their friendship had become stronger than most – the kind that endures. For the past few years they had scarcely been out of each other's company, so perhaps it wasn't surprising that Rebecca was missing her friend.

'Father is determined that I shall marry well,' Celia had told her with a sigh as they travelled home to England under the watchful eye of the chaperone Lord Braithewaite had sent to fetch them. 'All I want is to be happy, Rebecca. I want to fall in love with a handsome, charming who will love and cherish me.'

'At least you will have the chance to meet lots of men,' Rebecca had replied, feeling a pang of envy. 'I shan't meet anyone at home. Father is always too busy to take me anywhere.'

'You could come to us for the summer. My mother would be pleased to have you – you might even meet someone and fall in love.'

The offer was so tempting that Rebecca knew a moment of intense longing – a longing she hastily suppressed.

'My father wants me home …'

It would be useless to ask if she could stay with Celia for the summer. Her father had been reluctant to let her have that last year in Switzerland and from the tone of his recent letters she'd sensed that he had regretted giving way to Lord Braithewaite's persuasion.

'I'm a plain-spoken man,' he'd told her just before she left to join her friend at the school. 'I sent you to boarding school after your mother died because I had no choice. But don't lose sight of who and what you are, Rebecca. I'm Jack Cottrel, a publican, businessman and councillor – and don't you forget it. Your mother was a vicar's daughter and we're decent folk, worth a bob or two, but not gentry. Not like those fancy friends of yours.'

During the years of her friendship with Celia she had often stayed at the Braithewaites' home and despite her father's warning, Rebecca's head had undoubtedly been turned. She had for a while allowed herself to dream of a different life, but now she was home and back to earth with a bump.

7

She glanced round the large bedroom, which was crammed with dark oak, newish but rather ponderous furniture, Staffordshire pottery figures and several engravings of dogs and horses (mostly from pictures by Landseer, who was said to be a favourite of Queen Victoria and very fashionable), and compared it unfavourably with the elegance of Braithewaite Hall: there the best of many centuries combined to give the rooms a charm and stylishness that put her own home to shame.

This must stop at once! It was wrong and foolish and she was ashamed of her own thoughts. Her father had always made it plain that he wanted her home when she was eighteen and in a way she was glad to be back. She was grateful for the advantages she had been given and she loved her father – it was just that she could not imagine how she would fill her time.

Both the inn and the private rooms were kept clean by a woman who came in every other morning to scrub and polish, and her father's food was cooked by Eileen Henderson, who also did the cooking for the customers on market day and Saturdays. Eileen had taken over in the kitchen soon after Rebecca's mother had died, and The Cottrel Arms was popular with the people from neighbouring villages; they came to shop at the market and stayed to eat at The Arms before returning home.

At school Rebecca had discovered that she had a talent for cooking. She had suggested to her father that when she came home she might help Eileen in the kitchens but he had immediately squashed the idea.

'You're Jack Cottrel's daughter,' he'd told her with a flash of pride. 'There's no need for you to work. Eileen will take you along to some of the women's meetings at the hall – and there's always something needed for the church. You'll find enough to do, Rebecca, don't you worry.'

It all sounded so dull! The past year had been exciting and Rebecca's head was filled with pictures of glorious scenery: vast mountains, sweeping valleys and deep, pale lakes that sparkled in a cool, clear sunlight; of midnight feasts in the dormitories and all the plans that Celia and the other girls had made for balls and parties. On their return home her friends would be swept up in a whirl of excitement but she was faced with endless, empty days. If only she could think of something worthwhile … something that would stretch her mind a little. Perhaps marriage?

She had a very clear picture in her mind of the man she wanted to marry – an intelligent, cultured man with good manners and a gentle nature, someone who would cherish and spoil her. Or did she imagine him that way because Celia had described the man of her dreams to her so many times?

If she did marry it certainly wouldn't be to anyone like that arrogant farmer she had met a few moments ago!

Rebecca glanced at her reflection in the dressing mirror. Her heavy, reddish-brown hair was drawn back into a neat pleat at the nape of her neck, her complexion was creamy but not pale and delicate like Celia's, her mouth was full – perhaps a little too wide? – and her eyes grey. She was not ugly but certainly no beauty – yet there was nothing in her appearance to amuse Mr Sawle, was there?

No, she thought not. It was simply his tiresome manner and she would not allow it to upset her.

It was an hour or so later when she saw her father again and was immediately aware of a brooding anger beneath the surface.

'Is something wrong?' she asked. 'Have I displeased you in some way?'

'You?' Jack Cottrel glanced at her and sighed, reaching up to ruffle his wiry greying hair. 'No, it's not you, Rebecca. It was that young rogue earlier. He had the cheek to threaten ...'

'Are you speaking of Mr Sawle?' she asked as the words died on his lips and his expression became severe. She was surprised at his change of attitude. He had seemed to approve of the farmer, to welcome him ... though she had noticed a certain wariness towards him.

'Aye, that's the one. He tried to push me into – well, I told him straight. I've finished with him. He's no longer welcome here. You're to have nothing to do with him, Rebecca. Do you hear me? I won't have the rascal in my pub or my home.'

'I'm not likely to want anything to do with him. I don't know Mr Sawle and I don't wish to.'

'Good. You're a sensible lass. He's a rogue and a scoundrel, though a charming one, I'll admit.' Jack's eyes narrowed, his normally good-humoured features becoming harsh as his thick brows drew together. 'Let's forget him. I've news for you, Rebecca. Eileen has offered to take you to one of her meetings tomorrow afternoon. It's naught but a bit of gossip and a cup of tea, but you'll make friends – and you can ask any of your school friends to stay whenever you like.'

'Thank you.' Rebecca's eyes were misty as she leaned forward to kiss his cheek. His skin was slightly rough and he smelt of ale and spirits, though he drank little himself. 'Don't worry, Father. I'm finding it a bit strange at the moment but I'll settle down soon.'

'I hope so, Rebecca. I hope so ...'

He sighed and looked anxious as he left the room, leaving her to wonder what had so suddenly turned him against the impudent Mr Sawle.

It did not matter. She had other, more important things to concern her. Aden Sawle was nothing to her and she would think of him no more. She would not allow herself to wonder what kind of man he was or what he could have done to upset her father.

It had not been light when Aden left the drugging warmth of his feather bed that morning. He had splashed cold water over his face and body to sharpen his wits, towelling himself down vigorously. He needed to be alert, to keep his wits about him when he saw Jack Cottrel later – because he was going to do it: he'd made up his mind.

He stood at the landing window for a moment, looking out at the yard and the fields he could see stretching away behind him. Five Winds was an odd name for the farm but when he'd asked his father about it once he'd been told it had been named by his grandfather.

'You see the fifth wind is destiny,' his father explained with a wry smile. 'And a man rides the fifth wind at his peril.'

Downstairs in the kitchen the range was still warm. Aden raked up the fire and filled a kettle ready for his return, knowing that he would have no time once his chores were done – not if he wanted to drive the waggon into Chatteris before the cattle market got under way.

It was a clear, fresh morning. Outside in the yard he caught the sharp tang of cow dung and straw from a heap of manure behind the cattle sheds. He was filled with a sense of purpose as he carried water to the drinking troughs then brought in his herd of eight milking cows. After today he might be in a position to double the size of the herd and take on a lad to help him with the chores.

10

His brief service in the army as an officer's batman had opened Aden's eyes; there was another way to live and he had no intention of being poor all his life. Money was the key to freedom, he'd learned that from watching the sons of gentlemen rise through the ranks. In war there might have been a chance for someone like him to earn promotion but in peacetime it had not been possible. He didn't have the right background and his speech held him back. There was no real future for him in the army, though he believed he might have made a good officer if he'd been given the chance. Now, though, he was back home and things were about to change for the better.

The cows came to his call, their udders heavy with the rich, creamy milk that came from years of good husbandry. The Sawles were smallholders scraping a living from their few acres but they were known for being hardworking folk. The land had broken their backs and drained all their energy for generations, but Aden was determined not to let it crush him. He wanted more from life and he believed he knew how to get it.

Aden's expression was thoughtful as he watched the faces of the people thronging the streets of the little market town, sensing the atmosphere of excitement and anticipation. He knew most of them by sight and was on nodding terms with several, because his father had brought him into town on Saturdays when he was a lad and it was a small, friendly community.

'Morning, Aden,' a local farmer called to him. 'Lovely day for it.'

'Good day for drilling,' he responded. 'Morning, Mrs Bristow.'

The farmer's wife dimpled at him. Aden was generally liked. Tall, black-haired, with a healthy outdoor complexion and an infectious smile, he had been known to set a few female hearts fluttering.

Aden drove on unaware of the momentary excitement he had aroused in her breast, his mind fixed on more important matters.

Both his parents were now buried in the little churchyard in Mepal. Amos Sawle had died some nine months back, just two years after his wife had been taken in childbed – her baby, a stillborn daughter, was lying beside her in her coffin. Hester Sawle had been in her fortieth year, and, as all the prophets of doom had forecast, too old for childbearing.

It was his father's death which had brought Aden home to take over the farm that was both his living and a rod for his back. But not for much longer; if he had his way, things were going to improve!

The cattle market sale was just about to begin as he drove the waggon into the yard at the back of The Cottrel Arms and handed the reins over to a cheeky, freckle-faced youth.

'Wotcher doin' Aden? Come to drink us dry then?'

'Just you watch it,' he said, and laughed as the lad grinned in response. 'You need a spell in the army, my lad – that'll straighten you out, make a man of you.'

'Wot's it like then?' The lad wiped his nose on the sleeve of his patched jacket. 'I've always fancied bein' a sailor – girl in every port …'

Aden laughed again and winked at him. 'Why not a girl in every town? The army move you around the country a bit in peacetime.'

The lad chuckled as he began to lead Aden's waggon away. Aden was still laughing as he glanced up, his attention caught by a flash of white at the upper windows of the inn. A young woman was standing there watching him – she was rather attractive from what he could see, and disapproving by her expression. He smiled to himself as he walked towards the inn. He'd known a few lasses in his time but not quite as many as he'd hinted to the groom just now.

He liked to drink at The Arms after unloading his produce for the market. It was convenient, a meeting place where he could exchange news and gossip with friends – and he had known Jack for years. Threading his way through the packed taproom, he saw people he knew, nodding to them and smiling easily as he approached the bar.

'Pint of the usual, Aden?'

The barmaid gave him a saucy look. Dotty had an eye for him. Recently she'd hinted that she was free on Sunday afternoons but he hadn't taken her up on her invitation yet, though he was tempted. She was a pretty girl was Dotty, with blue eyes, curly brown hair and a slight upturn to her pert nose. Nice, trim figure, too.

'Jack around by any chance?'

'Upstairs. Rebecca came home from school this morning.'

He nodded in understanding: she must have been the woman watching him from the window overlooking the yard.

Aden paid for his drink, took a swallow and wiped his mouth with the back of his hand. He had large brown hands, the palms calloused from work, nails clean but broken. 'That's good, Dotty.' He jerked his head towards the stairs that led to the Cottrel's private living quarters. 'Do you think Jack would mind if I went up? There's something I want to ask him.'

'Well ...' She looked doubtful, her eyes losing some of their sparkle as she realized he wasn't in the mood for chatting. 'He did say as he wasn't to be disturbed. Still, seeing as it's you ...'

'Thanks.' Aden finished his drink and gave her a brilliant smile as a reward for letting him through. 'See you later, Dotty.'

'Promises!' she replied, and arched her brows.

He grinned to himself. She'd been hinting about the harvest dance for weeks and he knew she was hoping he would ask her. Well, maybe he would and maybe he wouldn't.

The dance was the last thing on his mind as he walked up the steep wooden stairs. There was a good-sized parcel of parish land coming up for letting by tender. It was across the road from the farm he'd inherited from his father, and Aden wanted it. The extra acres would enable him to live decently instead of scratching an existence from the soil as his father and grandfather had done before him. It was the first step on his way up the ladder.

There were ways of fixing a tender to make sure of getting it. Jack could do it if he wanted and he owed Aden a few favours. Maybe it wasn't exactly legal but it wouldn't be the first time it had been done. He was sure Jack would see it his way. Even if he didn't, it was worth a try. Aden needed that land and he was determined to get it, one way or another.

2

The weather continued fine and warm for a few days and Rebecca was able to get out, to go for long walks down pleasant country lanes where the hedgerows smelled sweetly of lilac and blossom. She gathered wild flowers and pressed them between the pages of her Bible, cooked special cakes and biscuits for her father and rearranged the parlour several times. Gradually, she was becoming accustomed to the slower pace of life. It wasn't always easy but she had her books and her needlework – and Eileen Henderson had gone out of her way to be friendly.

Eileen was a pretty, soft-spoken woman with fine pale hair and a well-rounded figure. Her husband was the local butcher and reputedly not as pleasant as his wife, though Rebecca had always found him civil. From little things Eileen said, though, she guessed he was a jealous man and could be violent.

'Frank has never liked me working at The Arms,' Eileen had confided once when they were on their way to a meeting at the church hall. 'But we've no children and there's never enough for me to do at home. I've put my foot down over it and that's that.'

There was something a little odd in her tone then but it didn't really register with Rebecca. She was more interested in the bazaar they were planning to help raise money for the church restoration fund.

'I could make cakes and jam,' she said as they entered the hall. 'Cooking is one of the more useful things they taught us at school.'

'Are you missing it all very much?' Eileen asked. 'Jack worries about you, Rebecca. He's afraid you won't settle after the life you've led.'

14

'You've helped me,' Rebecca replied, smiling. The older woman had taken her about with her, introducing her to her own friends and other young women she might not otherwise have met. 'If I seem restless it's because ... well, I do like to be busy.'

They were entering the hall as Eileen would have spoken again and someone called Rebecca's name. She turned to find herself staring into the blushing, eager face of the curate. He had been attentive to her from the very first time she'd attended a meeting at the church hall, drawing her into long, meaningful discussions whenever he got the chance.

'Mr Bently,' she said, and smiled. 'Did you want something?'

'It's so good of you to come. I was hoping I might interest you in joining a committee? It's for an overseas mission to the poor of India and we need new ideas for raising money ...'

'Now that sounds just what you were looking for, Rebecca,' Eileen said. 'Excuse me, I must speak to Mrs Jones for a moment.'

Her desertion was annoying but predictable. The curate was in his early-twenties, presentable and pleasant enough in his own way. His attentions had been quite marked and from remarks her father had made over the past week or so Rebecca believed that both he and Eileen thought Robert Bently might make her a suitable husband. She herself suspected it was only a matter of time before Mr Bently spoke his mind on the matter. His prospects were not exactly good but Jack Cottrel was a wealthy man and no doubt something could be arranged. Rebecca did not believe her father's wealth to be Mr Bently's only consideration but sensed it was a factor: she would make a good wife for a man of the church who could never expect to earn more than a small stipend.

He was the only suitable young man she had met since her return from school who had shown the slightest interest in her, but for the moment she was not ready to commit herself either way. She thought it might be a fulfilling life to be involved in the welfare of the community and devoted to good works but a part of her still hankered for something more exciting.

She had that morning received a letter from Celia asking her once again if she would go and stay with her. Perhaps this time she would show it to her father, though she doubted he would agree to the visit.

'Your life is here,' he had told her. 'You'd best make up your mind to it, Rebecca.'

He was right, of course, but it was easier said than done. She needed something more to occupy her time but she wasn't sure what – nor did she understand why she was so often restless. She ought to be satisfied with her life, it was the one she had been born to, but she could not help the vague feelings of discontent that plagued her now and then.

Surely they would go in time?

It was a blazingly hot August morning when Rebecca met Aden Sawle as she was walking back from the market, her basket heavy with the eggs and fruit she had purchased. She was feeling the heat and wanting to be inside in the cool, so when a man planted himself directly in her path, preventing her from walking on, she felt a surge of annoyance.

'Good day, Miss Cottrel,' he said, removing his cap to push back his thick, springy black hair. The sweat glistened on his forehead and she was aware of something threateningly masculine about him, something that challenged and yet intrigued her. She noticed an earthy smell about him that made her think of fresh-cut straw. 'Been to the market then?'

'It would seem obvious.' She remembered her father had forbidden her to have anything to do with him and gave him a frosty stare. 'I should like to pass, if you please.'

For a moment his eyes defied her, as if he would somehow force her to acknowledge him as more than a casual acquaintance, then they dropped away and she walked on into the taproom of The Arms. It was empty apart from Dotty, who was leaning on her elbows and looking bored. She raised her head as Rebecca approached, eyes narrowed and hostile.

Rebecca was momentarily taken aback. Why was the girl staring at her like that? They had never exactly been friends but she'd thought they got on tolerably well.

Dotty was a plump, pretty girl with curling hair and a sulky mouth. That day she was wearing a full red dress with a dipping neckline that revealed more than a glimpse of her breasts. There was a strong, sickly odour of perfume mixed with sweat emanating from her and her bodice was wet in places.

'Hot, ain't it?'

'Very warm,' Rebecca agreed, feeling sweat trickling down her own back. 'My clothes are sticking to me.'

'Was that Aden Sawle I saw you talking to just now? Didn't

know you two was friends ...'

Dotty had obviously been watching from the window and misread what she had seen.

'You saw him accost me,' Rebecca replied. 'He's not a man I would choose to speak with, however.'

'Aden's all right,' Dotty said, a spark of interest in her eyes. 'He's not a bad sort – and he'll be a rich man one day.'

'What makes you say that?'

'He put in a tender for some council land they were hiring and got it. There were a dozen or more in for them fifty acres – makes you think, don't it?' She gave Rebecca a significant look. 'I thought you'd know – with your pa being on the council?' Her expression was calculating, bordering on insulting, as if implying something underhand.

'We don't discuss parish business.'

'Aden don't drink here no more. Strange, ain't it?' She leered at Rebecca, challenging her. 'He was always in here market days, regular as clockwork.'

'That's his affair.'

Rebecca went past her and up the stairs. Something in Dotty's green eyes made her wonder if she knew more than she was saying ... but her father didn't even like Aden Sawle. He would never have ... even if it were possible ... no, of course not! Jack Cottrel would never help anyone fix a tender for council land. It was both morally and legally wrong – though possible, she supposed.

Rebecca dismissed the idea as ridiculous, but all the same, couldn't help remembering how angry her father had been the day Aden Sawle had come to their home uninvited.

Aden scowled as he walked past the pub to collect his money from the auctioneer in the market. She was a right stuck up miss, that Rebecca Cottrel! He was annoyed with himself for having behaved like any green youth: it *was* obvious she'd been to the market and if he'd hoped to capture her attention he should have thought of something more interesting to say. Not that he wanted much to do with Jack's daughter, of course.

'Well then, Aden Sawle, ain't you the stranger!'

He blinked as he looked down into Dotty's bright eyes. Lost in his thoughts he hadn't seen her there.

'Where did you come from?'

17

'Jack let me go early seein' as we weren't busy. He says it's the weather keeping folks home.'

'Happen he's right. I'll be glad to get home myself.'

Dotty shuffled her feet, hovering just in front of him so that he couldn't walk on without pushing her aside. She was smiling flirtatiously, her lashes fluttering against rosy cheeks.

'You don't drink at The Arms these days,' she said. 'Fell out with me, 'ave you?'

'Not with you, Dotty.' He eyed the girl. She was a tempting armful and clearly more than willing. 'I'm too busy to drink much since I got that extra land.'

'Done all right for yourself!' Dotty's eyes were warm with admiration. 'You're the clever one, Aden Sawle. There were a dozen or more in for that land.'

Her words were like balm to his wounded pride. She wasn't ashamed of making her feelings plain – no more was he. To hell with the Cottrels!

'Are you going to the harvest dance then?'

Her eyes lit with sudden excitement. 'Are you asking, Aden Sawle?'

'Why not? If you're not already promised ...'

'I've been waiting for the right offer,' she said, her mouth soft and provocative. 'You know where I live. I'll expect a spray of roses and you can fetch me from the house. I'm not meeting you there.'

'Know what you want, don't you?' He laughed. 'The word is corsage, Dotty. All the officers' ladies had them at their dances.'

'Oh, la, la,' she trilled, pouting her red lips at him. 'Ain't you the posh one then? Don't you be late, Aden Sawle!' Giggling, she ran past him and down the street.

He watched her go, noticing the froth of lace petticoats beneath her full skirts. That told him something about her. Fancy petticoats under a working dress: Dotty Prentice was a hot little piece and no mistake!

Whistling, he made his way to where his horse was contentedly chewing at its nosebag and unhitched the reins from the rail. Why should he bother his head over Jack Cottrel or his uppity daughter? Maybe he had gone a bit far that day in Jack's parlour, implying that he might tell Frank Henderson about Jack's affair with his wife ... he wouldn't have done it, of course. It had just been annoyance because Jack turned him down without a fair hearing.

It wasn't as if Jack was whiter than white himself. There *had* been something going on between him and Aden's mother years ago. Aden had seen them kissing in the pub yard. His father would have killed Jack if he'd known but Aden hadn't told him. He reckoned Jack owed him something for that …

To hell with him! Aden was young, heartfree – and that extra land was going to make all the difference. He had plans for the future. Plans that might include Dotty, who was an obliging sort of girl, but definitely didn't include Rebecca Cottrel … or was he kidding himself?

His mouth twisted ruefully as he admitted to himself that he was more than a little interested in Jack's daughter. If things had been different he might have gone courting her. It was too late now, though.

'Bloody fool, that's what you are!'

He laughed as he climbed up on the waggon. Best put such thoughts out of his head before they got him into trouble.

Rebecca forgot about Dotty and the arrogant farmer, finding a place to sit and read for most of the afternoon, though even her favourite books were unable to hold her attention for long. She had no idea why she felt so restless but somehow she just couldn't settle. She kept thinking about Celia, wondering what she was doing – and whether she had found the man of her dreams yet.

It was a long, dull afternoon and another lonely evening loomed ahead so when her father announced after dinner that they were going to the harvest dance, she was surprised.

'Isn't that this weekend?'

'Yes – why?'

'I would have bought a new dress if I'd known. I didn't think you would go. You haven't been for years, have you?'

'That's no reason I shouldn't start now. I thought you might enjoy it?' He looked hard at her. 'You must have plenty of clothes. I've paid for enough this past year.'

'I have one that might do …'

It was a pink velvet evening dress she'd had made the previous Christmas when she'd gone to a dance with Celia. It wasn't really suitable for a country affair but there was no time to make or even buy a new one so it would have to do. Besides, her father had seemed in such a mood lately that she didn't want to ask for more money.

'I'll get someone in to look after the bar,' he said. 'You'll enjoy it when you get there. You never know who you might meet.'

'Is Eileen going?'

'Yes – yes, I think so.' His eyes slid away from hers. 'She suggested that I should take you.'

Rebecca didn't particularly want to go, even though it would make a change from sitting alone in the parlour. Years before when her mother was alive she had been taken to the dance by her parents; it was a noisy, boisterous affair with children running around and the men gathered down one end drinking beer half the night. Her expensive dancing lessons wouldn't be of much use to her there but she couldn't refuse to go. Her father had made up his mind. Anyway, it might be fun.

She might even meet someone interesting.

The hall was swarming with excited people when they arrived that Saturday night. No one had thought to open the windows and it was very hot, the air thick with heavy perfumes, hair pomade and a faint undertone of mothballs emanating from clothes that were seldom worn and had been brought out for the occasion. It made the atmosphere oppressive in the crowded room and Rebecca was immediately aware of a slight headache, which she tried to suppress. Her father had made an effort for her benefit and she must repay him by at least looking as if she was enjoying herself.

A waltz was being played by the little group of musicians but apart from a few 'engaged' couples no one was dancing. Everyone was more interested in gossiping and chatting to friends they had met, the women ignoring their children as they ran wild around the room and the men arguing over their beer. Jack walked straight to a row of chairs occupied by Eileen and some of her friends, then glanced at the bar.

'Anything for you, Eileen? Rebecca?'

'No, thank you, Jack.' Eileen smiled up at him. 'Perhaps later.'

Rebecca was aware of something between them at that moment. It was a look or a slight softening of her father's voice: clearly he liked Eileen a lot but then, they had known each other for years – so why shouldn't he?

Rebecca sat beside Eileen, watching the dancers a little wistfully and wishing she knew more people – girls of her own age with brothers who might ask her to be their partner. The previous

Christmas she'd danced with several interesting young men. Celia had made certain that her brother asked her to stand up with him twice. Philip was the heir to his father's title and two years older than his sister. He was a terrible flirt but Celia had warned Rebecca and she had known better than to take him seriously. The Braithewaites had plans for their only son, plans which would not include marriage to a girl like her – a girl whose father ran a public house.

The Braithewaites had accepted her because Celia had made it plain that she was fond of her, but Rebecca had always known that they thought her a little beneath them socially. Here at this local dance she was set apart from the other young people because she had been away and they thought her different. For a moment she wished that she had never gone away, perhaps then she would have known where she belonged.

'Miss Cottrel.' She glanced up as the curate hovered shyly in front of her. 'May I have the honour? I mean, would you ... if it isn't too much trouble?'

Rebecca believed it was only his shyness that had kept him from speaking to her before this. If she wanted an offer from him she would have to encourage him, to lead him into it gently, but for the moment she preferred things as they were.

'I should like very much to dance with you, Mr Bently,' she said and stood up. 'Thank you.'

She gave him her hand for the military two-step. To her surprise he was an excellent dancer and executed the intricate steps with flair. She was sorry when the music ended and he escorted her back to her seat.

'Perhaps another dance later?' he asked diffidently.

'I shall look forward to it.'

She watched him walk away and found herself wishing they could have gone on dancing together as the engaged couples did, but that would have caused too much gossip. Unless she was seriously thinking of becoming a curate's wife, two dances during the evening were all she dare accept.

'Such a pleasant young man – and a good dancer,' Eileen observed with a satisfied smile. 'Don't you agree?'

'Yes, surprisingly good.'

Rebecca let her gaze stray round the large room with its cream-painted walls and chairs placed strategically at each end. She caught sight of Dotty. She was wearing a red silky dress with lots of frills and had a spray of white roses pinned to her shoulder. It suited her, making her look voluptuous and very much a woman. She was laughing, obviously having a wonderful time, and several men were watching her – some of them married. Rebecca envied her a little, then gasped as she realized who Dotty was actually with that evening.

She had never seen Aden Sawle in a suit before. His usual attire was a pair of worn cords with buckled leggings, boots, waistcoat and shirt sleeves rolled up to his elbows. Tonight he looked quite distinguished, almost elegant. At this distance he could be mistaken for a gentleman: of course the illusion would be shattered as soon as he spoke. There was nothing refined about him, though he wasn't coarse either.

He had become aware of her scrutiny and turned his head. Their eyes met and held and Rebecca's heart raced. She was the first to look away. That straight stare of his had unsettled her. She hoped he wouldn't ask her for a dance: it would be too embarrassing.

'Miss Cottrel. May I ask for this dance?'

She glanced up, surprised as she recognized the man who had spoken. Henry Barker was in his forties, a widower with two small children and the owner of a large furniture shop in the neighbouring town of March. His sister Annie lived alone in Chatteris and was with him that evening. Rebecca had met her a few times. She was nodding and smiling now and Rebecca knew she couldn't refuse without offending them both. She stood up and allowed him to take her hand, though he was not someone she cared to dance with. She thought him rather pompous – and far too old. She hoped fervently that Annie had not recommended her to him as a suitable mother for his children, suppressing a sigh as his clammy hands grasped hers and he leered down at her with thinly veiled lust.

Fortunately it was a country dance and a progressive, which meant that she moved from one partner to the next after each set of steps, giving her a chance to dance with most of the men in the hall – except for Aden Sawle, who had decided to sit this one out. As the music ended she thanked her partner and retook her seat, feeling uncomfortable. The pink velvet dress was too heavy for a summer evening and although someone had at last opened a window it was still overpoweringly hot in the hall.

It was nearly half an hour before she was asked to dance again, this time by a clumsy young man who managed to step on her toes several times. After that her father brought drinks for them all. She sipped her warm orangeade then asked to be excused, making her way to the cloakroom, where she splashed her face and arms with cold water. That felt better!

She was about to leave when she heard a loud burst of laughter from behind a silk screen that partitioned the rest room from the services.

'Old Frank would do his nut if he knew what his missus and Jack Cottrel was up to last Saturday afternoon,' said a spiteful female voice.

'Shush!' another voice hushed the first. 'You promised you wouldn't say anything if I told you.'

A chill ran down Rebecca's spine as she recognized Dotty's voice this time. She tried to recall where she had been the previous Saturday and remembered that Eileen had asked her to do some shopping for her in March town. She had even arranged for Rebecca to be taken up in a friend's carriage, which meant she was gone for the whole of the afternoon – so it was possible that Eileen and her father could have ... No, she wouldn't listen to such disgusting gossip! Eileen was her friend and it would mean that she had planned the trip just to get Rebecca out of the house for a while.

Rebecca was angry with the barmaid as she went back into the crowded hall. Dotty had no right to spread tales! She had always known she was a spiteful girl but this was wicked. Rebecca had wondered for a second – but it wasn't, it couldn't be true. Her father could not be having an affair with Eileen Henderson! And yet she had seen that look between them earlier this evening ... it might be true. Jack had lived alone for some years now; it was natural that he would want some female company. But Eileen was married to one of his friends ...

Immersed in her own thoughts, she wasn't looking where she was going and almost walked into a man. She caught the strong, sharp scent of his hair oil and a more familiar musk that she recognized instinctively without knowing why. Only his prompt action in putting out his hands prevented the collision. She glanced up, dropping her gaze again hastily as she realized why her senses had reacted to that particular combination of scents.

'Excuse me,' she muttered. 'I was thinking and didn't see you.'

'You're forgiven,' Aden said, preventing her from passing by.

'Are you ill? You look pale.'

'It's the heat. This dress is too warm.' It was only a partial lie. The sweat was trickling between her breasts and her hands were clammy. She felt uncomfortable and upset. How could she look Eileen in the face after what she'd just heard?

'I'll take you outside for a moment.'

'No, thank you. I'll be all right.'

He ignored her protests, capturing her arm and propelling her towards the door, through the covered porch and out into the tiny garden at the rear. In other circumstances she might have argued but people had already noticed and she didn't want to make a scene. Once outside he relinquished his hold and she moved away from him, breathing deeply, her back towards him. She was confused and upset, close to tears, and he sensed her mood.

'What's wrong? Do you want to talk about it? You can trust me not to repeat anything you tell me.'

For some reason she believed him, or perhaps she was simply desperate. There was no one else she could ask, no one she could turn to. She swung round to face him, her eyes smarting with the tears she was trying so hard not to shed. His expression was concerned, interested, inviting her confidence. This was not the man who had mocked her that day in her father's parlour but a man she could depend on – at least that was how he seemed to her now.

'Will you tell me the truth? If I ask you something – will you give me a straight answer? Please? –' Her eyes were a smokey grey, misted with the sheen of tears.

'If I can.' A wary expression crept into his eyes. 'What do you want to know?'

'It's about my father. Are people gossiping about him ... and someone else?'

He was silent for a few moments, then cleared his throat. 'I've heard no gossip. If you've heard something this evening, I should ignore it. People always drink too much at this sort of affair. Drink makes folk say and do daft things ... things they may regret afterwards.'

'Yes, I suppose it does.' She studied his face. Was he telling her the truth or being kind? What he said made sense and his manner was reassuring. She smiled, grateful for his presence whatever the truth. 'Shall we go back inside now? I'm feeling cooler and much better – thanks to you.'

He gazed down at her and there was something in his eyes now, an expression that shattered her hard-won calm and made her heart begin to thud.

'Why are you looking at me like that? Are you laughing at me?'

'Not at you,' he replied, wry amusement in his voice. 'I'm the fool, not you. We'd best get back or Jack will have a search party out looking for you.'

'Yes.' She remembered her father's warnings. 'Yes, he will. It might be better if we went in separately, don't you think?'

'You go,' he said. 'I'll stay for a while.'

'Good night then – and thank you.'

As she went inside she passed Dotty on her way out. The other girl gave her a hard, accusing stare but didn't speak. Rebecca heard her call Aden's name before the heat and the clamour of the hall claimed her once more.

Rebecca tossed and turned half the night. She could not stop thinking about what she had heard in the cloakroom. If it were true about her father and Eileen … but it couldn't be. It was just Dotty's spite. She had seen something and put two and two together to make five – just as she had when she'd seen Rebecca stop to talk to Aden in the street a few days earlier. Yes, that's all it was.

Having made up her mind to ignore the gossip she fell asleep at last in the early hours and the next day had something else to occupy her thoughts.

She couldn't believe it when she read Celia's letter, which arrived soon after breakfast. She was engaged to a wealthy baronet and getting married at the end of October. Rebecca had always known marriage was the object of her friend's season – but it was so soon! She was aware of a sharp pang of jealousy before she swiftly crushed it. Celia was her friend and she didn't grudge her her happiness. She just wished she could find love herself.

'Isn't it wonderful?' Celia had written in her scrawling hand. 'Mother is thrilled, though she thinks we should wait for a while, but Victor says he can't wait and because he's so gorgeously rich, Daddy has agreed to a wedding soon. The thing is, dearest Rebecca, I want you for one of my bridesmaids. Can you come and stay so that we can have your dress made? I'm longing to see you, do say yes!'

Rebecca thought for a while before taking the letter to her

father. He hadn't been happy when she'd asked to be allowed to visit the last time but Celia was her best friend and she couldn't miss her wedding.

Jack was in the parlour staring at a pile of bills on the table in front of him, but she sensed that his mind was far away. He looked up as she entered, an odd, regretful expression in his eyes.

'Celia is getting married. She wants me to be a bridesmaid. That means I have to go and stay so the dress can be made …'

'And you want to go, of course?' He nodded and she saw that his face had a strained, tight look, as though he was very worried or ill. 'Yes, you go, Rebecca. Buy whatever you need.'

She felt a pang of concern. 'Are you all right, Father? You don't seem well.'

'You mustn't worry over me,' he said with an attempt at cheerfulness. 'I've something on my mind, that's all.'

'Is something wrong?' she persisted. 'If you would rather I didn't go …'

'Miss your friend's wedding? No, of course you must go.' He stared at her and for a second she thought he meant to tell her something important, then he shook his head. 'There's naught wrong with me that a good tot of whisky won't cure. Nothing that need concern you. Go and stay with Celia. You'll enjoy that. I know you find life a bit dull here. You'll settle in time but it's not what you're used to. If your mother had lived it might have been different. Aye, a lot might have been different then.'

She hesitated, then kissed his cheek, still worried by his odd mood. 'If you're sure there's nothing I can do for you? Nothing you want to tell me?' He had withdrawn from her again, his eyes focused on something in the distance. 'I'll write to Celia then – let her know to expect me.'

She was uneasy as she went to write her letter. Her father had seemed in such a strange mood lately but she didn't know what was wrong. Was he troubled by the gossip circulating about him and Eileen? If she'd heard tales probably others had, too. She wished they could have talked about it but he had seemed deliberately to shut her out.

Perhaps if she had known her father better, been closer to him, he might have confided in her, but the years she had spent away at school had created a distance between them. They cared for each other but they did not know how to show it.

3

Celia's father had sent one of his servants to meet Rebecca at Winchester station with an elegant carriage; drawn by four beautifully matched bay horses, its black paintwork gleamed and there was an impressive coat of arms worked in gold leaf on the side panels. The groom jumped down to open the door for her and she was respectfully ushered up the steps and made comfortable with a soft travelling rug over her knees before the driver set off at a spanking pace through the town.

The carriage was luxurious inside, with soft squabs and velvet upholstery; it had such good springing that Rebecca felt utterly spoiled and pampered. She craned her neck to see out of the window as they bowled merrily along, looking with awe at the magnificent cathedral and many other fine buildings. How different it was from the small country town she lived in – and how lucky she was to be here!

The excitement was mounting inside her. She was to stay with the Braithewaites for three whole weeks; there would be endless parties, dinners and dances. Perhaps she would meet someone charming and fall in love. How wonderful that would be! To live in a world like Celia's and never have to go back to those dark, noisy rooms above The Cottrel Arms – never to return to the long, endless days when she felt so alone ...

She caught herself up almost at once. What an ungrateful, thankless child she was! She was shamed by her own thoughts. Her father was good to her and she did love him, truly she did.

For a few moments she was reminded of his recent odd moods. Something must be upsetting him, even though he had denied it several times. When she returned at the end of this visit she would make an effort to get closer to him, to show him that she loved him and see if she could help him with his problems.

The Braithewaites' home was a magnificent, sprawling gothic mansion set in acres of lovely landscaped gardens and parkland. In the park the carriage swept past a small herd of grazing deer and there were white doves on the lawns at the front of the house; the sound of their lazy cooing mingled with the rattle of wheels on the gravel drive as they finally came to a halt. She was helped out by a solicitous groom and paused for a moment to take in the timeless beauty of the scene before going up to the front entrance.

The pleasant-mannered but rather stately housekeeper met her in the hall and she was conducted to one of the many guest apartments. Although not one of the best rooms in the house, it was large, airy and tastefully furnished with polished walnut, heavy silk drapes and two deep-cushioned sofas in muted colours.

Taking off her bonnet and thick travelling cloak, Rebecca flung them on one of the sofas and went over to the window to look out. Her room was situated at the back of the house and the view was a splendid vista of smooth, seemingly endless lawns, ancient trees with branches that swooped down to embrace the earth and a lake glistening in the distance.

It was so lovely. She stood drinking it all in, letting the peace and tranquillity wash over her like a soothing balm. She could have happily spent the rest of her life in a house like this – and for the next three weeks she could do just that. Sheer bliss!

Sighing with contentment, she returned to the dressing table and picked up a pretty silver-backed brush, admiring the engraving of cherubs and flowers on the handle and thinking it was similar to one her mother had used. Suddenly the door was flung open behind her and Celia came rushing in.

She looked prettier than ever, her eyes alight with a shining happiness that told Rebecca more than words ever could – though enough of those came tumbling out of her as she burst into speech.

'I've just been told you've arrived,' she cried, seizing Rebecca by the waist and whirling her round in a flurry of excited kisses and hugs. 'Oh, Rebecca, I'm so happy! So very happy! Victor is everything I've dreamed of – all I could possibly want in a husband. So kind and gentle and loving. I've been longing and longing to tell you – but how rude I am! First you must tell me all your news. Have you found someone nice, too? Do say you have!

I've thought of you so often, missed you so much ...'

'I've missed you, too,' Rebecca assured her. She hesitated, reluctant to admit how dull her own life had been since she'd left school. Celia would pity her if she guessed the truth. 'Well ... there's a shy curate and – and Aden Sawle ...' Her cheeks flushed as her friend looked at her.

Celia dimpled and slid an arm about her waist. 'I knew there must be someone. Is Mr Sawle tall and handsome?' she asked, instinctively dismissing the shy curate.

'Yes.' Rebecca admitted it to herself: there was something special about Aden. 'I suppose you could say he is rather attractive.'

'How old?'

'Twenty-four or five.' She warmed to her theme. After all, Celia would never meet him. 'He has thick dark hair and ... eyes that seem to mock you even when he smiles.'

Celia nodded understandingly. 'I know just what you mean. I've met some of that type but they scare me to death. Is he rich?'

'He has his own land.' Rebecca became more cautious; she didn't want to give her friend the wrong impression. 'No, he isn't rich yet but everyone says he will be.'

'Are you engaged?'

'I'm not sure I want to be. I'm not sure I shall marry at all.'

Celia's fine brows arched in surprise. 'But of course you will! That is what it has all been about – our education, the finishing school – we've been groomed for the purpose of finding a husband. Marrying well is a woman's duty.'

For her perhaps that was true. Rebecca's father had sent her away simply because he had not known what else to do with her after her mother died; it had been too difficult to bring up a young girl alone when he had the inn to run, but with hindsight he might have done things differently. Sometimes she wished he had. She wasn't sure whether he had expected her to find herself a husband amongst the families of her friends, nor did she know if she had any real prospect of marrying anyone, let alone the kind of man Celia meant. Her father had forbidden her to speak with Mr Sawle and – she definitely did not wish to marry Mr Bently. She had at least made up her mind on that score.

Celia saved her the embarrassment of stumbling through some kind of explanation. Now her curiosity was satisfied she was full of her own affairs.

Sir Victor Roth was an extremely wealthy man, far richer even than Lord Braithewaite. He had his own private yacht, several homes in England and a villa in the South of France; they were planning to sail to the Greek islands for the first part of their honeymoon and then stay at the villa for another month or so before returning to the new house Sir Victor had bought for his future wife, which was situated just a few miles from her father's mansion and was one of the many wedding gifts he had lavished on her.

What a wonderful experience it would be to do all that! Rebecca was once again aware of that faint pang of envy. How lucky Celia was. She could not help wishing that she had had an opportunity to meet someone like Sir Victor but struggled to keep her feelings in check. Envy was an ugly emotion. She would not allow it to spoil things. She was lucky to be here now, to be allowed to share in her friend's happiness.

The whole house had an air of expectancy about it – it was alive with the scent of flowers, vases of which were everywhere, delighting the passer by with their perfume and colour; and there were voices, laughter echoing through the rooms as the servants hurried back and forth in the polished hallways. The wedding of Lord Braithewaite's only daughter was clearly a joyous occasion to be shared by everyone.

As the two girls turned into the elegant drawing-room, Rebecca noticed the wealth of paintings and huge, gilt-framed mirrors adorning the walls. Large sofas were placed in pairs at either end of the long room and there were little groups of chairs and occasional tables set between.

Two men were standing by the windows, gazing out at the gardens and talking in a casual manner. Rebecca immediately recognized Celia's brother but the other man was a stranger to her. He was perhaps forty, his thick dark hair slightly greying at the temples, but tall and attractive with an air of distinction about him.

'Victor,' Celia cried, her face lighting up as she saw him. 'Come and meet Rebecca. She's my very best friend from school.'

Rebecca was shocked, though swift to hide it. She had taken him for a friend of Lord Braithewaite. He was so much older than Celia, perhaps more than twice her age. Yet when he smiled at her she began to understand what had attracted Celia to him. There was such warmth, such tenderness in that look, and something so compelling about the man himself.

'Victor Roth,' he said, offering his hand. His fingers closed about Rebecca's with a cool, strong clasp that sent a tingle down her spine. 'I'm so pleased to meet you at last, Rebecca. Celia speaks of you so often that I feel we are already friends.'

'I'm delighted to meet you, Sir Victor.' The words came easily to her lips despite the sudden mad pounding of her heart. Her cheeks were warm and her head seemed to swim as she felt herself drawn to him so strongly that she was afraid everyone would see it in her face.

'No, no, it is Victor to you, Rebecca. I insist. There must be no formality with such a dear friend of Celia's.'

'Thank you, Victor.'

She managed to say the words and smile though she felt close to swooning. She wanted to go on holding his hand forever and felt bereft when he let go. A hot rush of shame followed swiftly. This was ridiculous! And wrong. He was about to marry her best friend. She must not allow herself to have such feelings – but they had descended without warning. Her mind was all confusion and she was fearful of letting it show.

Fortunately, his gaze had moved to his fiancée. Celia offered her hand to him and he took it, lifting it to his lips to kiss it briefly. Rebecca moved away, towards the window and Philip Braithewaite, who had not moved and was a silent, thoughtful observer. Had he noticed anything odd in her manner? She hoped not.

'Becky,' he said, his blue eyes scanning her with approval. 'You've grown up since last Christmas. You were still a child then … now you are beautiful.'

She raised her eyes to look at him. He had the same fair good looks as Celia but there was something weak about his mouth and chin, giving him a slightly sullen, spoiled expression.

'You flatter me, sir,' she replied, still flustered by the way she had reacted to Victor Roth. 'I believe I am passable but not beautiful.'

'Philip,' he chided. His manner at that moment was amused, indulgent … predatory? 'It was Philip at Christmas – have you forgotten?'

'No.' He had taken little notice of her then apart from the duty dances Celia had forced on him.

31

'And you are beautiful, believe me.'

Celia had noticed what was going on. Her pretty face was tight with disapproval. 'Stop it, Philip!' she commanded. 'Leave Rebecca alone. I won't have you teasing her. She's much too good for you – besides, she's practically engaged. You can't have her.'

'Tell me at once it isn't true?' he demanded, dropping his voice and giving Rebecca a mocking look. 'Promise me your heart has not been given to another … I quite thought it was mine, dearest Becky.' His suggestive, intimate manner made her uneasy and suddenly she was annoyed.

He was flirting with her outrageously, going beyond the bounds of politeness in a way that was not acceptable when she knew that he would never consider making her a proposal of marriage. He would never behave this badly with other unmarried girls of his acquaintance – so why do so with her? Did he believe that she was ripe for seduction simply because her father owned a country inn?

'I cannot imagine why you should have thought that,' she said, her head lifting proudly. 'My heart is my own and given to no one.'

'Then there is still a chance for me?'

'Don't be ridiculous!' Celia swooped across the room to rescue her. 'Rebecca has too much good sense to be another of your conquests, Philip. Come on, Rebecca, I'm taking you to see my wedding presents. We've masses of lovely things already and there's weeks to go yet. Mummy has them all set out on tables in the long gallery.'

Rebecca resisted the temptation to glance back as Celia swept her away. Her intuition warned her that Philip Braithewaite's predatory instincts had been aroused and she would be wise to be on her guard where he was concerned.

It was not of Philip she thought as she went to bed that night, though, but of Victor Roth. She had been placed next to him at dinner and after a momentary nervousness, found him to be a pleasant companion. He had gone out of his way to entertain her, making her laugh and banishing any embarrassment.

'Celia was so afraid you would not be able to come,' he confided in a husky whisper. 'She would have been so disappointed. I think she might even have cancelled the wedding.'

He was teasing her, of course, but his smile was so gentle and indulgent that she responded instantly, feeling herself drawn to him so strongly that once again she was afraid he must see it in her eyes.

'I'm sure she would not,' she replied. 'She is very happy – happier, I think, than I have ever seen her.'

'I shall try to make her happy always,' he said with a warm glance across the table at Celia. 'She is a darling girl and I am fortunate to have found her – do you not agree?'

'Yes. Yes, of course.'

Rebecca's agreement was both generous and genuine. She was fond of her friend and wished her only happiness. This attraction she felt towards Celia's fiancé was foolish and wrong. She had no right to think of him as anything other than the man her best friend had chosen to marry – but she did. She did!

She was torn with guilt as she lay sleepless that night, turning restlessly from side to side. How could she possibly feel this way about a man she hardly knew – a man who could never, never be hers?

'Are you sure you don't want to come?' Celia was dressed for riding in a smart black habit, silk hat and long leather boots, her delicate, swanlike neck swathed in the folds of a white linen stock. 'I hate to leave you here all alone. Everyone is going on the hunt.'

'You know I've never liked horses. Please don't worry about me, Celia. I can amuse myself for a few hours. I'll read a book or go for a walk – there's so much to do here.'

Celia shrugged, puzzled by what she thought of as Rebecca's odd dislike of horses. She kissed her cheek, then went clattering down the stairs in a flurry of excitement.

Rebecca was drawn to the window at the top of the landing by the noise and bustle in the courtyard below; a pale autumn sun warmed the old stone walls and worn brick paving, giving them a charming mellowness. She paused to watch what was undeniably a fascinating scene: horses and dogs mingling in a fever of impatience, their riders resplendent in scarlet or sober black coats with snowy stocks and York tan gloves.

Viewed from a distance it was indeed a stirring sight but not one she cared to be a part of. She could just about ride if she had to but would never have been able to keep up with all the others. Besides, she hated the idea of all those men, horses and dogs chasing after one poor little fox – not that she would have dreamed of offending her hosts by saying such a thing!

She turned away and went down the stairs to the library. The noise was much less now and she thought the hunt must have moved off. It was so peaceful in the long, quiet room with its shelves of leather-bound books and a clock gently ticking on the mantelpiece; some of the books were serious, heavy tomes, but there was also a wonderful selection of Shakespeare's plays, Byron's poems, works by Sheridan and Goldsmith as well as the novels of Dickens and the Brontë sisters.

She took her time selecting books that interested her, curling up in a deep wing chair by the fire to read for a while. It was almost noon when she stood up, stretched and looked out at the gardens. She had no idea what arrangements had been made for luncheon but supposed something cold might have been laid for her in the breakfast room. Leaving her books lying on one of the little tables, she wandered out of the French windows to the terraces. It was warmer outside than in the house. Perhaps she would go for a walk before lunch.

The lawns had been cut early that morning and the grass was dry beneath her feet as she strolled slowly towards the shrubbery. The weather was still fine and warm and the musk roses were blooming profusely in the shelter of crumbling stone walls, their scent wafting towards her on the slight breeze. She paused to breathe in their perfume, thinking again how lovely it all was.

Why was she so restless? In this wonderful place with such a wealth of books to enjoy she ought to have been perfectly content, but something was nagging at her, destroying her peace of mind. Her gaze travelled round the gardens. Surely she was not foolish enough to be grieving for something she could never …

Her thoughts were suspended as she saw the man striding towards her and her heart began to thudd madly against her ribcage. He was still wearing his riding dress, the fitted coat emphasizing his wide shoulders, the pale breeches clinging to his muscular thighs like a second skin. She felt a wild, surging longing. He was even more attractive than she had thought him the previous evening – and he was smiling at her, turning her knees to jelly and making her catch her breath as his pace slowed and she knew he had been looking for her.

'I thought it must be you. May. I join you on your walk?' His voice was soft, husky, as though he were slightly out of breath, had hurried to catch up with her.

'Of course, if you wish, Victor.' Her eyelashes flicked down to hide the excitement his sudden appearance had aroused. It meant nothing – could mean nothing! – that he had sought her out. It was mere politeness on his part but it thrilled her just the same. 'These grounds are pretty, are they not?'

'A little formal for my taste. I prefer the park – but perhaps you would not wish to walk that far from the house?'

She would have walked to the ends of the earth with him! Yet she knew she must conceal her eagerness. She must remember that this was her best friend's fiancé.

'I enjoy walking. It is my favourite pastime – apart from reading, of course.'

His smile crinkled the corners of his eyes. 'It seems we have much in common. What are you reading now?'

She told him and he nodded then added after a pause, 'You do not care to hunt?'

'I fear I'm not much of a horsewoman.'

His eyes were a kind of greenish-brown that made her think of warm afternoons in country lanes, and just now they held a sparkle of amusement.

'Not like Celia then. She was leading the field when I last saw her. My own horse went lame and I was forced to walk him home.'

'I'm sorry. You have missed most of the day's sport,' she said, and looked away as her heart took a giddy leap.

The air was heavy with the sweet fragrance of honeysuckle and musk roses, filling her with a sense of wanting, aching for something – something she could never have.

'I don't care for being in at the kill, though the chase itself is exhilarating. Besides, this gives me the chance to become better acquainted with you.'

'Do you wish for a closer acquaintance?' She held her breath, looking at him doubtfully. What could he mean? It was impossible to read his expression and she sensed that he had drawn a veil over his private thoughts. Had he guessed what she was feeling? Had he seen too much in her face?

Rebecca could not have known it but at that moment she was breathtakingly lovely, her face touched by a wistful appeal that would have melted the hearts of sterner men than Victor Roth.

'It is my hope that you will continue to be Celia's friend over the years and that you will visit us when we are settled. You must know that Celia is very fond ...' The sound of a gong being beaten in the house caused him to pause and glance over his shoulder. 'Do you suppose that is for us?'

'I think it must be.'

She was disappointed that their walk had been curtailed but it would seem odd if they ignored the summons. Victor was obviously of the same opinion for he turned when she did – just as a sudden gust of wind blew up. Rebecca gave a cry of distress as she felt a sharp pricking in her eye.

'Oh ...' She blinked as it started to water. 'I think I have something in my eye. It hurts ...'

'Stand still and tip your head towards me.' Victor's hands were cool and firm as he gently opened her eye. 'Look up ... now down ... ah, yes, I see it. A speck of grit. I shall remove it with my handkerchief. Keep still, Rebecca ... there, is that better?'

She had trembled as he touched her and the gentle tone of his voice turned her knees to jelly. The awful pricking sensation had ceased but her eye was still watering and she felt close to tears.

'Yes, I think so. Thank you. It was quite painful but it is better now.'

'I'm glad I was able to help.'

He was looking at her intently. His words were polite, formal, but as they gazed at one another in silence she was aware of a struggle within him and sensed that he was fighting a temptation to kiss her. She held her breath. For one brief, wonderful moment she thought he would take her in his arms – and she wanted it, she wanted it to happen so much. She seemed to ache for his touch, her body swaying towards him in anticipation of his kiss, then his expression changed, becoming almost stern as he refolded his handkerchief and replaced it in his pocket.

'I must change for lunch,' he said, his tone cool and remote. 'Please excuse me, Rebecca.'

She stood as if turned to stone as he strode away, fighting her disappointment and the tears that threatened to spill over. Her pulses were throbbing and her throat was tight as she fought the maelstrom of emotions inside her. Why could she not show the same control as Victor? Why did she feel as if she had been torn apart?

This was terrible! She had fallen in love with Celia's fiancé.

How could it have happened? It was wrong and foolish. Victor worshipped Celia. It showed every time he looked at her. She was the woman he loved, admired and respected, the woman he wanted to marry. She was also Rebecca's friend.

She must have imagined that look just now, that hot glow in his eyes when just for a moment she had felt something flare between them. Her own feelings had misled her, causing her to see something that was not there. It was all her own fault. She had allowed herself to envy Celia, to covet her life and her future husband – and this was the result.

It must stop now! She had to crush these wicked thoughts at once, to stamp out the creeping evil of envy before it flared out of control.

If she could have left Braithewaite Hall without causing a fuss and ruining Celia's wedding she would have done so immediately, but that would have been unpardonably rude. She might sometimes wish that she could exchange her life for her friend's but she was fond of her and would do nothing that might harm her.

Rebecca hurried towards the house, knowing that she must face Victor at luncheon with the calm friendliness he had a right to expect.

She would conquer this foolishness. She would smile and behave as though everything was as it ought to be, and she would never let Victor or anyone else guess that her heart was breaking.

'It won't be long afore Jack Cottrel gets his comeuppance,' Dotty said, a note of glee in her voice. 'And that snooty cat Eileen Henderson! Putting on airs the way she does – she's no better than the rest of us.'

Aden turned to look at her lying sprawled on the ground beside him and felt a surge of disgust, with himself as much as her. She was a spiteful little thing and he often wondered just why he had become involved with her in the first place. She was willing enough to spread her legs for him whenever he was in the mood for a bit of fun but he was not the first with her – nor would he be the last. He'd been a damned fool, but it had started on the night of the harvest dance – after Rebecca had walked away, leaving him feeling disturbed and regretful.

'I thought you liked Jack? What's brought all this on then?'

Dotty looked sullen. 'He's all right, I suppose. It's that daughter of his. Nothing's the same since she came home; she's always finding fault with my work, poking her nose in where it isn't wanted. Lady Muck! She'll come down a peg or two when she finds out what her pa's bin up to.'

Aden got to his feet, surveying the flat fields stretching away into the distance, hardly a tree in sight and only a few scrawny hedges to break the force of the wind. Pleasant enough on a summer's day but dank and dismal when the mist came curling up from the river and winter-bare branches dripped with moisture. Not everyone's idea of heaven, perhaps, but he had developed a feeling for this land ... his land. It wasn't black like the real fen soil but thick clay that stuck to a man's boots and dragged him down. It was land that needed the right master, someone who knew how to nurture and respect it. Not every man could work the clay soil. Go battling on it at the wrong moment and it went down flat and hard. Some of his neighbours made a pig's ear out of it, getting scrappy crops for their labours, but Aden knew how to coax the best from his land – though it took all his time and energy. He hadn't any to waste.

'I'd best be getting back then,' he said, not looking at Dotty. 'Make a start on the milking.'

'So soon?' She pouted at him. 'After I've walked all this way? We ain't even done it yet.' Her eyes narrowed suspiciously as she saw his expression. 'You going off me already?'

'Don't be daft,' he said. 'It's broad daylight. This field is too close to the road. Someone might see.' There were bales of sweet, dry hay in the barn and complete privacy, but he didn't want her.

'When shall I see you again?'

'I'm not sure.' She had rubbed rouge into her cheeks and it looked tawdry, sending a spasm of revulsion through him. He must have been out of his mind to start this! 'Maybe we'll leave it for a while.'

'You bastard!' Dotty screamed. 'You *have* gone off me.' She reared up, close to tears. 'Not good enough for you, am I? Don't bother to pretend. It's her you're after – that stuck up bitch! I've seen yer face when I mention her.'

'Don't go making anything of it, Dotty, or you'll be sorry.'

'You're the one who's going to be sorry!' She brushed at her skirt. 'If you get involved with that cold cat, you'll regret it 'til your dying day.'

'That's my business,' Aden said. 'Not that I've any intention of getting involved.'

'You will,' she said bitterly. 'You've got it bad, you poor bugger. Well, you'll get what you deserve.'

'Come on, Dotty,' he muttered uneasily. 'There's no call for us to part bad friends. We've had some fun together – and I wasn't the first.'

'Nor the best neither,' she retorted. 'I've had better men than you'll ever be.'

'Then you won't miss me, will you?'

'Go to hell!' she yelled, and started to run across the field towards the Chatteris road. 'You'll be sorry one of these days, Aden Sawle. Just you wait and see!'

He watched her go. He was sorry it had ended in bitterness but glad it was over. It had been a mistake. He'd always liked Dotty and it wasn't fair to use her the way he had.

She was right, he thought ruefully, he had got it bad as far as Rebecca Cottrel was concerned. Her image was in his mind day and night. Sometimes the ache inside him was so bad that he couldn't sleep for thinking of her ... wanting her. He'd used Dotty to try and ease that ache – only it hadn't worked.

What the hell was he going to do about this mess? There wasn't much he could do, given the fact that Jack hated his guts now. He had tried to make it up with him but the publican had told him to go to hell.

All he could do was bide his time. Rebecca had been grateful to him at the dance. It might be that she would need a friend in the future ...

4

Rebecca was very careful to hide her feelings whenever Victor was present. She spent as little time as possible in his company, often turning aside rather than meet him in a quiet corridor or the gardens, though of course she was always polite ... polite but distant. Once or twice she thought she saw him look puzzled, as if he were wondering whether he had offended her, but he made no attempt to break down the barrier she had erected between them.

The past weeks had not been easy for her, but because she had been so very careful she believed she had managed to deceive everyone ... until the evening of Celia's special dance.

It was to be a lavish affair, the climax of the celebrations leading up to the wedding – which was to take place just two days later – and guests had been arriving from all over the country.

That evening she was to wear a new dress made specially for the occasion; it was a heavy tussore silk with a low neckline that skimmed over her shoulders and revealed a glimpse of her cleavage. She and Celia had spent a long time choosing it with the seamstress and she knew it was the most elegant gown she had ever owned, but even when they were ordering it she had thought that perhaps it was a little daring. Celia had insisted that it would look wonderful on her but when Rebecca tried it on that evening she felt awkward. She was half-naked! Even when she had fastened a heavy silver locket around her neck she still couldn't help thinking that she had been unwise to agree to the style. However, she had nothing else suitable so she would have to wear it.

Celia gave a cry of delight when she went to her room a few minutes later. 'I was right,' she said. 'That dress looks wonderful on you.'

'You don't think it's slightly … brazen?'

Celia laughed and shook her head. 'No, of course not. It suits you, Rebecca. Really it does. Everyone wears this sort of thing now.' Her own dress was of a similar style but somehow it looked different on her: she still seemed an enchanting, innocent child, her body thin and immature – unlike Rebecca's, which was very much that of a woman.

Rebecca was reassured by Celia's approval. Perhaps her own dressing mirror had made the gown look more daring than it really was. She tucked her arm through her friend's and they walked down the stairs together, their heads almost touching as they laughed and whispered secrets in each other's ears.

Celia's excitement had reached fever pitch. She could hardly wait for her wedding day and her eyes glowed as she saw how charmingly the ballroom had been decorated with banks and banks of flowers. There was layer upon layer of gorgeous blooms around the dais where the musicians would soon assemble, their sweet perfume filling the room.

'Doesn't it all look wonderful?' she asked, giving Rebecca's arm a squeeze. 'Can you smell those gardenias? Victor had them specially grown in his hothouses for this evening.'

'They are perfect,' Rebecca replied. 'You're very lucky to be marrying such a thoughtful man.'

'Yes, I am, aren't I?' Celia looked a little smug. 'He adores me – and here he is now …'

She greeted Victor with a confident smile. He kissed her cheek, glanced at Rebecca and then turned away as the rest of the family arrived to line up at the entrance to the ballroom and the first guests began to drift downstairs. Many of them were staying in the house, as Rebecca was, but the rattle of carriage wheels outside announced the arrival of others, and the ballroom rapidly filled up, coming alive with the sound of laughter and excited voices.

Had that been approval she'd seen so briefly in Victor's eyes? Rebecca's pulses had quickened for a moment but she had dropped her gaze swiftly. Somehow she must keep her secret for two more days.

She moved further down the room, feeling a little out of things as she heard Celia's happy laughter. Standing by the long windows she gazed out at the gardens. Tiny lanterns had been hung in the trees nearest the house; they flickered like fireflies amongst the branches, creating a feeling of enchantment and making the night seem somehow magical. If only she … but it was useless to sigh for the moon, foolish to yearn for something that could never be hers. She must not give way to her feelings now. In a few days she would be home and no one need ever know how silly she had been.

Absorbed in her thoughts she was startled when someone came up behind her, standing so close that she could feel the warmth of his breath brushing her bare shoulder. She experienced a prickling sensation in the nape of her neck and knew who it was even before he spoke.

'You're beautiful, Becky,' Philip said in a low, caressing tone. 'Your hair is like rich brown satin and your skin has the texture of cream. I long to touch …'

'Philip! Please do not.'

She glanced uncertainly over her shoulder and her cheeks flushed bright red. She had been afraid of something like this. Several times recently she had noticed Philip watching her and the expression in his eyes now was disturbing.

'Not tell you you are beautiful?' His brows rose. 'You must know that there isn't a woman in the room who can hold a candle to you – especially in that dress.' His eyes seemed to dwell on her nakedness and she felt hot with shame.

'Celia chose it.'

'My sister always has had taste. You should wear gowns like this more often.' He leered at her, making her want to run away and hide – or cover herself! 'Do you know what you remind me of this evening, Becky?'

She shook her head, unable to speak and wishing he would go away and leave her in peace. He reached out, trailing the tips of his fingers down her bare arm and sending shivers the length of her spine. Warning bells were sounding in her head. When Philip rode to hounds he was always the first in at the kill and the look in his eyes now was that of a hunter stalking his prey.

'You could have held sway at the palace of the Sun King,' he said in a silky, persuasive voice. 'You are as seductive as any courtesan at his court … as lovely as any woman in history … more beautiful than Delilah herself …'

'I'm not sure I find that a compliment.' Rebecca frowned. The women he had mentioned were not famed for their virtue, while she valued her reputation.

'It was meant as one, believe me.'

He gave her another mocking look and moved away. Her stomach clenched. What could he mean by saying such things to her? It was surely not the language a lady might expect from a gentleman!

The ballroom was becoming crowded now and the musicians had begun to play. She forgot Philip Braithewaite as someone asked her to dance and she was swept away in a whirl of music and laughter. There was always a houseful of young men at the Braithewaites' and she knew her partner well enough to enjoy dancing with him. He was polite and friendly and she was soon completely at ease. When their dance ended she found herself in demand as one partner followed another and she was never permitted to sit out. She had never been quite this successful before and thought that perhaps Celia had been right about the dress after all.

Celia seemed to be dancing every dance, too, her pretty face alight with excitement as her laughter rang out again and again.

'Isn't this fun?' she whispered to Rebecca when they passed each other once. 'I'm so happy.'

Rebecca too was enjoying herself. She had forgotten about Philip and it was not until much later in the evening that he asked her to be his partner.

The ballroom was slightly less crowded now as some of the guests had gone into supper. Rebecca was about to leave when Philip caught her arm and she noticed the odd brilliance of his eyes as he asked her to dance. She hesitated, wishing that she could refuse, but knowing that it would be unforgivably rude.

Even as he led her on to the floor she was regretting her decision. His manner was belligerent, and, as his arm went round her waist, she caught the stink of strong drink on his breath. He had clearly been helping himself to more of Lord Braithewaite's excellent brandy than he should. She would have left him then if she could but it would have been too embarrassing.

They began to waltz but he insisted on holding her too tightly. She protested and tried to hold herself away from him but he pressed her even closer and she could feel the heat of his body through the silk of her gown. He was very warm and perspiring freely; the intimacy of his embrace made her uncomfortable and nervous.

'Please don't,' she whispered. 'You are making me too warm.'

'Methinks the lady doth protest too much.'

He refused to relax his hold on her, a malicious triumph in his face as though he had meant to punish her and was enjoying his success. Rebecca was upset and angry. She left him as soon as the dance finished and retired to a cool corner to fan herself vigorously as she agonised over his behaviour; he had deliberately set out to embarrass her and had succeeded all too well.

'May I have the honour of this dance, Rebecca?'

She turned with a little start, gazing up into Victor's smiling eyes. 'Thank you.' Her tension melted away as he offered his hand and she felt the pleasant coolness of his touch.

'This is the first chance I've had to dance with you this evening,' he said. 'And to tell you that you look ... charming.'

How good it was to be with a man as courteous and charming as Victor. She felt the relief wash over her as he led her on to the floor and rested his hand lightly against her waist, holding her at precisely the correct distance.

'I believe everyone is enjoying themselves.'

'Oh, yes.' Rebecca relaxed as he made polite conversation. 'Celia told me you had the gardenias grown specially. They are lovely.'

Glancing across the room she saw that Philip was watching them. Perhaps glowering at them would be a better description; there was such anger, such jealousy in his eyes!

She drew a deep breath and averted her gaze. Philip had no right to look at her like that – as if he were a simmering volcano about to erupt in a torrent of molten lava.

'You must promise to visit us as soon as we return?'

'Yes ... yes, thank you.'

Rebecca recalled her wandering thoughts. The music was drawing to an end and Victor had relinquished her. He thanked her and said that he was promised to Celia for the next dance. She nodded, watched him walk across the room, then took the chance to slip away up to her own room. It was so hot in the ballroom – and Philip was still watching her.

Upstairs, she splashed her face and neck with cold water. What on earth was wrong with Philip? Was he drunk? It was too bad of him to behave so foolishly at his sister's special dance. She was reluctant to return to the ballroom and found herself wishing that she could go home. The evening was spoiled and she longed to be alone ... to let this hurt inside her spill over into the tears she had been fighting for days.

No, she would not give in to self-pity! Her head went up and her eyes sparked with anger.

She had to return to the dance, of course. If she didn't someone was bound to notice and tell Celia or her mother – and she didn't feel like lying to either of them. Glancing in the mirror again, she smoothed a wisp of hair into place. Was Philip behaving badly because of the dress? She ought never to have let Celia persuade her into ordering it – though it was no more daring than others she'd seen that evening.

She had been up here long enough: she ought to go back. As she left her room she could hear the music floating up from the ballroom and knew they were playing another waltz. She walked down the stairs and past the library, jumping as the door suddenly opened and a hand shot out, grabbing her wrist.

'Philip!' she cried, alarmed by the feverish look in his eyes. 'What are you doing?'

'I want to talk to you …'

'Please let me go.'

'Not just yet.' His face was flushed and his manner was very odd. 'Not unless you want me to tell my sister about what you've been up to with her fiancé?'

'There's nothing to tell,' she protested, but a tremor went through her as she saw his expression. Somehow she sensed that he was vicious enough to carry out his threat regardless of the truth – and she was afraid that Celia might believe him, or at the very least become suspicious and upset.

'I saw you meet him in the gardens on the morning of the hunt,' Philip muttered. 'I wondered why he left the field so early so I followed him home. I saw you kissing …'

'No, that's not true!'

He must have seen Victor remove the grit from her eye and had misinterpreted the scene, mistaking it for something altogether more intimate.

'We did not plan to meet. His horse was lamed and he had to retire.'

'A convenient excuse to sneak away and meet you!'

'It was a chance meeting. Please believe me.'

He was pulling her into the library; she protested weakly, knowing that she had no choice but to give in to him. She could not risk his creating a scene in the ballroom. She had to reason with him, make him accept the truth.

'There is no sense in this,' she said. 'Victor wasn't kissing me. I had a piece of grit in my eye …'

'Don't lie to me!'

'Please let me go, Philip. I don't want to be here alone with you … you frighten me …'

'I'll let you go when I'm ready.' He pulled her against him suddenly, his fingers digging into the tender flesh of her upper arm. 'I want some of what you've been giving him all this time.' His voice grated harshly and she cringed at the crudeness of his words. No one had ever spoken to her like that. She had thought Aden Sawle arrogant but knew instinctively he would never have dreamed of speaking so rudely to a woman. Philip was supposed to be a gentleman but he was a drunken brute and she despised him.

'How dare you? Let me go at once!'

She tried to break away from him but he tightened his hold on her, forcing her head back as his mouth closed over hers, his teeth grinding against hers, bruising her lips. She struggled furiously, opening her mouth to protest, but his tongue thrust inside, making her gag and choke as she felt a surge of revulsion. Angry now, she made a tremendous effort and wrenched her head away, gazing up at him in fear and loathing. His face was ugly, contorted by lust, his eyes blood-shot, his mouth slack and wet with saliva.

'Don't … please don't!' she begged. 'Philip …'

'You've been driving me mad,' he muttered, breathing hard. 'You're a witch, Becky, and I want you more than I've ever wanted any other woman. If you please me I might even marry you – and that's more than *he* will. All he wants from you is this …'

His mouth moved feverishly against her throat, then he made a grab at her breasts, trying to thrust his hand down inside the dipping neckline of her gown. His roughness shocked her. He was obviously in no mood to listen to reason, nor to be satisfied with a few chaste kisses.

'I'm going to show you what it's like to have a real man inside you,' he rasped against her ear. 'You'll love it, Becky – you've been begging for it for weeks.'

Rebecca felt a surge of anger. How dared he? How could he do this to her? Treat her as if she were a slut from the streets! It was disgusting. She gave a cry of fury then pushed hard at his shoulders, managing at last to break his hold on her. She was more angry than afraid now, retreating backwards and away from him but further into the room, her eyes moving from side to side as she sought a way of escape. He came after her, slowly but with a determined look on his face.

'Please, no. I beg you ...' Despite her anger she was still trying to placate him, to avoid an embarrassing scene.

'You will beg me,' he murmured throatily. 'You will beg for more, you little whore! I know you love it ...'

She wanted to scream but knew she must not; if they were discovered it would cause a terrible scandal. Had Philip lost his senses? He could not mean to rape her, here in his father's library, two days before his sister's wedding? It would ruin everything. And yet – would she ever dare to tell anyone? He was probably counting on her fear of being disgraced to hold her silent.

'Come on,' he taunted. 'Don't play hard to get, Becky. I know you want it. You've been teasing me all this time.'

She had to get out of the room! But she must manage it without causing an uproar. Celia would never forgive her if she ruined her dance. Everyone would believe she had sneaked away to meet Philip. It would be her word – the word of a publican's daughter – against his. She couldn't risk it. Her only chance was to reach the safety of the ballroom, but to leave the library she had to pass Philip ...

Should she try to dodge past or ... Even as she poised herself for flight the door opened and a man came in. She stared at him, a little sob of relief escaping as she realized it was going to be all right.

'Victor ... please!'

She hesitated as he stared at her and she thought she saw doubt in his face. Surely he could not believe she had come here of her own free will?

'What are you doing, Philip?' Victor asked, his eyes narrowing as he saw Philip's flushed face and slackened mouth. 'You've had too much to drink this evening. Remember your manners and allow Rebecca to leave.'

Philip's face went even redder and then white with fury. 'Get out of here and mind your own business,' he snarled. 'Or I'll tell my sister what you've been doing with Becky.'

'There's nothing *to* tell!' Rebecca cried. 'It's your imagination, Philip.'

'I'm not imagining the way he's looking at you now. He's lusting after you as much as I ...'

'Be quiet, Braithewaite!' Victor's voice was sharp with anger. 'If you dare to upset Celia – or Rebecca – I shall see to it that your father learns of your gambling losses.'

The colour was wiped from Philip's face. 'Damn you, Roth! You swore it wouldn't go any further when you made me that loan. If Father finds out ... last time he threatened to disinherit and pack me off abroad.'

'Exactly.' Victor's eyes were forbidding as broken glass. 'I suggest you apologize to Rebecca and leave. And I would advise you to sober up before you return to your sister's dance. I will not have either her or Rebecca upset by your lack of manners. At least try to behave like a gentleman.'

Philip looked as if he would have liked to run him through with a sword, but he was beaten. Victor had the upper hand and he knew it.

'My apologies, Miss Cottrel,' he muttered, and strode from the room.

Rebecca was trembling and felt sick. What must Victor be thinking? When at last she dared to look at him she saw concern and not disgust in his face. She felt a rush of emotion, tears springing to her eyes as she tried to explain.

'I went upstairs to tidy myself. When I came down he dragged me in here and threatened to ...' She choked and could not go on.

'The young fool had been drinking too much. I noticed earlier that he had upset you and when I realized he had left the room soon after you.' He paused sympathetically. 'I do not believe he will bother you again.'

'Thank you. I'm so sorry that he ... of course it was ridiculous ...'

'Philip is more perceptive than I had thought,' he replied a little huskily. 'I do have a high regard for you, Rebecca. If we had met first ... before ... who knows?' His smile was tinged with regret. 'I love Celia and always shall – but there are different kinds of love. However, this is something we may not discuss. We shall forget it ever happened.'

'Yes, of course.' She was shaken by his admission but tried to appear calm and unconcerned. He was right, the subject was forbidden. Neither of them was willing to hurt Celia. 'Perhaps we should return to the ballroom before we are missed?'

'You go. I shall smoke a cigar – that was after all my excuse for leaving.'

'I understand.'

He was so sure, so gentle – so distant. Her senses were numbed as she left the room at once. Philip's attempt at rape had shamed her – and Victor's words had confused her.

What did he mean by saying that Philip was perceptive? He had admitted to feeling something for her, but it wasn't the tender, protective love he had for Celia. A different kind of love? Or was it simply lust?

Philip had tried to force himself on her but Victor was a true gentleman. That didn't stop him having the same urges as other men. Despite her sheltered life she knew that men often sought a certain type of woman to ease their needs – the baser needs they were too considerate to inflict on their virtuous wives. Did both Philip and Victor see her as that kind of woman?

She knew that neither of them had considered marrying her, though both wanted her in a physical way. They must both think her a wanton! She squirmed with shame and disgust. Philip had thought it a game to hunt her down, but Victor – how could he see her that way? Had he guessed how she felt despite all her efforts to hide it?

She was hurt and humiliated. If she could she would have run back to her own room but her pride would not let her. Somehow she would get through the rest of the evening.

There was a cold, biting wind blowing across the fen as Aden drove into Chatteris. More like winter than the end of October, he thought, shivering and turning up his coat collar. If he hadn't wanted to collect the money Frank Henderson owed him for some cockrels and a couple of bullocks he wouldn't have bothered to make the journey at all.

He drove into the stableyard behind The Cottrel Arms, made his horse comfortable, then began to walk towards the archway that led out to the main street. Suddenly, the back door of the inn was flung open and someone came flying out. Seeing that it was Dotty and that she was in a panic he went up to her, catching hold of her arm.

'What's wrong? What's happened, lass?'

She stared at him, then started blubbering and gabbling so fast that he could hardly make out what she was saying.

'Lying there ... the blood ... both of them ...' She wrenched herself away to vomit in the gutter. Aden waited until she straightened up, then gave her his handkerchief.

'Slow up, Dotty. I can't make head nor tail of it.'

'It's Jack and her.' Dotty drew a sobbing breath. 'They're lying there ... blood all over the place ... dead ... I think they're dead ...' Her voice rose on a note of hysteria.

'Dead!' A blinding pain went through him. 'Not Rebecca? My God, not Rebecca!'

'No, not her. Eileen Henderson and ...' Dotty looked scared as she gazed up at him. 'It's Frank what's done it,' she whispered. 'I never meant for this to happen. You've got to believe me, Aden. When I started them rumours I never meant it to end like this.'

'Wait here. I shan't be long.'

She plucked nervously at his arm 'Don't leave me.'

'I'd best have a look for myself. Stay here.'

Her face was white and she was reluctant to let him go but he knew he had to make sure that neither Jack nor his mistress was still alive – and that Frank Henderson wasn't still lurking upstairs.

It was cold in the pub, a damned sight colder than outside. He saw it as soon as he walked in – a dark, spreading stain on the ceiling and a patch of something on the floor that looked like half-dried blood. There must have been a hell of a lot of it to have caused that. He wondered just what he was going to find in the room above.

It was worse than Dotty had described and the stench was nauseating. Jack's eyes were open and staring, his face contorted in terrible agony, as if he had died hard, putting up a struggle against his attacker. Eileen was lying on the bed as if asleep, a huge knife sticking out of her stomach.

Aden backed out of the room as the vomit rose in his throat. Frank must have been crazy with jealousy to do this! He'd never seen anything like it in his life and hoped to God he never would again. For a moment he felt like running out the way Dotty had but he took a grip on himself and began to search the other rooms, calling out a couple of times in case Frank was hiding somewhere.

'Come on, Frank, best give yourself up now. It won't do any good to hide from it ...'

There was no reply but he hadn't really expected one. Still, it was best to be sure.

Dotty was waiting outside the back door. She looked at him and shuddered as he nodded grimly.

'Both dead, ain't they? It must 'ave been Frank. Couldn't have been no one else, could it? It weren't my fault … I didn't …'

'Frank always had an evil temper,' Aden said quickly. Her face was ashen and her teeth were chattering. 'Calm down, lass. They're gone and grieving won't bring them back. Now tell me – where is Rebecca?'

'Staying with some posh friends near Winchester,' Dotty said. 'Her friend got married. She'll be coming home on the train tomorrow.'

'Then there's no need for her to know until then.' He looked grim. 'This is a mess all right.'

'What are we goin' to do?'

'You hurry off to the constable's house and tell him what you told me.'

'What about you?'

'There's nothing I can do for Eileen or Jack but it might not be too late for Frank. I'll go round to his house now.'

'Rather you than me. He's run mad, that's what he's done.'

'Frank's a decent enough bloke. He was just pushed too far, that's all. Likely he's in a state and can do with some help.'

Dotty had calmed down now. Aden watched as she set off towards the constable's house then turned towards the butcher's shop, which was at the far end of the street. Frank lived over the top and there was a private passage at the side, leading to the back kitchen. It was there that Aden had often called in the past to collect money for deliveries of poultry, eggs and the occasional pig or bullock. Frank had been a good customer and Aden reckoned he owed him this. Maybe if he got to him first they could work something out …

The door of the shop was locked and the blind pulled tight over the window. Aden rang the bell but there was no answer. Of course there wouldn't be if … taking a deep breath to steady himself he went through the side passage to the back door. It was slightly ajar, as if someone had been in too much of a hurry to close it.

'Frank,' he called. 'Frank – are you about? It's Aden Sawle. Can I talk to you?'

There was no answer but as he watched the door began to open slowly, little by little. Ice trailed down Aden's spine. He called again. Then a cat squeezed through the opening, mewing pitifully as it pressed itself against his legs. He reached down to stroke it and felt something sticky on its fur. He knew even before he looked at his fingers that it was blood; it was still wet so whatever Frank had done, it couldn't have happened long before Aden arrived. Maybe there was a chance he was still alive.

Aden hesitated, steeling himself before going in. Frank was slumped across the kitchen table, his throat cut, blood oozing into the scrubbed pine and dripping onto the rush matting on the floor. Pawprints led away from the table to the door.

'Frank – you bloody fool!'

The gorge rose in Aden's throat. He moved gingerly towards the body, trying not to tread in the blood. His stomach heaved as he saw the sharp butcher's knife lying on the floor where it had fallen from Frank's hand.

'What a mess …'

There was nothing he could do for Frank now. The butcher had taken his own life after murdering both his wife and her lover; it was a terrible tragedy and the shock of it would reverberate throughout the small community, causing endless gossip and speculation. Rebecca was going to be caught up in it when she came home.

All he could do for the moment was report this to the police. Aden turned to leave, then caught sight of a cash box on the pine dresser. Jack must have been counting his takings earlier. He hesitated, then moved decisively towards it. Frank owed him ten pounds. No sense in going through the lawyers … he was stunned as he opened the box and saw the piles of gold coins. Why there must be close on a thousand pounds … no, nearer two, and all in gold sovereigns. This was more than a few days' takings. It was Frank's own little nest egg … but why keep it here and not in the bank?

Aden grinned to himself as he realized it was money Frank had hidden from the taxman. Like many others Frank still resented the imposition of income tax: first brought in in 1799 by William Pitt to finance a war, it had been abolished twice before being reintroduced by Peel in 1842. Nearly fifty years had passed since then but it was still fiercely resented by many.

'You crafty old bugger, Frank!'

Aden took out the ten pounds he was owed and closed the box. He was about to turn away when a thought struck him. Frank and Eileen had no children nor any relatives that he knew of. So what would happen to the money? It would be a waste to let it go to the Crown after all Frank's trouble.

His hand reached towards the box then dropped. It wasn't his and there might be a distant relative he didn't know about ... but he'd never heard Frank mention even a cousin. Aden thought of all he could do with the money. It was a small fortune, enough to set him up for life. He couldn't take it, it wouldn't be right. Yet Frank wouldn't want it to go to the taxman.

Aden wrestled with his conscience, then picked up the box and took it outside. Glancing round the yard, his gaze fell on a stack of kindling. He couldn't risk taking the box with him now but if it was still here in a few days ...

He hid the box beneath the wood and told himself it was in the lap of the gods. If it was there when he came back for it it would be his. If not ... He shrugged his shoulders. It was a chance he was willing to take.

For the moment he had more important matters to attend to. Frank's suicide must be reported, and Rebecca must be told. It would be a terrible shock for her. He couldn't let her hear it from anyone else so he was going to have to tell her himself.

5

The morning after the wedding, Rebecca stood watching with the family as Victor helped his wife into the seat of his new automobile. It looked a little draughty but he placed a blanket tenderly over Celia's legs and she was already wearing a voluminous dustcoat to cover her pretty clothes and keep out the wind.

Celia had been a beautiful bride, bringing a lump to the throats of everyone present as she took her vows – including Rebecca. She hadn't grudged Celia her happiness, despite her own feelings: fate was to blame for her situation, a fate that had decreed she should meet Victor when it was already too late.

After the reception Celia threw her the bouquet. Rebecca caught it, as her friend had intended. 'You'll be next,' she cried, and clapped her hands in delight.

Rebecca shook her head and smiled. It was hardly likely she would marry in the near future.

Now, after a night spent together at her parents' home, Celia and her husband were about to leave on their wedding trip.

Victor shook hands with the family then moved down the line to Rebecca. For one brief moment their eyes met and held, making her tremble inside, then he leaned forward to kiss her cheek.

'Take care of yourself, dear Rebecca,' he said softly. 'You must come and visit us when we return.'

'Thank you. I wish you both a safe journey and much happiness.'

Her throat tightened with emotion. He did care for her a little: it wasn't just lust. She blinked hard, waving at them both as the horseless carriage was driven away. How she longed to be sitting at Victor's side! It would be so wonderful to be his wife.

Suddenly, she sensed that she was being watched and turned her head to see Philip staring at her with a vicious, gloating expression in his eyes. He really believed that she had been Victor's mistress – and hated her for her rejection of his own advances. Thank goodness she would never have to see him again!

She felt miserable and wretched as she went into the house to finish her packing. This visit had promised so much but now she knew she didn't belong here: it was Celia's world, not hers.

She must put aside her foolish dreams and try to find a life for herself. Perhaps now that she had finally grown up she could talk to her father. She was suddenly anxious to see him – to show him that she loved him.

Chastened but a little wiser, she sat deep in thought throughout what seemed far too long a journey. Celia and the other girls had talked of marriage so much during that last year at school that she had allowed it to become too important in her own mind.

In future she would be content to be a companion to her father. Many women in her circumstances were obliged to stay at home and care for a parent – perhaps that was her destiny. She would learn to accept it, to fill her days with some kind of useful work.

She looked eagerly out of the window as the train drew into the station at last. Her letter had given exact details and she was expecting to be met. No one seemed to be waiting for her, however, so she stood a little disconsolately by her trunk, which the guard had dumped unceremoniously on the platform, feeling cold and anxious. Had her letter gone astray?

The weather had taken a turn for the worse and a chill breeze had sprung up, causing her to turn up the collar of her coat. Dark clouds scudded across the sky and it looked as if it might rain before long.

Just as she was beginning to think of asking a porter to store her trunk while she walked home she saw a man come on to the platform and look in her direction. Her heart jerked in sudden fright as the whistle blew loudly behind her and the man began to stride purposefully towards her. Surely he hadn't been sent to fetch her? Aden Sawle – the man her father had forbidden her to speak to!

As he drew nearer his expression warned her that something was wrong. She felt chilled and fear gnawed at her. This wasn't right. Her father would never have sent Aden to fetch her. Why was he looking so grim?

'What is it?' she asked as he reached her. 'Something has happened ...'

'Rebecca.' His eyes were compassionate, sorrowful. 'I wanted to tell you myself. Your father ... you'll have to be brave, lass.'

'Is he ill?' The fear had become a churning sickness in her stomach and all at once she knew. 'He – he's dead, isn't he? That's what you've come to tell me, isn't it?'

He was reluctant to answer, staring at her hesitantly for a moment before inclining his head. 'I'm sorry. So very sorry, Rebecca. It's no use trying to soften the blow. I had to tell you – you had to know.'

The ground had been swept from beneath her feet, leaving her stunned and dismayed. It must be a bad dream! The last few days – Philip's attempt at rape, Victor's admission that he wanted her but would still marry Celia, and now this – it must all be part of a continuing nightmare. Any moment now she would wake up in her own bed and hear her father calling to her that it was time for breakfast.

'How – how did he die?' She sounded so cool, so calm, but she had to hold back the screams because if she let go she would lose control.

Aden stared at her in silence, obviously seeking the right words to answer her. When at last he began to speak she understood that look of horror in his eyes.

'Jack was murdered in his own bedroom.' Aden took a deep breath. 'Eileen was with him. She's dead, too. Stabbed ... both stabbed.' His face looked grey. 'Dotty found them first and came running out into the yard, screaming. She was hysterical, babbling on so fast I could hardly understand her. After she told me I went up. I had to be sure before we called the police ...'

Rebecca could imagine the scene: blood everywhere and the horror of seeing them lying there. It must have been like walking into a living nightmare. The pictures crowded into her mind and she could smell the blood, taste it in her mouth and throat. She swayed, clutching at Aden's arm to stop herself falling as the world crumbled around her. It was so horrible, an evil dream, beyond comprehension: her father dead ... murdered with his mistress beside him.

'It was Frank, wasn't it? He killed them. She told me that he was insanely jealous.'

She thought of Eileen, so pretty and full of life … now she was dead, murdered in the cruellest way by a man who claimed to love her.

'Yes, he killed them – and then himself.' Aden's face had gone an odd colour. 'Afterwards, I went to the shop. Frank was in the back kitchen with his throat cut. There was a cat … its fur was sticky when I stroked it …'

'It must have been awful.'

'Best forgotten now,' he said, checking himself as if he felt he'd already said too much. 'The police are satisfied it was Frank. There'll be an inquest, of course, but you won't have to be there. I wouldn't let them contact you before – didn't want to spoil your friend's wedding. I thought this was the best way.'

A faint moan escaped Rebecca. She had gone very pale and clutched at her head as everything seemed to start spinning around her. She would have fallen but Aden was there to support her. She pressed her face into his shoulder, breathing in the scents of hay and body musk as she began to sob. His arms tightened around her and she felt the touch of his mouth against her forehead.

'That's it, my dear one,' he whispered huskily. 'Cry as much as you like. I'm here. I shan't leave you, not ever again. Hush, my little love. It's all right …'

She hardly heard the words; it was so comforting to be in his arms, to be held and soothed like a child. He was strong and reassuring – and there was no one else. No one she could turn to for help. Her father had been all she had. They had not been as close as they might have been and now she felt it was her fault.

'Oh, Father,' she whispered. 'I'm so sorry … so very sorry. Forgive me.'

If only she hadn't gone away. If she had been there she might have been able to do something – to have prevented the tragedy – but it was too late now. Her father was dead and she was left with a sense of guilt and a terrible emptiness.

Aden was leading her outside to where his waggon was waiting. She clung to him, needing the strength of his arms to support her. He spoke to a porter about her trunk and as she saw it being loaded on to the waggon, she panicked.

'I can't go back there – to The Arms! I couldn't bear it.'

'It's all arranged,' he said, and smiled. 'You're to stay with a friend of mine in Mepal. Sarah's a good old soul. You'll be safe with her until this is all over and you're more yourself.'

He gave her his handkerchief; it was large, clean and white. She wiped her face, gazing up at him uncertainly.

'Why are you doing all this for me? I've never given you cause to like me.'

'Happen I like you anyway. Don't bother your head over me, Rebecca. I do what I want. Always have, always will.'

A sound that might have been a sob or a laugh escaped her as he helped her up on the box seat of the waggon. 'Yes,' she said. 'I suppose you do.'

She was beginning to control her emotions now. Deep inside her there was pain mingled with regret and grief but she was determined to hide it, to behave as normally as possible, though whether out of a sense of pride or what was proper she didn't know. She blew her nose and slipped the handkerchief into her pocket.

'Tell me more about your friend,' she said as he flicked the reins and the waggon began to rumble through the streets. There was a bitter chill in the air but no sign of the rain that had threatened earlier; the sky was now a curious pearly grey that seemed to stretch endlessly into the distance over the flat land.

'Sarah Black is past seventy – or that's what she admits to. Some folk say she's nearer ninety. She lives just across the road from me and has been a widow for years. I've always found her goodhearted. She was a seamstress when she was a girl, still does a bit of sewing for folk now and then. I think you'll like her.'

The sureness of his deep voice was comforting, helping Rebecca to cling to normality, to push the horror of her father's death to a small corner of her mind, where it would lie dormant until she could bear to think about it.

'She sounds interesting.' A wistful note had crept into her voice. 'Like the grandmother everyone wants.'

'Aye, happen she does.' Aden glanced at her. 'You've no one of your own, have you?'

'Father had a cousin but he died two years ago. There's no one but me ...'

'You'll be needing some help with things then?' His eyes were fixed on the road ahead. 'I could talk to the lawyers for you, arrange whatever you like ... if you wanted?'

She wasn't sure how to answer him. There had been a quarrel between this man and her father – yet she had to trust someone.

'Sorry. You'll not be wanting to think of that yet. I'll mind my own business.'

'It was a kind thought. Perhaps we could talk about it later?'

'Of course.' His eyes never left the road. 'We shan't be long now. I'll soon have you out of this cold. You'll be safe and warm in Sarah's cottage. She'll look after you, lass. Don't you worry … don't you worry about a thing.'

Sarah was a little wizened witch of a woman with sparse grey hair and twinkling eyes. She clucked after Rebecca like a hen with her chick, drawing her close to the fire and settling her in a rocking chair with a mug of warming soup in her hands.

'Drink that, my lovey,' she crooned. 'It's a bitter, raw day outside and you need something inside you.'

'Thank you.' Rebecca was still too numbed to do more than watch as Aden carried her trunk upstairs. 'You're very kind.'

By the time he came down again she had begun to thaw out and take stock of her surroundings. The kitchen was the main room of Sarah's cottage, with a small parlour behind. Against one wall stood a painted dresser set with thick blue and white crockery. There were peg rugs on the quarry-tiled floor, a recently blacked cooking range, a scrubbed pine table and chairs – but its warm, homely atmosphere came from the scent of herbs and the soup pot, simmering on the hob.

'Off home with you now, Aden,' Sarah said as he hovered uncertainly. 'Leave Rebecca to me.'

'No …' She came to herself with a start. 'I shall be glad if you'll see to things for me, Aden. On the way here you said …' She faltered on a sob. 'Help me …'

'Of course. Leave it all to me, lass. I'll take care of things for you.'

'Thank you,' she whispered as the tears spilled over. 'I don't know what I would have done if you …'

'Come away, lass,' Sarah urged. 'Upstairs and take off your things. Happen you could do with a lie down.'

'Yes … yes, I think I should like to rest for a while.'

She was conscious of Aden's dark eyes following her as she walked up the stairs and she was grateful … grateful for his strength, a strength she would need to get her through the dark days ahead.

*

Rebecca's eyes were dry as she stood beside the yawning black hole into which her father's coffin had just been lowered. She had wept until there were no more tears and now she was angry – angry that she had never really known her father, angry with him for throwing his life away and ruining hers.

During the service she had been aware of the whispers and of the eyes watching her – watching and condemning. The church was packed with people who had ostensibly come to mourn Jack Cottrel and support her, but she sensed that many of them were there out of curiosity. She had been glad to have Aden's solid presence beside her, his steady manner reassuring her, giving her courage. She wasn't sure she could have borne it without him.

People were gossiping. Sarah and Aden had done their best to protect her but even John Bently had seemed shocked and awkward as he murmured empty phrases of sympathy. She thought he was relieved that he had never spoken the words which would have bound him to her, but at least he had tried to be kind. Other people she knew had actually crossed the street rather than speak to her. She was beyond the pale, smeared and tainted by the scandal of the murders. Everyone was embarrassed, even those who had tried to be generous – everyone except Sarah and Aden Sawle.

As she turned from the graveside Aden was waiting for her, standing a respectful distance away, his cap in his hands. They walked together from the churchyard, Rebecca's hand resting lightly on his arm as she nodded to the few folk still lingering outside. In the circumstances they had decided not to invite anyone back for the customary tea and sandwiches: it would have been a travesty, a macabre play.

'That's over then,' Aden said as he helped her up into his waggon for the journey home. 'You'll feel better in a day or two.'

'Yes, thank you.' Rebecca had been silent for a while, now she voiced what was on her mind. 'I want to sell The Arms as soon as possible.'

'Sell?' He was startled, surprised that she should choose to speak of business on this particular day, but she had to speak now, before the mood of despair overcame her. 'There's time to think of that once you're ...'

'I've made up my mind. Father told me ages ago that every-thing was left to me. I shall sell it all.'

Aden studied her in silence, then nodded. 'Happen that's best. You wouldn't want to go back there.'

'Nor could I run it alone.' She smoothed the fingers of her black leather gloves. 'Dotty must be compensated, her wages and a bit more – and the grooms. Will you see to it for me, Aden?'

'You know I will. Anything you want. You only have to say.'

'That's settled then. Now let's talk of something else please.'

'Well,' he said, easing the reins to let the horses walk slowly, 'happen you'd like to see Dolly's new calf? She's a right pretty little beast and as greedy as they come ...'

Rebecca relaxed as he talked, some of the hurt and anger draining out of her. Aden had proved himself a good friend and she was in no hurry to get home ... Where was her home? She could not stay with Sarah forever, though she seemed to be content to have Rebecca there, but eventually she must move on. Where could she go? There was no one to care, no one to mind what she did now.

During the next few weeks Rebecca became more and more aware of what it meant to have no family, no father, no friends, except for dear old Sarah and Aden Sawle.

She watched the autumn turn into winter, the bright red and gold leaves falling to fade under her feet. It was a depressing time of year with heavy mists and long, cold, lonely nights when she lay staring into the darkness, unable to sleep. Her thoughts were often as bleak as the dank, dark fenland. What was the point of going on? She was alone, her life overshadowed by the horror of the murders. If she had ever dreamed of marrying well that dream was over. She could imagine what Celia's family and friends would think when they heard.

She had not dared to write to Celia, nor did she expect her to get in touch. Despite their long friendship it would not be proper for Celia now to know someone who had been tainted by scandal.

Rebecca had fallen into the habit of walking by the river each afternoon. It broke the tedium of long, empty hours and somehow she was drawn by that sluggish, icy brown water. It would be so easy to slip into that water, to walk out until she could move no longer and the weight of her clothes dragged her down ... down and down to the twilight depths where she would feel no more pain.

This particular afternoon her thoughts were more than usually gloomy. She had been standing staring at the river watching the ripples for a long time. Why not? Why not end it now? The thought was strangely compelling and she moved towards the edge of the bank, half-dazed, drawn by the peaceful darkness of those murky waters.

'Rebecca! Rebecca ... wait!'

The man's shout made her start, breaking the odd trance that had held her. She turned as Aden came hurrying up to her, his breath making little white clouds on the frosty air.

'What are you doing here?' he demanded roughly, catching her arm and forcing her back from the edge. 'It's a raw day. You would be better inside by the fire.'

'I was just ... looking at the river.' It was not true. If he had not come she would have done something foolish and wicked. It was a sin to take a life, even her own. 'But you're right, it's too cold. I'll go back to Sarah's. She'll be worrying about me.'

How could she have contemplated an act that would hurt that kind old woman? She had done her best for Rebecca and would have blamed herself if any harm had come to the girl.

'I'll walk with you.' Aden's determined manner made her smile inwardly as he held her arm and marched her towards the road and out of danger.

'I'm not taking you from your work, am I?'

'I've always time for you, you must know that?'

'Yes.' Rebecca smiled and felt better. How could she have thought that she was all alone when he was her friend? 'Yes, I know that, Aden.'

'You got your things all right? Everything you wanted?'

'Yes, thank you.'

He had fetched her personal belongings from The Arms himself. The whole place had been thoroughly cleaned, all traces of the blood removed, and the furniture cleared to a saleroom in March market. There was nothing left to remind anyone of what had happened there, though it was bound to affect the price of the property.

'I've spoken to the auctioneers,' Aden went on. 'The Arms is up for sale, together with the stock. You've nothing to bother your head over, Rebecca. It's all taken care of.'

She pulled her muffler tighter around her neck. She had walked a long way, her head down, battling against the bitter wind and her even more bitter thoughts. The washes were bleak, lonely stretches of flat grass on either side of the river with huge docks sprouting here and there. Aden had told her that every year the broad green leaves had to be dug up before the stock was put out

62

to graze in the spring, because otherwise they ate them and made themselves ill. Aden was always telling her something … lifting her spirits … easing the ache around her heart. He was always there when she needed him.

'No,' she whispered as she looked up at him. 'Nothing to worry about.'

The tiny room under the eaves was crowded with the things she'd had brought from The Arms but at least Rebecca could be alone there. Sarah never disturbed her. She knew when to leave a body in peace and Rebecca had needed solitude; she'd needed time to think, time to let her raw wounds mend and heal.

For the past hour or more she had been staring into space thinking … thinking about Aden Sawle. It was strange how much she had come to depend on him, to anticipate his easy smile and listen for the sound of his deep voice at Sarah's door.

Rebecca's life had changed so swiftly, so irrevocably. Sometimes she felt as if the past were a dream and this the only reality. It was as if she had never been away to school, never danced with Victor Roth, never believed herself to be falling in love with the man who belonged to her best friend. She felt as if she had walked down a long, dark tunnel, looking neither to left nor right. It was night and there was no dawn, no way back to the girl she had been, the naive, slightly spoiled, foolish girl who had not realized how lucky she was. Her life had changed; she could not go back, only forward.

In the distance she could hear the sound of church bells calling the faithful to evensong. It was the first day of a new week, perhaps for her the first day of a new life. Putting on her coat she walked down the narrow staircase that led to Sarah's kitchen. Her decision was made.

'Going for a walk then?' she asked, her eyes mild and incurious. 'Wrap up warm, dearie.'

'I'm going to see Aden.'

Sarah was silent for a moment, then nodded. 'Yes, yes, 'tis the way for you now.'

Those mild, old eyes saw so much more than most. 'Yes,' said Rebecca, 'it's the way for me now.'

Aden looked surprised when he answered the door to her knock. He was wearing his Sunday clothes but had taken off his jacket and his shirt sleeves were rolled up to the elbows, revealing the crisp, dark hair on his forearms. She was very aware of the muscular body beneath those clothes, of his strength, both physical and mental.

'Rebecca, what are you doing here at this hour? Nothing wrong with Sarah, is there?'

'No. I've come to visit you. Won't you ask me in?'

'Yes, of course.' He stood back to allow her to enter. 'I was surprised, that's all.'

She smiled but didn't answer as she glanced round the large kitchen. Lit by two pretty oil lamps, it had low ceilings with blackened beams and white-washed walls; there was a sink of sorts beneath the window and a tap for water. The range was a combination of oven, hob and open fire, and it had been cleaned recently. The red floor tiles were polished and the table had a well-scrubbed appearance. Aden was either very capable of looking after himself or he had someone in to clean. By the fire there was an old rocking chair with bright chintz cushions tied to the splatted back; its worn seat was also fitted with a soft cushion. Against the far wall was an ugly daybed, and an equally ugly sideboard filled the space opposite the range.

The door to the adjoining parlour stood open. To reach it you had to step down, which accounted for the higher ceiling. A dull brown carpet covered the floorboards and the furniture had seen better days – but that was easily put right.

On the hob the kettle was beginning to boil. Rebecca sat down in the rocking chair and smiled to herself: there was a great deal to be done but it would serve her purpose for a while.

'Aren't you going to offer me tea?'

'Of course – if you're staying?'

'I'm staying.'

She watched as he moved about the kitchen, pouring water into a large brown pot and fetching a jug of milk from the pantry. It wouldn't take her long to make new curtains and that dreadful carpet would have to go. In fact she would discard all the furniture … perhaps not the pretty sewing table in the parlour, though: that had an octagonal top inlaid with marquetry and she liked it. With a little thought Aden's cottage could be charming, a real home, better than the rooms above The Arms. She accepted the tea he brought her in a thick mug and was glad she had kept her mother's best china.

Aden was watching her intently as she sipped her tea. 'Is it too strong for you?'

'I like strong tea – and I like your home.'

'It's all right,' he replied, looking about him doubtfully. 'I've been meaning to fix it up a bit. New curtains and maybe a carpet …'

'You can leave all that to me.' Rebecca glanced up, a teasing expression in her eyes. 'You've got your work, Aden. Besides, I shall enjoy doing it.'

'What do you mean?' There was surprise and a glimmer of hope in his eyes and she knew she had not been mistaken in him. 'Speak plainly, Rebecca. I'm maybe imagining things but that sounds as though …' He looked stunned as she put down her mug and stood up. 'You're not making fun of me, are you?'

'Why would I do that?' she asked in a soft voice. 'I want to make this place comfortable for you, Aden. Make it a proper home – a home to raise children in. Father left me several thousand pounds and there'll be more when The Arms is sold.'

'Rebecca.' He sounded breathless, his face working with emotion. 'Nay, don't say it, lass. You'd never look at me. I'm a plain working man, not good enough for you.'

'You're no fool,' she said, and the teasing note had gone. She was serious now as she saw the mixture of anxiety and disbelief in his face. 'You're ambitious. You want to make something of your-self – with a bit of help you could do it. Within a few years you could be a rich man. Rich enough to keep me in style, with a big house and a carriage.'

'It wouldn't take me long with a bit of money behind me,' he agreed, but was still hesitant. 'Are you sure about this? Do you know what you're doing – what you'll be giving up if you marry me? You could do better, lass – a man of your own sort, educated and …'

'Don't put me on a pedestal. What chance have I got of making that kind of a marriage now? Most men would run from the scandal. You've been the only one with guts enough to stand by me.'

'You think that now, but in a few months people will start to forget. In a year or two you could make new friends, start over somewhere else.'

'Run away! Is that what you think of me?' Her head went up proudly. 'No. I'll stay, and be damned to the lot of them!' She gave him a challenging look. 'Well, Aden Sawle, are you going to ask me to marry you?'

He stared at her for a moment, then his mouth began to twitch at the corners. 'I'm asking, Rebecca. Believe me, I'm asking. You may live to regret it but I'd be a fool to let a chance like this slip.'

The laughter bubbled up inside her. She had not been mistaken in him. Perhaps he was right, perhaps she would regret her impetuosity one day, but for now it seemed the only way forward.

'As proposals go that was probably the worst sort,' she said. 'But I accept. You can kiss me now if you like.'

'Becky ...' She stopped him with a frown. 'What's wrong?'

'Never Becky,' she said. 'My name is Rebecca.' She smiled to soften the words. One day she would tell him why she hated the abbreviation. 'We'd best start as we mean to go on.' She moved closer, tipping her face towards him. 'Well, go on then, kiss me.'

'Rebecca ...' He reached out for her hesitantly, afraid that she would somehow disappear as she did in his dreams, but she leaned against his body, offering herself for his kiss. 'Rebecca, my love. I'll be good to you. I swear I won't let you down.'

As their lips touched she was surprised at the surge of emotion it aroused in her. He was gentle, almost reverent in his manner, making her feel as if she were something precious, something to be worshipped and cared for; his tenderness soothed her hurts, restoring the pride Philip Braithewaite had crushed. Aden's mouth was warm and soft, not hard or demanding; the sweetness of his kiss drew a swift response from her, arousing passions and desires she had not known existed. She clung to him, needing, wanting, the strength of his arms around her. He was her rock, her refuge in a storm, and she believed she had made the right choice. With this man beside her the future no longer seemed so bleak. Rebecca had taken her decision for practical reasons but now she suspected that there might be more to be gained from their union than she had thought.

'I love you,' he said huskily. 'I have since I saw you that day after you came home from school. I hoped but I never imagined you would look at me.'

'Oh, I looked,' she said and laughed. 'I thought you were an arrogant devil, Aden Sawle, but then ... you were there when I needed you. I shall always be grateful ...'

'It's not gratitude I want, lass.'

She hardly hesitated. 'If it's love you want, Aden, then you'll have it. All I have to give is yours.'

As he caught her in his arms once more she closed her mind to dreams. She had believed herself in love with Victor Roth but all that belonged to another life, a different world; the girl who had danced with Victor had gone. That girl had been humiliated and hurt, carrying the sting of rejection with her as she struggled with her grief, and a woman had been born in her place.

The past seemed distant and unreal. This was what mattered. Aden wasn't the refined gentleman she had dreamed of, he wasn't Victor, but he was a good, decent man and he loved her.

It was enough. It had to be.

6

The solicitor's office was dark and had a dry, dusty atmosphere; there was an odd smell, which seemed to come from the shelves of ancient books and piles of yellowing documents spilling over table tops, out of cabinets and lying in seeming disorder on the floor. Rebecca wondered how anything was ever found and wasn't surprised that wills were often tied up in chancery for years; that thought made her frown but her attention was recalled as the lawyer began to speak.

'I'm not sure I can permit it, Miss Cottrel.' He faced her across the broad sweep of his imposing desk, which was cluttered with pen trays, inkstands and more documents tied with pink ribbon. 'Your father's will made me your trustee and I am in effect your guardian until you come of age.'

He was an elderly man, thin and sour-looking with skin almost the colour of old parchment. She had disliked him on sight but forced herself to smile.

'Yes, of course, I understand that, sir – but as a not inconsiderable heiress it would surely be best for me to marry. My husband would then be able to manage my affairs and save you the time and trouble. Do you not agree, Mr Ward?'

'Well, yes ...' He cleared his throat and glanced at Aden. 'I would agree but ...'

Rebecca was dressed all in black. Her blouse was a heavy self-striped silk with a high neck, to which she had fastened a cameo brooch that had belonged to her mother. It made her look older than her years. She touched a finger to the brooch as she considered her next move.

'Mr Sawle is my choice. His mother and mine were friends and

68

our families have known each other for years.' She smiled at him winningly. 'Mr Sawle has his own land and is well respected – what possible objection could there be?'

The lawyer's eyes met hers and dropped. He fiddled with the pens in front of him as he sought for his answer. She knew then that she was winning their little battle of wills.

'I'm just not sure your father would have wanted you to marry so soon. You are only just nineteen ...'

'My father would have wished me to be happy and safe. And since we cannot ask him for his opinion, I believe my own wishes should be paramount.' Her eyes challenged him. 'I have no relations to care for me. At the moment I am staying with a neighbour of Mr Sawle's but that cannot continue and I think you would agree that it would not be proper for me to live alone?'

'Of course. I was not doubting ... perhaps next year ...'

'In Scotland we could be married after three weeks of residence.'

'Miss Cottrel!' He was shocked. 'You would not elope? It is not to be thought of.'

'I shall do what I have to do, sir. If you are so unreasonable as to deny my request.'

'Miss Cottrel ... Mr Sawle ...' He opened his hands, looking from one to the other, then sighed deeply as he saw they were not to be dissuaded. 'Very well, if you are determined. Give me a few days and I'll have the necessary papers drawn up.'

He looked resigned, perhaps even relieved to have the matter resolved.

'Thank you.' Rebecca stood up and drew on her gloves. 'I shall need an advance of at least four hundred pounds. I want to furnish my new home.'

'That won't be necessary.' Aden spoke for the first time since greeting the lawyer. 'I've a bit put by. Keep your money until we decide what to do with it, Rebecca.'

'The sale of The Cottrel Arms will release a tidy sum,' the solicitor said. 'The rest of Mr Cottrel's money is invested and will take time to sort out.'

'Mr Sawle will be in touch with you to decide what's best. In future he will manage all my affairs.'

She swept out of the office, her long skirts and stiff silk petticoats rustling imperiously. Aden moved forward, offering his hand to the solicitor.

'You'll let us know when the papers are ready then?' he asked, and there was authority in his tone as they shook hands. He had remained silent throughout the interview, biding his time, but now he was clearly in charge. 'We've set our minds to a wedding in the New Year.'

'Of course. Certainly, Mr Sawle. When you come next time we can go through the papers together. Mr Cottrel had many different interests and I should appreciate your help in sorting out the estate.' There was a new respect in the lawyer's tone. 'Perhaps next week ... Thursday?'

'I'll look forward to that,' Aden promised with a nod. 'Thank you, Mr Ward.'

Moments later as they stood outside in the chill of a severe frost he turned to Rebecca and grinned. 'Well, you told him, lass. I thought he was going to stand on his rights but you shook him with your talk of running off to Scotland. You wouldn't have done it, of course.'

'Wouldn't I?'

Rebecca's eyes sparkled. The lawyer had annoyed her with his attempts to thwart her plans.

'Mebbe you would at that. Poor old Ward certainly believed you.'

She laughed, her annoyance gone. 'Was I too hard on him? He made me cross. As if he knew what my father would have wanted for me.'

'I doubt if Jack would be too happy about your marrying me.' Aden looked serious. 'We were friends once but we fell out.'

'Over that council land?' He seemed startled and she nodded, a little smile on her lips. 'I thought that must be it. Dotty Prentice hinted at something once – and Father was furious with you that morning.'

'It was business, that's all.' He was reluctant to discuss it. 'I've regretted the quarrel a thousand times – but I needed that land. At the time it was the only way I had of getting on a bit.'

'You're ambitious.' She gazed up at him, trying to read his thoughts. 'It's one of the things I like about you, Aden. You don't have to explain if you don't want to – it's over and my life is my own affair.'

'And mine ...'

'Yes, of course. I think I made that quite clear to Mr Ward just now.'

70

'Aye, you did that.' Aden chuckled.

She took his arm as they walked to the stables. The streets of the small market town were almost deserted but for a passing baker's van drawn by one tired old horse and two women with baskets on their arms gossiping outside the draper's shop. She stopped to glance in the window at an array of foulards and creamy white Broche Japanese silks, thinking that she might purchase some for her trousseau, and was reminded of something Aden had said earlier.

'Why won't you let me use my money for the cottage?'

'It's just a whim.' A puckish smile touched his mouth. 'I've a bit put by. We'll invest your money in land, Rebecca. There's a hundred acres of good fenland coming up for auction soon. I reckon we'll put in a bid for it. We may not see much return for a year or two, but trust me – I'll make you rich one day, lass.'

'I've every confidence in you.' She tipped her head to one side. 'Can you afford to give me four hundred pounds? Some of it is for wedding clothes, you know. Just fripperies and foolish things.'

'I had a little windfall, found some money ... in the loft. My father must have tucked it away for his old age. You're welcome to the four hundred, lass.'

'Thank you.'

She accepted his word. There was more to Aden Sawle than met the eye but she didn't particularly care if the money had been found or gained through wheeling and dealing. He was ambitious. He would take risks for profit. She sensed a certain ruthlessness in him over business but that suited her purpose. Her father had left her a reasonable sum of money but she wanted to be rich. Aden was the man to give her all the things she wanted.

'All right, I'll take your money. I doubt I shall need the half of it. I was just trying to make that old skinflint pay up. He'll hang on to my inheritance for years if we let him.'

'Oh, no, he won't.' Aden set his jaw. 'You just leave Arthur Ward to me, lass. Once we're married I'll make him put a move on. Believe me.'

Rebecca was tempted to giggle as she saw his determination. She almost felt sorry for the lawyer. Aden was obviously not going to stand for any nonsense.

The morning of their wedding was fine and clear. She glanced out of the window, her spirits soaring: it was the beginning of a new year, a new life.

She turned back to the small dressing mirror, which was a rather fine one set in a wooden stand so that it tipped freely and she could see most of herself. She fiddled with the lacy veil around her face. Her dress was a simple style in creamy silk, very suitable for the ceremony in the village church. It was to be a quiet affair. Neither she nor Aden had invited many guests. Just a distant cousin and a few friends on his side, Sarah, and one or two people who had been polite enough to call on Rebecca recently. She had prepared the refreshments herself the previous evening and they were laid out under cloths in Aden's cold pantry.

There was to be no wedding trip. It would have cost more than six guineas each for a few days in Geneva, though they could have sailed from Dover to France for five, but Aden could not really spare the time away from the farm and she wanted to make a start on refurbishing the cottage. Besides, the money would have kept a family for more than a month and was needed for more important things.

For a moment as she stared at her reflection in the mirror she thought of what might have been. If Victor had met her first ... if she had been other than the daughter of a publican.

'Forget him,' she whispered to the image in the mirror. 'He was a dream, only a dream. This is reality ...'

'Did you say something, lovey?' Sarah had come into the room and was looking at her anxiously. 'Not regretting it, lass? Aden Sawle is a good man, he'll look after you better than most.'

'No, of course I'm not regretting it,' she replied, and gathered up the posy of snowdrops Aden had sent round that morning. He must have picked them from a sheltered spot in his garden: the dew was still on them and they smelt like spring. 'Is it time to leave?'

It was only a short walk to the church but Aden had borrowed a pony and trap to carry her there. His yardman had groomed the pony until its coat shone, and the harness was decorated with burnished brasses. As he helped her up to the seat she saw it was covered with velvet and pinned with ribbons to give it a festive air.

'Thank you, Arthur,' she said. 'You must have been up early to get all this ready for me.'

'Pleasure, Miss Cottrel.' He tugged awkwardly at the stiffness of his starched collar, looking uncomfortable in his Sunday clothes.

A wedding was a big event in the village and a small group of women, old men and children had gathered outside the church to watch her arrive. Since she had no one of her own the vicar's brother had offered to give her away. He was waiting for her in the porch, an elderly man who smiled and came forward to offer his arm. She laid her hand on it, blinking away sudden tears as a picture of her father flashed into her mind. He should have been here today – and yet if he had lived she would not have been marrying Aden Sawle.

Walking down the aisle on a stranger's arm she knew a moment of fear. What was she doing? Was she making a terrible mistake? She hardly knew Aden …

She had reached him now. He turned to smile at her and her panic receded. It was foolish to regret, foolish to doubt. Sarah was right, Aden was a good man. Neither her doubts or her dreams were important. Aden was real. And soon she would be his wife.

At last they had the cottage to themselves. Although small the reception had been a merry gathering, and Rebecca had begun to think their guests would never go. Sarah had insisted on staying on after the others eventually left to help with the dishes, lingering by the fire to sip the glass of sweet sherry Aden had pressed on her until it was dark outside. He had seen her safely home but now he was back and they were finally alone.

Rebecca watched as he banked up the fire so that it would hold overnight. He moved confidently about the kitchen, attending to all the necessary chores as he usually did. Now that it was almost time for bed she had begun to feel a little nervous, unsure of what she ought to do next.

'Perhaps I should go up now?'

'Aye, you do that, Rebecca. I'll not be long. I've a few jobs to see to outside but they'll not take a minute.'

She was grateful for a few minutes to herself. She knew nothing about the intimate side of marriage, except what she had learned at school. There was of course a remarkable booklet which promised to tell young women everything they ought to know about the ideal husband and was available by post for one shilling, but she had not liked to send for it, even though it was advertised in a respectable magazine. Her friends had whispered to her about what went on behind bedroom doors but they were as ignorant of the truth as she. Not that she was unaware of the facts of life – it was just how people went about these things that teased her as she walked slowly up to the room she would share with Aden. What would he expect of her? How should she behave when he came to her?

She ought to have asked Sarah but she'd been too embarrassed. Slipping off her stays and then her heavy winter petticoats, she pulled on a warm, high-necked nightdress that covered her from just beneath her chin to her ankles, then flicked her long hair over her shoulders and sat down to brush it.

In the soft yellow light of the candles her dark hair seemed thick and luxuriant, falling about her face and down her back almost to her waist. Was she attractive? Her face was a little thin. She wasn't delicate and she didn't have Celia's fragile prettiness. Would Aden find her pleasing?

She picked up a pot of Clubb's cucumber balm and applied a dab to her hands, feeling they were a little red and needed soothing, then, hearing Aden's step on the stairs, she felt a tingle of apprehension and ran for the bed, instinctively drawing the covers up to her neck and trembling inwardly as she waited for him to come in. His eyes were drawn straight to her and she saw them light with anticipation.

'Everything's tucked up for the night,' he said. 'We're safe and cosy now, lass.'

He went behind a painted screen to undress. As she listened to him moving about it dawned on her that he was nervous, too. That made her feel better and when he came out from behind the screen wearing a nightshirt she was sitting up against the pillows with a smile of welcome on her face. She held out her hand to him as he sat on the edge of the bed.

'Rebecca,' he said gruffly. 'You're that lovely ...'

'Am I, Aden?' She lifted her face, inviting his kiss. A tingle of pleasure danced along her spine as she felt the warm caress of his lips. His mouth was soft yet firm and seeking, coaxing, a response from hers. 'Do I please you? Only I don't know what you want me to do – will you tell me?'

'Just be yourself,' he said huskily. 'I'll be gentle with you. You know I love you, don't you?'

'Yes. Yes, I know.'

He drew back the covers and lay down beside her, gathering

her against the length of his hard, muscular body, and she felt the pulsating heat of his flesh through her nightgown. She sensed that he was in the grip of some strong emotion and responded to the urgent need in him instinctively. His tongue traced the delicate shape of her ear, stroking and caressing as he whispered to her, then he unfastened the strings that tied her nightgown so that he could kiss the little pulse at the base of her throat. She trembled, feeling a sudden surge of excitement low in her belly, and began at last to understand desire.

'Just a moment,' she whispered, and as he released her, looking puzzled, she pulled her nightgown up over her head and dropped it on the floor. 'We don't want that getting in the way, do we?'

The expression in his eyes made her breathless; they seemed to dwell on her breasts with a kind of hunger mixed with reverence, then travel downwards over her flat navel to the mass of crisp curls at the source of her femininity – and she sensed that to Aden she was beautiful.

'Your skin is so soft ... like cream silk,' he murmured throatily. 'A pale goddess ...'

'Oh, Aden ...'

Tears of happiness caught at her throat. It made her feel humble to be loved so much. No one had ever said such things to her. His hand moved slowly down the length of her and he moaned softly in his throat, then he threw his nightshirt off and, as his naked body covered hers, she felt the burn of his thrusting manhood against her thigh. Her stomach spasmed with excitement as he began to kiss her breasts, taking her nipples into his mouth with little teasing movements of his tongue that made her gasp with pleasure. She had not dreamed it would be like this and her nails curved into the flesh of his shoulder as she moved and moaned beneath him.

'I'm not upsetting you, lass?'

'No,' she whispered. 'I like it, Aden. It feels nice – no, better than nice. It's ... I can't explain but I don't want you to stop.'

He chuckled deep in his throat, then ran his hands down over her body, exploring the soft, secret places of her femininity, his fingers so sure and gentle that they made her tingle and burn with pleasure. Her cries were stifled beneath his kisses as she felt the moisture run between her thighs and her body moved in response to his caresses, lifting, opening as a flower to welcome rain, and then he was on her, the lance-hard heat of him thrusting deep inside her. She felt a sharp, tearing pain and jerked back in fright. He was instantly still, his face anxious as he looked down at her, afraid of causing her too much pain. She reached up, pulling his head down so that his face was close to hers and their breath mingled.

'Don't hold back,' she whispered. 'I want to be all yours.'

'It only hurts once,' he said, his voice a harsh crack of emotion. 'Forgive me ...'

He thrust into her again and for a moment she felt the hugeness of him filling and stretching her and she thought the pain was more than she could bear, but then it began to ease and there was a warm sluggishness between her thighs. She was breathing faster now, her hips arching to meet his frantic thrusts – then he gave a moaning sigh and collapsed on top of her. It was over. A small sigh escaped her and he raised himself on one elbow to look down at her face.

'The first time is never easy for a woman,' he said. 'I promise it will be better another time.'

'I believe you.' She touched his cheek. 'How long do we have to wait before we do it again?'

'Not very long if you look at me like that,' he murmured and chuckled deep in his throat. 'Rebecca, Rebecca my love – you are a woman of surprises.'

'It doesn't disgust you that I liked what we did?' she asked anxiously. 'Only I've heard that some women don't welcome their husband's attentions in bed.'

'Pity the husbands then,' Aden said, and drew her close, his hand moving lazily in her hair. 'You're the woman for me, Rebecca, never doubt it. A warm-hearted woman is God's blessing – and I think perhaps I've been blessed more than most ...'

She smiled as she turned into the warmth of his body. He smelt of salt and an earthy musk she found appealing. If this was a foretaste of the future she was well content.

As he drew her to him once more she gave herself up to the pleasures of his caresses. His strong loving arms held her tightly, his kisses driving out any lingering regrets she might have had.

Rebecca awoke the next morning to find Aden's side of the bed cold and empty. She sat up, realizing that she was naked, and blushing as memories of the previous night came rushing back. Whatever must he think of her?

'You're awake then, lass?'

She was startled to see him bring a cup of tea into the bedroom. He was dressed as usual in his working clothes and looked as if he had already been out in the fresh air.

'You should have woken me when you got up, Aden.'

'You were sound asleep, lass. I didn't want to disturb you.'

'I wish you had – there's so much to do and I mean to start as I intend to go on.' She sipped her tea. 'Don't you want me to help with the milking? I thought that's what farmer's wives did?'

'Not my wife. You've enough to do with the house and the dairy. You'll make butter and cheese when you've a mind to it – and the chickens are your responsibility. The eggs will be yours to use or sell as you please.' He gave her a look of such warm intimacy that she knew she had no need to blush for her response to him the previous night. 'I'll be in the yard and in for my breakfast in half an hour.'

Rebecca threw off the covers as he left, feeling eager to make a start in her new home. There was so much to do ... so much to look forward to that she need never be bored again.

'If that's a taste of what I'll be getting in future, I shall be well satisfied.' Aden pushed back his plate with a laugh and stood up. 'Leave the clearing up for a moment, Rebecca. I want to show you something.'

She looked regretfully at the dirty plates as he took her hand and led her outside. 'Where are we going?'

It was cold after the warmth of the kitchen and it had been raining, making the yard slippery beneath her feet – and she was still wearing her house shoes. Why was he in such a hurry to show her whatever it was?

'Not far.' He held her firmly, hurrying her through the yard to the paddock. 'See those fields ...' He waved his hand to encompass the paddocks and a ploughed field beyond. 'Forty acres ... land that has been in my family for generations. The land I hire from the council is on the opposite side of the road and it's good land, but this land, Rebecca ...' He bent down to scoop up a handful of earth, sniffing it before showing it to her. 'This land is ours.'

'Yes, I know, you've told me before.' She glanced up at him, surprised at the fierce pride in his face. She had known he was ambitious but hadn't realized how much the land meant to him before this. 'And soon you'll have a lot more land, Aden.'

'When I was a lad my father told me always to be true to the land because it was a sacred trust,' he said, his eyes looking beyond her and across the fields. 'You mebbe don't feel it yet, lass, but you will one day. When you've sons to come after you …'

'We don't know that I can have a son yet,' she said on a teasing note.

His eyes moved over her, seeming to devour her. 'You'll have sons,' he said, 'the Sawles always have sons.'

'And the Cottrels have daughters.'

Aden chuckled as he saw the look in her eyes. 'Then we'll have to keep trying, won't we, lass? I need sons … sons for the land. Always remember, Rebecca – no matter what – this land we hold … it may break our hearts and our bodies at times but always, always, we hold to the land.'

7

The first few months of their marriage were so blissful that Rebecca sometimes had to pinch herself to make sure she wasn't dreaming. Aden was as caring and attentive in their daily life as in their bed and she knew that she had been lucky – perhaps more so than she deserved. She had not married for love but she was being given an abundance of it and tried to make her husband happy in return, to give back a little of what he gave her.

The busy regime suited her, filling her days so that she had neither the time nor the energy to waste on reflection. Aden had offered to employ a girl to help her but she had refused, finding pleasure in her daily tasks, whether it was baking, brewing her delicious home-made ale, or pounding away at the dolly tub in the wash-house.

Aden had taken on a young lad to deliver the milk locally but it was a country tradition that eggs and cheeses were the province of a farmer's wife and that any excess could be taken to market or sold at the farm gate. Rebecca soon found that it brought a stream of visitors to her door, children on errands for their mothers or women who came as much for a gossip as the eggs.

It was a busy but rewarding way of life and Rebecca settled quickly, discovering a new kind of contentment – a fulfilment that she had never known before.

Occasionally, she would think of Celia and a small cloud hovered in the background, but then someone would call and she would forget as she listened to her neighbours' idle chatter.

There was no point in looking back. She was unlikely to see or hear from her friend ever again, and perhaps that was a good thing.

They had been married for three months and Aden could still hardly credit his good fortune. Sometimes when he came home after a hard day in the fields to find Rebecca waiting for him, he felt as if he had stumbled into paradise. He'd known when she came to him that winter night that she was proposing a marriage of convenience, but her warmth on their wedding night had surprised and delighted him.

He paused in his task of loading manure on to the muck cart, watching as Rebecca bent to take a shirt from the laundry basket and peg it to the line in the back garden. Such a simple action but it could stir him to hungry desire. The taste of her was imprinted on his mouth as he recaptured the passion of the previous night, his body remembering the welcoming wetness of hers as he'd thrust into her again and again until he was spent. The thought of her opening to him so eagerly made his loins throb. She was some woman! As eager for their loving as he, even initiating it on occasions when he would have been content to have her close.

She worked as hard as he did, cooking, cleaning and sewing, always on the go and never idle even when they sat by the fire in the evenings. Now that the evenings were drawing out again she had started to tend the flower beds under the kitchen and parlour windows.

'Let me do that,' he'd protested when he saw her struggling with a clump of twitch. 'You'll strain yourself.'

'You've enough to do.' She had refused to give in. 'I can manage.'

She'd won her battle with the stubborn grass roots, just as she conquered every obstacle of her working day. It still surprised him to walk into the cottage and see how she had transformed it. Gone were the drab colours and ugly, ungainly furniture. The parlour floor was covered by the rich reds and blues of a Persian carpet, and the colours were picked up exactly in the curtains and velvet of a comfortable sofa and two deep armchairs. Gone was the ugly sideboard in the kitchen, in its place a traditional oak dresser with shining brass handles and Rebecca's best china set out on its shelves.

The cottage had become a home. Rebecca filled it with flowers, bright colours and the delicious aroma of her cooking. Sometimes it worried him because she devoted so much time to the house and seemed to have no real friends. Sarah hobbled over to visit now and then, and both the Vicar and his wife had been to tea, but it wasn't what she had been used to. When he mentioned it, though, all she did was shake her head and smile.

'I was bored with all that visiting. I've never been as happy as I am now, Aden.'

'You are happy then, lass?'

She moved towards him, inviting his kiss, though when he'd slipped his hand inside her blouse to fondle her breasts she'd laughingly pushed him away.

'Get off with you. Time enough for that tonight, Aden Sawle.'

As he fastened the tail of the cart, she lifted her hand to wave. She had known he was watching her and he sensed that she enjoyed his silent homage. She was proud, his Rebecca, and maybe a wee bit vain, but he wouldn't have changed her.

Clicking on his horse, Aden was thoughtful as he drove out of the farmyard and along the high road before turning off down the lane that led to the field he was spreading. Life had been good to him of late. The money from the sale of The Arms had amounted to more than they'd hoped; it was lying in the bank, waiting to be spent on the land they were already buying – and then there was the rest of Frank's gold lying up there in the attic. He hadn't dared touch it, except for the money he'd given Rebecca.

On his last visit to Chatteris he'd heard gossip about Frank having died owing money. Now that his lawyers had finished sorting things out there wasn't enough to pay his debts.

'Strange that,' the landlord of The Bull had said to Aden. 'I allus thought as Frank were a warm man – strange him leaving debts, don't you think?'

'Mebbe he had a bit hid up somewhere.'

'That's what folk are saying.' The landlord looked at Aden. 'You knew him as well as anyone – did you ever hear him mention a nest egg? Only he owed me ten pounds.'

'Can't say as I did.'

The look in the other man's eyes gave Aden a few uncomfortable moments, but there was nothing he could do short of taking the cashbox to Frank's lawyers – and that would be awkward. Best not to get involved.

Aden pushed away the uneasy thoughts. When they got that new land he would need to take on another man to help him, then maybe a skilled worker and a lad to do the mucking out. Yes, things were going just as he'd hoped, he mustn't do anything to rock the boat. Frank would have hated all the talk – but what could he do?

The cart was empty now. He paused, surveying the twenty-acre field. It was decent land this, but not worth the bother it had caused him. By quarrelling with Jack Cottrel over that tender, he'd almost lost the chance of getting Rebecca. He'd hinted at blackmail that day in Jack's parlour but he would never have actually told Frank about him and Eileen – things like that left a bad taste in the mouth, though, making him feel guilty even when he'd done nothing wrong. It was strange how it had all worked out.

Fastening the tail of the cart, he was about to remount the driving block when he saw someone standing by the field gate. A woman … Dotty! What the hell was she doing here?

He led the horse and cart towards her. She saw him coming and lifted her hand in a tentative wave. As he drew closer he was shocked to see that she was obviously with child, her body heavy and ungainly. A warning bell sounded in his head.

'Where did you come from?' he asked, his voice sounding harsh even to his own ears. 'You didn't walk all the way from Chatteris in your condition?'

Dotty flushed and looked down, shuffling her muddy boots. 'I hitched a lift on a milk cart for part of the way,' she said. 'I had to see you, Aden. I need help.'

'Why not ask the father for help?'

'Don't look at me that way.' She bit her lip. 'You know it's yourn. There ain't bin no one else since you.'

Aden saw the distress in her eyes. She looked awful, her face puffy and unhealthy and her hair lank with grease. The child might or might not be his, but he couldn't deny the possibility.

'What do you want from me, Dotty?'

'I don't want to cause no trouble.' She sniffed and looked for her handkerchief. 'Only … after The Arms closed, I worked in a shop for a while but they sacked me a month ago.'

'Because of the child?'

She nodded miserably. 'I've spent all I had, Aden. Ma says she can't keep me and me pa – well, he's hit me a few times. I'd clear off to London if I had a bit of money.'

His eyes narrowed. 'How much do you need?'

'Hundred pounds would see me through nicely.'

It was a small fortune, as much as a skilled man might earn in a year and far more than a labourer could expect.

'Do you think I'm a fool?' Aden's mouth hardened. 'I'll give you fifty and not a penny more. Not ever – do you understand me, Dotty?'

She nodded and he could see from her smile that she hadn't expected that much.

'I promise I won't ask again. And I won't tell anyone who the father is neither.'

'You'd best keep your word on that. If I hear rumours I shall know who to blame.'

She flushed as he looked at her. 'I never meant Frank to find out, Aden. Cross me heart and hope to die.'

'That's in the past, but if I hear gossip about this I shall be angry.' He sighed and ran his fingers through his hair. 'I'll meet you at Chatteris market. I'm giving you the money for old times' sake, Dotty, that doesn't mean I'm admitting it's mine.'

'Ain't no doubt about it,' she said, then as he frowned, 'you needn't admit it if you don't want to, so long as I get that money.'

'Next week then,' he said. 'And don't come here again. I shan't be so easy in future.'

He climbed on to the driving board as she turned away. His little frolic had cost him dear, but it might have been worse. Dotty wasn't a bad sort. Some girls would have held out for the hundred pounds. If she had he might have given in. He couldn't risk Rebecca finding out, not now when everything was going so well.

His frown cleared as he remembered his secret hoard in the loft. He would never have found the gold in the first place if it hadn't been for Dotty. Perhaps she was entitled to her share. He toyed with the idea of giving her more, then decided against it. She would think he'd gone soft and then she'd be back again and again. No – best settle it once and for all when they met, make it quite clear the fifty pounds was all she would get from him.

Rebecca felt a sense of satisfaction as she looked round the parlour. The room smelt of beeswax and everything was clean and shining – as it ought to be after she'd spent the past two hours polishing. She ran her fingers lightly over the faded mahogany sideboard and opened the pretty musical box Aden had given her as a wedding gift. It had several metal cylinders which played a variety of tunes once it was wound up and fitted in well with the gentle elegance of the room. Perhaps it wasn't quite Braithewaite

Hall, but it was comfortable and she enjoyed sitting there when she had time.

She went upstairs to wash and change, thinking that now the house was finished she would be able to pay more attention to the garden. She wanted to plant tulips and daffodils ... perhaps even roses.

When she came down again she saw that the sky had become overcast and grey. It looked as if a storm was threatening as she picked up the linen basket and hurried outside to fetch in her washing.

She had thought Aden might be back by now. It must be well past three. As she went to the gate to see if there was any sign of him she noticed a woman walking round the bend in the road. She was walking slowly with her head down and it was obvious that she was several months gone with child, her dress stretched tightly over her bulging stomach. Rebecca was shocked as she suddenly realized it was Dotty.

'Dotty! Dotty Prentice,' she called. 'What are you doing in Mepal?'

Dotty hesitated, then walked reluctantly towards her. 'Nothin' much,' she said, looking sullen. 'I've been visitin' a friend, that's all.'

Her face was puffy and unhealthy, her hair hanging limply about her collar. 'You don't look well,' Rebecca said. She hadn't heard that Dotty was married and a glance at her finger revealed that she wasn't wearing a ring. 'Are you ill?'

'It's just ... you can see for yourself.'

'I'm sorry. I had no idea that you were ...' Rebecca hesitated. Most girls in her situation would have married long before this. 'It must be awkward for you.'

'There's no need to be sorry for me.' Dotty flashed a look of dislike at her. 'He's going to wed me soon.'

'I didn't mean to sound disapproving. I'm not criticising you, Dotty. I'm just sorry ...'

'Don't pity me,' she snapped. 'I don't need pity from you – nor anything else.'

'No, I'm sure you don't.' Rebecca was taken aback by her vehemence. 'It looks like rain. You'll have to hurry or you'll get wet before you're home.'

'There's someone waiting for me up the road,' she said, a gleam of triumph in her eyes. 'I'll soon be safe and dry. Don't you worry about me, Mrs Sawle.'

Rebecca watched as she walked away. What did she mean – someone waiting? Had her man got a waggon of some kind? The only carrier who plied a trade between Mepal and Chatteris that Rebecca knew of was married.

She glanced up at the gathering clouds. Dotty was probably lying. They had never been friends but Rebecca had tried to compensate her for the loss of her job so why was she so resentful? If anyone had the right to resentment it was Rebecca, because Dotty's spiteful gossip was probably what had driven Frank Henderson to murder.

She wouldn't allow it to bother her. Dotty Prentice wasn't important. Rebecca had felt sorry for her because it was hard for a woman to bear a child out of wedlock – but perhaps she was getting married soon.

As she felt the first drops of rain Rebecca hurried inside. It was almost four o'clock. Aden would be home at any minute and she hadn't started the dinner.

She forgot Dotty as she began to peel the potatoes. What difference could it make to her whether the girl was going to marry the father of her child or not?

She stopped with her knife in mid-air – how long would it be before she was carrying Aden's child? Until this moment she had not given it much thought but now she realized that she wanted her husband's child. It would be wonderful to hold Aden's son in her arms. Surely it could not be long ... not when they made love as often as they did? And it could only make their lives better.

She smiled as she heard the rumble of waggon wheels in the yard. Aden was back at last. Perhaps they would have that early night ...

'Surely you don't want to drag all the way into Chatteris for nothing?' Aden asked as Rebecca came downstairs. 'I'm only going to take those geese and some eggs to the market. I shan't stop long.'

'I thought I would come for the ride. Besides, I want to do some shopping.'

He had been asking her to go with him for weeks. She usually refused but this time she had decided there were a few things she needed from town.

'If you really want to come ...' He shrugged. 'Not that I'm not pleased to have you with me, mind.'

'Well, you don't sound it. Anyone would think you had something to hide in Chatteris.'

'Don't talk daft, woman.' He helped her up on to the waggon, his mouth a little tight. 'I thought you liked to have the house to yourself once in a while – so you could read those books of yours?'

'I've read most of them a dozen times over. I want to order some new ones. I thought I might like to read *The Mayor of Casterbridge*. Celia said she enjoyed it but I haven't see a copy yet.'

There was a shop at the far end of town that sent away for parcels of new books on subscription. Rebecca planned to visit the market first then the shop. It was a pleasant day and would make a nice outing, but she felt a bit upset that Aden didn't seem to want her along.

'I'll drive you to the shop then come back to the market.'

'No, drop me at the stalls, please. I want to buy several things – perhaps some material for a new bedspread in the spare room.'

'Just as you like.'

He sounded odd. Rebecca shot a glance at him but his eyes were fixed on the road ahead. What was the matter with him? Why didn't he want her with him?

'If things go well we might buy a small carriage soon,' he said, giving the reins a flick. 'Or a pony and trap. I've always fancied one of those high-stepping ponies.'

She nodded agreement. 'I was thinking the same thing. Once that new land is yours you'll be one of the biggest farmers in the area. You shouldn't have to drive a waggon into town.'

'I'm used to it. It was mostly for your sake.' He gave her a sideways glance. 'It would be more comfortable for you. Especially if ... well, there might come a time when the waggon wouldn't suit you.'

'If I were with child, you mean? What made you think of that?' She looked at him curiously.

'It's bound to happen sooner or later.'

'Yes.' She turned her wedding ring. 'I saw Dotty Prentice the other day. She was walking past the yard – just before that storm broke. It was the day you'd been muck spreading and I'd walked out to the gate to look for you.'

'What was she doing out this way then?' Aden's tone was disinterested but she noticed a little pulse flickering in his throat. 'You didn't mention it.'

'I'd forgotten by the time you came in. I was excited because the postman brought me a letter from Celia – don't you remember? It arrived just as you came in. It was the first time I'd heard from her since I wrote to tell her we were married.' He nodded and she thought he seemed relieved. 'You reminded me just now – about Dotty. She's with child and she's not married.'

'Well ... you know Dotty. Always one for the lads.'

'Was she?' Rebecca was surprised. 'I didn't realize that. How do you know?'

'Common knowledge. Ask any man in Chatteris, they'll all say the same. Nice enough girl in her own way, though. Pity if she's in trouble.'

'Do you think I should offer to help her?'

'Shouldn't bother if I were you. She always seemed an independent lass to me. Wouldn't thank you for interfering.'

'No, she wouldn't. She seems to resent me. I don't know why she should.'

'Stands to reason. She ruled the roost at The Arms until you came home. Probably didn't like you telling her what to do.'

'She was sloppy with her work sometimes. I did tell her about it but she ignored me.' Rebecca glanced at him. 'How did you know we'd had words over it?'

'I know you, the way you like things neat and tidy. Dotty was always a bit of a slut. I noticed it when I used to drink at The Arms.'

'But you stopped – after that quarrel with my father.'

'It was parish business, nothing important.'

'I know I said I didn't need explanations, but I hate lies, Aden. Don't you think it's time you told me the truth?'

He hesitated, then nodded. 'Jack was on the committee for leasing that fifty acres. I asked him to fix a tender for me to make sure my bid was the highest. I wanted to be certain of getting those acres ...' He arched his brows. 'Does that shock you?'

'It's wrong, but no, I'm not shocked. Why did you think my father would do it?'

He sighed deeply. 'You won't like it – but you may as well know. I saw him kissing my mother in the pub yard once. I was a bit of a lad then and my father was still a strong man. If I'd told him he would have had a go at Jack. My father adored Ma: after she died of a miscarriage he couldn't go on – just gave up bothering. It left me on my own with the farm to run and barely a shilling to my name. I've had to struggle for everything since. I reckoned Jack owed me something for keeping quiet and I asked for a favour. He didn't seem inclined to help me so I told him I knew about him and Eileen. I wouldn't have told Frank, of course, but Jack couldn't be sure of that so he agreed to do it – but it finished us as mates.'

'No wonder he was so angry that morning. He warned me never to speak to you again.' Rebecca looked at him straight. 'He ought to have called your bluff and told you to do your worst.'

'Happen you're right but he didn't.' A pulse flickered in his cheek. 'It's one of the things I regret most. Especially after the way things turned out. But at the time it was the only way I could see of making something of my life. I watched my father wear himself out trying to keep body and soul together and I swore I wouldn't follow him into an early grave. There's more to life than that, Rebecca.'

'Yes, I know. I like it that you want to be better than you are. I want to be rich one day. I want to send my children to the best schools and have a house they can bring their friends back to without feeling ashamed.'

'And I'm going to do my damnedest to give you what you want.' He shot an anxious look at her. 'Has the truth shocked you then?'

'I'm glad you told me. I can stand anything except lies. If you ever lied to me about something important, I might not be able to trust you again.'

He was silent for a moment and she noticed that throbbing pulse again. Was he angry with her?

'Why should I lie to you? Believe me, Rebecca, if there's one thing in this life that means more than all the rest – it's you.' His tone was rough, almost harsh.

'Don't say it like that. I may not agree with what you did but if my father had been more circumspect in his own behaviour he wouldn't have been at risk. Men who think they can use women for their pleasure – that's the worst, the very worst thing. At least I know you're faithful to me. You never have time for anything else.'

'Nor the inclination for it,' he said with a chuckle. 'It takes all my energy to satisfy you, lass.'

'Aden!' Her cheeks flushed but she was laughing inside. 'You make me sound wanton.'

'Well, if you are, that's the way I like you. Don't ever change, will you?'

'Not unless you give me cause, Aden Sawle!' She teased him with her eyes but his were fixed on the road ahead as they turned into the town's main street. Again she sensed something in his manner ... as if he were on edge or hiding something from her ... feeling guilty.

'Well, here we are then,' he said. 'You get down here, Rebecca, and I'll be off to the auction.'

'I know you're busy. I shan't delay you long.'

'Take your time, lass. Do as you like. I'll be a while myself.'

'I thought you were in a hurry to get back?'

'We might as well make the most of it now we're here. You don't often have a day out.'

He helped her down, then, as she began to wander round the market stalls, he led his horse into the yard at the back of The Arms, which was once more functioning as an inn, though the name had been changed.

Suddenly, she thought she understood his odd manner: he had been worried that she might be upset at seeing her old home again. Of course, that must be it. She hadn't been to Chatteris since The Arms was sold. How thoughtful Aden was – and she had suspected him of hiding something from her.

She spent half an hour choosing the books she wanted, then, glancing at the pretty silver fob watch pinned to her coat, she felt guilty. She had promised Aden she wouldn't be long! She paid for her order and left the shop, walking hurriedly in the direction of the market place.

A woman's shrill laugh caught her attention and she glanced across the road, wondering what was going on. A man was standing outside The Bull public house and roaring with laughter in a rather coarse way. In his mid-twenties, he was tall with long, greasy black hair and dressed in dark trousers, a striped shirt with the sleeves rolled up and a fancy waistcoat. He looked attractive in a foreign, flashy way and the large gold ring in his ear made her think he might be a gipsy. She would not have given him a second look, except that the woman laughing with him was Dotty. They were obviously both very pleased about something, and, as she watched, the man grabbed Dotty and kissed her on the mouth.

No decent woman would have made such a display of herself in the street. Rebecca turned her head at once. Had Dotty not been behaving so badly she might have gone over to speak to her – to ask if she needed anything – but now she realized Aden was right. Dotty was a flirt and not worthy of her pity. If a girl took up with gipsies she deserved all she got!

As she approached the marketplace, Rebecca saw that Aden was waiting for her. His face lit up as he saw her and she felt a pang of guilt. Until she'd seen Dotty with the gipsy she had suspected Aden of being involved with her. He had after all taken her to the harvest dance and she thought Dotty might have had hopes of him, but now she knew how wrong and wicked her thoughts had been. Shame engulfed her as she noticed the tiny posy of violets in his hand.

'Are they for me? Oh, Aden, how lovely. Thank you so much.'

'I've got something else for you,' he said, touching his breast pocket. 'To say thank you for all the joy you've given me since we were wed.'

'Another present? You spoil me, Aden.' He was so good to her and she had suspected him of being the father of Dotty's child! 'I don't deserve all this …'

'I wouldn't say that, lass. You deserve the best – and one day I'll get it all for you. The moon as well if you want.'

'Give me your present then,' she said, holding the violets to her nose and sniffing. 'These smell wonderful.'

'Wait until we get home,' Aden replied with a tantalising grin. 'Come on, we'll have a bite to eat before we go – make a day of it.'

His moodiness had gone and he was his usual cheerful self again. Almost as if he had shed his cares …

'It's beautiful!' Rebecca gazed with pleasure at the tiny brooch lying on the palm of her hand. It was no bigger than her thumbnail, square and made of silver. A row of pearls surrounded a removable glass, under which could be placed a lock of hair. 'I love it, Aden. Thank you so much.'

'It's just a token.' He looked slightly sheepish. 'One day it will be diamonds and rubies. Everything you ever wanted.'

'They will be no more precious to me than this proof of your love.'

Her eyes misted with tears. How good he was and how wrong she had been to doubt him. Thank goodness she hadn't accused him of betraying her with Dotty!

She wanted to make up for her wicked thoughts and knew exactly what to do. Aden was a very sensual man. She opened her arms to him.

'Love me,' she whispered. 'I'm so glad I married you, Aden Sawle. Love me now – don't wait for tonight …'

He made a low, moaning sound in his throat. His kisses were feverish, hungry, as he swept her into his arms. Then he was tugging at her fine linen blouse, pulling it from her skirt as his hands slipped beneath, covering her breasts, squeezing and caressing with sudden urgency.

'Up them stairs with you,' he muttered low in his throat. 'I'm bursting out of me breeches already.'

'No …' Her voice was husky with desire. 'Take me now on the floor as we are.'

Her words seemed to drive him crazy with passion. Still kissing, they sank to their knees in the middle of the kitchen floor, Aden's hand reaching for the buttons at the front of his trousers. He was lance-hard, throbbing with the urgency of his need. She laughed as they came together with a wild sweet passion that had them both gasping as he drove inside her, thrusting and groaning as he lost all sense of control. Their loving was frantic and swift, but, oh, so good. As he collapsed on top of her she shuddered convulsively, curling her legs around him and sobbing his name over and over again.

'Aden … Aden … Aden …'

'That was the best, the best ever,' he murmured huskily against her throat. 'I love you so much, Rebecca. You'll never know how much you mean to me …'

There was an odd desperation in his voice that touched her. 'And I love you,' she whispered. 'I love you, Aden.' And in that moment she meant it. Surely this must be love? It was so good, so true, so real.

Her words stirred him to fresh desire. He was moving inside her again, slowly, sensuously. She moaned softly as the relentless, endless assault on her senses went on and on, bringing her to a climax long before he was done.

She stroked his head, her fingers moving at the nape of his neck, closing her eyes and letting the pleasure flow over her. How could she have doubted his love for her? She was so relieved they had not quarrelled over Dotty. He was her husband and a good, decent man. She was glad she had married him despite the vague longings that still came to her now and then when she thought of Victor Roth.

She must never think of Victor again, not as someone she might have married. It would be wrong and cruel of her to make comparisons when Aden tried so hard to please her. He had brought her through the worst crisis of her life and she was grateful.

Aden was lying quietly now, his expression serious, almost as though he could read her thoughts. He smoothed the line of her brow with the tips of her fingers.

'A penny for them?'

'They're worth much more than that,' she teased. 'I was just thinking how lucky I am.'

'I'm the lucky one.'

'Then we both are,' she said and smiled. 'Now let me up, Aden. I've work to do.'

He laughed, stood up and pulled her to her feet. 'And so have I,' he said. 'If you've done with me, woman, I'd best be off and see to it!'

8

An auction was being held in the market square. Aden stopped out of curiosity, smiling to himself as he heard two matrons gossiping about a young woman who was getting married that weekend.

'And not before time if you ask me ... any later and the child will be here before she's got the ring on her finger.'

At least they weren't talking about Rebecca – or Dotty! Aden's smile disappeared. It had given him a fright that day Rebecca had insisted on coming to town with him, but in the end it had turned out well. He'd managed to give the money to Dotty without being seen and she'd kept her word about clearing off somewhere.

'Any advance on eighty pounds?' The auctioneer's voice rang out and Aden suddenly realized what was going on. 'It's a good grazing field, gentlemen – going for nothing. Make no mistake, I'm selling ...'

'Ninety pounds.'

There was a mild murmur of interest from the crowd as Aden's voice rang out; the field was worth a hundred and going cheap.

'One hundred pounds.' The bid came from a stout, red-faced man who owned the land adjoining the field.

'One hundred and ten.'

'And twenty.'

'And thirty.'

'A hundred and forty pounds.'

A hush fell over the crowd as they waited expectantly for Aden's next bid. It did not come and the auctioneer's hammer fell.

'Sold to Mr Hauxton.'

The red-faced farmer turned dark purple and glared at Aden as he pushed his way clear of the spectators. He had paid too much for the field and he knew it.

'Damned upstart,' he muttered. 'More money than sense.'

Aden heard the remark and smiled inwardly. He hadn't meant to attend the auction but he was always in the market for more land.

'Now, ladies and gentlemen,' the auctioneer's voice broke into his thoughts. 'Here's an opportunity – a butcher's shop with living accommodation over the top. I'm instructed to sell without reserve.'

Aden's attention was caught. Frank's place had been empty for months despite all attempts to rent it.

'What am I bid – come along, gentlemen. You must be willing to start me somewhere – say a hundred and fifty pounds?'

There was absolute silence. The shop and house were worth much more but with the murders still fresh in everyone's mind no one was buying.

'Fifty pounds.'

This time there was an excited buzz as Aden spoke and several heads turned towards him.

'Fifty pounds?' The auctioneer sounded hopeful. 'Here's a man with an eye for a bargain, gentlemen. Come on now, you know it's cheap – who'll advance me?'

There were a few murmurs in the crowd, but no one spoke and the auctioneer's hammer fell on the third asking.

'Sold to Mr Sawle for fifty pounds.'

Aden turned away, a smile on his lips. The shop was an even better buy than that grass field would have been at ninety pounds; with a lick of paint, a few changes to its structure and some patience, he would eventually earn a nice bit out of it. He might have to wait a few years but in the end …

'You crafty young bugger!'

Aden's progress was halted by the bulky figure of The Bull's landlord.

'Mornin', Sam,' Aden said. 'Fancied the place yourself then?'

'If I'd had the money to spare. Especially if I knew as much as you.' He winked and nudged Aden in the ribs. 'Don't forget me if you find old Frank's nest egg.'

'You never know your luck.'

Aden was thoughtful as he walked on. No doubt others would be thinking the same thing. Maybe after a decent interval he'd give Frank's lawyers a few pounds to settle those outstanding debts.

He was pleased as he turned towards the pub. Might as well have a drink before he went home; he quite liked the new landlord of The Arms. Besides, he'd got himself a cheap bit of property and a way of easing his conscience into the bargain.

As he went into the taproom he saw a group of men playing cards at a table in the corner. With a tankard of best bitter in his hand, he walked over to watch them. He hadn't played since his army days but he'd always been lucky at poker …

Two months had passed since the trip to Chatteris that had ended in a wild and passionate loving – and Rebecca was now certain in her own mind that she was carrying Aden's child.

Until now she hadn't been confident enough to mention her hopes to Aden, but all at once she was quite, quite sure. She had missed her second period by several days and this particular morning she had been sick three times. Sarah had come in just as she was vomiting into a bowl and had given her a knowing look.

'You'll be like this for a while yet,' she said. 'But it passes soon enough. I've seen many a lass in your condition – though I was never able to have a child of my own.'

'You must have grieved over it, Sarah?'

'For a bit,' she agreed. 'But I've lived through it. It's surprising what a woman can bear if she has to. I'll enjoy seeing your little ones grow, Rebecca. You'll bring them over to visit me now and then?'

'Of course.' Rebecca smiled at her. They had become even closer since her marriage and Sarah was her dearest friend. 'Now sit down and I'll make a cup of tea. You won't mind waiting while I put these towels to soak?' She picked up the pound packet of Borax dry soap and showed it to her. 'I tried this as you advised and it's much better than the soda mixture I was using.'

'They make a lovely starch glaze too,' Sarah said. 'Try it on your linens and lace – it stops the iron sticking.'

Rebecca nodded and wiped her hands as the kettle boiled. Sarah had given her many useful household tips, the kind of things they hadn't bothered to teach her at the expensive boarding school she'd attended. But of course most of the girls they taught there would have housekeepers and servants to attend to these things – as Celia now had. Her last letter had been full of how troublesome it was having to listen to her housekeeper's complaints about the maids.

Sarah stayed to gossip for an hour or so. Rebecca was glad of her company but impatient for Aden's return. He had gone to the auction in Chatteris as he did most weeks and she couldn't wait for him to come home.

It was past three in the afternoon when his waggon finally rolled into the yard. As soon as he entered the kitchen she sensed that he was feeling pleased with himself, and, as he kissed her, she smelled whisky on his breath. He seldom drank anything stronger than a glass of beer with his meal and for some reason she was irritated by his lateness and his drinking. She had been longing to tell him her news and he'd been in a pub!

'Where have you been? I should have thought you had better things to do than waste your time drinking!'

'What's wrong?' He was surprised at her sharpness. 'It was just a bit of a celebration, that's all.'

'A celebration of what?'

'I had a bit of luck today. I brought a property cheap. It was going for fifty pounds and no one seemed interested so I bought it.'

'What kind of property?'

'As a matter of fact, it was Frank Henderson's old shop,' he said. 'It has been empty since ...' He stopped as he saw the look on her face. 'I know it's got a bad name but in a few years everyone will have forgotten and we'll sell it for many times what I paid ...'

'Is that all it means to you?' she cried. 'How could you be so insensitive? That man murdered my father – and you've bought his shop! How could you?'

'Oh, that's it.' Aden combed his fingers through his dark hair. 'Sorry, lass. I didn't think it would upset you. I just saw a bargain and went for it.'

'Get rid of it!'

'Can't do that. No one would buy it. Not until I've had it done up.' He moved towards her, giving her a persuasive smile. 'Don't take on so, Rebecca. It's only a bit of property.'

'Only!' She jerked away from him. She was furious, though she didn't really know why. 'Don't you touch me, Aden Sawle! I'll never forgive you for this – never!'

'Rebecca ...'

He called after her as she rushed from the room but she ignored

96

him. It was their first real quarrel and she wanted to be alone so that she could cry. She rushed upstairs and flung herself down on the bed. How could Aden hurt her like this – and when she was carrying his child?

'Rebecca ... Rebecca, I'm sorry. Please forgive me.' He stood in the doorway looking bewildered and anxious. 'I'll burn the damned place down if it means that much to you. It was for you, lass – for the future. I want to make lots of money as fast as I can, to give you all the things you want ... for our children.'

'Oh, Aden,' she sobbed as he came to sit beside her on the bed. 'I've been feeling wretched all morning and you were so long coming ...'

'Are you ill? Shall I fetch the doctor?'

His alarm brought her out of herself and she laughed. She pushed herself up against the pillows and looked at him, her anger and frustration draining away as suddenly as they had come. He had only been thinking of the future and perhaps he was right, perhaps it was just bricks and mortar.

'No. There's nothing wrong – nothing the next few months won't cure.'

'What ...' He stared at her as enlightenment dawned and his eyes lit up. 'Rebecca – do you mean ... ?'

'I've been sick all morning,' she said. 'I wasn't sure before but now I am. We're having our first child, Aden.'

'A child.' His eyes dropped for a moment but when he raised them again they were glowing with love. 'I did wonder but you said nothing ...'

'I didn't want to raise your hopes too soon.' She held out her hand to him. 'You are pleased, aren't you, Aden?'

'You know the answer to that.' He bent to kiss her softly on the mouth. 'You've given me more happiness than any man deserves, and now this – I reckon I *am* pleased. More pleased than I can tell you.'

'I'm glad.' She lay back against the pillows and sighed. 'And I'm sorry I was so silly just now. Of course you must do what you think best. I trust your judgement, Aden. I expect it was just nerves.'

'It takes women different ways,' he said. 'You'll not be feeling yourself. Bide there, Rebecca, and I'll bring you a cup of tea.'

'Go and put the kettle on,' she said. 'I'll be down in a few minutes.'

'If you're sure?'

She assured him she was and he went out. For a few minutes she stayed where she was, then she got up to wash her face and tidy her hair, pausing to look at her face in the mirror. There was nothing different yet except perhaps something in her eyes ...

Had she imagined it or had there been a second when she'd told Aden she was with child, a fleeting instant when his eyes had been shadowed by a secret grief?

No, of course not! He was overjoyed at her news, and yet for a moment ... but that was her imagination, a sign of nerves. She was in an emotional state but she would not let herself dwell on such foolish thoughts.

Aden's smile of greeting when she went downstairs was so loving that she chided herself. How could she doubt this man? He had shown her over and over again how much he loved her – so why did she have this sense of unease?

Why couldn't she get Dotty's image out of her mind? It had been hovering there all morning, even when she was chatting to Sarah, and she didn't know why. Dotty's child must be about to be born anyday now – why was she haunted by the idea that her child would be Aden's first son?

There, she had admitted it now, the suspicion that she'd been trying to suppress all day; it must have lain dormant in her subconscious ever since that trip to Chatteris.

It was stupid, wicked and disloyal but she couldn't get it out of her head. For some reason she was haunted by Dotty's pale, bloated face for the rest of that day, and then, all of a sudden, in the middle of the night, the sense of fear and pain had gone and she could laugh at her foolishness.

It was probably the discovery of her own pregnancy that had made her have such strange fancies. Already it was clear that she was becoming more emotional and easily upset. Yes, it was just a symptom of her condition ... something she would have to live with over the next few months.

9

Dotty had been bitterly angry when she first met Lorenzo. It was the night after Aden Sawle had told her they were finished and she was still hurting inside. The gipsy's dark eyes followed her as she moved about the bar serving drinks, hot and lustful; she knew what that look meant all right. Usually, she stayed well clear of the gipsies who sometimes drank at The Arms. They were a surly lot, their tempers as black as their flashing eyes, especially on a Saturday night when they'd been drinking for hours. But something about Lorenzo had aroused Dotty's interest that night. Perhaps because he reminded her of Aden. Not in looks. No, in that way they were very different. Aden had the manner and appearance of a gent, but the gipsy was rough and coarse-featured. It was just the way he had of meeting her eyes straight on.

He'd been waiting for her in the yard when she'd finished work. Dotty had seen him in the shadows and her heart beat faster. For a moment she'd thought it was Aden. When he called her name, she'd stopped and smiled, tipping her head flirtatiously to one side. When he offered to walk her home, she knew exactly what was going to happen and she didn't care. She didn't much care about anything anymore.

Lorenzo had had her up against a wall, with her petticoats up round her waist and her legs spread wide. It was quick and not much fun, but the next night he was waiting for her again. This time he took her to his caravan. It was a real Romany waggon, and as clean as a new pin inside. There were pretty ornaments and shining brasses, and it was warm. Lorenzo undressed her slowly, kissing her breasts and fondling her so that she was ready for him this time. He took his time and when she felt the heat of him inside her she was already climaxing, her legs curled around his naked back.

'Are all gipsies like you?' she asked afterwards, when he gave her a bright scarf as a keepsake. 'You're a good lover, Lorenzo. I should like to see you again.'

'Tomorrow we leave,' he murmured, white teeth gleaming in the light of a pink-globed oil lamp. 'Perhaps when we come back?'

Gipsies were always on the move. Dotty hadn't expected to see him again. She'd lost her job when the pub closed, and then she'd discovered she was having a child. Working in a shop hadn't suited her because of the strictness. Shop girls were only allowed to assist the supervisor and say 'Yes' or 'No, madam'. If she was late in in the morning, she was fined sixpence from her wages and severely reprimanded. She began to realise how easy Jack Cottrel had been with her and to wish she'd never told anyone about the afternoon she'd seen him and Eileen at it in the snug room. If she'd kept her mouth shut, Jack would have helped her out. He would never have put her out with a week's wages and no reference.

Beset by her own problems, Dotty had almost forgotten the gipsy. Then, one day when she was walking up the high street, he suddenly came out of The Bull and saw her. He stared at her for several minutes, his eyes narrowed intently. Then he ran across the road and caught her arm.

'The child,' he said, his black eyes shining with excitement. 'Is the child mine?'

Dotty didn't know why she said yes. She was sure in her own heart that it was Aden's, but Lorenzo had given her that scarf. He might give her money if he thought that the child was his, and she was in trouble. Her father had hit her a couple of times and threatened to throw her out of the house.

'Yes, I reckon it's yourn,' Dotty said, grinning up at the gipsy. 'Ain't bin no one else anyways. I never thought you would come back.'

'We come and go.' There was a look of wonder in Lorenzo's eyes as he stared at her bulging stomach. 'The old one was right,' he muttered, giving such a yell of delight that Dotty jumped. 'Dena has foretold truly. My manusha is to be a gorgio.'

'What are you on about?' Dotty asked, eyeing him askance. 'What's a masui ... whatsisname?'

Lorenzo laughed. 'It's the word my tribe uses for special woman ... wife, you would say.'

'Your wife?' Dotty looked at him speculatively, her heart thumping with excitement. She remembered how clean and pretty the caravan had looked. 'You're kidding me, ain't yer? You gipsies stick to one another. You wouldn't marry me. Against your law, I shouldn't wonder.'

'Maybe, but it can be done sometimes, if the elders agree.' Lorenzo looked at her hard. 'You're sure this child is mine?'

'I told yer, there ain't bin no one else.' Dotty's heart was pumping wildly. 'You don't mean what you said just now, 'bout me being yer wife?'

'Dena has foretold my future. It is bound with a fair-skinned gorgio woman who is already carrying my child. If I take her as my manusha, she will bring good fortune to me and mine.'

'That's all fairytales, like they do at the fairs.' Dotty stared at him. 'You don't believe that, do you?'

'It is the way of our people.' Lorenzo's eyes were like burning coal, smoky and yet lit with a clear flame. 'Dena is a wise woman. She can see the future as others see the past.'

'And she said I would bring you money?' Dotty's eyes narrowed as she thought of something. There was a way she might get some money, but she couldn't tell Lorenzo about it. That would ruin everything. 'I've got a few pounds put by,' she lied. 'Will you marry me if I give it to you?'

Lorenzo grinned at her. 'If that child in your belly is mine, I will marry you anyway, but the money will be a present for Dena. It will set the seal of approval on our union.'

'It will take me a day or two to get it,' Dotty said anxiously. 'You ain't going to run off again, are yer?'

'We are here for a few days,' Lorenzo said. 'When we leave you must come with me, money or not.'

'It's money owed me,' Dotty said. 'A legacy, you might say. I'll get it and then I'll be your manusha, won't I?'

Lorenzo's dark eyes gleamed. The old one had foretold great riches for his son and his son's son if he took the gorgio woman for his own.

'Bring the money to me by the end of the week,' he said. 'I'll be waiting for you here.'

Dotty decided she would keep a part of the money Aden had

given her. Lorenzo was going to give it away so there was no sense in parting with the whole of the fifty pounds. She sewed twenty gold sovereigns into the hem of one of her skirts, smiling as she pushed the clothes into a bag. Lorenzo had been delighted with what she'd given him. He'd told her she would bring him good fortune and he'd wanted her to go with him straight away.

'I've got to go home and get me things,' she'd told him. 'I want to say goodbye to me mother.'

'Come to the caravan then,' he said, kissing her full on the lips in the middle of the street. 'Tonight we shall give the money to Dena and then you will be my manusha.'

When she went downstairs with the bag in her hand, her mother looked at her suspiciously.

'And where do you think you're going?' she asked.

'I'm off,' Dotty said, her eyes bright with triumph. 'You won't see me no more.'

'Promises!' her mother snorted. 'Off with some man, I suppose. You'll be back when he throws you out.'

'Lorenzo won't throw me out,' Dotty said proudly. 'I'm going to be his manusha. It's bin foretold. I'm going to bring him riches.'

'A gipsy!' The older woman looked at her in horror. 'You've never bin going with a gippo? They're bad trouble, Dotty. You don't know what you're getting yerself into, my girl.'

'You're like a lot of other folk,' Dotty said. 'You look at them and think they're dirty, but Lorenzo's van is cleaner than this house ever was.'

'You just watch yer lip or I'll tell yer father to take his belt to yer!'

'He won't do that no more.' Dotty stood with her hand on the door knob. 'That old bastard had me when I were eleven, did you know that?' As her mother's eyes widened in disbelief and disgust, Dotty laughed harshly. 'I reckon Lorenzo is as good as your old man any day.'

Leaving her mother staring, she ran laughing from the house. It served the old bitch right. Dotty was glad to be clearing out. Living in that pretty van and travelling all over the country was going to be fun, she reckoned. Gipsies didn't do much, everyone said they were lazy. Selling a few pegs or telling fortunes would be a lot easier than serving behind a bar in a public house …

It didn't take many days for Dotty's illusions to be shattered. The

102

very first night, when Lorenzo took her into the camp on his waggon, she could sense the hostility of the other women. Their dark eyes watched her, simmering with a deep, slow anger because she had dared to enter their world.

At first Dotty didn't care much what the women thought of her. Lorenzo was glowing with pride. Holding tight to her hand, he took her straight to a caravan in the centre of the camp, where an old woman was sitting on a stool outside, smoking a pipe. Her face was wrinkled and as brown as a walnut skin, and her eyes had a queer silvery point in the pupils. For a moment Dotty felt as if those eyes could see into her very soul, then Lorenzo whispered that she was blind. Dotty felt better after that.

'This is the one you spoke of,' he said in a clear ringing voice. 'She has brought a tribute to you, old one, as is the custom.'

'Bring her nearer,' Dena commanded. 'I want to lay hands on her.'

Lorenzo pushed Dotty forward and Dena's skinny hands reached out for her, fastening about her arm. The old woman was surprisingly strong and the pressure made Dotty stumble and then fall to her knees beside the elder. Grasping tightly with one hand, Dena ran her fingers over Dotty's face and hair. Her touch sent shivers down Dotty's spine and she recoiled but a frown from Lorenzo prevented her from pulling away.

'Does she carry your child, Lorenzo?'

'She does. When you told me the prophecy, old one, I knew that it could be only one woman. Then I saw her and with my own eyes I witnessed the truth of your words.'

Dena nodded, puffing on her pipe. 'You have done well, Lorenzo. This gorgio woman will bring riches to your son and your son's son. Now, give me the tribute.'

Lorenzo opened the purse and poured the money into her hands as she held them cupped before her. The gold made a chinking sound that brought a startled expression to Dena's face. She ran her fingers over the coins and then put one to her mouth, biting it with teeth that were still strong though yellowed with age.

'Gold,' she muttered. 'Thirty sovereigns. Where did this woman come by so much money? You have not abducted a girl of good family?'

'Don't worry, Dena,' Lorenzo laughed. 'She was working behind a bar when I first saw her.' He turned to Dotty, encouraging her. 'Tell her where the money came from, Dotty.'

'It were a legacy,' she said. 'From a man I used to work for. It were in his will.'

'And you give this tribute freely?'

'I give it to Lorenzo because he said I was going to be his wife,' Dotty said. 'He said it must be given to you, because of what you'd told him.'

'Do you give it freely?' The old woman's fingers dug into her arms.

Dotty glanced at Lorenzo, who nodded and frowned. 'I give it freely,' she said.

The grip on her arm relaxed. 'Then it is accepted. I give my permission, Lorenzo. You may take this woman as your manusha.'

Dotty wasn't sure what she'd expected to happen. Folk talked a lot about gipsies and their strange ceremonies, but all that happened later that night was that Lorenzo led her into the clearing in front of all his people and bound their wrists together with a leather thong.

'This woman is mine,' he said. 'Let no man here dishonour her lest he dishonours me.'

Some of the men yelled and cheered and they started passing the beer jugs round, but the women merely looked on sullenly. It was all a bit of an anti-climax for Dotty. She didn't feel any different and she wasn't sure it had been worth the thirty gold sovereigns. As far as she could see she was just living with Lorenzo. Becoming his manusha wasn't quite what she'd expected. The women still resented her and no one went out of their way to make her welcome.

In the days and weeks that followed, she became aware that to most of the gipsies she was an outsider. She might be Lorenzo's manusha, but they didn't like her and they didn't want her amongst them. When they went to draw water from the river, Dotty was always the last in line and no one helped her, even though she was big with child. She had thought to ride on the waggon and do little else, at least until the child was born, but she discovered she was expected to earn her keep from the very beginning.

Lorenzo showed her how to build a fire for cooking the first morning, but after that, he left the gathering of wood to her. When he threw a rabbit in front of her and told her to skin it for their meal, she stared at him in horror.

'I ain't never done nothing like that. We always bought 'em ready skinned from the butcher.'

'Then you must learn to do it,' Lorenzo said. 'I'll show you, but afterwards you must do it. Preparing food is a woman's work.'

Dotty had watched fearfully, almost throwing up as she saw the careless way he sliced through the skin. She didn't want to do it, but there was a look in Lorenzo's eyes that told her she would be in trouble if she didn't. As the days passed, she discovered that most of the work in the camp was done by women. The men saw to the horses and trapped animals for food, though the women were quite capable of doing both. They looked at her with contempt when she struggled to hold the horse's head for Lorenzo while he took a stone from its hoof, and she heard the whispers behind her back.

'A gorgio woman,' they murmured. 'Lorenzo has shamed us by bringing her here. Were there not enough of the true blood for him to choose from that he must take her for his manusha?'

Lorenzo was good to her in his way, though. He watched her with pride in his eyes and he would often reach out and touch her belly, as though fascinated by the thought of the child growing inside her. Because of his patience, she learned to make pegs and baskets as the other women did, though hers would never be as pretty as the blind Dena's. It was a marvel to see how Dena wove the rushes into intricate patterns, her fingers moving swiftly and surely. Sometimes, watching her finding her way about the camp, Dotty was sure that she wasn't truly blind. Yet every time the gipsies moved on, one of the men would take a turn in driving her waggon. It was the only thing she could not do for herself.

Dotty had been with the gipsies for three months when the pain struck. She had been gathering rushes from the bank of a river, enjoying the warmth of the sun and the pretty scenery. They were somewhere down in the south of the country now, many miles from Cambridgeshire, and she was beginning to think that there were compensations in being a traveller, despite the hard work. Then the pain began. At first it was just backache, and she put it down to her condition, ignoring it as she went about her work for most of the day. She was huge and it was an effort just to drag herself around. At about four in the afternoon, she looked at her bundle of rushes and decided that it was enough, then, as she straightened up, the pain seared her. She screamed out loud in her sudden fright and one of the women turned to look at her.

This woman had a child of nearly nine months herself and Dotty had sometimes watched her nursing it on the steps of her waggon, her full round breasts hardly covered by her red shawl. Lorenzo had told her that the woman was alone. Her man had died just before the birth of her child. Since then she had driven her own van and worked twice as hard as any other woman in the camp. Dotty had spoken to her a few times as she wandered through the camp on her way to fetch water or wood, but the woman had ignored her.

'Oh, gawd,' Dotty cried. 'It's the baby. Help me somebody, for the Lord's sake!'

The woman's eyes flashed with contempt and she turned back to her work. Dotty thought she was going to be ignored, but then Dena spoke to the others in that strange, unintelligible tongue that Dotty had not been able to master. Her words were a powerful force, bringing instant obedience. One of the women picked up Dotty's bundle of rushes, and the woman who had looked at her so contemptuously came to support her.

'It will be some time yet,' she said. 'I am Sadie and I look after our women when they give birth. Most do not need me. A true Romany woman will often lie down in the field, give birth and nurse the babe like any other creature without help. You are not of our blood, but you have chosen to live amongst us. You must not expect sympathy, but I shall do what I can to help you. There are ways of easing the pain, but you must trust me.'

'I'll do whatever you say.' Dotty's fingers curled on her arm as the pain tore through her again, but she held back her scream. She didn't want the other women looking at her with scorn. She'd show them she was as tough as they were!

Sadie helped her back to the van, then left her alone. Dotty lay down on the bed, her brow beaded with sweat as she fought her terror. Why had she ever gone with Lorenzo? If she'd stayed in Chatteris at least she would have had a midwife or the doctor to help her now. It was inhuman the way they expected her to manage all alone. Even Sadie had deserted her.

In that, however, she had wronged the gipsy woman. She returned in half an hour carrying a jug of liquid, some torn linen scraps and a kettle of hot water. Dotty was writhing on the bed but she was determined not to scream again.

'How close are the pains now?' Sadie asked, pouring some of the liquid into a cup. 'Drink this. It will help you.'

Dotty looked at the brown liquid suspiciously. 'What is it?'

'I make it from herbs and wild flowers,' Sadie said. 'If you had come to me, I would have given you some before. If you drink it for a few weeks before the birth it gives both you and the child strength.'

'No one speaks to me,' Dotty sniffed miserably as she sipped the drink. To her surprise it tasted much better than it looked. 'I didn't even know your name.'

Sadie frowned, looking at her hard. 'You must have patience,' she said. 'Lorenzo is of the true blood, the old blood. He is honoured by our tribe as a prince. It was thought that he would take a manusha from amongst our women. They are bound to resent you. If you want respect here, you must earn it.'

Dotty gasped and convulsed as the pain struck again. She drew a deep breath, panting hard to stop herself crying out. Sadie nodded her approval and soaked one of her cloths in cool water, then she bathed the girl's forehead.

'That's good,' she said. 'Drink it all. It will make the pain less sharp.'

Dotty swallowed obediently. The pain was just as bad as before, but the gipsy woman's presence eased her. There was something reassuring about her and some of the fear disappeared.

It was a long and difficult labour. Hours passed, endless hours of agony such as Dotty had never known. It was night and then it was not. Day dawned and then passed in a timeless blur and it was night again. The pains came and went, then eased before returning with a vengeance. Dotty didn't know whether it was the gipsy's potion or sheer weariness, but gradually a haziness came over her so that she was no longer aware of what was going on around her. All she knew was that the pain was unbearable. She did not want to fight anymore. It was too much trouble and her strength had almost gone. She did not know when she began to talk, to speak a name over and over again in her agony.

'Aden ... God damn you, Aden Sawle! You're going to finish me, you bastard ... You and this brat of yours ...'

In the act of delivering the child, Sadie stiffened and looked at the woman. The child was not Lorenzo's. The gorgio woman had cheated him. She had lied and because of that, the prophecy would not come true. If Lorenzo were ever to learn the truth, he would kill her ... and the child.

'Hush,' Sadie said. 'Hush now, foolish one.'

Dotty was no longer aware of her. She had slipped into the darkness where the pain could not reach her.

Sadie worked on, knowing that the woman was dying. As the huge male child came slithering into the world, the door of the van was thrown open and Lorenzo entered, his eyes going expectantly towards the bed. Cutting the cord, Sadie took the child, still covered in its mother's blood, and naked, slapped it hard to make it cry, then put it into his arms.

'Your son, Lorenzo,' she said. 'Your child.'

As he took the child outside to show it off to his people, Sadie bent over the woman lying on the bed. The struggle to give life had been too much for her. If she had been attended by doctors she might have lived, but now she was slipping away. Sadie was moved to pity as she bent over her. The gorgio woman was not born to the travelling life. Perhaps it was better that she should die now, before she learned how hard it could really be.

For a moment Dotty's eyes opened, and she gripped Sadie's arm.

'Please,' she whispered harshly. 'You must fetch Lorenzo to me. You must help me. I have to tell him. I have to tell him the truth ...'

'No.' Sadie's black eyes bored into hers. 'If you care for the child, you must keep your secret. Lorenzo would kill him if he knew the truth.'

'But he should know, my son!' Dotty cried, tears of weakness slipping down her cheeks. 'His father is Aden Sawle of Mepal. Tell him, Sadie. When he is old enough, tell him. Promise me ... Promise me ...'

Seeing her distress, Sadie nodded once. 'When the time comes. When he is a man and can choose for himself,' she said. 'Then I will tell him.'

'Thank you ...' Dotty's eyes closed. 'Thank ... you ...'

Sadie waited until she was sure the gorgio woman was dead, then she went out to where Lorenzo was showing the child to the other men. She saw the pride in his face as he turned to look at her, and she knew that it was very unlikely that she would keep her promise to Dotty. Sadie was older than Lorenzo but she was still an attractive woman, and Lorenzo would need someone to care for his son ...

Lorenzo turned to her then, his eyes glowing. 'My son shall be called Shima,' he said. 'The fortunate one.'

'The woman is dead,' Sadie said. 'I did all I could for her, but she was not strong enough to give birth to such a big child.'

'He will be strong and tall like his father,' Lorenzo said. Then, frowning, 'He needs a mother. A woman of the true blood to care for him.'

Sadie's own child, a girl of nine months, was almost weaned, but Sadie's milk still flowed. Several men had offered for her since her husband had been killed in an accident but Sadie had rejected them all. Now, looking into Lorenzo's dark eyes, she knew that the choice was made. It was for Lorenzo that she had waited. Opening her dress, she took the boy into her arms and held him to her breast. He began to suck greedily. Lorenzo watched and smiled.

'You will be my true manusha,' he said. 'Nourished on your milk, Shima will be a good Romany. We will never tell him that his mother was a gorgio.'

10

'I would never have believed carrying a child could be so uncomfortable,' Rebecca said as Nan Barwell passed her a cup of tea and one of her home-baked ginger biscuits, which were still hot from the oven, crisp and delicious.

Nan was a lively, fair-haired woman with a pretty face and a turned up nose, and was just a few years older than Rebecca. She was the new vicar's wife, and the two women had become friends since Nan's arrival in the village a few weeks earlier. The old vicar, who was a dear and would be missed, had finally retired at the age of seventy-nine and gone off to live with his daughter in Dorset.

'I thought once the sickness stopped I should feel so much better, but I don't,' Rebecca went on. 'I'm irritable and moody – nothing Aden does is right. It's a wonder he puts up with me – but he seems to have so much patience.'

'Then you're very lucky,' Nan said, and laughed, her blue eyes alight with mischief. 'Some men spend the whole nine months in a pub just to get out of the way. I was fine after the first two months but it's obviously different for you.' She sipped her tea. 'You're not worried about ... well, giving birth, are you?'

'A little,' Rebecca admitted. 'Women do die. I knew someone ... she died a few months ago.' She felt a chill trickle down her spine.

Just that week, while shopping in Chatteris, she had met Dotty Prentice's mother. She had stopped to speak to her, asking how she was and if she had heard from Dotty. For a moment Mrs Prentice's eyes had clouded with grief but then she scowled as if she preferred anger to sorrow.

'She's dead – died having that gipsy's bastard. He had the

110

cheek to come and tell me. Lorenzo his name was – nasty, flashy brute, foreign-looking. She got what she deserved if you ask me. I brought her up decent.'

'Dotty's dead?' The shock of it made Rebecca feel faint. The world seemed to spin and she clutched at the other woman's arm to steady herself. 'And ... and the child?'

'He told me it died,' Mrs Prentice replied, scowling, 'but he was lying. I could see it in his face. He needn't have bothered. I wouldn't have taken the brat even if he'd brought it to me. He's welcome to keep it – a boy, he said, but that may have been a lie, too.'

Rebecca hadn't been able to put the incident out of her mind – though she hadn't yet mentioned it to Aden. She wasn't sure why.

'Rebecca, are you all right?' Nan asked, her anxious voice breaking into her thoughts. 'You've gone a bit pale. It isn't the baby, is it?'

'No. No, that isn't for another month yet.' Rebecca dismissed the memory of Dotty's bloated face. She wouldn't let the tragedy haunt her, even though the girl's shadow still visited her in her dreams now and then, almost as if she wanted to tell her something. 'I'm all right, Nan. I just wish this was all over and I could get back to normal.'

'I know how you feel – we all go through it. And you've had it worse than most.'

'I want my baby,' Rebecca said with a rueful smile. 'It's just that I get so tired – but that's enough moaning from me. Let's talk of something else. How are you getting on with your plans for the bazaar?'

'Oh, you know.' Nan gave her a sympathetic look. 'You can't help being moody, Rebecca. Once the baby is born you'll feel wonderful.'

'Yes, of course – besides, I shouldn't grumble. I'm so lucky. Did I tell you I'd had another letter from Celia?'

'You didn't mention it.' Nan's expression was serious. 'Is she getting over the miscarriage?'

'Yes, I think so. Victor has taken her away for a long cruise on his yacht so that she can rest and recover.'

'It was such a shame. She must be so upset.'

'I expect so – that's why I mustn't grumble. At least I've managed to carry my baby full term. Or almost.' Her voice shook slightly.

'You're going to be fine.' Nan got up to add boiling water to the pot. 'Believe me, I'm sure of it.'

'Yes, I know.'

She sighed, thinking of Celia. How disappointed she and Victor must be that their child had miscarried.

Nan was right. It could not be much longer now and once the child was born she would be able to shake off the mood that had hung over her for so long. She wouldn't be like Dotty Prentice: she would live to hold Aden's child in her arms.

It was a miserable, cold morning, the sky a leaden grey that threatened rain later. When she felt the first pain in her back she thought it was because she had been working too hard. For the past two days she had been driven by a restless desire to turn the house upside down, scrubbing and cleaning everything in sight.

Aden had grumbled at her, asking her if she was trying to kill herself and the child.

'You should let me get a girl in to help you,' he said when he discovered she'd washed all the curtains. 'May Harris's sister is looking for a little job.'

'I don't want help. I can manage. Stop fussing, Aden! You know it gets on my nerves.'

She had flown at him in a sudden temper, accusing him of being unfeeling, then broken down in floods of tears. For a moment he'd stared at her in bewilderment, then he reached out and took her in his arms, stroking her hair with gentle hands.

'It's not your fault,' he said softly. 'This is too hard on you, Rebecca. I can't bear to see you this way.'

'I'll be all right soon,' she said, forcing a smile. 'How can you put up with me? I look awful and I'm impossible to live with.'

'Not impossible.' He grinned at her. 'Difficult – but not impossible.'

Some women blossomed in pregnancy but Rebecca knew it didn't suit her. Now, as the pain struck again, she realized the baby was coming at last and felt both relieved and frightened. She needed help!

She opened the back door and beckoned to the red-haired lad Aden had taken on to help out in the yard.

'Ned, I want you to do something for me, please.'

'Yes, missus?'

'Go to the doctor's house and ...'

112

His eyes widened with shock. 'Is it the babby, missus?' He was a skinny stick of a boy who was mostly put to bird scaring and odd jobs, a little slow on the uptake sometimes but good at heart. 'Be it coming now?' Ned knew about babies, his mother had had enough of them.

'Yes. Yes, I think ...' She gasped as the pain tore through her, swifter and sharper this time. 'Hurry, Ned. Tell him to come straight away.'

'Yes, missus.'

She went in and sat down as Ned sped off, looking as if the devil himself were after him. The lad should have been at school but his parents needed the few shillings he earned each week to help feed their large family. Most country folk earned barely enough to keep body and soul together and Aden had taken the boy on more out of kindness than anything else.

The pain struck again, turning her thoughts back to her own problems. What was it Nan had told her to do? Breathe deeply and keep calm. That wasn't easy when the pain was so bad and she was on the verge of panic. Oh God, how could she stand much more of this? It was far worse than she had imagined.

Something else Nan had said: the water. She would need plenty of boiling water. She filled two kettles and put them on the stove, gasping in agony as the pain pierced her like a knife.

She couldn't stand it. She couldn't!

She had to get upstairs. Their meal wasn't started yet but she couldn't think about that now. She had to lie down, to find the strength for what was coming.

She struggled upstairs, took off her outer clothes and lay down in her petticoats. Why had she ever thought she wanted a child? Why did any woman ever want to give birth when it hurt this much? It hurt so much ...

She started to breathe deeply as another pain came on, then, after what seemed like an eternity, she heard the back door open. Thank goodness, the doctor was coming! But it was Aden's voice that called up the stairs to her.

'Rebecca – where are you?'

'Up here. Lying down.'

She heard his boots clattering up the stairs. He rushed in and looked at her, concern in his face. 'How are you, love? The doctor will be a while but I've sent for Sarah. She's coming now.'

Rebecca bit her bottom lip to stop herself crying out in frustration. Sarah was old – what could she do? Why wasn't the doctor here? She was in terrible pain. She needed something to help her cope with the pain.

'Is there anything I can do?'

She opened her eyes as Aden hovered beside the bed. At this moment she almost hated him. It was all right for men; they shared the pleasure but the pain was all for their womenfolk. If men had to go through this they wouldn't be so keen on having children, she thought bitterly.

'No,' she said and sighed. 'When the doctor comes you may be needed downstairs but ...' She stifled a scream as the pain returned with a vengeance.

'Rebecca!' Aden caught her hand, his face working with emotion. 'I would go through it for you if I could.'

'Whist, what nonsense is that?' Sarah asked as she came puffing into the room, bringing the smell of fresh herbs and lavender water with her. 'Be off with you, Aden. Send the doctor up when he comes, then get yourself out of the house and find something to do. I'll look after Rebecca. I've seen a dozen or more babies into the world and yours is no different from the others.'

Her commonsense attitude eased the tension between them. Aden went with a smile for Rebecca and a look of regret. She couldn't return his smile, though she knew he meant well. She was relieved Sarah had sent him away; she didn't want him to see her like this.

'Don't hold back when the pain comes,' Sarah said after he had gone. 'Scream if it helps, Rebecca. I'll tie something to the bedrail. Sometimes it's better if you have something to hold on to.'

'I can't scream. It upsets Aden. He's worried enough as it is.'

'Be damned to him,' Sarah muttered. 'I've warned him not to stay here. You'll scream, lass, believe me. When it comes to it, you'll scream ...'

Aden stood in the hall and listened to Rebecca's screams. Each one tore through him like a knife. He had never expected it to go on for this long and he felt helpless. This wasn't the same as when one of the beasts gave birth; it was his wife up there and it was his fault she was in so much pain. He ought to have been more careful, made sure they didn't have a child so soon. She was only twenty ... if she died ... but she wouldn't. He couldn't bear it if she did: he loved her so much.

114

She was screaming again. How much of this could she stand? He went to the bottom of the stairs, straining to hear what was going on up there. There were three of them up there with her now, the doctor, Sarah and the midwife, yet still nothing was happening. He wanted to be there but he knew Rebecca would hate it; she would feel humiliated if he were there witnessing her ordeal. She liked to queen it over him; their relationship was based on his love for her and sometimes he wondered if she really cared for him. He had a feeling that she believed she had married beneath her, that he was second best – not that he blamed her. She had been brought up to expect more than he could give her. She should have married a gentleman, someone like Victor Roth perhaps.

Scowling, he went back to the kitchen and put on his coat. He would go and give a hand with the milking; it would be better than mooning about like a gutless fool!

He worked but didn't forget for a moment what was going on in the house and it seemed forever before Sarah came to tell him he had a son – a son who was perfect in every way.

'And Rebecca?' he croaked. 'Is she ... ?'

Sarah grinned toothlessly. 'She's as well as can be expected after what she's been through. Your son is a big 'un, Aden. Now you just get on up there and tell her how proud you are of her!'

He needed no prompting, taking the stairs two at a time, his heart thudding as he peeped cautiously round the door. Rebecca was sitting up in bed looking tired but happy. She held out her hand to him.

'You can come and see him now – he's so beautiful. He looks just like you, Aden.'

'Just for a few minutes, mind,' the doctor warned. 'Mrs Sawle is very tired.'

Aden perched on the edge of the bed and reached for her hand. He squeezed it gently, then turned as the midwife brought the child for his inspection. He looked down at the scrap of humanity in the blanket – such a little thing to cause so much pain, but so perfect. His throat caught with emotion and he found it difficult to speak.

'Look at all that hair ... and those eyes,' he said hoarsely. 'Thank you.'

'Your first son,' Rebecca said proudly. She had forgotten all the hours of agony as soon as they'd shown her the child. 'Your first

115

son … look at his hands, those tiny fingers …'

'He's beautiful … perfect,' replied Aden, and bent to kiss her. 'My son.'

'What's the matter?' she asked as he choked on the words. 'Aren't you pleased?'

'Of course I am. It's you – I've been that worried …'

'It wasn't pleasant but it's over,' she said. 'Forget it, Aden. What shall we call our son?'

'You choose. Do you want to name him for your father?'

'No.' She shook her head. 'Something different – what about Richie?'

'Richie Sawle … sounds all right to me. Short for Richard. Yes, Richie. I like it.'

'Mrs Sawle should rest now,' the midwife said in a tone of command.

Aden stood up obediently. Rebecca lay back against the pillows, closing her eyes. She looked pale and exhausted but relaxed.

Aden felt the relief flow over him as he walked downstairs. Maybe things would get back to normal now. Rebecca would soon be well and he had a fine son – a son to come after him on the land. There would be a new generation of Sawles at Five Winds and that gave him a sense of quiet satisfaction.

His father had been so proud of his land, land that had been passed down for several generations. It had sent him to an early grave but that wasn't going to happen to Aden or his sons. The Sawles were going to be rich. Rebecca's money had given him a start but he would build an empire to pass on to their children.

For a moment his feeling of satisfaction was marred by a prick of conscience – what about Dotty's child?

He'd heard nothing of her since that day he'd paid her off in Chatteris market. He hadn't thought of it then but now it had suddenly come home to him that the child might really be his – his own flesh and blood. Where was it now? Was it alive or dead? And what about Dotty? Perhaps he should ask her mother or … no, he couldn't do that.

Best forget the whole thing. He didn't know whether the child had been his or not. For all he knew Dotty could have been with half a dozen others.

11

The doctor had forbidden Rebecca to put a foot to the floor for three weeks and Aden had insisted that she should do as she was told. He wanted her to have May Harris's sister Ruth in to help her but Rebecca was still resisting.

'It would be better if you let me get a girl in,' he said when she protested that she could not lie abed for all that time. 'But Sarah will pop in to keep an eye on you, and so will Nan Barlow. Besides, I can look after most things myself.'

He was as good as his word, fetching and carrying for her and even changing Richie's napkin in the middle of the night. His uncomplaining attitude made her ashamed of her stubbornness. It wasn't fitting for a man to do these things and at last Rebecca came to the conclusion that she would have to give in over May Harris's sister.

She didn't want a girl in the house but it was too much to expect Aden to do everything and the doctor had warned her she must take things slowly, not work too hard for a while.

At last she reluctantly agreed to let Ruth Perry come on a trial basis. She was sixteen, pretty and pert with a way of tipping her head to one side that Rebecca thought flirtatious. She didn't really like her very much but was forced to accept her for the moment.

Ruth certainly did her work well, running up and down the stairs a dozen times a day to see if her mistress wanted anything. She was cheerful and obliging and laughed a lot, especially when Aden was around. Rebecca noticed her staring at him in a way she didn't care for when she didn't know she was being watched. If he had looked at the girl she would have sent her packing but he never seemed to notice her other than to greet her when she arrived, and Rebecca had no reason to be jealous.

At last the three weeks was over and she was allowed downstairs again. It felt so good to be out of that bed and almost back to normal! And it would be even better when they had the house to themselves again. When Aden came in she would tell him she didn't really need Ruth for much longer.

However, when he came in for his breakfast a little later he had a letter for her and in the excitement of opening and reading it she forgot about the young girl.

'It's from Celia,' she cried and took it from him eagerly. 'She must be back from that cruise ... Oh!' She stared at him, half-thrilled, half-dismayed. 'She and Victor want to come and visit us next month.'

'You'll enjoy that, won't you?' Aden was washing his hands at the sink, his back towards her so that she couldn't see his expression.

'Yes ...' She glanced round the kitchen. It was much improved from what it had been before they were married – but still the kitchen of a farmhouse. What would Celia think? She was used to far grander surroundings.

'What are you thinking?' She was startled by the question and glanced up to see that Aden looked serious. 'They'll take us as they find us, Rebecca.'

'Yes. Yes, of course.' She flushed and could not meet his searching gaze. 'Only ...'

'I've wondered if you've regretted marrying me,' he said, and there was a note of wounded pride in his voice. 'I told you at the start that you could do better ... that you could find someone of your own sort.'

'Don't be silly,' she said quickly. 'Celia's house was always grander than mine but we're still friends. I thought after the scandal of Father's death she would drop me, but she didn't. I don't suppose she'll care where we live.'

'There's money to spare if you need anything before they come. That's if you want them here?'

'Surely you don't grudge me a little pleasure?'

'That's not what I meant and you know it.' He turned away from her. 'I'll be off. I've some work to catch up on in the yard.'

He was reminding her that he had neglected his chores for her sake and she felt guilty. Aden was good to her and she ought not to be ashamed of what they had – or what they were.

118

'You will be here when they come?'

'You won't want me around.'

'Of course I shall. You're my husband. Besides, they would think it odd if you weren't here.'

'We'll see.'

'Aden, please …' She stopped as Ruth entered the kitchen, her eyes bright and curious, as if she knew they were having a quarrel.

'I shan't be late, Rebecca.'

He didn't smile as he left and she knew he was angry – angry and hurt. She would have to think of a way of making it up to him later.

'I've made the bed, Mrs Sawle,' Ruth said. 'Shall I do the washing now – or would you like me to bath Richie?'

'I'll look after Richie myself,' Rebecca said, more sharply than she'd meant to because she was upset. 'This was only a temporary arrangement. In a week or two I shall be able to manage the house without help.'

Ruth looked at her, a glint of resentment in her eyes, but didn't say anything as she went out to the wash-house.

'Why don't you like Ruth?' Aden asked that evening after she had left. 'Doesn't she do her work properly?'

'I haven't said I don't like her.'

'You don't need to. You show it when you speak to her – and she told me you were letting her go soon.'

'I didn't say that. I simply said I would be able to manage in a week or two.'

'That's the same thing.' He took his pipe down from the mantle. 'You don't mind if I smoke?'

'Why should I?'

'I thought it might upset you.'

'It made me feel unwell while I was carrying Richie but it won't upset me now.'

'As long as you're sure.' He struck a match and sucked on the stem of his pipe until the tobacco glowed, then stretched out in his chair and reached for the newspaper.

'I wanted to talk to you about Celia's visit. You will be here to meet them, Aden? They will expect it.'

'Then I suppose I shall have to be, shan't I?' There was humour but also a touch of resignation in his voice.

'Don't say it like that.' She went to kneel at his side. 'I want

119

things to be the way they were before I fell for Richie. Please don't let's quarrel.'

He laid the paper down and held out his arms to her. 'Sit on my lap,' he invited. 'Sorry if I've been touchy, love. It's a difficult time …'

She slid on to his lap and put her arms about his neck, lifting her face for his kiss. 'It doesn't have to be, Aden. I'm better now.'

He looked uncertain. 'Isn't it a bit soon? The doctor said …'

'I know what he said but …' She whispered in his ear and he chuckled. 'There's nothing to stop us doing that, is there?'

'No – not if you're sure?'

'I am.' She slid off his lap and held out her hand. 'Let's go to bed.'

It was three days later and Rebecca was in the kitchen when she heard a thump and then a wailing sound from upstairs. Richie! He had been sleeping peacefully when she left him – what was going on up there? She ran upstairs, her heart racing. Richie was screaming as if he were in pain.

As she rushed into the bedroom she saw Ruth Perry kneeling on the floor, trying to comfort the baby. The girl whirled round in guilty fright as Rebecca entered.

'What have you done to him?'

'I didn't mean …' Her face was white. 'I just wanted to nurse him but I … dropped him.'

'You wicked, wicked girl! You might have killed him.'

She was getting to her feet. Rebecca thrust her aside and swooped on her son, touching his soft cheeks anxiously and running her hands over his head. Was he hurt? Were any bones broken?

'Did you drop him on his head? You could have damaged him for life.'

'No, I swear.' Tears filled Ruth's eyes. 'He didn't fall hard. It was an accident …'

Rebecca was too concerned for her son to notice the girl's fear. 'I'm taking him to the doctor. If you've harmed him, you'll be sorry. I shall go to the police!' She walked to the door and glanced back. 'Don't be here when I get back.'

'Please, Mrs Sawle. I didn't mean …'

Rebecca was in such a state that she didn't stop to put on a coat, even though it was cold out, simply wrapping Richie in a warm shawl that she snatched from the wooden peg behind the kitchen door. She ran all the way to the doctor's house, pounding on his front door in a panic until his wife let her in. Richie hadn't stopped screaming and she was sure something was terribly wrong.

'Calm down, Rebecca,' Mrs Roberts soothed. 'Sit here, my dear, and I'll fetch the doctor straight to you.'

It seemed forever before he came but could have only been minutes. When he tried to take Richie from her she gave a cry of fear and clung on to him, tears streaming down her cheeks.

'What's wrong with him? She dropped him ... that wicked girl dropped him on his head ...'

'No, I don't think so,' the doctor said soothingly. 'He isn't concussed, Mrs Sawle. He's just had a nasty fright – as you have. He's maybe a little sore but otherwise no harm done.'

'No harm? Are you sure?'

Richie had stopped screaming at last. He was making little noises of distress and there were tears on his cheeks but his eyes were open and he was breathing normally.

'You've had a shock,' Doctor Roberts said, seeming more concerned for her than the child. 'You really shouldn't be out, Mrs Sawle.'

'Are you sure Richie is all right?'

'Keep an eye on him for a few hours. If you notice anything unusual send for me at once – but I'm sure you won't. He's fine, just a little shaken, that's all.'

'Will you have a cup of tea, Rebecca?' Mrs Roberts asked as her husband went back to his surgery. She smiled knowingly. 'We all have these little frights with the first one, my dear. But Doctor knows best.'

'Yes, I suppose so.' Rebecca felt foolish for having made such a fuss. 'Thank you, but I won't have that tea. I'd better get back.'

Richie started to gurgle happily as she carried him home. She remembered the frightened look on Ruth's face when she'd accused her of harming him and felt guilty. She ought not to have said those things to her. Ruth was wrong to have disobeyed her, and to have been so careless, but she hadn't done it on purpose.

Rebecca called the girl's name as she went in but the silence told her that she had already left. She sighed as she took Richie into the parlour and put him in his little wicker basket where she could keep an eye on him. She shouldn't have been so fierce with Ruth but she wasn't sorry she had gone.

*

121

Aden didn't say much about Ruth when Rebecca told him what had happened, though a few days later he mentioned that she had gone away to stay with an aunt.

'Ashamed to face you, I expect,' he said. 'Sid says she has been in floods of tears ever since you sent her home.'

'I thought Richie was badly hurt. If you had heard him screaming ...' Rebecca was defensive.

'Well, he seems all right now, doesn't he?'

'Yes.' She sighed. 'I'm sorry Ruth was upset. Tell Sid that I didn't mean what I said to her. I was worried.'

'He knows that. May was upset for her sister, of course, but Sid thinks the girl was at fault for picking Richie up when you'd told her not to.'

'She shouldn't have done it – but I shouldn't have shouted at her the way I did.'

'Forget it, love. I just feel it's a shame you're having to do all the work yourself.'

'I can manage. Honestly, I'm fine now.'

He accepted her word and the subject was dropped. She felt guilty about Ruth for a few days, then forgot about it as the time for Celia's visit drew nearer.

She had spent days getting the house ready and was almost sick with excitement as she glanced at the clock. They should be here at any moment!

Aden had left early that morning to supervise the ploughing of their top field but he had returned half an hour before their guests were due and was upstairs getting ready.

Rebecca had bought a new dress for the occasion. It was dark green with a fitted bodice, long, tight sleeves and a velvet collar – much finer than she would normally wear about the house but not as elegant as the gown Celia was wearing when she arrived.

She had hardly changed at all. Rebecca had thought she might look older, but she was still a pretty and obviously spoiled girl. Victor's manner towards her was more that of an indulgent father than a lover. Had it always been that way? Rebecca hadn't noticed it before.

'Rebecca!' Celia cried and hugged her. 'I've wanted to see you so much. I've missed you. You look wonderful.'

'Thank you. So do you.' Her dress was so elegant that it could only have come from Paris, and her little shoulder cape was trimmed with dark fur. 'And thank you, Victor, for bringing Celia to see me.'

They had arrived in a smart carriage drawn by four matched greys and driven by a groom in a green coat and cream breeches.

'You didn't bring your automobile then?' Rebecca said to cover a moment of shyness as she glanced at Victor. 'Aden was looking forward to seeing it.'

'It's so silly,' Celia cried with a little laugh. 'Victor was almost arrested because he refused to have a man walk in front of us with a red flag. He nearly came to blows over it with a police constable.'

'It's a stupid rule and I told the fellow so. They do not behave in such an antiquated way abroad. If we continue to bury our heads in the sand we shall fall far behind the rest of the industrialised world. It's no wonder the Empire is crumbling ...'

'Victor – don't!' Celia implored. 'Rebecca doesn't want to hear all that.'

'I'm very interested in what Victor has to say.'

Rebecca smiled at him. He was just the same – tall, distinguished and confident.

'Rebecca ...' His voice seemed to throb with emotion. 'You look ... beautiful.'

'Thank you.' She blushed as she heard a sound behind her. 'Celia – Victor ... I want you to meet my husband. Aden, this is Celia and her husband.'

'Rebecca has spoken of you often.' Aden extended his hand. He had washed and the smell of soap clung about him. Rebecca noticed that he had put on his Sunday suit and a starched collar. 'Sir Victor – it's good to meet you at last.'

There was a quiet dignity about Aden, and as she saw the two men side by side for the first time, Rebecca was aware of a fierce pride in her husband. Their cottage might not match up to Celia's various homes but Rebecca had nothing to blush for in the man she had married.

'We had hoped to come before but Celia has not been well.' Victor's eyes were soft as he glanced at his wife.

'I'm better now so don't look like that,' she cried. 'Talk to Aden for a few minutes. I want Rebecca to myself.'

'You stay here,' Aden said. 'I'll put the kettle on. But perhaps you would care for something stronger, Sir Victor?'

They moved into the kitchen together, clearly at ease with one another. Above Celia's inconsequential chatter, Rebecca could hear snatches of what they were saying.

'How much land have you now?'

'Around three hundred acres.'

'Is it all fen soil?'

'Some of it. The land here at Five Winds is clay and the very devil to work if you don't know what you're doing. We're ploughing the top field today ...'

'You're not listening to me!'

Celia sounded petulant and Rebecca turned her full attention to her.

'I was asking if you liked living here?'

'It's all right. Yes, I like it. Of course you travel so much ...'

'Yes.' Celia pulled a face. 'Victor's bailiff looks after the estate. Victor likes to travel but I find it tiring.' She did not sound as if she really enjoyed her life.

'About two thousand acres ...' Victor was saying. 'Most of it arable ...'

Celia sighed. 'It's always business, business with men, isn't it?'

'Aden talks to me about the land when he comes home. I find it interesting to know what's going on – don't you?'

'Celia has no interest in business.' Victor rejoined them, sherry glass in hand. 'All she cares for is her parties and the latest fashions, isn't it, darling?' His voice was light and teasing but there was an underlying note of irritation.

'I know you spoil me – but why shouldn't I enjoy those things?' She gave him a dimpled smile.

'Why not indeed?' He smiled at her, irritation gone. 'You have no need to think of business, my love.'

'I prefer to dance or hunt.' She wrinkled her brow. 'But you won't let me hunt, because it's not good for me.'

'It was hunting that caused your ... Forgive me,' he apologized as her face crumpled. 'I'm sorry, darling. I shouldn't have mentioned it.'

'I'll make the tea.' Rebecca paused as she heard a wail from upstairs. 'Oh dear. I was hoping Richie would sleep through your visit. I may have to fetch him down.'

'Please do,' Victor said. 'We were hoping to see him, weren't we, Celia?'

'Yes ... of course,' she said, and turned her face away.

'I'll fetch Richie,' Aden offered.

He returned several minutes later with the child wrapped in a lacy shawl. The baby's cries had stopped and Rebecca knew Aden must have changed his wet napkin – a chore he did with sure, deft hands whenever she would let him. He stood nursing the child as she finished serving tea, looking as proud as a peacock.

'This is delicious,' Celia said, nibbling at a light sponge filled with plum jam and whipped cream straight from the dairy. 'Did you make it, Rebecca?'

'I make all my own cakes.'

'You must give me the recipe for my cook.'

Victor was looking at Aden and in that moment his emotions were there in his eyes for all to see. He might own many times the acres Aden worked but Rebecca believed he would have given it all for the tiny scrap of humanity in her husband's arms.

'He's beautiful,' Victor said, and there was envy in his voice. 'You're a lucky man to have such a fine son.'

'Yes.' Aden's eyes sought Rebecca's. 'Some things are beyond price – and a man's first son is special.'

Celia winced. Rebecca felt a surge of sympathy for her. It must be hurtful not to be able to give her husband the one thing he wanted.

'Did you enjoy your trip to Greece?' she asked. 'I've always thought I should like to go sailing. Is it fun?'

The conversation was successfully turned and after a while she took Richie back upstairs. When she came down again Celia and Victor were preparing to leave.

'You must come and stay with us one day,' she said, kissing Rebecca's cheek. 'Do say you will.'

'Perhaps …' It was impossible for Rebecca to leave Aden and the cottage but Celia wouldn't understand. She had a houseful of servants to see that everything ran smoothly when she was away. 'One day.'

'Yes, you must come,' Victor said. 'All of you.'

Rebecca smiled but said nothing. Aden went to the gate to see them off. When he came back she was loading the tea things on to a tray.

'That's that then,' he said. 'I'll change and get back to work.'

'What did you think of them?'

'She's a bit petulant. Still a little girl, really. He's all right, though. Felt a bit sorry for him …'

'Sorry for Victor?'

125

'He wants a son badly and I doubt she'll ever give him one. She's not half the woman you are. No wonder he looked at you the way he did.'

Her heart jerked. 'What do you mean?'

'He couldn't keep his eyes off you.' There was a touch of jealousy in his voice.

'Don't be silly. He's very much in love with Celia.'

'Is he? He may have thought so when he married her but I dare say he has regretted it since.'

'That's not fair! I'm very fond of Celia. She can't help it if she lost her baby. We were lucky, Aden.'

'Yes, I know. I almost lost you.' He sighed, and looked rueful. 'I shouldn't have said that. She's nice enough in her way. I'm a jealous fool. You can't stop other men looking – and as long as that's all he does, I'll have to put up with it.'

'Aden!' Her cheeks burned. 'Victor isn't interested in me.'

'That's your opinion. It's a good thing we shan't see them for another year or more – or I might really be jealous.'

'You've no need. I'm a respectable married woman.'

'I know.' He grinned at her as he went to the door. 'But don't forget, I know the other side of you, lass.' He was chuckling as he went out.

Rebecca began to wash her best china, rinsing it carefully before letting it drain. Was Victor beginning to regret his marriage? Did he sometimes wish that ... No, she must not let herself have such wicked disloyal thoughts!

She was Aden's wife and they had a son. Their life was a good one and Aden loved her. She might occasionally think of a different life but only when she was tired or feeling down. Besides, it was too late to dwell on what might have been. She must be grateful for what she had.

126

12

Aden attended the auction which had brought him to Chatteris and secured the parcel of land he was after, outbidding Joshua Hauxton, who glared at him before moving away, still muttering under his breath. It wasn't the first time they'd clashed over land recently, and from the dark looks Hauxton was throwing him, Aden sensed he'd made an enemy.

Immersed in his own thoughts, he stepped backwards without looking and was startled by a woman's cry of pain. He turned quickly, apologizing as he realized he had trodden on her foot.

'I beg your pardon,' he said. 'I didn't know you were there.' He frowned as he suddenly recognized her. 'Mrs Prentice – you are Dotty's mother, aren't you?'

'Yes.' She gave him an odd look. 'You're Aden Sawle. You took her to a dance once.'

'Yes, that's right.' He hesitated, then cleared his throat. 'Have you heard from her lately?'

'Don't you know?' Mrs Prentice gave him a cold stare. 'I should have thought your wife would have told you – Dotty's dead. She died having that gipsy's bastard. I told Mrs Sawle about it soon after it happened ...'

That must have been almost three years earlier. Aden felt as if he'd been punched hard in the stomach. Rebecca had known all this time but she hadn't told him. Why?

'It must have slipped her mind,' he said in an odd, muffled voice. 'Or perhaps she did tell me and I forgot. I'm very sorry. I wouldn't have mentioned her if I'd known.'

'I miss her, you know,' Mrs Prentice said, her eyes suddenly misting. 'For a while I was angry but she was my only child ...'

'Yes, of course. It's very sad for you – and Mr Prentice.'

'That old devil couldn't care less one way or the other,' Mrs Prentice said, her face looking grey and tired all at once. 'If it hadn't been for him she might have stayed at home and then I'd have had the child ... if it had lived.'

'You don't know what happened to the baby then?'

'The gipsy told me it died,' she said and sniffed. 'I think he was lying but I've never known for sure.'

Aden nodded, feeling an odd, clenching sensation in his stomach. She winced and he glanced down at her foot, which still seemed to be causing her pain. 'Will you let me take you for a drink, Mrs Prentice? You need to rest that foot for a while – and then perhaps I can drive you home in my trap?'

'Well, that's very kind of you.' Her eyes brightened. 'I do take a little drop of brandy now and then – just for medicinal purposes, you know.'

'It's good for shock,' Aden agreed with a little smile. 'And that's just what you need. I think I might join you – but I'll have a whisky.'

He offered her his arm; she leaned on him heavily as they went into The Arms and he settled her at a table by the window.

He bought a double brandy for Dotty's mother and a single whisky for himself and carried them back to the table.

'This is ever so good of you,' she said and sipped at the drink. Then she gestured to something behind him. 'Is that a friend of yours? Over there ...'

Aden glanced over his shoulder and saw a couple of farmers he knew sitting in their usual table in the corner.

'Yes, it's Ted Harvey and Gerald Matthews,' he said as they beckoned to him. 'Would you mind if I left you for a moment?'

'You go,' she said. 'I'll sit here for a few minutes, then I'll get off home.'

'What about your foot?'

'It's feeling much better already. Don't you worry about me, Mr Sawle. You'd best see what your friends are after.'

Aden drained his glass and strolled over to the table. He already knew what Ted and Gerald wanted; they'd been asking him to play poker with them for months and he'd been resisting – but right now he was in the mood for company.

He was uneasy in his mind. Rebecca had known about Dotty dying for years and she hadn't told him ... it wasn't like her to keep something like that to herself.

Suddenly, he felt angry. Damn it! Why should he feel guilty after all this time? It had only been a bit of fun, nothing a thousand men before him hadn't done. He'd never cheated on Rebecca since they were married and he was damned if he was going to let something so trivial worry him now.

He pulled back a chair and sat down at the corner table.

'What are you drinking, lads?' he asked. 'I think I'll have another whisky myself.'

Rebecca glanced out of the window. It had turned out fine and warmer than they'd expected after a recent spell of cool weather. The sky was blue and blessedly free from cloud which augured well for the church fête.

Aden was coming across the yard and would be in for his breakfast soon. She was thoughtful as she went to the stove and turned the bubble and squeak in the pan so that it would be browned and crispy the way he liked it. He had been in a strange mood for a couple of days – ever since that last trip to Chatteris.

'That smells good,' he said as he came in and went to wash his hands at the stone sink. She laid a plate of bacon, eggs and the fried vegetables in front of him and he glanced at her own plate, which contained only a thin piece of buttered toast. 'You don't eat enough, Rebecca.'

'I felt a bit sick this morning,' she said, placing her hands on her stomach protectively. 'It seems to be hanging around forever this time.'

She was almost five months into her second pregnancy. It had taken her longer than they'd expected to recover from Richie's birth and it was now the spring of 1894, which meant that Richie would be almost three when the baby was born. He was a lively child, adventurous and strong-willed.

'You shouldn't be helping at the fête,' Aden said. 'Tell Nan you don't feel up to it, she'll understand.'

'I want to help and I'll be fine once the sickness goes. It's just in the mornings, you know that.'

He shrugged, demolishing his meal with evident enjoyment. 'Have you thought anymore about getting some help in the house? You should find someone before the baby is born, Rebecca. I might be away in the fen when it happens and I don't like the idea of your being alone in the house.'

Aden's empire had been growing steadily over the years and some of his land was in the Chatteris fen, which meant that there were days when he was gone from early in the morning until after dark. And he went regularly to market once a week, come rain or shine. His business seemed to take up more and more of his time and energy, and sometimes she found herself resenting that, though she knew he had no choice if they wanted all the things they had planned and dreamed of in the early days.

'I might talk to Mrs Green about Molly ...'

Aden was silent for a moment then asked, 'Did you know Ruth Perry was staying with her sister? She came back for a visit because their mother is ill but she's not staying long. I understand she's done very nicely for herself.'

'I hadn't heard.' Rebecca knew what he was waiting for and sighed. 'But if I see her, I'll have a word.'

'That's right,' he said and nodded his approval. 'I've asked Sid Harris if he'll come and work for me and we don't want to be bad friends with May, do we?'

'No, of course not. I've always liked May Harris. I'll make sure I see Ruth before she leaves.'

Sid Harris was one of Aden's closest friends and he'd been talking about offering him a job for a while now. Aden's hard work was beginning to pay dividends and the milking herd had increased to such a size that he needed a head stockman to look after it. He was looking for a decent cottage for Sid and his family, because the cottage they were living in now was tied to the job he already had – a job that paid a good deal less than Aden was prepared to offer him. Rebecca was sure that he would take the job at Five Winds, even if his wife still felt resentful over the way her sister had been summarily dismissed. But Aden was right: it was better to be on good terms with everyone. Besides, she had often wished that she had tried to make it up with Ruth, reassured her that she hadn't harmed Richie.

After she'd finished tidying up she popped round to the Vicarage to see how Nan was getting on and found her in high spirits; half of the stalls were already set up in her large garden and there were several willing helpers at work.

'We're going to have a beautiful day, Rebecca,' she said. 'Come and look at all the hats. That was an inspired idea of yours.'

They were always looking for something different to sell at the

130

fêtes and Rebecca had suggested that all the members of their little institute should make or trim a spring hat. They would be auctioned at the end of the afternoon and the hat that raised the most money would win a prize. She had told Celia about her idea and she had sent Nan a beautiful Derby porcelain teapot; it was painted with exotic birds and flowers in beautiful jewel-like colours and almost every woman in the village longed to own it. They would all be sure to muster their friends and relations to bid high for their own hats, which meant that they should raise a lot of money for the church.

Nan was right to be pleased with the hats; they had all been lovingly trimmed and made and were of a very high standard but Rebecca was particularly interested in one of them.

'I love this black straw with the silk roses,' she said. 'Who made it?'

'That's Sarah's,' Nan said with a smile. 'You should buy that, Rebecca, it would suit you.'

'I shall certainly bid for it,' she promised. 'Now – what can I do to help you?'

'Are you sure you did everything we discussed?' Aden looked at the lad shuffling his boots in front of him. 'Daisy's one of my best milkers, Ben, and I don't want to lose her. Yesterday that infected teat seemed to be getting better but now she looks worse.'

'I did what you told me, sir.' Ben Woods stared at the ground, knowing full well that he was lying. He'd taken shortcuts to get the work done and if his employer knew the truth he'd be out on his ear – and it wasn't that easy to find work in the area. 'She don't seem to be responding.'

'All right – get back to the mucking out. I'll see to her myself.'

Aden watched the youth walk away. He suspected Ben of lying but he was generally a good worker and Aden didn't want to get rid of him. What he needed was an experienced man to look after the cows, because he couldn't do everything himself.

'Mr Sawle ... Mr Sawle! Come quick!'

Aden heard the urgency in Ben's voice as he came running out of the cowshed where the sick cow was being kept away from the others. Damn it! This was what he'd been afraid of when he'd looked at Daisy earlier. The infection had been neglected and now they were going to lose her ...

131

Rebecca was serving on the cake stall, which was always one of the most popular and had been very busy all afternoon. Molly Green had volunteered to help her, and she was such a sweet, reasonable girl that after an hour or so in her company, Rebecca had decided to speak to her mother about letting her come to help out in the house. Aden was right, she would need someone when the baby came – and he was too busy to help as he had done when Richie was born.

By four o'clock they had almost sold out of cakes and Molly suggested that she could manage if Rebecca wanted to go for a walk round the other stalls.

'You ought to put your feet up and have a cup of tea, Mrs Sawle,' she said.

'I'll just go and have a word with Nan if you're sure you don't mind?' Rebecca accepted her offer gratefully. 'I'd like to see the rest of the hats.'

Nan was presiding over the needlework stall, which had been covered with masses of cushion covers, aprons, oven gloves and table runners, all beautifully sewn and embroidered by local women. The best had gone and it was obvious by her flushed face that she had had a successful afternoon. The stall next to her was set out with all the hats that were soon to be auctioned.

Rebecca's own offering was a lace mobcap with a puffed caul and frilled border; it was pretty but not exciting and she didn't expect to win the teapot, but since it was all her idea it wouldn't have looked right if she had.

She was surprised to see that there were now two very similar hats. Sarah's hat was not new but she had trimmed it with two pale cream silk roses and that morning it had seemed likely that she would win, but now there was a very new black straw with a wide sweeping brim and a cluster of white silk roses scattered across the crown.

'Who made that?' she asked, turning to Nan. 'It looks professional.'

'I suppose it is in a way,' she said. 'May Harris brought it along. Her sister Ruth made it and I believe she works in a milliner's shop in Cambridge.'

'But she did make the hat herself?'

'That's what May told me – so we can't refuse it, can we?'

'No ... no, of course not. Anyway, it doesn't mean it will win, even if it is by far the best. Remember, it's what someone is prepared to pay for the hat that counts – and I shall bid for Sarah's.'

'Good for you,' Nan said. 'I think I've done my share for today. Let's have a cup of tea, shall we?'

'I could do with a sit down,' Rebecca agreed and glanced round. 'Have you seen Aden? He said he might come if he had time.'

'No, I haven't seen him. I expect he was too busy.'

Rebecca nodded. It didn't really matter, except that he had promised to come if he could.

The tea tent was busy; it smelt of damp canvas and grass and the women behind the counter were rushed off their feet, but Rebecca and Nan managed to find a couple of chairs and sat down. It had been a good fête and often by this time of the afternoon people were drifting away but no one looked like moving that day; they were all waiting for Nan to announce the auction, which she did as soon as she'd finished her tea.

An excited buzz went round the little crowd and women looked anxiously for their relatives who had been primed to do the bidding, because of course no one could bid for their own hat.

Rebecca had suggested that Nan should start with her cap, which, as no one had been asked to bid for it, sold quickly for one shilling. Rebecca smiled as she said goodbye to any chance of winning Celia's teapot. Nan grinned at her and sold her own knitted tammy next, achieving just tuppence less for her efforts – but after that it was a very different story. Very ordinary hats began to sell for ten and twelve shillings, a pretty straw bonnet trimmed with bows and fresh flowers reached fifteen, and then it was Sarah's turn. Rebecca bid sixteen shillings for it, topping any earlier bids, someone else went to a pound and she offered another five shillings. Her bid was topped by half a crown and she went to thirty shillings.

She heard a muffled cry of annoyance behind her and turned to see Ruth Perry shake her head at the young man who had been bidding against her. From the look of annoyance on Ruth's face, she suspected that he had been bidding for the wrong hat and she had only just managed to stop him.

Sarah's hat was knocked down to Rebecca for thirty shillings and she smiled, thinking that it ought to secure the teapot for her friend.

'You were silly,' Sarah said as she came to join her. 'It was only an old thing and I would have made you one for nothing. That's the one you should have bid for.'

Nan was holding up Ruth's hat. 'Now this is very pretty,' she said. 'Who will bid me a pound for this? It has to be worth at least that.'

It was a pretty hat and Rebecca knew it would suit her. She put her hand up. 'I'll give you a pound,' she said.

'Twenty-five shillings,' a voice said behind her, and she didn't need to turn round to know who was bidding.

Rebecca hesitated, torn between wanting Sarah's hat to win and a sense of fairplay; Ruth's was after all the best hat in the auction.

'Twenty-seven shillings and sixpence.'

'Thirty shillings,' the young man behind her chipped in confidently.

'Thirty shillings,' Nan said. 'Is that your last offer?'

'Bid another two shillings,' Sarah whispered as there was silence from the onlookers. 'The girl deserves her prize, Rebecca – and the hat will suit you. Besides, I don't need another teapot at my age.'

Rebecca looked at her, still hesitating, but she nodded, her eyes twinkling.

'Thirty-two shillings,' Rebecca said, and there was a little sigh from the women standing round her as Nan brought the hammer down. No one was going to bid more for any of the other hats and so Ruth had won.

The other hats raised only a few shillings each and Nan announced what everyone knew already, that the teapot was awarded to Miss Ruth Perry.

'And now I'm going to ask Rebecca Sawle to present the prize,' Nan said, beaming at her. 'It was her idea to have this competition and I think we all agree that it was a good one.'

Rebecca shook her head at Nan – this wasn't what she had expected. Considering who had won it was very awkward and she held back, but Nan was smiling and beckoning to her and she was forced to join her on the little stage. She took a deep breath and summoned a smile as Ruth came towards her.

She had grown up since they'd last met and looked very smart and attractive in a striped poplin blouse and a dark skirt with a matching fitted jacket; her long thick hair was swept up under a pretty straw boater.

'It is my pleasure to present you with this prize,' Rebecca said, and picked up the teapot, holding it out to her. 'It was a very attractive hat and I know I'm going to enjoy wearing ...'

How it happened she would never be sure but as she handed the delicate pot to Ruth it seemed to slip through her fingers and fell to the floor with a crash. She stared in horror as the lid flew out and the knob broke off. There was a little groan from the watching women and she felt as if she had committed a terrible crime.

'Oh ...' she whispered. 'I'm so sorry, Ruth.'

Ruth stared at her with tears in her eyes as she bent to pick up the pieces. 'You did that on purpose,' she said. 'You couldn't bear it because I'd won.'

'Ruth ... I never meant it to happen. I'm so sorry. I thought you had it safely ...'

'You're not sorry. You did it on purpose because you hate me,' she said in a loud voice, and turned away with her head in the air.

Rebecca looked at Nan, her cheeks on fire. 'I thought she had it. I wouldn't have ...'

'Of course you wouldn't,' Nan agreed, a flash of annoyance in her eyes. 'It was her fault. She drew her hands away as you let go.'

Nan had been close enough to see but others might think she had done it out of spite; they would remember that Ruth had been unfairly dismissed and think Rebecca still bore a grudge against the girl.

'Take your hats,' Nan said as she turned away. 'You paid enough for them.'

'Yes.' Rebecca held on to her dignity, refusing to let anyone see she was upset. She would take the hats but she would never be able to wear the one Ruth had made. 'I think I'll go home now, Nan. I'll see you tomorrow.'

The whole thing had upset her. She felt embarrassed and guilty, as if she had done something awful – and when she saw the slaughterhouse cart standing in the yard she took little notice, except to press a hand to her nose to shut out the stink of rotting carcasses.

'It was very unfortunate,' Aden said that evening. 'I know you didn't do it out of spite, Rebecca, but some will think so. May was in tears over it. I think you ought to give Ruth a new teapot.'

'She pulled her hands away, Aden,' she said, feeling annoyed that he seemed to have taken her side. 'If I hadn't bid that extra two shillings she wouldn't have won anyway. Sarah wanted me to but I wish I hadn't now.' She gave him a resentful glance. 'If you'd been there you would have seen what happened.'

'I was busy.' He frowned as he knocked his pipe against the side of the grate. 'It might have been better if you hadn't bid for the hats at all. I'm not blaming you. I'm just saying how it looks.'

He yawned and went upstairs. Rebecca followed more slowly, feeling hurt and irritated. Nan had seen Ruth deliberately pull her hands away but Aden was acting as though it were her fault.

She turned away from him in bed, not returning his kiss as she usually did. He didn't say anything, merely closing his eyes and falling asleep while she lay staring into the darkness and going over it all in her mind. Why should she give Ruth a new teapot? She didn't deserve it – and it wasn't fair of Aden to take her side.

It took her three days to calm down enough to see it from his point of view. Perhaps Ruth had behaved badly but in a way it was Rebecca's fault. Anyway, it wouldn't hurt her to give the girl a teapot; she had lots of pretty ones and it was worth it if it made things easier for Aden. He had been quiet for a few days, as if he had something on his mind.

She packed the pot in tissue and placed it in a withy basket, then set out to the Harrises' cottage, which was across the bridge and a fair walk down the Chatteris road. Although not as warm as the day of the fête it was quite pleasant and she enjoyed being out in the fresh air.

May Harris opened the door. She was a thin woman in her early-thirties and the mother of two sons, but very attractive still with light brown hair and hazel eyes. She looked a bit stern until Rebecca explained why she had come, then she smiled and invited her in.

'I told Ruth you wouldn't have done it on purpose,' she said. 'But she thinks you hate her because of what happened with Richie.'

'I wanted to apologize about that,' Rebecca said. 'I was so upset at the time that I said things I shouldn't have done.'

May took her into the tiny kitchen. The cottage was neat and clean, though obviously too small for her family. Besides herself, her husband and two sons, May had her elderly bed-ridden mother to care for and she needed more room.

'I'll call Ruth down,' she said. 'She's upstairs with Ma ... ah, here she is.'

'May ...' Ruth stopped speaking as she saw who their visitor was and flushed a bright red. 'What's *she* doing here?'

'I've come to bring you a new teapot,' Rebecca said. 'I was sorry the other one ...'

'I don't want your charity!'

'Now then, Ruth,' May said in a chiding tone. 'Listen to what Mrs Sawle has to say.'

'You keep out of it.' Ruth rounded on her in a fury. 'I hate her and I don't want her pot. She's a spiteful bitch and I'll say what I like ...'

'You just wash your mouth out with carbolic,' May Harris said angrily. 'Mrs Sawle came here to put things right, not to be insulted by the likes of you.'

'It doesn't matter,' Rebecca said and looked at Ruth. 'I wasn't offering charity – just recompense for what you've lost.'

'Well, you needn't have bothered because your husband gave me ten pounds to buy myself something nice.' She shot a look of triumph at Rebecca. 'Aden always had a soft spot for me when I was working for you. I reckon he fancies me – and that's why you couldn't wait to get rid of me!'

'Ruth!' May was shocked. Before Rebecca really knew what she was doing she stepped forward and slapped her sister's face. 'Now you just take back that wicked lie!'

Ruth stared at her and the tears welled up in her eyes, then she turned and ran out of the room, back up the stairs to her mother's sickroom.

'Come back here!' May called after her. 'You apologize this instant or ...'

'It doesn't matter,' Rebecca said quickly. 'It's so silly that I'm not going to take any notice of her. When she calms down, please tell her that I'm willing to forget all this nonsense if she is.'

'You've been fair with her,' May said. 'More than she deserves if you ask me. I shall tell her so, believe me.'

Rebecca nodded, then left the cottage to walk home; she looked calm but inside she was seething. How could Aden go behind her back like that? He had made her look such a fool!

She couldn't get it out of her mind all day and when he came in that evening she rounded on him in a fury.

'Did you give Ruth Perry ten pounds to make up for that teapot?'

Aden looked sheepish. 'Don't take on so, Rebecca. I just felt sorry for the lass, that's all. Besides, I need Sid for the stock and I couldn't afford to let a rift develop between us over this nonsense.'

'That's all it is to you, isn't it?' Rebecca demanded bitterly. 'It looks as if you have taken her side instead of mine. As if you think I dropped that pot out of spite.'

'You know better than that,' he said, a note of irritation in his voice. 'But you did dismiss her unfairly after the incident with Richie, you won't deny that?' He met her angry gaze and she nodded. 'I was just trying to save you the trouble of apologizing. You said you wouldn't … if you'd told me you'd changed your mind, I wouldn't have interfered.'

'Why didn't you tell me?'

'I didn't think it was important.' There was something odd in his eyes at that moment. 'You don't always tell me everything … Besides, I had other things on my mind. We lost one of our best milkers the day of the fête and now I've got another going down with the same thing. Sid Harris is the best stockman I know and I'd have paid the girl twice as much if it meant getting him.'

Rebecca felt the sting of tears and turned away. Was he saying the farm meant more to him than she did?

He came up to her, slipping his arms about her and turning her to face him. 'Don't get foolish ideas into that head of yours,' he said softly. 'I'm sorry if you were embarrassed but I did what I thought right. You know I love you, don't you?'

'Yes,' she sighed and let him hold her. 'Yes, I know.'

He had probably acted with the best of intentions but she felt it was a small betrayal all the same.

13

It was hot and sultry and would probably end in a thunderstorm. Aden was in the yard looking impatiently at his pocket watch. He had been waiting for George Tubbs for hours. One of the mares was in season and George was due to bring the stallion to her that morning.

Rebecca moved away from the window with a sigh. She ought to pop across the road and see Sarah. Her health had been failing this past month or so and Rebecca sat with her as often as she could.

'Watch out for Richie when he wakes up,' she said to the young girl who was washing out a few towels at the sink. 'I don't want him in the yard when the stallion gets here – and he mustn't watch what's going on.'

'Yes, Mrs Sawle. I understand,' Molly Green replied, glancing over her shoulder. 'I'll be sure to keep him inside. I don't like horses much myself.'

Molly was a plump, homely sort of girl but very good-natured. Rebecca still liked her as much as she had when she'd helped her on the cake stall at the fête. She was very good with Richie, who was forever into something and needed constant watching.

Rebecca pressed a hand to her back and sighed. 'Aden says Canuden Quicksilver is as gentle as a lamb but it's the whole business that I don't care for, though I know it's necessary.'

During the three and a half years of their marriage she had grown used to seeing the mares served by the huge stallion that George Tubbs walked from farm to farm, but she still found it distasteful. She was beginning to think it was time Aden built her the new house he'd promised. Richie was growing up and her second child would soon be born, which was a mercy because her ankles were permanently swollen now. She was always tired and felt so irritable she could scream. Aden was being patient, though perhaps not quite as patient as he had been with the first one – but she knew her moods had put a strain on their relationship, which had never been quite the same since he'd given that money to Ruth Perry. Neither of them had mentioned the incident again but it still niggled Rebecca, even though the girl had left the village after her mother died.

'Going across to Sarah then?' Aden asked as she went into the yard carrying a jug of nourishing broth. 'Stay for an hour or two. This should all be over when you get back.'

Rebecca nodded but didn't speak. Aden knew that she didn't care for this sort of thing but of course he didn't understand why.

George was walking down the road with the horse, which even Rebecca acknowledged was a proud sight, its rich chestnut coat glistening with sweat and its noble head tossing restlessly. He waved to her as she crossed the road and went into Sarah's cottage.

It was so hot! She had been feeling the oppressive atmosphere all morning and her back was aching. All she really wanted was to lie down in a cool room with the curtains closed.

'Sarah – it's me,' she called as she went up the narrow stairs. 'I've brought you some soup.'

Sarah was confined to her bed now. Rebecca had been over earlier to help her wash and make her a cup of tea. She ate very little these days but might take a little of her favourite oxtail broth.

Sarah smiled as Rebecca went in but she could see that her old friend was weaker. The doctor had told them days ago that it was only a matter of time.

Sarah sipped a little of the soup, then sighed as she lay back against the pillows. 'You shouldn't be looking after me, lass. You look worn out yourself.'

'I'm well enough to visit you. The baby isn't due for another week or two yet.'

Sarah nodded but seemed restless. 'Ask Aden to come over, will you? I want to see him about something while I've still got my wits about me. I've not got much time left.'

'Hush, Sarah. Don't distress yourself.'

'I'm not afraid.' She took Rebecca's hand in her skinny claws.

140

'It's my time, Rebecca. We both know that – but I want to see Aden. He's been like a son to me.'

'He's very fond of you.'

'Aye, he's a good lad.'

Her eyes closed and Rebecca knew she would sleep. She sat in a chair beside her, thinking how much she would miss her when she was gone. She had been Rebecca's first friend in the village, and though there were many others now, Sarah was special.

'There you are then,' Aden said as George brought the horse into the yard at last. 'I was beginning to think you had moved on.'

'It was this silly bugger,' George said with a grin. 'Frisky as a two year old he were this morning. Took me two hours jest to catch him and then he kicked me. You try walking from Sutton Gault with a sore shin.'

Aden chuckled. He'd heard George's tales before and he knew the strength of the great shire horses. Canuden Quicksilver was as gentle as he was strong but he could be contrary and took some handling, which was why Aden wanted to be there himself when the mare was served.

'Let's hope he hasn't worn himself out then. That mare is as ready as she'll ever be. Put him in the stable and let him cool down for an hour or so while we have a beer. You look as if you could do with one.'

George was sweating hard. He nodded and led the horse into the stable, then followed Aden towards the cottage. As they approached, the door opened and a young girl of sixteen or so came out. She was carrying a child but set him down and he came toddling to meet them.

'Richie was asking for you,' Molly said. 'So I thought it was all right.'

Aden bent down to sweep up his son and swing him round on his shoulders.

'This your boy?' George asked. 'Fine lad.'

'Richie wants to see the stallion,' Molly said. 'But Mrs Sawle said he wasn't to see … anything.' She blushed furiously as George winked at her.

Aden nodded in agreement. 'You make sure he doesn't slip out when you're not watching. His mother wouldn't be best pleased if young Richie learned the facts of life too soon.'

'He's a mite young,' George agreed, 'though I wasn't much older when my father took me out to see what was what.'

'It's not as if he'd know what was going on,' Aden said as Molly went to fetch a jug of beer from the cold pantry. 'But Rebecca's strict where the boy is concerned.'

'Aye, well, women are like that.' George winked at him. 'That's a comely lass you've got looking after him. I'd give my right arm for ten minutes behind the barn with her ... I'd want it back, mind.'

'Don't you let Rebecca hear you talk like that,' Aden said. 'She thinks the world of that girl.'

'Respectable woman, your Rebecca. I didn't mean no harm. It was jest my bit of fun like.'

Aden nodded and sipped his beer. It surprised him how vehement Rebecca could be over anything in the least bit risqué, considering what she was like in the privacy of their bedroom. She disapproved of coarse talk from his labourers and she was down on any man who got a girl into trouble or went with women other than his wife. She had a sharp tongue on her when she liked, as he'd found out a few times this past month or so. Not that he really minded. A bit of tongue was nothing when you considered how good things were between them most of the time.

And it was this pregnancy that was pulling her down. Aden had been thinking that he might take her and the children away for a few days by the sea after harvest – after the baby was born and Rebecca was on her feet again. Sid should be working for him by then and Aden could leave him in charge. He hadn't mentioned it to Rebecca yet but he thought a little holiday might do them all good, not that he could see Rebecca wanting to dip her toes in the water.

'They reckon it 'ull be a bad year for oats,' George said, wiping the beer froth from his mouth. 'What do you think? Should I buy now or later? Can't risk Canuden going short this winter.'

Aden blinked, bringing his mind back to business. 'Can't say I've heard that. Tell you what, I'll pay you in kind if you like?'

'Build a new house in the high street?' Aden paused in the act of unbuttoning his shirt and turned to look at her. They were in the bedroom and Rebecca had taken the pins from her hair to brush it; it looked thick and glossy as it glowed in the candlelight. 'I was thinking that could wait for another year or so. There's fifty acres coming up for sale in Sutton Gault soon and ...'

She glanced over her shoulder, feeling annoyed. 'It's a chance we can't afford to miss,' she said. 'Nan is sitting with Sarah tonight, and she told me that now that old Mr Abbs is dead, his son is going to sell that barn and the yard next to it. If you pulled the barn down you could build a fine house and have room for a big garden at the back for the children to play in.'

'Richie has plenty of room to play here,' Aden objected. 'I was thinking we could build on a couple of bedrooms out the back and maybe a second bathroom ...'

'No!' She was suddenly angry. He had put a bathroom in the previous year and now he was talking of making the cottage bigger to avoid moving. 'You promised me a decent house, Aden. We agreed on it when we married. You gave me your word.'

He reached out to touch her hair. 'I'll keep my word, Rebecca. I promise. I just thought it could wait for a few years, until the children are older and we can afford it.'

She stood up, resisting his attempts to soothe her. 'We could afford it now – at least, we could if you didn't put every penny you earn back into the land.'

'I thought that was what you wanted?' His tone was reasonable but she could see he was annoyed underneath. He wanted those fifty acres at Sutton. 'You're the one who wants to be rich. Really rich ... so that you can show off to those friends of yours.'

'I knew that was coming.' She felt a surge of irritation. Her back was aching so much that she could hardly bear it and she was so very, very tired. 'You've always resented Celia and Victor, haven't you? You can't bear it that I've kept up my friendship with them – that they've asked me to go to France with them this winter.'

'I don't like the way he looks at you,' Aden said gruffly, a hint of jealousy in his eyes. 'It's not right for another man to look at my wife like that. I know just what he's thinking ... wanting.'

'Oh, don't be so ridiculous,' she snapped, her irritation boiling over. 'Victor is head over heels in love with Celia and always has been.'

'Maybe – or maybe he's discovered that she's a child and always will be,' Aden muttered, his expression brooding in the pale light of the candles. The friendship did niggle him. He tried to hide it but she knew. He was jealous of Victor. 'It's not that I think you would do anything ...'

'I should hope you know me better than that, Aden. I don't believe in infidelity – I've always told you that.'

143

'Yes.' He turned away from her. 'I'm sorry. You're tired, love. I didn't mean to quarrel. I'm a jealous fool I suppose, but I can't abide any man to look at you the way he does.'

'You are a fool,' she agreed but in a softer tone. 'You needn't worry because I'm not going to France. I couldn't leave you and Richie.' She paused and sighed. 'But I do want you to think about that house. Please, Aden, for my sake?'

'I will,' he promised, and kissed her cheek. 'Get some rest now.'

'I am very tired. Nan may come for me before breakfast. I don't think Sarah will last much longer. You must go over and see her, Aden. She has been asking for you.'

'I will, first thing,' he promised. 'Now get to bed. You're exhausted.'

The thunder woke Rebecca with a start. For a moment she lay trembling, then, realizing it was just a storm, she got up and began to pull on the clothes she had worn the day before. Aden's side of the bed was cold so he must have been up for a while.

She gave her hair a quick brush and knotted it at the nape of her neck. Sometimes she wished she could have it all cut off but Aden liked her hair; he often remarked on how thick and soft it was and it would have upset him if she'd had it cut short.

Another terrific clap of thunder overhead made her jump and she heard a shrill whinney from the yard below. Remembering that the stallion had been lodged in their small barn overnight, she jumped up and went to the window. She was always uneasy when that great brute of a thing was around and now her blood ran cold as she saw Richie below, still in his nightshirt and toddling innocently towards the small barn.

She screamed to him to stop but he couldn't hear her. Her heart was racing with fear as she ran from the room and down the stairs. If Richie went in with that horse ... The fire was lit in the kitchen and the back door was open, swinging on its hinges. Aden must have left it unlatched and Richie had got out. How could he be so careless? He must know how adventurous their son was getting.

She rushed out into the yard, calling to her child. Thunder and lightning rent the air and she could hear the stallion crashing against the stable door with his great hooves; obviously he was terrified of the storm. Richie was at the door, stretching up as he tried to reach the bolts.

'Aden!' Rebecca screamed as the stable door was split by Canuden Quicksilver's heavy hooves. 'George! George Tubbs!'

Someone had to help her she thought wildly as she screamed their names over and over again. She raced across the yard, bending to scoop up her son seconds before the door fell back on its hinges and the huge horse burst out, rearing up on its hind legs and snorting in terror.

'Aden ...'

'Get back, Mrs Sawle! Get back and he won't hurt you,' George Tubbs shouted from somewhere behind her. 'He's jest scared of the thunder.'

She backed away, her heart thudding with fear as the horse surged past her in a wild dash for freedom, missing her by a hair's breadth and causing her to stumble and fall with Richie still in her arms. She lay on the rough ground, shaking and sick with fright, as the stallion charged across the yard and out into the road. George went chasing after it, still fastening his breeches and calling to Rebecca as he ran.

'Gentle as a lamb that horse is,' he cried breathlessly. 'But mortal afeared of storms. Like a big babby, that's him.'

Like a big babby! But a babby that had almost killed her son!

Rebecca rose shakily to her feet. She was on the verge of hysteria, clutching Richie in a suffocating hold and fighting the desire to scream. Another few seconds and he would have been trampled beneath those hooves! They might both have been badly injured or killed. She was trembling and felt dizzy, and because she was so terrified she was holding Richie too tightly.

He struggled against her. 'Want to see horsey,' he demanded imperiously. 'Want to get down, Mama. Stroke big horsey.'

'No!' Her voice was sharp and brought a wail of protest from him. Richie screamed loudly as he fought to escape her restraining arms. He had a violent and disturbing temper when thwarted and was difficult to control. 'Stop it, Richie. You're a naughty boy to creep out like that. Mama told you not to go near the stallion. Bad boy!'

She carried him back to the house, setting him down only after she had secured the door. He lay on the floor screaming and beating at her legs with his fists until he wore himself out, then he was suddenly calm. Rebecca was calmer, too. She picked him up and carried him to the rocking chair, soothing him as he whimpered against her neck, his wet, sticky face burrowing into her. He was such a naughty child sometimes but she loved him so much. So much! A wave of sickness swept over her as she thought of what might have happened if she hadn't glanced out of the window at the precise moment she did.

She was still sitting by the fire with Richie asleep in her arms when Aden came in. He looked at her face, then poured some brandy into a glass and brought it to her.

'Drink that,' he said. 'You look terrible.'

She knocked the glass from his hand in sudden fury.

'You left the door open,' she cried accusingly. 'Richie was almost killed. That horse nearly killed our son.'

Aden bent to retrieve the glass as she got up and laid Richie on the sofa. 'Canuden Quicksilver was frightened,' he said. 'He wouldn't normally hurt a fly. It was an accident, Rebecca. My fault for not fastening the door properly, I'll grant you that, but …'

'For as long as we live here, I shall never feel safe again.'

'Rebecca.' He sighed in frustration. 'Be reasonable, can't you?'

'Reasonable! When my son was almost killed?' She gave him a scathing look, then moved past him to reach for the kettle. A sudden blinding pain struck her and she gasped. 'Oh God! Aden, it's the baby. Fetch the doctor and Molly. She must look after Richie.'

He stared at her in dismay. The baby was coming early. It was the shock of seeing their son almost trampled beneath the horse's hooves that had brought on her labour.

'I'll be back!' he said, and rushed out into the yard.

Rebecca doubled up with pain. Surely it hadn't been this bad the last time – or perhaps she had forgotten. The pains were coming quicker and stronger. She hardly noticed that Aden had returned until he spoke.

'Ned has gone for the doctor and Molly is on her way. She won't be long,' he said, offering her his hand. 'Let me help you back to bed, love.'

She shook off his hand angrily. 'I can manage. Look after your son until Molly gets here. You can do that, can't you?'

Her voice was harsh and complaining. She hated the sound of it and knew she was being unfair but she was still too upset by what had happened to stop herself.

Aden stood at the bottom of the stairs, watching her as she walked slowly up them, hanging on to the banisters with all her strength. She was in terrible agony but refused to let him see it.

146

She was angry with him. It was his fault for not fastening that door, his fault for not building the house he had promised her – it would be his fault if she died having his child.

'Don't die,' Aden said over and over as he hammered nails into the door of the barn. 'Please don't die and leave me, Rebecca. I'll build that damned house. I'll do anything you want ... just don't die.'

The sound of her screams had sent him outside. Her labour seemed to have been going on for an eternity and he was close to despair. If she died there would be no reason for all this ... no reason to carry on.

Most of Frank's gold was still in the attic where he had hidden it. Perhaps because of his guilty conscience he hadn't got round to using it – but he would now, for Rebecca's sake. She would want to know where the money had come from but he would think of something.

He went on hammering long after the door was fixed, then Sid came and fetched him into the cowsheds and as he buried his head against the side of a cow, his fingers stroking her teats, coaxing the rich milk from her with practised ease, he began to calm down. Rebecca wouldn't die ... she wouldn't die ... she wouldn't ...

It was evening when the doctor finally came down to the kitchen where Aden was brewing tea and told him it was over.

'You've a fine son, Aden,' he said. 'Eight pounds and ten ounces. Not the biggest child ever but he was difficult.'

'Is he all right?' Aden's fists curled at his sides. 'And Rebecca?'

'As well as you can expect in the circumstances. The midwife is tidying her up. You can visit in a few minutes – but not for too long. She needs rest.'

Aden nodded. 'She's had a bad time all the way through – and then, well, you know what happened.'

'Maybe it was just as well. I'm not sure she could have gone on much longer. She's worn out, Aden. She shouldn't have another child ... not for a long time, anyway.' He gave Aden a hard look. 'Do you know what I'm saying?'

'Yes. Yes, I understand. Thank you for making it clear.'

'I've spoken to her before this,' Doctor Roberts said, 'but you know how stubborn she is. If she were to have another child too soon, I couldn't be responsible for her well being.'

'It's that serious then?' Aden felt sick and shaken. 'She's always seemed so strong ...'

'She is strong in every other way. Give her a real rest, Aden. Ideally, she should go away somewhere for a few months – to a warmer climate.'

'Did she suggest that?' Despite his anxiety he felt a surge of jealousy.

'She's in no condition to think of anything but sleep. This is my personal opinion, Aden. She'll recover in time but a change would do her good. Especially after that incident this morning.'

'Yes, I understand.' Aden pulled himself together. 'Would you like a cup of tea, Doctor?'

'Thank you, but no. I'll be on my way.' He smiled at Aden. 'Go up to her now. She won't break if you touch her – but she needs care and consideration.'

'Aden will be up in a minute,' Nan said. 'The poor man was nearly out of his mind. He kept saying he had killed you – that it was his fault you were suffering so much.'

'I thought I was going to die for a while,' Rebecca whispered through dry lips. 'It was even worse than the last time.'

'You have a very large, beautiful son,' Nan said. 'The doctor had to put a few stiches in you but he says you'll be fine in a month or so. He's talking to Aden now.'

'Ask him to come up, please.' She caught Nan's hand as she turned. 'Did I say awful things, Nan? When the pain was so bad – did Aden hear me?'

'Good gracious, no,' said her friend. 'He was out there murdering that barn door, cursing and swearing enough himself to raise the dead. Besides, you're entitled to say what you like when you're giving birth. I believe I may have sworn a little myself when my son was born.'

Rebecca closed her eyes as Nan laughed and went out. Had she screamed out that she hated Aden when the pain was at it's worst – or was that part of the nightmare? She knew she had been barely conscious for part of the time, so demented by her agony that she might have said anything.

Aden looked very subdued when he came in. She held her hand out to him and he took it, holding it carefully as if he were afraid to touch her.

'You've got another son,' she said, beginning to feel pride now

148

that it was all over. 'I thought we might call him Jay. What do you think?'

'Whatever you want.' His voice was husky with emotion.

She smiled down at the child lying in the cot beside her. He was so beautiful, his face flushed and his eyelids blue-shadowed. 'Isn't he perfect? Richie was red and wrinkled when he was born but this one is lovely.'

Aden glanced at the child and nodded. 'Yes, he is a fine boy – but he gave you such a terrible time. I was so afraid you would die and I should never have forgiven myself ...' He choked back his emotion. 'It was all my fault.'

'No, don't blame yourself,' Rebecca said, and pressed his hand. 'The horse was frightened. You couldn't have known what would happen.'

'I must have left the back door open.'

'Perhaps. Richie is so ... adventurous. He might have opened it himself.'

'You're trying to make me feel better – but I think it was my fault. I shall never be sure.'

'Accidents happen. A farm is a dangerous place for young children. That's why ...'

'I know.' He touched a finger to her lips. 'You are right, Rebecca. I've made up my mind. I'm going to build you that new house.'

'Oh, Aden,' she said, torn between relief and regret. 'I shouldn't have nagged you. If we built on extra rooms Molly could live in and ... I know you want that land in Sutton.'

'After what happened the house must come first.' A nerve flicked in Aden's throat. 'If I'd lost you and the children ... nothing else matters, Rebecca. Nothing.'

'Aden ...' Her eyes closed. 'I'm so tired ...'

He bent to kiss her. 'Rest then, love. It's all over now and we'll be more careful in future. I'll not put you at risk, no matter what it costs me.'

She wondered what he meant but was too weary to ask.

Ten days passed before Aden told her what the doctor had said to him after Jay was born.

'What do you mean – I mustn't have another child?'

'That's what he said – at least, not for a long time.' Aden avoided looking at her. 'For at least three years. You're not strong enough, Rebecca.'

'That's ridiculous!' She was upset and angry. 'Besides, we can't … children come when they're ready.'

'Not if we don't …' He held her hand tighter. 'I'll have to take more care of you, not be so selfish.'

'You're not selfish. Oh, Aden.' Tears welled up in her eyes and trickled down her cheeks. 'I want more children. I want a little girl.'

'Don't cry, love.' He kissed her cheek, wiping away her tears with his gentle hands. 'We'll talk about it when you're better.' He stroked her hair back from her face. 'I thought you would want to know that I'd seen about a headstone for Sarah.'

'Poor Sarah.' She gulped and wiped her face with his handkerchief. She had not been able to be with her old friend at the end and that had hurt her. 'You did see her before she died?'

'Yes. That's where I was the morning of the storm. She … wanted to tell me she had left everything to me.'

'Poor, dear Sarah.' Rebecca sighed, feeling sad that she would never see that kind old face again. 'She was so fond of you – but I don't suppose she had much to leave?'

'There's her cottage. I'm going to have that done up a bit for Sid and his family. Their eldest boy is a bit older than Richie and the second lad is a year younger; they are quite a handful and need a bigger place than they've got now. And … Sarah had some shares her husband bought over fifty years ago. For tuppence each, I understand.'

'What kind of shares?'

'In an old copper mine. Sarah always thought they were worthless but …' He paused tantalisingly.

'If you don't tell me, I'll get out of this bed and hit you, Aden Sawle!'

'Nay, don't do that, lass – they're worth just under a pound each. I've had an offer of fifteen hundred pounds. It appears that they discovered a rich seam a few months back and the mine is working again.'

'Oh, how sad,' Rebecca said. 'To think Sarah had all that money and it never did her any good.'

'What difference would it have made? She never went short of anything – we saw to that.'

'You're right, of course. Even so …'

'It means you'll be able to have your new house – and I can still buy that land in Sutton.'

'Yes, I suppose it does.' Rebecca smiled at him. 'Sarah would be so pleased to think she'd helped you.' She moved restlessly in the bed. 'Do I really have to stay here for another three weeks?'

'It's for your own good.' Aden hesitated, his eyes staring at a point somewhere above her head. 'I've been thinking – maybe you should accept that invitation to stay with Celia in France this winter? It would do you the world of good to get away and ...'

'I couldn't leave you, Aden. It wouldn't be fair. Besides, what about the children?'

'You could take Jay with you and Molly could look after Richie.'

'She would have to sleep in. We couldn't ask her to do that. Not with me away. People would talk.'

'I've thought of that. I had a word with Molly and she said her sister would come every night and share her bed, then go off to school after breakfast. No one could make anything out of that, could they?'

'I'm not sure ...' Rebecca was still doubtful. 'I should be away for two months.'

'I'm prepared for that. I'll get someone to help Molly with the rough work. I'll miss you, love, of course I shall, but I think it might be for the best. After what the doctor said ...'

'I know I need a rest, but two months? That's a long time, Aden.'

'It won't be easy for either of us,' he replied, 'but I was really frightened this time, Rebecca. I thought you were going to die. We have to be careful, at least for a while – until you're stronger. It might be easier if you were away ... just for a time.'

He had given this a great deal of consideration and she was grateful for his concern. 'Perhaps you are right. Let me think about it.'

'You do that.' He bent and kissed her. 'I'm off to see how the threshing is going. I shan't be back before supper but Molly will look after you and Nan said she would call in this afternoon. Is there anything you want before I go?'

'No, thank you. I'll just lie here and think.'

Rebecca closed her eyes as the door shut behind him. Surely it wasn't possible? She couldn't go to France with Celia and leave Aden alone – or could she? He didn't seem to mind, in fact he was encouraging her to go.

She felt a tingle of anticipation. She had never seriously considered the possibility, but it would be so wonderful to get away for a while. For years she had read Celia's letters and envied her her life, wishing that she could travel to all the exciting places her friend wrote about. Now she had the chance to do just that. It was wrong of her to feel so much pleasure in the idea but she couldn't help it.

It wasn't that she regretted her marriage. No, she was happy enough most of the time – but sometimes she still wondered what her life might have been like if Victor had asked her to marry him.

14

The visit was scheduled to take place in November, which was almost three months away and seemed a long way off, in a distant future that might never happen. Once Rebecca was on her feet again, though, the time just flew by. Before she really knew what was happening her friends had come to collect her and they were on their way to France.

She suffered a few pangs of guilt at leaving Aden and Richie – particularly Richie, who wasn't old enough to understand. Her eldest son was a little jealous of his brother; she had caught him standing by the cot pinching Jay once and had had to scold him for it.

She was taking her darling Jay with her, of course. Already he had found a special place in her heart and she had to be careful not to make more fuss of him than Richie but it wasn't easy. Jay was such a good child, sleeping peacefully between feeds; Richie had always been fretful and restless and his tantrums had increased after Jay was born.

Victor had engaged the services of a nursery maid for her. He was disappointed that she had decided to leave her eldest son at home.

'Richie is difficult,' she explained. 'Aden wanted me to have a complete rest and Richie demands so much attention. Besides, I couldn't leave Aden all alone. He loves his children. It will be hard enough for him as it is.'

She was a little emotional when she thought of Aden coming home to an empty bed. He had smiled at her cheerfully as she left, telling her to have a good time and not to worry.

'I love you,' he'd said as he kissed her goodbye. 'Just get well and come home to us safe.'

153

Even as he spoke she had known he was trying to hide his doubts and anxiety. His face haunted her for the first part of the journey but by the time they reached Paris her guilt had begun to ease. This was her first visit to France and she couldn't help feeling excited.

They spent three days in Paris and Rebecca was enchanted with everything she saw: from Les Halles fruit market, where they ate gooseberry-flavoured ice-creams, to the exciting and slightly wicked Moulin Rouge, where they sat at a table in a secluded corner and enjoyed the rather decadent atmosphere without being a part of it. Rebecca absorbed and savoured it all. She felt as if she could have walked forever along the wide avenue of the Champs-Elysées, listening to the music from Cafés Concerts or simply feasting her eyes on the magical city itself.

After nearly four years at the farm, during which time she seemed to have done nothing but work and produce babies, it was like stepping into another world – a world of laughter and light and music. She was in love with Paris, charmed by the impudent little workgirls, as they hurried about the city, their voices like the chirping of sparrows, enchanted with the elegant carriages and their beautifully dressed passengers, the flower sellers and the artists who offered to sketch her likeness for a few sous. It was like waking from a long sleep and she was reluctant to leave.

'If we stayed here longer you would soon tire of it,' Celia said. 'Paris makes my head ache.'

Rebecca caught a note of petulance in her voice and wondered what lay behind it. Sometimes she thought she noticed friction between Celia and Victor but she wasn't sure what was wrong. It was not until after they had been at the villa in Provence for three days that she learned the truth.

It was such a wonderful place. Rebecca felt at home within minutes of settling into her own room. Cool and white-walled with thick marble floors and exquisite furniture, it was a little palace. The views out over the hills and sea beyond were so lovely that they gave her a deep sense of peace and tranquillity. Now she was truly glad she had come. Aden had been right; she did need this time to recoup her strength and heal her spirit. She still felt a pang of guilt when she thought about the husband and son she had left behind, but it was fading as she began to relax and let the gentle winter sunshine warm and restore her.

Just as she had finished feeding Jay one morning, Celia walked

154

into her room without knocking. She blushed and apologized as Rebecca fastened her gown.

'Forgive me. I should have knocked and waited.'

'It doesn't matter. I wouldn't have minded you being here while I was feeding him. Aden likes to watch so I'm not shy about it.'

'Oh, well, that's different.'

Celia walked over to the window and looked out. The view was of a wide sweep of bay with wooded hillsides, white villas tucked in amongst the secret hollows, and a deep turquoise sea in the distance. It was breath-taking but Celia did not seem impressed. Her face looked sulky and bored, her mouth drooping at the corners.

'I should have thought you would employ a wetnurse or wean him to a bottle,' she remarked. 'It must be awkward having to … you know, when you're in company.'

'I'm seldom in company, not of the kind you mean. Besides, I've always enjoyed feeding my babies. I wouldn't feel right doing anything else, especially as I have so much milk of my own.'

'It's your choice, of course.' Celia pulled a face. She could not see the charm in breast-feeding – but then, she had no children of her own. 'Victor wants us to try for a child again but after the last time …' Her expression showed her dislike of the idea. 'I was so ill when I miscarried. I couldn't bear to go through all that again. It was so … messy.'

'But don't you want children? Victor seems to like them.' He was always picking Jay up, taking him from the nurse when he cried, looking at him in that hungry way which showed so much of his inner feelings.

'He's always talking about them.' There was a hint of bitterness in Celia's voice. 'Most of our friends have children. Victor can't understand why I don't want them.'

'Surely it isn't a matter of choice? They … well, they just come.'

'There are ways of preventing it,' Celia said, her mouth hard. 'I know you live in the country, Rebecca, but you must know it isn't necessary to have a child every time you make love.'

'Well, I suppose there are ways, but it seems unnatural to me.'

'Most of the women I know do something,' Celia said. 'It doesn't always work, of course. The best way is simply not to have intimate relations with your husband, or no more than you can help.'

'But that's so cold! It would be like having no marriage at all.'

Rebecca recalled the first months of her own marriage and smiled to herself.

'I can do without all that bother. I was never very interested and now ...' Celia shrugged eloquently. 'Victor is very good about it, apart from wanting a child. If we'd had our son the first time I think he would have given up all that nonsense for my sake.'

'I see.' Rebecca was careful with her answer. 'You're not afraid that Victor might ... men do need physical relief, you know.'

'Oh, I'm certain that he has someone.' Celia's expression was tightly controlled. 'A mistress, I suppose you would call her.'

'Don't you mind?' Rebecca would be so hurt, so angry if Aden betrayed her with another woman. For a moment she thought of Dotty Prentice but squashed the irritating thought swiftly – that was just her imagination! She must forget it, just as she had forgotten the hurt she had felt when he'd taken Ruth Perry's side over that teapot – or almost. That still niggled sometimes, though she knew she shouldn't let it.

'If he were in love with her I should mind very much,' Celia said a little too carelessly. 'But he's madly in love with me. I only have to crook my finger and he comes rushing back to my bed. It's my choice.'

'Are you frightened of having a child?' Rebecca wondered if that was the real problem. 'It's not so very bad, Celia. You soon forget once it's over. Jay gave me a terrible time – but he's worth it.'

'I'm not frightened. I just hate all the fuss and the mess – don't let's talk of it!' She took a restless walk about the room, the skirts of her elegant gown swishing over the marble floor. 'I came to ask if you would like to go out on the yacht? Victor says it's a perfect day for it.'

'I should like that very much. Jay will settle now and I do love sailing – it's so restful and yet so exciting.'

She had already been out once and had discovered a previously unsuspected love of the sea. The sound of the waves against the ship's sides thrilled her and she loved the feel of a warm breeze on her skin, the taste of salt on her lips. It was pure delight, an experience she would always treasure.

'That's what I thought.' Celia smiled at her with satisfaction. 'If you go with Victor he will be happy. I don't feel well. I'm going to lie down for a few hours.'

156

It was such a lovely day. Rebecca sat in a reclining chair on deck, her face turned up to the sun and her eyes closed. The sun had a warmth that was almost sensual as it soothed her skin and relaxed her; it was difficult to remember if was November. They often had cooler days in summer at home and now the fens would be damp and grey, at their bleakest. The soft winds here were like a welcome kiss on her brow, caressing but not biting into her flesh as the bitter winds did at Five Winds when they swept down from the north.

She closed her eyes, wondering what Aden was doing at that moment. Was he missing her, or was he too busy to notice whether she was there or not?

'You look peaceful.'

She glanced up as Victor spoke, shading her eyes to see him properly as he stood with his back towards the sun. He was dressed in immaculate white flannels and a striped linen jacket worn with an open-necked shirt and a silk cravat. He seemed both relaxed and pleased with life.

'Isn't it lovely? The water is so blue ... almost turquoise. I never realized it could be that colour.'

'A perfect day.' He sat in a chair beside her, crossing his legs and resting his hand on the wooden arm. 'It's a pity Celia doesn't care for sailing. It would have done her so much good to come out today.'

'She does seem a little low.'

'She hasn't been well since that last miscarriage. I'm afraid she's delicate, not like you, Rebecca. Aden must be proud of you ... two wonderful sons.'

She hesitated, not wanting to sound critical of Celia. 'It hasn't been easy even for me.' She blushed as he stared at her in surprise. 'In fact the doctor has warned us that I shouldn't have another baby for at least three years.'

'I didn't realize.' Victor was immediately concerned. 'You always look so strong and healthy.'

'I am.' She laughed at his expression. 'No, really. I think it is all nonsense but Aden was worried and ... we have decided to take care for a while, but I hope to have more children when I'm able. I want a daughter.'

Victor's expression was warm and deeply admiring, making her blush and turn away from his intense gaze. 'You really do want more children despite what you've been through, don't you?' His voice seemed to throb and when she looked at him again her heart missed a beat. 'Aden is a lucky man. I wonder if he knows how lucky …'

What was he saying? His manner seemed to convey all kinds of thing … sweet, forbidden, wanton things that set her body trembling. She felt a deep, aching yearning for the touch of his lips on hers – but she knew she must resist.

'It is natural for a woman to want children. I'm sure Celia will feel the same in time. She's young and she has suffered.' They were almost exactly the same age but Celia seemed to be still a pretty child, while Rebecca had blossomed into a beautiful woman.

'You mean she is completely spoiled and can't be bothered with motherhood?' Victor's tone was light but there was a grim set to his mouth. 'It's my fault, of course. I began by treating her as if she were a china doll and now she's come to think of herself as one. I had hoped she would grow up but …'

'Oh, Victor! You know you adored her for her silly ways. You would not truly want her different, would you?' Rebecca's heart raced as their eyes met.

His hand closed over hers on the arm of the chair. His touch made her tingle all over and she gasped as she felt a swift surge of desire. She moved her hand away, knowing that Victor had felt something, too. It was there in his eyes. He wanted to make love to her – wanted it badly.

She was shocked and confused by the sudden intense feeling between them. A long time ago she had dreamed of this moment, pictured it over and over again in her imagination, longed for it with all the eager yearning of a young girl's heart – but she was married. And so was Victor. All she had ever been taught or believed in rose up to mock her. Where was her passionate belief in fidelity now?

She jumped up and walked to the ship's rail, gazing down at the foaming water, watching the changing colours deep beneath the surface, green and black and midnight blue, her pulses surging with the wild, tempestuous ocean. She was in the grip of a fever, a madness that raged through her blood and cried out for satisfaction: a longing to turn and throw herself into Victor's arms. What should she do? Aden had been right all the time. Victor was more attracted to her than he had any right to be. His eyes held a hot, flagrant desire that told her how deep and urgent his need was –

how lonely he was ... Her head was spinning and she felt as if she were losing control. Victor had always been special to her – a vision of another life, something to be cherished and enshrined in her heart, a source of refreshment when her spirits were low ... a way of easing the dullest day when Aden was in a mood and she was tired ... but this was reality. Somehow she knew that if this feeling between them was allowed to develop it would flare out of control like a forest fire, consuming everything in its path, destroying all it touched.

'Forgive me,' Victor said as he came up to her. 'You know I've always admired you, Rebecca. You're so beautiful – such a fine, passionate woman. A real woman.' His voice throbbed with emotion and she trembled. Her knees felt as if they had turned to water and it was all she could do to stop herself falling into his arms.

'You mustn't ... must not say such things,' she whispered, breathless and weak with longing. She was aching for the touch of his mouth on hers but she had to be strong. 'It isn't fair to Celia – or Aden.'

His eyes seemed to devour her and she felt as if she were suffocating. She wanted to lie in Victor's arms, to know the touch of his hand, the heat of his flesh against hers, but it would be wrong.

'You sense it, too, don't you? This bond between us?' His words seemed to plead for understanding. 'It was there from the start but I was too blind to see what it meant ... too foolish to realize that I was letting true happiness slide through my fingers ...'

'No!' she denied him and moved away but he caught her hand. Her eyes pleaded with him then. She was weakening. She could feel her resolve dissolving in the flame of his passion – but it must not. She must not! 'Please don't ... it would not be right. You know it would not be right. I can't ...'

Even as she protested he was reaching out for her, his arms closing about her; she trembled as she gazed up at him uncertainly. His lips were warm and tender, undemanding but persuasive. Perhaps it was his very gentleness that awoke such a fierce response in her. Her arms went up around his neck and she returned his kiss, pressing against him with a desperate need. She was melting, dissolving in the heat of desire, then, realizing what was happening, she suddenly wrenched away from him, the hot colour rushing to her cheeks.

'We cannot do this, Victor. It is wrong, deceitful. I will not break my marriage vows and nor must you on my account.'

'If I had only met you first, before my word was given to Celia ... I couldn't jilt her, Rebecca. It would have been a terrible thing to do when everything had been arranged. You must see that?' There was such utter wretchedness in his voice that it almost destroyed her. How could she ignore such a cry from his heart? She had always cared for him – why shouldn't she take this chance of knowing how it felt to be in his arms, his bed? He was the man she would have married if she could. And now he was telling her that he loved her ... needed her! Her thoughts were confused, tortured, as she was torn between loyalty to Aden and her dreams.

'Rebecca, I want you ... need you so much ... so much.'

'Please don't, Victor.' She made a last desperate appeal to his sense of justice. 'Don't make me do this, please.'

He gazed down at her, his eyes blazing with passion, and she knew she was lost. They both wanted this so much that it was wickedness to deny it; she was on the verge of giving in, of saying the words he wanted to hear, and then, all at once, the heat faded from his eyes and he was in control once more.

'Forgive me,' he said huskily. 'I have behaved badly. I don't know what you must think of me.'

'Oh, Victor my dear ... my dearest,' she whispered, tears hovering on her lashes. 'If things had been different ... I'm so sorry ... so very sorry.'

For a moment longer he looked at her, the passion still simmering deep within him, and then he laughed. 'I, too, my wise and wonderful, most dear Rebecca. I shall always regret that you were too strong for me – and yet, and yet ... if you gave lightly of your love you would not be the woman I admire so much. You are strong and loyal and beautiful – and I shall never cease to regret that I was not strong enough to make you my wife.'

She watched as he walked away from her, experiencing a deep, searing regret. Her nails curled into the palms of her hands digging so deeply that they drew blood as she held back the words that would have recalled him. It would have been far easier to give in to her senses, to let herself forget duty in the pursuit of pleasure, but she had done what was right. She had resisted temptation.

Alone in her room that night she found sleep elusive. Had she been a fool to waste the chance Fate had given her? Aden's loving was both passionate and satisfying, but with Victor might she have found something more? A meeting not just of their bodies but of hearts, minds and souls ... She would never know.

Yet even as she felt the pangs of bitter-sweet regret she knew that she could never have left her husband, never have taken their children from a father who loved them. Aden was a good, decent man and he did not deserve a disloyal wife. He must never, never guess how close she had come to betraying his trust.

Victor made no further advances towards her after that day on the yacht but Rebecca had not expected he would. He was a gentleman and would not dream of pressing her into something against her will. Her steadfast refusal had cost her some heart searching and a few restless nights but she had come to terms with herself at last. And now she was going home. Her visit had come to an end without causing embarrassment or heartbreak for anyone.

Celia embraced her when she went to say goodbye to them on her last morning, then gave her a present wrapped in silver paper.

'Victor and I both wanted you to have this as a memento of your stay with us,' she said, and smiled as Rebecca opened the velvet box. 'I do hope you like it?'

Inside was an oval brooch. It was set in a surround of diamonds and white gold and had a dainty miniature of a woman and child painted on ivory in glowing colours at the centre.

'It's beautiful,' Rebecca said. 'I shall always treasure it. Thank you both very much.'

'And now we have some news for you,' Celia said, looking shyly at her husband as she reached for his hand. 'I think – I believe I am expecting a child.'

'That's wonderful, Celia. I'm so happy for you – for both of you.'

Victor glanced at her and she thought there was a plea for understanding in his eyes. Rebecca avoided his gaze and kissed Celia's cheek, her thoughts a little mixed. As she recalled that brief moment of madness on his yacht she was aware of guilt, anger – and an overwhelming sense of relief that she had not given in to him. Despite all his impassioned words Victor was still Celia's husband and he would never dream of leaving her.

Rebecca was suddenly very glad that she could go home to Aden with a clear conscience. She had known temptation but she had fought it – and won.

Aden was waiting at the station to meet her. Molly stood just behind him, keeping a tight hold on Richie, who was struggling to get free. All at once Rebecca was swept away on a tide of emotion and ran to Aden, crying foolish tears of relief as he swept her up in his arms and kissed her.

'Aden,' she cried as he held her so tightly that poor Jay was crushed between them. 'I've missed you all so much ... so much!'

'Not half as much as we've missed you,' he said hoarsely. 'Never leave me for that long again, Rebecca. I thought I should die or lose my senses.'

'Oh, Aden,' she whispered as she saw the anguish in his eyes and felt the guilt strike deep into her heart. 'I'm sorry, my dearest. I ought never to have gone.'

He kissed her again and laughed. 'Take no notice, love. I'm just that pleased to see you. You look wonderful, like your old self again.'

'I feel wonderful.' She brushed away her tears and smiled. 'So much better – you wouldn't believe how well I am.'

'I can see that,' he said, and there was a hint of the old jealousy in his eyes. 'Let me take Jay. He has grown a lot.'

'Yes, hasn't he?' She gave the baby to Aden, then turned to Richie. He looked at her with big, resentful eyes and screamed, clinging to Molly for all he was worth. 'Richie, it's Mama, don't you remember? Don't you know me?'

'No, no, no!' he screamed. 'Don't want you ... want Molly.'

'I'm sorry, Mrs Sawle,' the girl said, looking upset. 'He has been a bit fretful lately. He cried for you for days after you left, wouldn't eat or sleep for nearly a week, and he's been talking about you coming home all day. He's just overexcited.'

'Yes, of course.' She was hurt by Richie's rejection but also aware of guilt. It was her fault her son preferred his nurse. He didn't understand why his mother had left him. 'He'll soon get used to me again.'

'Of course he will. Come on, let's go home,' Aden said, a hint of mischief in his eyes. 'I've got a surprise for you, Rebecca.'

'Alone at last,' said Aden, and drew her into his arms as she rose from the dressing stool, her hair flowing over her shoulders and down her back. 'The party was Molly's idea – were you pleased?'

'It was very nice but I'm glad they've all gone. Not that it wasn't a lovely surprise.'

'That wasn't my surprise,' he said, releasing her and going across to the chest in the corner of their room. '*This* is my surprise.'

'What is it?' She stared as he brought out the cylinder of paper and laid it on the bed, then gasped in dawning excitement as she realized what it must be. 'You've had plans drawn up for the house. Oh, Aden, let me look!'

'Six bedrooms,' he said. 'Two bathrooms, both with airing cupboards. Three good reception rooms, a kitchen, scullery and a sitting-room for Molly. And a nursery floor with two bedrooms.'

'It looks wonderful.' She pored over the drawings, her thick, glossy hair falling forward, unaware of how lovely she looked with those eager shining eyes. 'I love it, Aden. It's exactly what we want. Oh, you're so good to me!' She moved towards him, slipping her arms about his waist. 'I'm so glad to be home again.'

'Are you?' he asked, one finger tipping her chin so that she looked up at him. 'Are you truly, lass? I thought you might have got a taste for high living with your friends?'

She gazed up at him, her expression serious as she saw the doubts in his eyes. 'It was exciting, especially those few days in Paris. I told you in my letter how much I liked Paris, didn't I?'

'Yes.' He was watchful and quiet. 'And you enjoyed sailing on that yacht?'

'I enjoyed it all and it did me good – but I'm glad to be home just the same. I think perhaps I should be bored if I lived the way Celia does all the time.'

'Truly?' He raised his brows. 'I've wondered if you might regret having married me ... met someone else you preferred?'

'Aden Sawle!' she cried, her cheeks warm. 'What nonsense is this? You were the one who wanted me to go, remember?'

'You weren't hard to persuade.'

'No – no, I wasn't,' she admitted honestly. 'I was tired, Aden, after Jay was born. I needed to get right away but now I'm back and I intend to stay.'

He drew a ragged sigh of relief. 'Thank God for that! I want you here lass, never doubt that – but I wouldn't have held you against your will.'

'Oh, Aden.' She was close to tears 'Don't ... please ... don't make me feel so guilty.'

The strain of the past two months showed in his face and she knew he had been afraid she wouldn't want to come back. She

163

understood then how much it had cost him to let her go, to wait for her return, not knowing whether he had lost her.

'You'd have been better off with a man of your own sort. Someone more like Celia's husband.'

'You're daft, Aden Sawle,' she said, and put her arms about him. 'Victor can be a little pompous, you know. He's forever going on about the Empire and how wonderful Mr Gladstone was – says things will never be the same again now that he has resigned. It bores Celia so.'

'I've never bothered much about politics,' Aden said, still frowning. 'I don't reckon there's much to choose between them – and won't be until the ordinary folk start to stand up for themselves.'

'Celia would agree with you, she finds it all very tedious. They have a lot of Victor's business friends and government people to dine and she hates it. I don't think she is particularly happy. She might be rich but she doesn't have two wonderful sons or a husband she can trust completely. She told me Victor has a mistress. I couldn't put up with that, Aden.'

'You won't have to,' he said. 'You've always been woman enough for me, Rebecca.'

'What are you waiting for then?' she whispered with a teasing smile. 'I've been away for two months and all you want to do is talk.'

'We'd best be a bit careful for a while yet,' he said doubtfully. 'You know what the doctor said.'

'I went to another doctor in France, a specialist. He thinks I'm perfectly fit, though he agrees that it might be as well to take certain precautions for a time. He gave me something to use, Aden. It won't affect you and I don't mind a little bit of bother afterwards.'

'I didn't like to suggest it, knowing your views.' He looked relieved. 'But you know best, love.'

'It means you don't have to worry.' She smiled at him invitingly, then moistened her lips with the tip of her tongue. 'So stop looking at me as if I were made of china and show me how pleased you are to have me home ...'

Rebecca was still sleeping, her glorious hair spread on the pillow and her nightgown discarded on the floor beside the bed. She had thrown it off just as she had on the first night they were wed, giving herself to him with such generosity that he had been swept along on a tide of passion.

Yet even as he moved quietly about the room so as not to wake her, Aden could feel the knot of jealousy tighten in his stomach. Thoughts of her – perhaps alone – on that yacht with Victor Roth had haunted him day and night while she was gone. He was a damned fool to let it bother him, but he'd always had a suspicion that she'd married him because she couldn't have the man she really wanted – and he'd known when he first saw Victor that there was some feeling between them.

Why had she gone to that French doctor? Was it for his benefit or so that she could ... Aden squashed the worm of jealousy as it wriggled inside him. No, she wouldn't do that and he was wronging her to think it.

He walked downstairs and filled a kettle, putting it on the hob while he made up the fire. Now that Rebecca was home he wouldn't be going into Chatteris so often ... he'd fallen into the habit of driving over sometimes of an evening to drink a couple of whiskies and play a hand of cards with some friends. It was a harmless pastime, because they never risked more than a few shillings on a pot, but the last time he'd been asked to join the game in the landlord's back parlour ... and that was for very different stakes.

The men who were invited to that private game were all wealthy farmers or businessmen. Joshua Hauxton was one and his cousin Keith another. Aden liked the cousin but made it a rule to avoid Joshua whenever possible. Besides, now that Rebecca was home he wouldn't need to find a way of filling the lonely evenings.

Aden nodded to himself as he made a cup of tea to take up to her. Maybe it was just as well she hadn't stayed away any longer or he might have got drawn into something rather dangerous.

165

15

Sadie paused in the act of lighting her fire as Lorenzo strode through the gipsy camp with his eldest son on his shoulders; her black eyes were angry as she heard Shima's laughter ring out again and again. Lorenzo was so proud of the boy. It was always that gorgio woman's brat he favoured, never her own son by him, Leyan – always it was Shima who was held up as an example to the other members of the tribe.

The fire was catching now, the flames beginning to crackle as they ate up the dry wood. A young girl came to place a bundle of thin sticks near the waggon, glancing at Sadie with eyes as dark and resentful as her own. Tarina was her daughter but she had no time for the girl, not since she had given birth to her second child.

'Was that all you could find?' Sadie grumbled, taking her anger out on her daughter. 'You're a lazy good-for-nothing and I should beat you!'

She had given Lorenzo a son a year after he had taken her for his woman, but Leyan was a slight, thin child, small for his age and nervous. Even his mother could see why Lorenzo preferred Shima, but that didn't stop her anger or her resentment – because she knew the truth about the gorgio woman's son.

But it was not surprising that Lorenzo should be proud of the boy. Shima was a tall, strong boy, bigger than lads two or three years his senior, with dark, curling hair, a cheeky grin and wicked eyes. He could run faster than other boys his age and when they worked in the fields he did more than his share, while Leyan pulled at her skirts and got in her way – but Sadie favoured him as much as she could, never sparing a kind word for either her daughter or Shima.

166

She had not forgotten the gorgio woman's dying words. Shima was the son of Aden Sawle of Mepal – his mother had lied to Lorenzo and cheated them all. Dena had been dead these three years past but the prophecy was still spoken of with awe, and no one could doubt that Shima was special. He had a way with horses; there wasn't one that wouldn't come to his call, and he had been riding them bare-backed since he was three. The other women of the tribe doted on him, swearing that he could charm the birds from the trees. Sometimes, when Sadie watched the way Lorenzo praised Shima, ignoring his younger son, she was tempted to tell him the truth.

It was fear that held her silent. Lorenzo had a violent temper. He would not believe her; would accuse her of lying and then beat her. He might even kill her. So she held her silence, just as she had when she'd found the twenty gold sovereigns sewn into Dotty's skirt.

It was their custom to burn everything belonging to a member of the tribe who had died, and although Dotty hadn't truly been one of them, Sadie had gathered her things to burn as usual. The weight of the skirt made her suspicious and she had ripped open the hem, letting the coins cascade on to the ground. The money should have been buried with the woman but Sadie had kept it, saying nothing to anyone. If Lorenzo had known he would have taken it from her.

Sadie's mother had lived amongst the gorgios for a while and she had learned to read and write, passing on her skills to Sadie in turn. She had written down the name of the man who had fathered Shima. Perhaps one day she would give both the money and the name to Shima – one day she would reveal the truth and then Leyan would take his rightful place as Lorenzo's eldest son.

Rebecca walked through the empty rooms of her new house. It was almost ready; they were only waiting for the plaster to dry out so that it could be decorated, then they could move in. And she couldn't wait! It was all going to be so exciting, so wonderful, a dream come true.

Unlike so many of her other dreams – but she had put them away now. She ran her hand over the oak panelling in the hall and sighed. This was all that mattered now – the future. Her future and her family's.

She turned her back to the wall and closed her eyes, letting her thoughts drift aimlessly like thistledown on a summer breeze.

The first few months after Rebecca returned from France had passed so swiftly that she often wondered where the time had gone. Her memories of that special time gradually faded, became hazy and distant, seeming like a dream.

She was too busy to dwell on regrets or what might have been as she watched their new house take shape and grow. Besides, she had decided to put the past behind her and make a new start. She had ceased to yearn for a life that could never be hers.

For months now all her dreams had been centred on her new house. She was impatient for it to be finished and grumbled when things went wrong – like those special marble tiles Aden had ordered from Italy, which did not arrive until a month after they were due.

'It won't hurt to let the plaster dry out,' he had told her, amused by her impatience. 'We'll have water running down the walls if we move in too soon.'

She knew he was right but she still couldn't wait. She visited the site daily, checking every stage of the construction and getting in everyone's way.

The house was going to be everything Aden had promised her and he had spared no expense. Besides the marble tiles in the hall there were to be French silk wallcoverings in the best rooms, silk brocade or velvet drapes at the windows – and a large billiard table, which was bound to cause a great deal of curiosity in the village when it arrived.

'I dare say it's as good as Victor Roth's,' Aden said carelessly when she teased him about ordering it. 'He can use it when you ask them to stay.'

Aden was very proud of that table, despite his casual manner. He thought of it as a symbol, a sign that he had left his humble beginnings behind – and that meant more to him than he would ever have admitted.

'Yes, I'll ask them when we're settled,' Rebecca replied. 'If Celia is well enough.'

She had lost the baby she had conceived in France. Her letter made Rebecca cry when she read it.

'Victor says I must be very careful,' her friend had written in a rather shaky hand. 'He insists that we must not think of having children now.'

So Victor had given up any hope of a son. Rebecca knew what that must have cost him and wept again for his sake.

She felt the tears on her cheeks and realized she had been day-dreaming again. She glanced round the empty rooms once more, went out, shut the door behind her carefully and walked across the road, feeling the warmth of the sun touch her face. Only a few weeks to go now and she would be able to move into their new home.

It was, however, nearly two years after the French visit before they finally moved into their new house, and almost at that same moment Rebecca discovered she was expecting another child.

Jay would be almost three when her daughter was born. She was convinced that she would have a girl this time and refused to contemplate anything else. All the new baby clothes she made were white or pink and she trimmed the new cot with layer after layer of pretty lace.

'You're tempting Fate,' Aden warned though she wouldn't listen. 'It might be another boy.'

Rebecca knew that she was carrying a girl. Everything was different. The boys had made her ill but this time she was full of energy, cheerful and happy, able to enjoy her pregnancy for the first time.

'Life is so good,' she told Nan when they sat sewing together in the afternoons. 'Aden is doing well and I feel wonderful.'

Aden was in fact becoming more and more prosperous with each harvest. He employed so many men that she no longer knew them all, and they now had a woman in to do all the rough work in the house, leaving Molly to take over many of the jobs that had once been Rebecca's.

'I shall soon be a lady of leisure,' she said. 'There's so little for me to do these days.'

'And why not?' Aden asked. 'It's what you wanted, Rebecca. You can entertain your friends and take up good works.'

'Yes, of course,' she agreed, but in her heart she wasn't as convinced as she sounded. Aden worked longer and longer hours, coming home for his supper late at night, and sometimes she regretted the old days when they had had more time together. She no longer saw him when he drove a waggon into the yard, nor could she feel his eyes on her as she hung out the washing, and sometimes felt an odd pang of regret, as though she had lost something special.

Yet she could not complain. The scandal of her father's murder had long been forgotten by most people. She was respected and looked up to as the wife of one of the most important farmers in the district. What more could she ask?

She had chosen well when she married Aden and now that she had at last put her foolish dreams behind her, she was sure that nothing could destroy her peace of mind.

Part Two
Dreams Die Hard

16

The morning of Richie's ninth birthday was fine and bright. He was so excited he could hardly eat a mouthful of his breakfast. Aden had promised him a pony of his own, despite Rebecca's protests that he was still too young.

'He won't be able to control it,' she had argued over and over again. She might as well have saved her breath. Aden was almost as excited as his son. If Rebecca had let him he would have bought ponies for all the children – including her darling little Fanny.

Fanny was her angel. She was the most beautiful child imaginable, like a little porcelain doll that Rebecca could dress in lovely clothes and spoil to her heart's content – and she adored her.

Since her daughter's birth four years earlier, she had taken good care not to fall for another child and so far had been lucky. The years at the new house had been good ones for them all; Aden was becoming steadily richer, amassing money and land in such quantities that she sometimes wondered how he managed it, but she never questioned him even though their income had grown far beyond her expectations. He was always generous, providing everything she asked for – for the children, herself and her various charities – without complaint. It was a comfortable life, and had she thought about it, she would have said she was happy – but happiness was a strange thing. One only noticed it when it had gone.

After breakfast on Richie's birthday Aden had the pony brought round from the farm, where it had been kept overnight, and they all trooped out to the paddock behind the house. Rebecca kept a tight hold of Fanny's hand, though she struggled and pulled against her as the boys followed their father into the field.

'Fanny want see pony,' she said, her mouth set rebelliously. 'Mama let go.'

'No, darling, you stay with me,' Rebecca said, and called after her eldest son: 'Be careful, Richie. Do exactly as your father tells you.'

Richie looked back at her, his eyes glittering with a mixture of excitement and fear. He was such a headstrong, unpredictable child. Sometimes his violent mood swings frightened her; he could be sweet and loving one moment and then ... but he was on his best behaviour at the moment and waved excitedly to her.

Jay was running to keep up with his father's long strides. He wanted a pony of his own but Rebecca had put her foot down over that.

'You can have a pony when you're nine, Jay, and not before,' she had told him over and over again, despite his protests and sulky looks.

'But that's ages away. It's not fair!'

'Fair or not, I've made up my mind.'

The arguments over the ponies had been going on for weeks, and Rebecca knew they were all ranged against her, but she could n t forget the day of the thunderstorm when Richie had almost been trampled, and her own subsequent fear of horses.

Jay was the most adventurous of all her children and very like his father; not in looks so much – all her children looked like her – but in manner and temperament. Aden and Jay were equally stubborn when they chose, but had the same loving smile, a smile that could charm even when they had done something they knew would make her angry. Rebecca often felt guilty because she preferred Jay and Fanny to Richie. Somehow she had never been as close as she would have liked to her eldest son – not since that trip to France. It was as though he had decided she was not to be trusted ... and yet sometimes he would throw his arms about her and cling to her as though his life depended on her loving him.

And she did love him, of course, but perhaps not as much as the others – though she did her best to hide it, sometimes giving in to him too easily because of her sense of guilt.

'Look at me, Mama!' Richie called and waved as Aden put him up on the pony's back. She thought perhaps he was a little scared underneath but determined not to show it. 'I'm riding ... I'm riding!'

'Mum, can I have a ride?' Jay's face was desperate with

longing. 'Father says it will be all right if you agree. Please let me … please!'

'Let Jay have a ride,' Aden said as he passed her on his way round the field. 'There'll be no peace unless you do.'

A chill breeze had blown up all of a sudden. Rebecca pulled her warm shawl over her shoulders and shivered. Sometimes she was haunted by an odd fear that life was too good, that she had too much, and was afraid that she would be punished – that she would lose those she most loved.

'Me too. Me too,' Fanny chanted, tugging at her hand. 'Fanny want ride pony. Fanny want ride …'

Rebecca smothered her irrational fears as she sighed and accepted the inevitable. It was no use. She would have to let them both have their turn or there would be tears and tantrums. Fanny was trying to wriggle free but Rebecca held her tightly as she unlatched the gate and went into the field. Richie had got down and the boys were patting the pony, obviously enchanted with the new pet.

'Fanny ride horsey now!'

All eyes had turned on Rebecca and she knew she was beaten. The children and Aden would have their way or there would be sulks in the house for days.

'Let Fanny go first,' she said with a look of resignation. 'Then I'll take her in. You can have a ride, Jay, but only when your father is here. You must promise me that you will never try to ride the pony on your own.'

'I promise,' he said, face glowing eagerly. 'Honest, Mama. I shan't fall off so you needn't worry.'

'Very well. Fanny first then.'

There were shouts of triumph from Jay and Fanny chuckled with glee. Her face was wreathed in smiles as her father lifted her on to the pony's back and led it round the field. When he tried to take her off she clung on and yelled her disappointment.

'Fanny want go again,' she cried, pouting as Aden gave her back to her mother. 'Fanny want go again …'

'Another day,' Aden promised. 'Be a good girl and go with Mama now.'

'It's Jay's turn now, darling,' Rebecca said. 'Come along, there's a good girl. Mama wants her little angel with her. It's too cold out here for us.'

Fanny screamed and protested as she was carried into the

house. Glancing over her shoulder, Rebecca saw that Jay was already on the pony's back, and sighed. It was only a matter of time before Aden bought him his own mount.

Richie was looking a bit disgruntled at having to share and there were bound to be arguments between them over who was going to ride the wretched animal next.

Once inside the house Fanny ceased to struggle. She squatted contentedly on the floor of Rebecca's little parlour and sang to herself, playing with her large collection of wax-faced dolls in fashionable clothes and a pretend house full of exquisite miniature furniture. She was the spoilt darling of the family and both Aden and Rebecca tended to give her far too much – and Celia was worse than either of them, petting her continuously whenever she came to visit.

Rebecca wound the key of the automaton Celia had given her on her last visit: it was a pretty music box with three monkeys dressed in human clothes and seeming to play on violins and a tiny piano. Fanny loved it and would sit for hours watching the monkeys go through their routine.

She was soon immersed in her own little world of make believe. Rebecca smiled as she watched her. Sometimes she felt the boys were growing away from her, becoming independent, but Fanny was all hers. A daughter was always closer to her mother. When she grew up there would be all the fun of buying her lovely clothes and taking her to parties. It was Fanny who would do all the things Rebecca had dreamed of as a young girl. She would travel, go to dances and exciting places. As the years passed the boys would belong more and more to Aden and the land – always the land – but Fanny was hers.

Since the move to their new home Rebecca had begun to devote more and more of her time to charitable work and through that she had made many friends, mostly business people or wealthy farmers. Sometimes she wondered where all the years had gone.

It hardly seemed five minutes since they had celebrated Queen Victoria's Diamond Jubilee but now it was 1901 and the newspapers were full of stories about the new era. The old Queen had died and was mourned by everyone, as if her people knew that they would not see her like again.

Rebecca had been asked if she would organize a party for the village children in honour of the new King, who was soon to attend the first Parliament of his reign. She sat watching Fanny, making her plans. They would give every child a commemorative mug and five shillings as well as a party they would remember all their lives. She would ask May Harris to help organize the tea.

She and May got on well together these days, perhaps because May had a little girl of almost the same age as Fanny. Sorrel was a pretty child, though not as beautiful as Fanny, of course. Because Sorrel was that few months younger, Rebecca often passed on little dresses that her daughter had outgrown, and May always seemed pleased. Yes, she would ask her to serve on the committee.

The village had collected about fifty pounds and Rebecca's plans would cost more but Aden would give her the rest. She did not even have to ask; she simply drew whatever she wanted from their bank in Chatteris. Aden had arranged the facility to make it easier for her.

'It's your money as much as mine,' he'd told her at the time. 'Take what you need, Rebecca.'

Besides, there was always more than enough money, so much that they could afford to be generous.

Perhaps she would ask Aden to have a pig killed and roasted whole. They might as well have a little celebration for the whole village. Yes, they would have a pig, a few barrels of cider, beer and a fruit punch. It was spring after all and a time for celebration.

'Fancy a game of poker?' Keith Hauxton asked as Aden joined him at a corner table in The Arms. The name of the inn had been changed years before, after it was sold, but everyone still called it The Arms. 'Joshua has booked a private room for this evening. We'll be playing for a few guineas a hand, to make it worthwhile.'

'Can't manage it this evening,' Aden replied. 'Rebecca has an important dinner party – friends staying.' He shrugged carelessly. 'You know how it is.'

'Right!' Keith grinned at him. 'My wife would kill me if she knew where I was half the time. Especially if she knew ...' His smile faded. 'But you're always so lucky, Aden. Joshua says you have the luck of the devil.'

'Your cousin and I don't exactly see eye to eye,' Aden replied. He hesitated then asked, 'Are you in a spot of bother?'

'I lost three hundred last night,' Keith replied. 'Trouble is, it was three hundred I didn't have. I shall have to borrow from the bank ...'

'Bad policy that,' Aden said, and frowned. He had borrowed money himself recently and it had annoyed him that it should be necessary. 'I could let you have a hundred or two if you ...'

'No! No, thanks, Aden. It was good of you to offer but I'd rather not. Besides ...' he grinned again '... I've every intention of winning it back from Joshua this evening.'

Aden finished his drink, stood up, took his watch from his waistcoat pocket and checked it. 'I have to see someone ... appointment at my bank. Good luck for this evening, Keith. Don't be too rash.'

He was thoughtful as he walked from the taproom, nodding to a couple of men he knew. He'd had to make the offer to Keith, because he liked him – and because he'd won a bit from him himself over the years – but it would have been awkward if he'd accepted. Money was a little tight at the moment; it was a temporary thing, of course, due to a couple of unwise investments and some bad luck. For years he'd seemed to turn everything he'd touched into gold, but just recently he'd hit a bad patch. Nothing too terrible – nothing he couldn't get over, given time – but he was going to have to be careful for a few months ...

17

'Why must we stop here?' Sadie asked, scowling at Lorenzo. 'Why not go on to Chatteris as we used to?'

'Mind your business, woman, and leave the decisions to me,' he said. 'When I want your advice I'll ask for it.'

'But there's bound to be work in Chatteris ... good work ... and the land's easy.'

Lorenzo turned with a snarl and struck her across the face. 'Hold your tongue, damn you! I've been told that Aden Sawle wants help in his potato fields. He's planted more than he can handle and he's offering a good price – more than we'll get elsewhere. Now get on with your work and leave me be.'

Sadie turned away. Her face was red and stinging where he had hit her and her dark eyes burned with an angry resentment. She had known she was risking a blow if she pressed him, but she was frightened – frightened that Lorenzo might discover the truth. If he ever guessed that she had known from the beginning he would kill her.

She had a bad feeling about this place. The fens were damp and the years had begun to catch up with her, making her bones ache during the long, cold days of winter. She wished Lorenzo had stayed down in the south of the country, where they had been for the past few years. Life was easier there and she had felt safe ... safe from the fear that had haunted her since the gorgio woman died and she had given her son to Lorenzo.

Fear had kept her silent all these years. It was a long time since Lorenzo had chosen to bring his people this far east but times had been hard for them and he was hoping that a return to Cambridgeshire would bring them luck.

'Shall I light a fire for you, Sadie?'

She turned as the boy spoke, her eyes narrowing with hatred. It was all his fault – and his mother's for lying to Lorenzo about the child!

'Get out of my way!' she snarled, and slapped his head as hard as she dared. Once she would not have dared to touch him at all but Lorenzo's mood had turned more and more surly of late and even Shima had come in for some blows. 'Go and look for some work for us – you were supposed to bring us luck but we've not seen much of it.'

She started to build her own fire, muttering to herself about false prophecies and cursing the day he had been born. She should have left the gorgio woman to give birth and die alone.

Shima watched her bend over her fire and wondered what he had done to make her hate him, then he set off down the road. It was the first time they had camped in Mepal and he wanted to see what the village was like.

'Gipsies camping along Witcham Road?' Rebecca pulled a face as Molly told her the news. She had an unreasonable but deep-rooted dislike of the travelling people. It was without foundation and she was a little ashamed of her feelings but could not help them. 'I hope they won't cause trouble. Perhaps they'll move on soon.'

She glanced out at the garden, noticing that the leaves on the cherry tree had begun to turn brown and would soon fall. Autumn mists had brought that sense of unease and inner loneliness that still came back to her now and then, stirring memories of the brutal murders of her father and Eileen Henderson and the isolation she had felt then.

It was all so long ago! She shivered, then gave herself a mental scolding, telling her herself that she was being foolish, letting that old fear of insecurity creep into her mind.

'Someone told me Mr Sawle has given the gipsies work in the potato fields,' Molly said, wiping her hands as she left the sink. 'I saw some of them this morning walking through the village as if they owned the place. They give me the creeps with their black eyes and their dark faces.'

'I must admit I don't like them much,' Rebecca admitted. 'But I suppose they are are harmless enough or Aden wouldn't have employed them.'

180

Molly sniffed to show her disapproval. It was obvious that she did not agree and Rebecca made up her mind to speak to Aden about it that evening – but first she had to go into Chatteris to a meeting about a new Temperance mission she was setting up for battered wives. It was a cause that both she and Nan had taken up after a woman from one of the nearby villages had been beaten to death by a drunken husband.

Rebecca had her own carriage now. It was kept in a special brick-built barn on the farm and brought round whenever she needed it. Aden employed so many men that there was always someone available to take her wherever she wanted to go, though occasionally he drove her himself in his pony and trap.

'I've been thinking of getting a motor car,' he'd told her recently. 'I had a chat with Victor last time they were here and he says they're improving all the time – especially since they got rid of that silly nonsense over the flag.'

The law which forced everyone to have a man with a red flag walking in front of their automobile had been abolished in 1886 and some of the new vehicles were actually reasonably reliable these days.

'If you did, I could drive myself,' Rebecca said. 'I should quite enjoy that, I think. You could ask Victor what make is best next time they are here.'

'I've had my eye on a De Dion for a while,' Aden said. 'I can make up my own mind without help from Victor, thank you.'

There had been a little glint of jealousy in his eyes as he spoke and she was surprised that he should still feel that way after ten years of marriage. She had thought he was more interested in his land these days, but it seemed he still cared enough to feel jealous sometimes.

He had struck a good bargain with the gipsies! Aden was feeling pleased and so busy with his own thoughts that he didn't notice the boys were in the field with the pony until he heard the commotion. When he looked he saw that there were three lads having a scrap and it seemed as if his sons were both fighting the third, who was taller and appeared to be giving a good account of himself.

'What's all this then?' They hadn't noticed him and fell apart in dismay as he reached them. 'What's going on here?'

Richie and Jay stared at each other in alarm. They had been forbidden to ride the pony without their father – and now they had been caught in the act of fighting with the gipsy boy. If their mother heard of it they would probably both get the strap. They remained silent, their faces guilty as they shuffled their boots and stared at the ground.

'I asked what was going on?' Aden said. He glanced at the pony, already saddled and bridled. 'I told you to wait until I came to catch Brindle. Who did catch him anyway?'

Again there was silence, then the gipsy spoke. 'I caught him, sir. I was only tryin' to help – but the young 'un fell off.'

Aden noticed the bruise beginning to appear on Jay's forehead. 'Are you in pain?' he asked. 'Anything broken?'

'No, Dad. It was my fault, honest it was,' he said. 'Don't blame Shima. I wanted to ride. He just showed us how to catch Brindle.'

'Shima ...' Aden transferred his gaze to the gipsy boy and experienced a shock. He felt as if someone had thrown a bucket of icy water over him and for a moment he could hardly believe his eyes. It was like looking at himself when he was ten or eleven years old. Face, hair, eyes ... it couldn't be! His imagination was playing a cruel trick on him. 'Who are you?'

'Shima, sir. I'm Lorenzo's son – you give us work in the potato fields. Didn't mean to do no harm, sir. I was jest walking past when I see these lads tryin' to catch the pony.'

'So you did it for them?' Aden nodded. Yes, it would be easy for a lad brought up the way this one must have been, taught to work from the moment he could walk. Life was hard in the gipsy camp, even harder than it was for village folk. But the boy couldn't be his – no, it wasn't possible: he must be at least eleven or more. His first shock was receding now and he was beginning to think it through. 'How old are you, Shima?'

'Ten ... at least that's what Sadie says.'

'Who is Sadie? Your mother?'

'No.' A shadow passed across the boy's face. 'She's Lorenzo's woman ... his wife, sir.'

Could this lad be Dotty's son? There was certainly a likeness but perhaps not quite as marked as he'd first thought. No, he must be mistaken. The boy couldn't be his ...

'Why were you fighting just now?'

None of the boys ventured an answer. Aden hadn't really expected they would. He gave the gipsy lad a friendly smile.

'You get off now, Shima and you two ...' He turned and

182

frowned at his sons. 'I'm not sure what to do about you. If your mother hears about this there's going to be trouble.'

'Don't tell her I fell off,' Jay begged, waving to the gipsy as he set off across the field. 'Please, Dad, you know what she'll say.'

'We'll see. She's going to notice that bruise, though we could just say it was a fall ... but I want you both to promise me that you won't do this again? Not until you can both handle the pony properly.'

'Yes, Dad.' They spoke together. 'We promise.'

Aden ruffled Jay's hair. 'No doubt we're lucky it wasn't worse,' he said. 'Now I'd better give you both the ride I promised you, I suppose.'

The first thing Rebecca noticed when she saw Jay was the bruise. It was just above his right eye, beginning to turn purple and looking nasty.

'What have you been doing?' she demanded. 'You haven't been fighting with Richie again? Let me look at you, Jay.'

He was growing fast, as tall as Richie now and in some ways seeming older, stronger and more independent – very much his father's son.

'I'm all right,' he said, and threw a guilty glance at his brother. 'It's nothing. I ... I fell, that's all.'

'Were you climbing trees again? I've told you over and over again not to do that, Jay. You could break your arm – or your neck!'

He didn't answer. She was about to turn away when Richie spoke. 'It was the gipsy boy's fault.'

'Gipsy boy?' Rebecca stared at Jay. 'Were you fighting with him?'

Jay shook his head. 'We were trying to catch Brindle ... Shima showed us how, that's all.'

'Shima?' Rebecca felt a surge of irritation. 'What kind of a name is that? And what has he to do with your bruise?'

'Jay was riding,' Richie said and Jay shot a look of fury at him. 'The gipsy slapped Brindle's rump. He took off across the field and Jay ...'

'You rotten telltale!' he cried. 'You promised you wouldn't say anything.'

'Jay!' Her heart caught with fear. She'd known how it would be when Aden bought the wretched pony. 'You promised you wouldn't ride that pony alone. You gave me your word.'

'I can ride him easily,' Jay replied with more bravado than truth. 'It was just that it took me by surprise when Shima slapped him like that but I wouldn't have come off if Brindle hadn't stumbled ...'

'You won't be riding him again,' Rebecca said angrily. 'Neither one of you. I shall tell your father to sell the wretched pony.'

'But he's mine,' Richie protested. 'You can't do that just because Jay broke his word. I wasn't riding him.'

'But you were intending to,' Rebecca said, giving him a withering look. 'You both broke your promise to me. It's no use pulling a face, Richie. I shall speak to your father this evening.'

'You're mean,' Richie said, staring at her as if he hated her. 'You don't care about me at all ...'

He turned and ran from the room, ignoring her demands that he should return. She felt a familiar flicker of annoyance: Richie was always so difficult. When she looked at Jay she saw reproach in his eyes.

'Don't sell Richie's pony, Mama,' he begged in a choking voice. 'He loves Brindle. It was my fault I fell – and I'm not hurt. Please, please, don't sell Brindle.'

'Let me have another look at you.' She smoothed the hair back from his brow and looked closely at the bruise. 'Does it hurt?'

'No, honest. Please don't sell Brindle. I promise I won't ride him again ... unless Father is there,' he added hastily.

'Brindle is too big for you to manage.' She sighed. 'I suppose that's my fault. I should have let your father buy you a pony of your own. It would save all the arguments between you and Richie.'

'Do you mean you won't tell Dad to sell him?' Jay's face lit up, reminding her sharply of his father.

'He probably wouldn't if I did,' Rebecca admitted. 'All right, I'll forgive you this time – but don't do it again. And don't play with gipsies!'

'Can I tell Richie he can keep his pony?'

'Yes, go on then.' She ruffled his hair and smiled as he ran after his brother. Why were they so different – why did one of them pull at her heartstrings so much more than the other?

She ought to have told Richie herself that the pony was safe but she had other things on her mind. Those gipsies ... she couldn't rid herself of the feeling that they would bring trouble.

*

It seemed to have been raining forever and the high land was soggy, despite all the ditch clearer's attempts to keep it well drained. Rebecca knew Aden was having a problem with lifting the potato crop so she hadn't said much to him about the gipsies, apart from mentioning her surprise that he'd taken them on in the first place.

'They don't seem a bad lot,' Aden replied with a shrug. 'Their leader is a dark, rather foreign-looking chap but I quite like him. He seems honest enough – and his men are working like dogs. The women and children, too, poor devils!'

Rebecca felt a tingling sensation at the back of her neck. Something was tugging at her subconscious but she didn't know what; it was too deeply buried in the mists of time.

'But still, gipsies, Aden. You know what everyone says. You'll have eggs and chickens missing from the yard.'

'Not if Lorenzo knows anything about it.'

'Lorenzo?' The tingle was spreading down her spine. Lorenzo … that was the name of the gipsy Dotty had run off with, wasn't it? She remembered the conversation with Mrs Prentice. The dark, flashy man she had seen kissing the girl in the street that day in Chatteris. It had all happened so many years ago but the memory was still there, waiting to surface. Why? Why had she let it haunt her all these years? 'I still think you'd be better off without them.'

'I can't get all the potatoes up without them,' Aden said, and looked away from her. 'Anyway, what's this about Jay having a pony of his own?'

The subject had been changed and Rebecca let it go. Perhaps she was just being silly but her sense of unease was growing. Was it just the dank mist that seemed to hang over everywhere, making the trees drip and the paths slippery underfoot – or was it something more?

Aden seemed to feel it too. He had been odd for a few days, quiet and withdrawn, as though he had something on his mind. Rebecca had problems of her own. She and Nan were meeting opposition to their proposals for the Temperance mission, which meant that funds weren't coming in as fast as they had hoped.

They should have expected it, of course. Country folk liked their beer and it was often part of the deal struck over wages – so much for the day plus beer or cider. Rebecca could understand the men needing it during the long hot days of harvest, but too many of them spent most of their wages at the pubs then went home to mistreat their wives, who often had nowhere to go and no choice but to put up with brutal husbands. The mission would give sanctuary to those who needed it most and she was determined to get the money from somewhere, even if she had to fund it herself. So the subject of the gipsies slipped from her mind until something happened to bring it back.

She came downstairs one morning about a week later just as Molly closed the back door with a little snap. From the look on her face Rebecca could tell she was annoyed about something.

'Who was that? I thought I heard voices.'

'It was that gipsy lad,' Molly replied. 'Asking for Mr Sawle.'

Rebecca went to the door and glanced out. A youth who looked as if he might be a year or so older than Richie was standing just inside the gate talking to Jay.

'Yes – what did you want?' she called. 'You, boy!'

The youth turned to look at her and her heart stood still as she saw his face – those eyes and that way of holding his head, of staring straight at you. She felt an icy tingle down her spine and for a moment the world seemed to spin around her. She had known of him before. She had always known, though her heart denied it … but no, it couldn't be true. It was her imagination!

'Who are you and what do you want?' she asked coldly.

'I'm Shima, ma'am.' He took off his cap and held it respectfully in front of him. The likeness was even more marked now: there was a faded photograph in a drawer somewhere, a picture of Aden as a lad. It could have been this boy. 'I was lookin' for Mr Sawle, ma'am. Me da sent me with a message.'

'He's at Five Winds, I believe,' she said. 'If you've got a message for him you'd better get off.'

'Yes, ma'am.'

As he ran off Rebecca looked at Jay. She was feeling numbed, hardly aware of what she was saying. 'I would prefer it if you stayed clear of that boy,' she said, her tone harsh. 'It's a pity your father chose to harbour those gipsies here but since he has you must stay away from them – and the farm while they're here.'

'But Shima's all right,' Jay protested. 'I like him.'

'It's what *I* like that counts. You will do as I say. Do you hear me, Jay?'

'Yes, I hear you.'

He gave her a stubborn look. Rebecca turned and went inside

the house, walking past the curious Molly without a word and into the study. The photograph was in Aden's desk. She searched feverishly for a few minutes, then gave a cry of triumph as she found it. It was brown, poor quality and faded with age, but as she stared at it she was certain – the gipsy boy was Aden's son. The child Dotty Prentice had died giving birth to. The boy Lorenzo had told Mrs Prentice was stillborn. Mrs Prentice had sensed that he was lying and now Rebecca knew she had been right. Suddenly she knew everything, saw it all just as it must have happened ...

Dotty had come to Mepal that day to find Aden. She had told him she was carrying his child and he had promised her money. He had given her money that day in Chatteris, the day Rebecca had seen her laughing with the gipsy.

She had always known deep down inside herself. She had always known that Dotty's child was also Aden's.

Her hand was shaking as she held the faded photograph and she felt sick. That gipsy youth was Aden's firstborn ... not Richie. Not her son! The truth pierced her like the point of a sword, then the pain was swept away before a tide of anger. She tore the picture into tiny pieces and tossed it back into the drawer, shutting it with a snap. Aden had betrayed her. He had betrayed her with that slut! It had all been a lie. Their whole life together was based on deceit.

What ought she to do? She wanted to scream and shout, to tear her hair out and rend her clothes. She wanted to hit out at something ... someone. If Aden had been there at that moment she could cheerfully have thrust a knife into his heart.

'Mrs Sawle?' Molly had come to the door of the study. She was wiping her hands on her apron and looking anxious. 'Is something wrong?'

Rebecca took a deep breath to regain control of her emotions. It was important to keep calm, important not to betray herself.

'No, Molly, there's nothing wrong,' she said, and forced a smile. 'I have a little headache, that's all – but it will soon go. I'm going to see Nan now. Excuse me.'

Rebecca walked past her and out of the back door without her coat or hat despite the bitter cold. Her heart felt as if it had been torn to shreds but her head was high as she walked through the village. No one must guess that her whole life had just fallen apart.   *

'What's the matter?' Aden asked when she moved away from him in bed that night. 'Have I upset you?'

Rebecca lay with her back to him. She could not bear him to touch her, not yet. If he tried to make love to her she thought she would scream. He was not the man she had married, not the man she had believed in. He had betrayed her, lied to her. Her whole life had been a lie.

'I have a headache, that's all,' she said in a muffled voice. 'Please go to sleep, Aden.'

'Why didn't you say so?' He kissed her shoulder. 'Go to sleep then, love. I shan't bother you.'

She didn't answer him. Long after he was asleep she lay wakeful, staring into the darkness. How could she ever forgive him? How could she continue to live as his wife? She wished that she could somehow walk away and never see him again.

He was the father of another woman's child! How could he do that to her? He must have gone with Dotty only a short time before he took her to Mepal ... perhaps even after ... and she had believed that he loved her. He had told her that he'd fallen in love with her that first morning at The Cottrel Arms ... and yet he had gone to Dotty. Lies, all lies! How could she trust him again? How could she be sure he wouldn't betray her again?

Why had he married her? Was it only for the money? She had never thought herself beautiful, though Aden swore she was to him. She had always known he was ambitious ... and yet he was always telling her he loved her. If he could lie about one thing, he could lie about everything else!

He had lied to try and stop her going with him to Chatteris that day; he'd lied because he was afraid she would see him with Dotty and guess the truth. It all made so much sense now ... his unease and Dotty's hostility. She must have hoped he would marry her. How she must have hated Rebecca when he chose her instead. But she had chosen him!

She had gone to him at his cottage and offered herself ... and her father's money.

Dotty's pale face had haunted Rebecca down the years and now she understood why. She was laughing at her, waiting for the chance to destroy Rebecca's marriage and her with it. This was her revenge from beyond the grave.

18

A week passed, a week in which Rebecca hardly spoke to Aden, lying as far away from him in their bed as she could. He looked at her with bewildered, half-angry eyes and yet he said nothing, nor did he attempt to touch her. It was guilt, of course. He must have seen Shima, too. He must know the boy was his son.

She wanted to scream and rave at him but instead she was silent, as if she knew that silence would hurt him more – and she wanted to hurt him. Oh, yes, she wanted him to feel pain ... the pain she was feeling inside her, a pain so deep and raw that she hardly knew how to bear it.

The silence might have gone on forever but then something happened to break it, something more fateful than either of them could have known at the time.

It was the following Saturday and she was in the kitchen baking when Molly came rushing in, looking as if she'd seen a ghost. Her face was a ghastly white and when she saw Rebecca she burst into noisy tears.

'What's the matter?' Rebecca asked in alarm. Molly was usually such a cheerful girl that something awful must have happened to upset her this much. 'What is it?'

'It was terrible,' she sobbed, fumbling for her handkerchief. She was trembling, in a dreadful state. 'I was coming over the bridge when they walked out of the pub. There were three of them and ...' She drew a shaky breath. 'They started whistling and calling out to me ... cheeky things. I was frightened.'

'Gipsies?' Rebecca asked instinctively, and frowned as Molly nodded. 'I was afraid of something like this. Go on, tell me all of it.'

189

'Well ...' Molly bit her bottom lip. 'They blocked my path, stopped me going on. Every time I tried to pass they moved in front of me, laughing and winking at each other. I got scared and screamed, then they let me go.'

Rebecca was furious. Some girls would have laughed it off, but Molly was the shy, vulnerable sort and the incident had really upset her.

'Did they touch you? What exactly did they say to you, Molly?'

She blushed and hung her head. She was nearly twenty-three but, so far as Rebecca knew, had never had a boyfriend.

'I can't tell you what they said,' she whispered, her cheeks bright with shame. 'I can't say it, Mrs Sawle. I'm too embarrassed. Please, please don't make me repeat it.'

'Very well, there's no need. I can imagine the kind of things men like that would say.' Rebecca handed her a clean handkerchief because her own had been twisted into a crumpled rag, then she took off her own apron, reached for her coat, which was hanging on a stand in the hall, and buttoned it up to the fur collar. 'I'm going to speak to my husband about this. I won't stand for such disgusting behaviour in our village. Something must be done.'

'They didn't hurt me,' Molly said quickly. 'It was just what they said ...'

'It's what they *might* have done. It's getting so that it's not safe for a decent woman to walk in the street. Make yourself a cup of tea and sit down by the fire, Molly. I shan't be long.'

Rebecca put on her hat, driving a long steel pin through the crown and wishing she could have stuck it into the wretches who had frightened poor Molly. If it was up to her she would have seen they had a good birching! It might teach them how to behave amongst decent folk.

She went out of the house and across the road, taking the lane that wound round behind the church to Five Winds. The path was slippery underfoot because of all the rain and a slight frost that morning. The trees had lost their leaves now and looked bare, their branches silvered with little trails of frost. It had turned cold overnight and Rebecca pulled her warm collar up to keep out the biting wind. She was so angry. So angry!

She hadn't been near the farm since they'd moved into their new house but knew Aden would be there at this time of day, supervising the dairy. Even though Sid and May Harris were

190

living at the farm now with their two sons and their daughter Sorrel, Aden liked to see how things were going. Besides, he enjoyed a chat with his friend.

As she had expected, she found the men in the dairy. They were inspecting the cheeses set out on little straw mats. May made excellent cheeses and people called regularly at the gate to buy them as well as jugs of fresh, creamy milk.

'You'll see to that then, Sid?' Aden looked up in surprise as she entered the dairy. 'Rebecca – what are you doing here? What's wrong? Are the children ...'

'It's Molly,' she said. 'She was accosted by gipsies on her way back from visiting her mother. They had been drinking, Aden – at this time of day!'

'It's payday,' he replied, immediately defensive. 'Is Molly hurt?'

'Not physically, but she was very frightened and upset. I won't stand for this, Aden. You must get rid of those gipsies. Send them packing at once.'

'We need them for another week ...'

'So the women of the village are to go in fear because you need fieldhands?' Rebecca lost her temper. She could guess why he wanted to keep them here. 'That is disgraceful, Aden! Why can't you use local labour as you usually do? You've never needed gipsies before.'

'It has been so wet. We have to get the potatoes up quickly or they may rot. If you knew what a mess the land is in, Rebecca ... They're working like slaves. Our land isn't the easiest, you know.'

She was in no mood to be placated. 'That doesn't excuse what they said to Molly. She's a respectable girl and they were rude; they made her cry.'

'Well, leave it to me.' Aden looked at her uneasily. 'I'll sort something out.'

'You had better. I'm warning you, Aden. If you don't do something about this, I shall!'

She turned on her heel and marched away. She wasn't sure whether she was so angry because of what had happened to Molly or because Aden had kept the gipsies here, knowing that one of them was his son.

Aden stood on the bridge by the river, waiting for the late drinkers to leave the pub. It was a clear, frosty night and the sky was sprinkled with stars. Several local men he knew walked past him on their way home, tipping their caps politely in acknowledgement.

'Night, Mr Sawle.'

'Good night, Jess. Good night, Fred.' He answered each one with a nod or a smile. They were all decent blokes, out for a drink and no harm done, though a couple of them looked as if they'd had more than enough. Maybe Rebecca was on to something after all with her stand against the evils of heavy drinking.

It was beginning to freeze hard, and Aden cursed the necessity for standing here at this hour. He would much rather be at home beside his own fire with the paper and his pipe. Having thought it through, however, he had decided that there was only one way of dealing with the problem. He had to keep the gipsies for a bit longer but he couldn't let them run wild. He would just have to show them who was boss.

As soon as the three men came out of the pub he knew that they were well on the way to being drunk. He heard them swearing at each other, their voices loud and coarse. Maybe he'd been wrong to encourage them in the first place – and he'd probably paid them too much, because he needed that crop.

He moved to confront them. They halted, looking at each other uncertainly as they saw him.

'This lunchtime you insulted a girl who works for me,' Aden said. 'Now I find you drunk and using foul language. This isn't the behaviour I expect from men who work for me.'

'We ain't doin' no 'arm.'

'Jest 'aving a bit of fun like.'

They shuffled their feet, obviously uneasy. Lorenzo had warned his men to leave the local girls alone, and he had an evil temper if he was crossed.

'It were naught but a bit of a laugh, sir.'

'To you perhaps,' Aden said coldly. 'For the girl it was a terrifying ordeal. I'm afraid I'm going to have to teach you lads some manners.'

The gleam in his eyes suddenly got through to them. He was challenging them to a fight. They stared at him warily, unwilling to go for a man who carried the stamp of authority. They might end up in prison for attacking a solid citizen. It was sure to be them who took the blame, no one ever listened to the word of gipsies.

'Come on,' Aden said. 'One at a time or all three together. It's all the same to me.' He took off his jacket, throwing it over a fence and holding up his clenched fists. 'What are you waiting for then – not scared of me, are you? If you're not, then by God you will be when I've finished with the lot of you ...'

It was past eleven in the evening and Aden still wasn't home. He never stayed out this late even on the rare occasions when he went for a pint with his friends. He had told her that he was going to sort out the trouble with the gipsies ... but that was hours ago. Rebecca was beginning to wonder if something terrible had happened to him when she heard a sound downstairs. Was that the back door? She listened intently for a moment and heard someone moving around. He must be home at last. She picked up a lighted oil lamp and went to the head of the stairs, shivering slightly in the cooler air of the hall. She was wearing only a warm flannel nightgown, her long, thick hair hanging down her back as she peered into the darkness.

'Is that you, Aden?'

'I'm coming up now.'

As the light from her lamp fell on his face, she gasped. 'Just look at the sight of you – you've been fighting!'

He was laughing, obviously pleased with himself. 'I've been teaching those gipsies a lesson they'll not forget in a hurry.' He followed her into the bedroom, wincing as he took off his jacket. 'I thrashed all three of them – took on the lot of them at once and thrashed them!'

'Aden!' She was stunned, shocked. His face was bruised, his mouth cut and bleeding. 'Fighting with gipsies! And so pleased with yourself. What on earth possessed you to do such a thing?'

'I had to show them who was boss,' he replied. 'It's the only way to deal with them – the only thing they understand. I need them, Rebecca. We'll lose half the crop if they go. Besides, they'll be no more trouble now. They know when they're licked.'

He grinned at her, looking so much like a cheeky schoolboy that she saw the funny side of it. 'If you won, I dread to think what *they* look like,' she said in a severe tone, but her mouth quivered and inside she was laughing. This was so typical of Aden. He had his own way of settling things, his own sense of fair play. 'What am I to do with you? And you a respectable man!'

'I can think of something,' he murmured throatily. He took the lamp from her and set it on the table, then drew her against him. For a moment she stiffened and he looked at her oddly. 'What's wrong, Rebecca? I've felt something lately but I don't know …'

'It doesn't matter,' she said, and touched her finger to his lips. Perhaps she should have spoken out then; it might have cleared the air and prevented so much pain but she couldn't, the hurt was too raw, too deep to speak of just yet. She had thought her marriage was over but now she knew she still cared for him. 'Aden …'

His hands moved over her breasts, caressing and fondling. As their lips met he winced and cursed. 'Damn those beggers, they must have landed a lucky punch.'

'Men!' She smiled despite herself. 'You're all the same. If it's not fighting or drinking it's the other thing. Behave yourself, Aden, and let me do something about that cut.'

He sat patiently on the edge of the bed while she fetched a bowl of warm water and bathed his face, then, when she returned after swilling the water into the basin, he put his arms around her, pulling her down with him to the bed, his hands pushing beneath her nightgown to cover her breasts.

'I might be bruised about the face,' he murmured against her ear, 'but there's nowt wrong with the rest of me that you can't cure.'

Her pulses raced as her body responded to his touch. It was a while since they had been together like this and she had missed him. The picture of a young gipsy boy's face rose up in her mind to haunt her but she smothered it, banishing it to a tiny corner of her mind where it could not hurt her. Aden was her husband, nothing could change that. They were bound together for life, for better or for worse.

If she had pushed him away then and demanded explanations, would it have saved all the anguish and pain of the years to follow? Perhaps if they had talked then the bitterness would not have built up inside her – but she did as she had always done when things hurt her too much. She held the pain deep inside her, pretending it wasn't there.

She ought to have raged at him then; she should have told him what she knew, made him confess the truth – but instead she lay in his arms and let him love her. Only afterwards, as she lay staring into the darkness, did she understand that things could never be quite the same again. Her body had responded to Aden's loving but her heart was encased in ice.

*

'I came to say goodbye,' Shima said. 'I wanted to give you this. It's to say sorry for any trouble our men caused.' He held out a beautifully carved wooden peg doll. 'I made it for your daughter. It needs clothes but perhaps Mrs Sawle will dress it for her. You have got a daughter, ain't you?'

'Yes.' Aden stared at the boy and it was as if a knife twisted inside him, wrenching at his guts. He was almost certain in his own mind that Shima was his son and longed to touch that dark, curly head – to take him in his arms and claim him as his own – but that was something he could never do: he had forfeited that right long ago. 'This is good work, Shima. I'm sure Fanny will be pleased with it.' He put his hand in his pocket, fingering a gold coin. He wanted to give his son something but he knew that Shima wouldn't be allowed to keep the money. 'Thank you, lad. I've enjoyed having you here.'

Shima grinned, his white teeth flashing against the weathered tan of his skin. 'I like you, Aden Sawle,' he said cheekily. 'You were a good master, the best we've ever had. I shan't forget you.'

And then he was off, running down the road. Aden watched him go, his heart heavy with a grief he could never share. 'I shan't forget you either, Shima,' he murmured softly. 'God be with you, son.'

He felt the sting of tears. The bible said a man reaped what he sowed, and for the first time Aden was beginning to understand what that meant. He had sown his seed carelessly and because of that his eldest son was living like a gipsy. The knife cut into his heart, dealing him a wound that was all the more severe because he must hide it from the world.

He must not inflict his pain on anyone else. Rebecca must never be hurt because of what he had done.

Sighing, he turned away. He had other problems pressing on him. Sid had discovered there was blight in one of the potato stores. They would have to destroy tons of the crop and hope that the rest was not affected, because if it was he was going to be in big trouble.

How cruel fate could be! Rebecca could not believe it when she realized she was once more with child, now when she least wanted or expected it – and even more bitter was the knowledge that it must have happened the night Aden fought the gipsies.

Almost two months had passed since then and they had not

195

made love in all that time. Aden had tried to hold her a few times when they lay in bed, but she always turned away from him, denying the clamouring of her own body, punishing him with her silences and coldness. She still wanted him but she was angry – angry and bitter. He had lied to her; he had deceived her. She was not sure she would ever be able to forgive him.

'Are you certain?' he asked the morning she told him she was carrying their fourth child. She nodded and he sighed, looking at her doubtfully. 'I'm sorry, Rebecca. I should have been more careful. Let's hope you don't have too bad a time with this one.'

'I was all right with Fanny …'

'Yes, you were.' He forced a smile. 'Let's pray it's another girl then. I'm sorry, Rebecca, I must go. I'm meeting the mole catcher and I want to show him where I saw the little pests. We'll talk later.'

'Yes, you must go.' The mole catcher was obviously more important than the news that she was carrying Aden's child!

After he had left she sat on at the breakfast table, her toast and coffee turning cold. The usual sickness had robbed her of her appetite and all she had to look forward to was several months of feeling unwell – and for what? To give Aden another child, a child he did not seem to want.

Why should he? He already had three sons … perhaps more. He might have a dozen children for all she knew. How could she be certain that he didn't have a mistress? How could she ever really trust him again? She knew it had happened a long time ago, that it shouldn't matter after so many years of marriage – but if it didn't matter, why hadn't he told her?

She tried to fight her bitter thoughts but they would not leave her in peace, returning again and again to mock and haunt her. If she could not trust Aden then what did her life mean? What was it all for?

She went upstairs to change. Nan had asked her to help with sorting out the boxes of jumble she had collected for her latest charity bazaar. This time the money was for the poor of London's East End. Rebecca stopped to look at herself in the mirror. She was not yet thirty but thought she looked older. Was her face getting puffy already? She had never thought herself beautiful, but soon she would look bloated and ugly. Was that when Aden would turn to another woman, once she began to swell up and get irritable – or did he already have someone else he visited? He was often out until late in the evenings these days – where did he go? She had thought it must be business but now – now she was no longer sure ... of anything.

'Stop feeling sorry for yourself,' she told herself sharply. 'It was your choice. No one forced you to marry him.'

Perhaps she was being unfair to him. It had all happened so long ago. She shouldn't let the fact that her husband had once had a son by another woman spoil what they had together, but she couldn't stop her bitter thoughts. She felt humiliated, hurt, angry. She had resisted temptation but Aden had indulged his senses even when he was supposed to be in love with her. More than that, he had lied to her ... that's what hurt the most.

When she went downstairs she found a letter waiting for her on the hall table. It was from Celia. She and Victor must be back from their latest travels; they had been to America this time and Rebecca was looking forward to reading all about it. She slit the envelope and took out the one thin sheet of paper. How unusual! Celia always wrote long, newsy letters ... suddenly her blood ran cold as she saw what she had written.

'Victor died yesterday. He had a heart attack and collapsed at home. It was very quick so he did not suffer too much. I wanted to tell you at once because I know how very fond ...'

The letter fluttered from Rebecca's grasp. She gave a little moan and then crumpled into a heap on the floor.

'Are you all right now?' Aden looked at her from the end of the bed an hour or so later. 'Do you want the doctor?'

'No, of course not. It was just a faint, Aden. I'm perfectly well again now. There was no need to send for you – no need at all.'

'Molly was worried,' he said. 'She saw the letter after you dropped it and thought you might need comforting.'

'I told her I would be all right.' Rebecca sighed and closed her eyes, trying to hold back the wave of grief. Victor was dead. It was years since she had ceased to dream of anything between them but it was still painful to know that she would never see him again. 'I shall have to go to Celia at once.'

Aden looked serious when she opened her eyes and glanced at him. 'Do you think you should?' he asked. 'In your condition? You know how ill you always are for the first few months.'

'Victor has just died,' Rebecca said coldly. Her head was aching and she wanted to be alone so that she could come to terms with her grief. 'Celia is my friend. She will need me. I must go to her.'

'I was thinking of you but ...' Aden's expression was very odd. Rebecca had a sudden feeling of foreboding. She could hear the wind whistling in the trees outside, an eerie, chilling whine, and downstairs the longcase clock was striking the hour, sounding like a death knell rather than the comforting chime she was used to. 'I suppose you'll do as you want. You always do.'

'And what does that mean?'

'You know that as well as I do.'

'You don't want me to go. You were always jealous of Victor.' The bitter, accusing words tumbled out before she could stop them and she gasped as she saw the sudden fury in Aden's eyes.

'I had cause, didn't I, Rebecca?' he asked bitterly. 'It was him you wanted. Victor Roth. You would have married him if you could, wouldn't you? I was always second best, wasn't I?'

She was horrified. How could Aden have known? She had never said anything ... never done anything to make him jealous. But he had known somehow.

'That's ridiculous,' she said in a hoarse whisper. 'I've never been unfaithful to you, Aden. Never!'

'Maybe not.' His mouth hardened and he was giving no quarter. 'But you wanted to ... you wanted to!'

The words lay between them; long unspoken they had festered in his heart and now they were out. She was ashamed and then angry. How dare he accuse her of betrayal?

'I've never betrayed you.'

'There are different kinds of infidelity, Rebecca. I'm not saying he had you ...'

'The way you had Dotty Prentice?'

The colour drained from Aden's face. He stared at her as if he had seen a ghost, and the knife turned in her breast. Any doubts she might have had about the gipsy boy vanished as she saw the guilt in his eyes.

'That was a long time ago – before you and me.'

'Before you met me? No, I don't think so, Aden. Dotty's child must have been conceived after the harvest dance.'

'I never thought I had a chance with you ...' He moistened his lips, his eyes seeming to plead with her. 'You saw the boy. You knew he ... ?'

'Did you think I wouldn't?' she asked coldly. 'He was the image of you as a lad. Did you think I wouldn't know?'

'Dotty said the child was mine.' His voice was a strangled whisper. 'I couldn't be sure. I wasn't the only one to go with her … but I gave her money.'

'She took your money and went to that gipsy,' Rebecca said, wanting to hurt him. 'I saw them laughing together that day at Chatteris. She probably didn't know who the father was but you were the easiest target for blackmail … because you had married a woman with money.'

Aden was silent, his face white and tight-lipped. 'Lorenzo believes Shima is his. He thinks the lad will bring his people luck. There was some kind of a prophecy before he was born, that's why he took Dotty as his woman.'

'So she deceived both of you? She was brighter than any of us realized.' Rebecca laughed harshly, remembering the triumph in Dotty's eyes the day she had seen her in the village. 'How does it feel to know that your first son has been brought up as a gipsy – a dirty, thieving, little gipsy brat?'

Aden stared at her as if he didn't know her and she sensed that her taunt had driven deeper than she had intended. She had wanted to hurt him but now she wished the words unsaid; they were too cruel. She knew how much his sons meant to him. It must be hurting him not to be able to claim his firstborn.

'Aden, I'm sorry. I didn't mean …'

'But you did,' he said quietly. 'We both meant what we said. Perhaps it would be best if you went to Celia's for a while.'

She stared after him as he left the room. They had both said such bitter, hurtful things. Could their marriage survive or was this the end?

19

Rebecca had thought her marriage was over when she first saw the gipsy boy but she was wrong. A marriage did not die all at once but little by little, drop by drop, like a bleeding heart.

The rift with Aden was not repaired before she left to stay with Celia. He was seldom in the house and when he was they passed each other without speaking, though on the morning she was due to leave he came in as she was having breakfast and handed her a hundred pounds in crisp five-pound notes.

'For your journey,' he said as she lifted her brows. 'Please give Lady Roth my regards.'

'Thank you, Aden. I shall do so, of course.'

She accepted the money without comment. Perhaps it was meant as a peace offering, time would tell. They had both said such bitter things and it would not be easy to learn to live with each other again, but they must try, for the sake of their children. This time apart would give them both time to think and heal. For the moment she could think only of her friend ... of how Celia must be suffering.

Rebecca spent a month with Celia at her home in Hampshire, helping her through the funeral and the first terrible days afterwards. Celia was tearful but surprisingly strong: at some time over the years she had grown up without anyone really noticing it. Somehow Victor's death had brought the two women closer than ever before. They were united in their grief.

For Rebecca it was a time of peace and healing. Away from Aden she had been able to think clearly and had made her decision. She would try to forgive him and to forget. Life was too short for recriminations. Surely they could at least live peaceably together if nothing else?

Celia's marriage had not been perfect but she had made the best of it – and now was determined to remember only the good things.

'I have no regrets,' she told Rebecca as they sat talking by the fire the night before she was due to return home. 'Victor loved me, I know that. He wanted a son and I couldn't give him one – but he always loved me.' Her eyes were very bright as she looked at Rebecca. 'He did love me, didn't he?'

A log crackled and spat on the fire, sending a little shower of sparks up the chimney. Outside the wind whistled and howled through the trees, warning of a rough night ahead.

'You know he did,' Rebecca replied, and got up to kiss her cheek. Celia smelt of a flowery, expensive perfume and her skin was as soft as silk. 'You were his darling girl and he adored you. Always.'

She was still so delicate and so pretty. Rebecca thought she would always be that way – one of those women who never seemed to grow old.

'Yes.' Celia smiled contentedly, satisfied now that her friend had reassured her. 'He was so fond of you, dear Rebecca. He often used to talk of you – tell me how much he admired you. Did you know?'

'We were friends,' Rebecca said. She returned to her chair and took up her embroidery. 'Just as you and I are friends.' And it was the truth. For many years now Victor had been simply that – a dear and valued friend.

'We shall continue to be friends.' Celia held out her hand to the fire, her beautiful diamond rings sparkling in the light from the flames. 'You will visit me as often as you can and I shall visit you. You will bring Fanny when you next come, won't you? She's such a beautiful child. If I'd had one, I would have wanted a daughter just like yours.'

When Rebecca left Celia the next morning, she was preparing to go and stay with one of the many friends she had made on her travels over the years. She would not be lonely. Her memories of Victor were happy ones and Rebecca was glad that she had done nothing to spoil them. It was always easier to take what you wanted from life than to deny yourself, but selfishness could cause so much pain.

It was with mixed feelings that she returned to her own house.

Fanny had been with her all the time, of course, but she had missed her sons and the familiar things of home. A tiny part of her had missed Aden, too, but she shut the regrets and faint yearnings out of her mind. Her anger had worn itself out but the hurt remained. She was prepared for reconciliation but it was up to him now. He had begun their quarrel; he must be the one to make the first move.

She arrived home in the middle of the afternoon and only Molly was there to greet her, but of course she should not have expected anything else: Aden was sure to be busy. After drinking a cup of tea in the kitchen with her housekeeper, Rebecca went upstairs to take off her things – and it was then she discovered that Aden had already made his feelings clear, but not in the way she had hoped.

She noticed something different as soon as she entered her bedroom but it wasn't until she opened the wardrobe and found it half-empty that she realized what had happened.

'Mr Sawle asked me to move his things,' Molly told her awkwardly when Rebecca questioned her later. 'He said you might prefer to be alone now that you're … having another baby.'

'That was thoughtful of him,' she replied in a cool, emotionless voice that revealed nothing. 'I must remember to thank him.' Inside she was seething.

How could he ask Molly to move his things while she was away? Without even discussing it with her first! She was angry but she was also hurt – deeply hurt. It was such a final, cold thing to do. How could he?

'You might have waited until I came home,' she said when they were alone in the parlour that evening. She was standing by the fire with her back towards him, her hand pressed against her stomach as if to protect the child inside her. 'You could have asked me what I thought, Aden.' She looked proud, dignified – untouchable.

'You made your feelings clear for weeks before you left,' he replied in a flat, hard voice. 'I thought it would suit you – at least for the next few months.'

'We may as well make it a permanent arrangement,' she said, matching her tone to his. If this was how he felt there was no point in anything else. 'At least then I shall be certain that this child is the last.' Her words were chosen with care, each one barbed and meant to strike deep at his heart.

'That's hardly fair,' he retorted, rising to her bait. 'I've never forced you – never done anything you didn't want.'

She turned to look at him, her head going up, her eyes cold. 'Nevertheless, that side of our marriage is over.' It was her pride talking. He had already made the choice.

Aden stared at her and for a moment something flared in his eyes. She thought he was about to protest, to say he wouldn't accept it ... wouldn't let their love wither and die like this. She wanted him to be angry, to shake her until she screamed the hurt out of her – but he didn't. He just stared at her in silence, then nodded his head and turned away to pick up his overcoat.

She suddenly realized he was about to leave the house and was filled with a sense of dread.

'Where are you going?'

'I have a business meeting.'

'At this hour?'

'Since my whereabouts can no longer concern you, I see no need to answer that.' How proud and hard he was – how different from the man who had worshipped at her feet! When had he changed? Had it happened all at once, or little by little?

'Are you going to another woman? Is that why you asked Molly to move your things?'

'There is no one else at the moment.'

'I see.' She turned her face aside, struggling to hide the pain his words had caused her. There was no one yet but he clearly intended there should be. Her expression gave nothing away, she was as white and cold as a marble statue. 'You have made yourself quite plain. Our marriage is over in all but name – but I shall expect you to be discreet. Good night, Aden.'

She walked past him and up the stairs without looking at him again.

'Rebecca ...' She heard the exasperation in his voice as he followed her into the hall, but did not turn round. 'Damn you, Rebecca! If I do go to another woman, remember you drove me to it!'

The door slammed after him as he went out; it seemed to shake the house to its very foundations and she jumped. How could he be so thoughtless? He had probably woken the children.

Fanny was still asleep when she glanced in, so was Richie. She wasn't sure about Jay, even though his eyes were tightly closed.

She gazed down at him, resisting the temptation to stroke his hair. He looked so angelic lying there, so beautiful it caught at her heart. She loved her children so much and they were all she had left now. She did not know what she would do if she lost them.

Aden was going to another woman. She wondered who it was. Not Ruth Perry: she was married to a draper and living in Cambridge. May Harris was very proud of how well her sister had done and told Rebecca snippets of news whenever they met. No, it wasn't Ruth but there was someone.

She walked along the corridor and went into her own room, closing the door behind her.

Aden strode across the fields to the brow of the hill. It was a clear, moonlit night and he could see for miles across the low-lying land. He had lied to Rebecca when he'd said he had a business meeting, but he'd had to get out of the house before he did something he would regret. For a moment he had wanted to take her white throat in his hands and ... he shivered and cursed himself for a fool. He should never have asked Molly to move his things but after Rebecca left him to rush off to Celia he had felt angry. She had always made it clear where her priorities lay. Well, he'd had enough of it. He was tired of being second best.

His marriage was over. There would not be a divorce, neither of them wanted that, just a parting of the ways – a separation of hearts and minds. But that had been happening for a long time, before Rebecca discovered the truth about Shima.

He wasn't sure what had gone wrong between them. Perhaps it was his pride ... he'd let his jealousy fester and grow so that he'd needed something to drive it out and that something had made him withdraw into his own world.

Besides, there were problems ...

What had it all been about? The struggle to heave himself up the ladder of success? Where had he gone wrong? Why had he shut himself more and more into his own world, a world of increasing loneliness? He thought it might have started after she left him for two months and went to stay in France with Celia and Victor. He'd been haunted by his fear that she might have ...

He'd tried so hard to give her everything she wanted. She had never known where the money had come from to build her house – she would kill him for that!

She had been angry enough when he'd bought Frank's place but that had turned out well. He'd recently let it to a pleasant widow who had turned it into a wool shop. Frank's shop was now a warm, comfortable place where expectant mothers met to discuss their problems and buy balls of pink and blue knitting wool.

He hadn't told Rebecca but she must have noticed it when she was shopping in town. Of course they hadn't been talking to each other much recently.

Had it all been worth the effort? He'd found it so exciting at the start; the building up had taken all his time and his energy ... was that when they started to drift apart?

He wasn't sure exactly when things had started to go wrong with the business; that had crept up on him and now he owed more than he felt comfortable with. A couple of bad investments, some shares that dropped like a stone after he'd bought them – and a disastrous potato harvest.

Of course he still had the land. Far more than he could really keep an eye on – perhaps that was why some of it wasn't producing as well as it should.

He kicked at the earth, then bent down to pick up a handful and crumble it through his fingers. This was all that really mattered, the rich, fertile soil that his family had worked for years. To hell with all the rest!

He retraced his footsteps towards the road. Damn the debts and damn Rebecca's coldness, her silences! He supposed they would get over this somehow. He wasn't going to worry over something that couldn't be helped; there was a big, private card game on at Joshua Hauxton's house and he had been invited. He might as well go ...

Rebecca stared out of the window, noticing that the blossom was just coming out on the cherry trees. It was spring again, a particularly warm spring. The past few days had been almost like summer and she had spent some time walking on the riverbank as she'd done long ago – in those dark days after her father was murdered. Her thoughts were almost as gloomy as they had been then as she reflected on the rift between her and Aden ... a rift that did not seem to heal. They were polite to each other, of course, but they didn't really talk – they were like strangers living under the same roof.

She sighed and went to sit down, picking up a newspaper from the small table beside her. The news did nothing to cheer her up.

All anyone seemed interested in writing about was the end of the Boer War, a horrific murder and some trouble at the docks.

'Mrs Sawle ... Mrs Sawle!' Molly sounded hysterical and Rebecca let the paper fall to the floor at her feet as her housekeeper rushed in. 'Come quickly – it's Master Jay!'

There was such panic in her voice that Rebecca knew something was very wrong. She moved awkwardly across the room; she was in her seventh month and carrying badly, and was frowning with the effort as she hurried out into the hall. She gasped with shock as she saw Aden carrying an unconscious Jay up the stairs.

'Aden – what happened?'

'He collapsed playing cricket at school,' said Aden, his face white and strained. 'The doctor is on his way.'

She followed him up the stairs, her heart jerking with fear. What had happened to make Jay pass out? As she saw his blue-shadowed eyes and flushed face her throat tightened with emotion. He was clearly very ill. She touched his forehead and felt the heat of his skin.

'He must have taken a fever,' she said. 'Molly told me his clothes were soaking wet when he came home on Saturday afternoon. He had been swimming in the river with the Harris boys. I told him it was too soon, that it wasn't really summer, but he wouldn't listen to me.'

'He'll be all right,' Aden said. 'Don't look like that, Rebecca. He'll pull through ...'

'How can you be so sure? He should never have gone swimming – it's too early. The water was much too cold even though the sun was warm.'

'It was hot on Saturday.' Aden raked his fingers through his hair, obviously beside himself with worry but determined not to admit it. 'Besides, you know what Jay is – tell him not to do something and it makes him all the more determined.'

'You've no need to tell me how stubborn he is,' she said as she pulled back the covers for Aden to lay the boy down. 'And you encourage him. You taught him to swim ...'

'And you begged me not to.' Aden was grim-faced. 'So it will be my fault if he has pneumonia. You are very cruel, Rebecca.'

'I didn't say that ...'

'But you meant it, didn't you?'

They were quarrelling again. It seemed they never met without exchanging harsh words these days – even over the unconscious body of their son.

Rebecca was saved from making a reply by the doctor's arrival. He examined Jay, listened to his chest and then confirmed Rebecca's worst fears.

'He has a nasty infection, I'm afraid. He will need constant nursing – something you shouldn't undertake in your condition, Mrs Sawle. It would be best if he went to the fever hospital.'

'No!' She couldn't bear to leave her precious son to the care of strangers: too many people died in that hospital. 'Tell me what I must do, Doctor Roberts. Molly and I will look after him here.'

'Rebecca ...'

'No, Aden!' She stared at him defiantly. She was like a tigress at bay, all teeth and claws, prepared to defend her young to the death. 'He'll die if we let him go, I know he will. I want to nurse him myself.'

'Is it possible?' Aden looked at the doctor.

'Of course. My concern was for Mrs Sawle.'

'We'll manage,' Aden said. 'We have friends who will help. If it's what Rebecca wants ...'

She was already bent over Jay, sponging the sweat from his brow as they spoke. Nothing would make her part with her son, because she knew he would die if she let him go away.

'Make sure she gets some rest,' the doctor was saying as he left. 'You'll need some steaming kettles and you should try to erect some kind of a tent over his bed ... it may help the tightness on his chest ... ease his breathing.'

Their voices faded into a blur as they left the room. She bent over Jay, stroking the soft hair back from his face. He was so hot and had begun to moan and toss restlessly.

'I won't let you die,' she whispered to him. 'I gave you life. I carried you in my womb for nine months and you almost killed me when you came but I won't let you die. I won't let you leave me ... you have to live. You have to live for me, my darling.'

'Mama – what's wrong?'

She swung round as she heard Richie's voice behind her. 'Go away, Richie!' she cried harshly. 'I don't want you in here while Jay is ill. I can't have you here.' She didn't want to run the risk of his taking the fever but as she saw his scowl she knew he had mis-understood. He thought she didn't want him ... didn't care about him. 'Richie!' she called as he turned away. 'Come back. I didn't mean to hurt you ...'

He had gone and once again she had trampled on his feelings. He would think she was neglecting him for Jay, as she had when he was very small and she'd taken his brother to France, leaving him at home. She would have to talk to him, to explain – but not now. For the moment she could think of no one but Jay.

It was nearly three weeks before they could be sure that Jay would live. During all that time Rebecca hardly left her son's side, day or night. She was consumed by a terrible fear that if she was not with him he would die. It was irrational and foolish but so strong that she could not rid herself of the idea that she must not leave, even for a moment.

Aden was angry because she would not go and rest even when he was there. 'Surely you can trust me to watch over him for an hour or so?' he asked. 'You're exhausted, Rebecca. If you're not careful you will kill yourself and the baby – is that what you want?' His look was so accusing and bitter that it broke through the mist of pain that surrounded her.

She went to her bed then but within an hour she was back at Jay's side. He was feverish, calling out for her as he writhed amongst the tangled sheets.

'I'm here, my darling. I'm with you.'

Jay quietened at the sound of her voice. She stroked his brow until he stopped his restless tossing – and when she looked round Aden had gone.

It had been a long, terrible time but at last the fever had abated and Jay was over the worst. He was conscious but still weak and fretful, clinging to her, demanding all her attention, all her strength. She was so tired that she hardly knew how to stand, going through the motions in a kind of daze.

The doctor looked at her oddly when he called that morning and pronounced that Jay was on the mend. 'You've worked a little miracle,' he told her as they left the room together. 'It was a particularly virulent fever and I thought we might lose him, but you pulled him back. He owes his life to you, my dear.'

'Will he be strong again? This won't leave him with a weak chest, will it?' Her concern was all for Jay. She could not bear to think of her beautiful son as an invalid: he would rather have died.

The doctor patted her hand reassuringly. 'No more swimming

for a while – but, yes, I think you can be sure he will soon be back to normal, up to all kinds of mischief. He just needs to take care for a while.'

'Thank you.' She smiled at him gratefully as they stood at the head of the stairs. He had played his part in Jay's recovery, as had Molly, Aden and her friends. 'I'll see you to the door ...' She gasped as the pain struck suddenly. 'Oh ... it can't be the baby. It's not due for at least six weeks ...'

'Perhaps I ought to examine you?'

'Yes, I think perhaps ...' She could feel a strange sensation low in her belly. It was a slow, sluggish warmth spreading between her thighs. 'I – I think I'm bleeding ...'

'I was afraid of something like this, Mrs Sawle. With your history I think we should have you in hospital just to make sure ...'

She tried to shake her head. She wanted her child to be born at home as the others had been but his voice sounded so strange. She could no longer see his face and there was a roaring in her ears. She had never felt like this before. She was losing her balance, falling ... tumbling down the stairs ... into the blackness.

Afterwards, she was to discover that her loss of consciousness was a blessing. She was not aware of being rushed to the small cottage hospital, nor of what followed. It was only much, much later when she lay weeping in a pleasant little side room that a doctor told her she had lost her child.

'You were brought here because we were afraid that you might have injured yourself in the fall and we had to act swiftly to save your life,' he told her. 'I'm sorry but we could not save your daughter.' He looked grave. 'I'm afraid that you will never be able to have another child. There was irreparable damage internally.'

He said it so sorrowfully that she felt close to hysteria. 'Thank God,' she whispered as the tears slipped slowly down her cheeks, partly in relief. She was grieving for the child – but did not want the pain and discomfort of bearing more children. It was a blessed relief to know that it could never happen again. Yet it hurt that she had lost the baby she had been carrying. 'My poor little girl. I was going to call her Celia.'

'Your husband is here.' The young doctor looked at her anxiously, as if he feared for her sanity. 'Would you like to see him?'

'I'm too tired,' she said, and turned her face to the pillow. 'Please ask him to come tomorrow. I'll see Aden tomorrow ...'

Rebecca didn't want to see him. She hated him so much that she couldn't bear to have him near her – even after she had been through so much!

Aden was distraught; he hardly listened as the doctor told him how close his wife had come to dying ... that she must never have another child. As if he didn't know that! As if he wasn't already wracked with guilt for what he had done. It was his fault she had been carrying the child in the first place.

And she blamed him for Jay's illness. She hadn't wanted him near the boy or her all the time Jay was so desperately ill. Of course he couldn't blame her. He had let her down, lied to her. And if she knew what a fool he had been, losing that money to Joshua Hauxton ... three thousand pounds! He still couldn't believe he'd done it. It had happened because he was torn with guilt and anguish over the discovery that Shima was his son – and the quarrel with Rebecca, of course – but that was no excuse. He'd had to borrow the money from the bank to pay his gambling debt and he had already mortgaged some of the land ...

But what the hell did any of it matter compared to the fact that Rebecca had almost died on the way to the hospital? The doctors said it was a miracle she had survived – and she must never have another child. Had the doctor said that – or was he remembering what Roberts had told him years ago? Not that it made one jot of difference. What it boiled down to was that if he ever gave way to temptation again, he might as well take a gun and shoot her.

20

Rebecca glanced round the small private room at the cottage hospital. She seemed to have been here for ever and it must be costing Aden a fortune. She knew she was lucky to have survived the ordeal of a childbirth that was far from natural; if she had not been the wife of a rich man she would no doubt have had to remain at home and it was more than likely she would have died – and yet she longed to be home. This room was so dull and dark with its shiny cream walls and olive green curtains. Thank goodness they had said she was well enough to leave it at last! She had thought she would go mad or die of boredom if she were forced to remain much longer. She longed to see her children again.

It was almost a month since they had brought her here and Aden had visited her no more than four or five times, though Nan made the journey almost every day and Molly had come as often as she could; the children had been allowed to visit only for a few minutes one Sunday afternoon.

'You don't seem to understand how ill you've been, Mrs Sawle,' the doctor told her when she begged him to let her go home sooner. 'We almost lost you. And you will need to take things easily for a while yet.'

Now, at last, they had agreed to let her go home, providing she promised to rest every afternoon.

Aden had said he would come and fetch her that afternoon. She couldn't wait, pacing restlessly round and round the small room like a caged animal. He was late. Surely he hadn't forgotten his promise?

When he came in at last he hardly looked at her, just asked her if she was ready and picked up her bags. Rebecca made no mention of his lateness; she did not want to quarrel again so she just smiled and nodded, feeling oddly shy – as if he were a stranger.

They walked out of the hospital together, stopping once to say goodbye to Matron and some of the nurses.

'You have been very kind,' Rebecca said, and gave them the box of bon bons she had asked Aden to bring in specially. 'Thank you for looking after me so well.'

'Take care of yourself, Mrs Sawle,' one of them replied, and looked curiously at Aden as if wondering why he hadn't visited his wife more often.

Rebecca shivered as they went outside. It was a dull, overcast day and it looked as if it might rain throughout the journey. He insisted on laying a warm rug over her knees once she was settled in the carriage, but then he sat up front with the driver. He didn't even want to be with her during the short drive home.

There was a fire burning in the parlour. Molly had polished everything so that the scent of lavender and beeswax was everywhere, and there were tears in her eyes as she welcomed Rebecca home.

'I'm that glad to see you …'

Rebecca thanked her and kissed her cheek. Her children came in once she was settled in her chair by the fire. Fanny ran straight to hug her, clinging to her as if she were afraid she would suddenly disappear again. Jay gave her his sweet, loving smile and kissed her cheek, gazing at her pale face anxiously.

'Are you truly better now?' he asked. He came and knelt at her side, gazing up at her in a way that reminded her of Aden and caught at her heart. 'Was it my fault – because I was ill and you looked after me? Did I make you lose the baby?'

'No, of course it wasn't your fault. It was just me. Something was wrong inside me.' She smiled and kissed the top of his head. 'You mustn't feel guilty, Jay. I promise you, it wasn't your fault.'

'I'm better now,' he said, and looked at his father who was standing by the sideboard, watching them all. 'Good as new, aren't I, Father?'

'He's up to his usual mischief,' Aden replied, but still he didn't look directly at her. She felt as she had when he'd fetched her from the hospital – that he was a stranger, someone she didn't know. It was as if the good years had never been, as if they had never laughed together … never made love or kissed.

'Richie.' Her eldest son was standing by the window, ignoring everyone. 'Aren't you glad to have me back?'

For a moment he didn't move, then he turned to face her, a cool, remote smile on his lips. 'Of course I am, Mother.' He walked over to kiss her on the cheek. 'I hope you are quite well now?'

'Thank you. Yes, I am.' She stared at him uncertainly. He seemed to have grown so much older in a few weeks. 'How are you, Richie?'

'I'm very well, thank you. I've asked Father if I may go to boarding school next year. He says I may if you agree.'

'I said we would ask your mother what she thinks.'

'I think a boarding school is an excellent idea if it is what Richie wants. I've always hoped for a good education for my children.'

'I've quite made up my mind, Mother. I should like to apply as soon as possible.'

He had the manner of a much older boy, so reserved and polite. Richie had never been like this before. What had happened to her son while she was away? He was a stranger ... a stranger with cold, distant eyes. Rebecca began to feel frightened. What was happening to her life? Why were the people she loved turning away from her?

'Mama ... Mama!' Fanny tugged at her sleeve. 'Look, see the new doll Father bought me.'

She turned to her daughter with relief. At least she hadn't changed.

'Yes, darling, I can see,' she said as Fanny held the doll up for inspection. 'It is very pretty.'

Fanny claimed her attention for the next hour or so, then Molly came to take her away while Rebecca went up for the rest she was supposed to have every afternoon. It was such a nuisance but she did feel tired; the journey had taken more out of her than she would have thought possible. She had just taken off her dress and was standing in her petticoat when Aden came in.

'I'm sorry,' he said as she held it against her defensively. 'I didn't mean to disturb you.'

It had begun to rain hard. She could hear it beating against the window, a constant drumming – or was that the pounding of her heart?

'I was about to lie down for an hour.' It was like talking to someone she had never met before. He was so cold, so remote. This was not the man she had married so many years before, the man who had given her so much love, laughter and tears. 'The doctor said I should.'

'Yes, of course. You must rest.' He hesitated, then cleared his throat. 'I need to talk to you but I can come back later.'

'You may as well say it now.' She wanted to talk to him, too – but she wanted the old Aden, not this hard-eyed man who looked at her as if he didn't know her.

'I thought it right to tell you myself … before you hear it from someone else.'

Her heart jerked with fright. She knew what he was going to say and wanted to stop him before it was too late.

'Aden, I thought that now …' The look in his eyes stopped her. 'Can't we …'

'Let me say this first, please. You made it clear months ago that the intimate side of our marriage was over. We shall stay married for the sake of the children, of course. Everything will be just as it was – except that I shall never bother you in that way again.'

There was a terrible noise in her head, cymbals crashing, pagan horns blaring, as the world she had known came tumbling about her ears. She wanted to scream or shout at him to stop but of course she didn't. It was important to keep control. She must give no sign of the torment his words had caused; she must exercise icy control.

'There's someone else, isn't there?'

'Yes.'

'Are you in love with her?'

'Beth is a pleasant woman – a widow. We suit each other. She lives in Chatteris and is a tenant of mine. We've known each other for a while. There has been nothing intimate between us before this but now we have come to an understanding …'

She guessed that he must be talking about the woman who had rented Frank Henderson's old shop from him. Rebecca had noticed it had been turned into a wool shop the last time she'd been in town and she knew the woman who ran it was a widow. She had glimpsed her as she'd passed by, but only from the back. She had never been inside the shop because it held too many memories.

'I see.' She turned away so that he should not see her anguish. 'Thank you for telling me.'

214

'It will make no difference to you, Rebecca.'

'No, I suppose not.'

No difference? When her heart was breaking!

She remained standing with her back to him until she was sure he had left the room, then she sat down on the edge of the bed, still clutching her dress to her breast. She was shaking but she wasn't cold. Aden no longer wanted her as his wife. She had killed his love.

'Aden ... Aden ...' she whispered, bending her head as the grief tore at her. 'I loved you so ... I loved you so.'

Why had she never known it until now? All those years when he had loved her and she had hankered for the moon! What a stupid, foolish girl she had been. How could she not have known? How could she have been so blind? Not to have recognized true happiness ... not to have realized how lucky she was. But she had envied Celia her life and because of that she had believed herself in love with Celia's husband ... and all the time she had been married to a far better man.

If Victor had been half the man Aden was he would have married her instead of Celia – or he would have kept his thoughts to himself. He ought never to have let her believe he cared for her when he loved Celia. He had led her on and so destroyed any chance she'd had of forgetting him. She could see it now, when it was too late.

She must have hurt Aden so badly over the years. He had given her so much love, striven so hard to provide her with all the things she had craved – and she had taken it all, giving too little in return. She hadn't realized how fortunate – how happy – she was until now.

Happiness was a strange thing. You never really noticed it until it had gone.

'Aden ... please come back to me ... love me again.'

The words were only in her head, of course. She would never say them aloud to him. She was too proud to beg. The beautiful, shining thing they had had was broken and could not be mended. She had lost Aden.

The years seemed to stretch endlessly in front of her ... empty, bitter years that might have been filled with laughter and loving.

Her head went up. Tears glittered in her eyes but she would not give way to self-pity. She had lost Aden, nothing could change that. Richie too had withdrawn from her because she had hurt him too many times, but perhaps it wasn't too late to win his love back. Jay was well again and there was Fanny ... her darling, beautiful little girl. She would live for her children. Fanny would not leave her. Fanny was all hers. All she had to live for now.

21

'This is going to make the difference between life and death for some of these women,' Stuart Monroe said, giving Rebecca a look of warm admiration. 'Your generosity astounds me at times, Mrs Sawle. I can't thank you enough for such a generous donation.'

The young lawyer was a handsome, well-built man of medium height, a Scotsman who had lived in England for much of his life and had lost all but the faintest trace of his native accent. Since he had come to join the small country firm of lawyers just over a year earlier, he had proved to be a tower of strength, joining several of the committees for good works on which Rebecca served. She liked him and had come to trust his judgement, which was why she had asked him to help her set up the trust fund for her home for unfortunate women.

'It has always been my aim to help women in distress,' she said, twisting her wedding ring on her finger as the lawyer's expression became almost too admiring, too intense. She stood up, pulling on a pair of soft kid gloves, smoothing them over her fingers to cover a moment of confusion. This was so silly! Her heart was fluttering and she felt as shy as any green girl. 'I must go now. You will see that the trust fund for the new home is set in place immediately, won't you? We hope to move our first occupants in next week.'

'You may safely leave everything to me.'

She gave him her hand and he held it just the tiniest fraction longer than necessary.

'Perhaps I could call on you one afternoon at home? Just to keep you informed of our progress.'

'If you wish. I am usually at home to my friends on Tuesdays and Fridays.'

Her cheeks were pinker than they should have been as she left his office and went out into the crisp air. It was the end of March and they were still in the grip of winter, the wind bitterly cold as it swept down from the north.

She stood in the street for a moment, taking deep breaths to calm herself. How foolish it was of her to imagine that there was anything other than friendship in Stuart Monroe's eyes. He could be no more than twenty-seven at most and she was nearly six years older – a woman who had given birth to four children and was plumper than she ought to be. No, no, she told herself sternly. If he seemed to admire her it was merely because they shared the same ideals, the same desire to improve life for less fortunate people – and because they just happened to enjoy each other's company. Stuart had taken an interest in the mission from the beginning – and she *had* made a very generous donation to the cause.

The truth of the matter was that in her loneliness she had become susceptible to flattery. She was in danger of turning into one of those foolish, wealthy women who simper and sigh after any passable young man. Of course Stuart Monroe was rather more than passable with that soft fair hair of his and the bluest eyes she had ever seen. If she had met him years ago, when she was younger …

'You're a fool, Rebecca Sawle!'

She spoke the words aloud as she walked down the street and a woman turned her head to stare at her in amazement. Rebecca smiled wryly. Yes, she was all kinds of a fool but not fool enough to let herself get entangled in an affair of that nature – even if Mr Monroe's smile did make her heart beat a little faster.

She left such things to Aden. The bitter thought flashed into her mind without warning, lying there like a white maggot, eating away into her flesh like the vile thing it was.

Aden's betrayal still hurt. Even now, some two years later, she occasionally woke with tears on her cheeks and there were times when she reached for him in her dreams, when she turned in bed seeking the warmth of his body and found nothing.

And there were other times – times when the anger raged through her … as now. She was still smarting from her encounter with Ruth Perry two days earlier. Ruth was married now, of

218

course, but Rebecca would never think of her by any other name.

She had been coming from the village hall and they had met face to face in the middle of the narrow path. For a moment Rebecca had felt like ignoring Ruth but good manners would not let her pass by without a word.

'Good morning, Ruth,' she said. 'How are you?'

'Very well, thank you.' Ruth's eyes glittered with dislike. 'And you?'

'Quite well, thank you. May tells me that you have a son now – and that your husband has bought another shop.'

'Cyril is a man of property these days,' Ruth replied, her mouth twisting in a kind of bitter triumph. 'Like Aden. I heard he's been buying a house in Chatteris ... for that friend of his. She's a widow, isn't she? Beth Jones.'

Aden had bought a house for his mistress! Ruth's spiteful words struck deep at Rebecca's heart, wiping the colour from her cheeks. She knew that she had shown too much of her feelings when Ruth smiled.

'You didn't know? I'm so sorry. Everyone else does. I thought you must ...'

Rebecca had not bothered to reply, simply walking past with her back straight and her head up, but inside she felt humiliated ... angry.

How could he do something like that? He might at least have had the courtesy to tell her.

But Aden had withdrawn from her. He was polite but remote; there was an invisible barrier between them, a silence that lay like a suffocating blanket over their lives. Sometimes she wanted to scream at him, to claw that barrier down and let the blood run. She longed for the days when they had argued; at least there had been something between them then, even if it was only anger.

These days Aden no longer cared what she did.

'What the hell did you think you were doing?' Aden raged at her across the room. He had burst into her bedroom as she was dressing for dinner and she was wearing only a satin robe that clung to her like a second skin, making her very aware of her nakedness underneath. 'Two thousand pounds, Rebecca. Two thousand pounds for a home for unfortunate women – you must be out of your mind!'

The suddenness of his attack unnerved her. Such fury! Such a look in his eyes! She moved to put the width of the bed between them, her stomach clenching with fright. What was the matter with him? He looked almost demented.

'I've always given to charity. You've never complained before.'

It was over a week since she had made the donation and nothing could be done about it now. The fund was already in place, the papers signed.

'I don't mind you giving a reasonable amount. I've never objected, you know that – but this is ridiculous.'

Still such anger! She could sense the violence simmering beneath the surface.

She and Nan had managed to raise enough to purchase the building but the funds for running the home would have taken years to collect and Rebecca had decided to endow it herself with what was, she admitted, a huge sum of money – but not beyond their means, surely?

'It was necessary to set up the trust fund. The home will now be completely independent and have no need of additional funding.'

'It's too much. You must get it back – at least, most of it. A hundred pounds to start up the fund would be sufficient. I don't know what you were thinking of – that was every penny we had in the account.'

His autocratic manner made her defiant. 'The money will already have been invested. Besides, it would make me look a fool. I won't do it, Aden.'

'You had no right to draw out such a sum without asking me first.'

'I think I had every right.' She glared at him, defiance turning to anger. 'You may be a rich man now, Aden, but don't forget how you started.'

'Do you think I could?' A nerve twitched at the corner of his mouth. Recently he had grown a moustache and she didn't like it; it made him look older and sterner. 'I am well aware that it was your inheritance that gave me a start – but that isn't the point. I needed that money.'

'So it's all right for you to buy a house for your mistress now that she has given up the shop but when I want money ...' Aden's mouth had gone white with temper and she should have been warned but couldn't hold back the bitter words. 'This is a small village. People talk. I met Ruth Perry ... she has been staying with her sister, did you know? She told me you had bought a house for your fancy woman. She enjoyed that, Aden. But she isn't the only one. Everyone knows about it apparently.'

'Is that why you did it – to pay me back?'

'Don't be ridiculous!'

He gave a sigh of exasperation. 'Beth has nothing to do with this. I bought her the house because … well, it doesn't matter.'

'Really? You think not?' Rebecca curled her nails into the palms of her hands as the anger began to mount inside her. 'You may not think it important but I feel otherwise. It was bad enough that you should hurt and humiliate me but …'

'It wasn't done to hurt or humiliate you.'

'Wasn't it?' Her laugh was harsh and bitter. A bitterness born of lonely nights spent imagining him with Beth – the woman he had put in her place. 'I thought that was your reason, Aden – or at least one of them. Of course I realize that I no longer appeal to you physically but …'

'It was you who wanted it finished,' he said, his eyes fixing her with an icy stare. 'You made your feelings very clear.'

'Don't make excuses, Aden. I was ill. You gave me no choice in the matter. When I came home from hospital you had made your arrangements.'

'You never wanted me. I was always second best – because you couldn't have him.'

'You can't complain. You got what you wanted.'

'Which was?'

'My father's money!'

'Damn you for that! It was never the money, Rebecca.' He raised his fist, towering over her as if he would strike her. She lifted her head, staring proudly at him until his hand fell to his side. 'Take that back. Take that back, damn you!'

'You mean it wasn't the money, not even a little bit?' she asked tauntingly. She felt reckless, wild. She wanted to draw blood, to push him to the limit. 'You were ambitious, Aden. There were other women even then … Dotty …'

'You'll never forgive me for that, will you?' There was real anguish in his voice. She caught her breath, staring at him in disbelief. 'No matter what. I knew it was useless when you wouldn't see me …'

What was he talking about? Pain made her deaf to his words and she heard without understanding.

'I might have been able to forgive in time … if you hadn't taken up with her … that woman in Chatteris.' Suddenly the words she had held back for so long were spilling over in a rushing torrent. 'But you couldn't wait! I could have died when they took our child out of me. If you'd cared, tried to see things my way – but you went to her while I was in the hospital … that was unforgivable!'

'No, Rebecca – not until afterwards. I told you!'

His face had gone a ghastly putty colour. She gazed up at him and a flicker of something began way down deep inside her. Was there still a little of the old passion left between them? For a moment she felt hope but it died as his face became cold and distant; the barrier was in place once more.

'You wanted him but he's dead, isn't he, Rebecca?' He spoke in a flat, emotionless tone. 'You can't have him. Not now – not ever. I was always a convenient substitute.'

'I could have had him if I'd wanted!' She flung the words at him as if they were a spear, wanting to wound him as he had wounded her so many times. 'On his yacht … He tried to make love to me. He wanted me, Aden. He begged me … pleaded with me … kissed me … told me he had always regretted not marrying me …'

She watched as Aden's hands curled at his sides; his expression was so murderous that she thought he would try to kill her, and she laughed. She was so proud, so full of passion – like the old Rebecca.

'Are you saying he had you – that you were lovers?' Aden's voice was harsh with anguish.

'I'm saying that he wanted me.' She gave him a withering, soul-destroying smile. 'Not everyone is as faithless as you, Aden. I was tempted, I don't deny it. I was attracted to Victor and it would have been easy to go to bed with him – but I resisted temptation. I remembered my vows. I remembered that I had a husband waiting for me …'

Aden's fists clenched and unclenched in frustration. He wanted to hit her but he was controlling his temper – just.

'Damn you,' he muttered through bloodless lips. 'Damn you, Rebecca!'

Suddenly he turned and strode out of the room. She heard him clatter down the stairs and slam the front door as he went out.

So she still had the power to hurt him! For a few seconds she was filled with elation, as if she had won some kind of a victory, then it drained away, leaving her empty. He had gone to that woman. Rebecca could hurt his pride but his heart was no longer hers.

Silent tears trickled down her cheeks and she tasted salt. Why did it still hurt? Why did she care what he did? She ought to hate him for what he had done to her ... but she loved him. She wanted him back. She wanted the loving, slightly arrogant but gentle, caring man she had married.

She dashed her hand across her eyes, annoyed with herself. What a fool she was to carry this hope inside her, like a flickering torch that wavered with every breeze. Aden had made his feelings plain enough. He didn't want her. He resented it when she spent his money – money that was as much hers as his.

Resentment stirred, drying her tears. She would not ask Stuart Monroe to return the money. Never! If it had spoilt some of Aden's plans, so much the better. It was a small revenge but it was something.

Somehow she had to carry on as if nothing had happened. Nan and her husband were coming to dinner. Aden had promised to be there but perhaps it was best that he had forgotten. She would have to find some excuse for his absence.

Sighing, Rebecca went to the mirror to brush her hair. It was too bad of him to force a quarrel on her this evening. The action of brushing soothed her. Anger was driving out the pain. That was better. It was easier to cope with anger.

Aden swallowed the whisky, feeling it burn all the way down his throat. It warmed him, taking away some of the numbness that had possessed him as he drove the pony and trap into Chatteris. What the hell was he going to do? Rebecca had no idea what she had done when she drew out that money ... damn her and her charities! She'd had no right ... no right ...

'Your call, Aden.'

He looked up as Keith Hauxton spoke, coming to himself for a moment. Glancing at his hand he saw that he had three aces and two kings – and he hadn't even noticed. He pushed ten guineas into the pot, then another ten.

'Raise you,' he said, his eyes meeting those of the man sitting opposite him. 'Not too steep for you, Josuha?'

For a moment pure hatred glittered in the other man's eyes. The enmity had grown up between them over the years and it was foolish of Aden to have let himself be drawn into a feud that would probably ruin him. He knew it but he was caught up in a reckless mood – one that bordered on black despair.

'I'll see you.' Hauxton paid the twenty guineas and waited as Aden laid down his hand, then scowled. 'Your luck is in tonight, Sawle. Too good for me.'

Aden reached for the small pile of coins and notes. About sixty or seventy pounds. Enough to tide him over the next week. He ought to leave the table now, call it quits while he was ahead.

'What do you say we raise the stakes to twenty guineas?' Hauxton's eyes glittered with deliberate malice, as if he had somehow guessed that Aden was in trouble. 'Or have you had enough?' His brows rose as Aden was silent. 'Too deep for you perhaps?'

'Take care,' Keith said in a low voice. 'He's the very devil, Aden. Don't let him get his hooks into you the way he has me ...'

Aden glanced up as the door of the private room opened and the landlord came in. 'Bring us another bottle of whisky, will you?' he said, his eyes never leaving Joshua Hauxton's face. 'Twenty guineas? Why not? I feel lucky this evening ...'

22

The evening was not a success. Rebecca did her best to appear at ease but knew she hadn't made a very good job of it. Nan was obviously sympathetic but didn't know what was wrong, and her husband was bewildered by Aden's absence. He kept asking if he would be much longer, forcing Rebecca to invent excuses. She felt humiliated and annoyed. Aden had always insisted on keeping up appearances in public – now he had left her to entertain their guests alone. If it had been anyone but Nan the news would have been all over the village by the next morning.

'It was business, I'm afraid,' she apologized as she saw them to the door at the end of a long and difficult evening. 'Aden must have been delayed. He will be so sorry to have missed you.'

'It was a wonderful dinner.' Nan kissed her, whispering in her ear: 'It doesn't matter, Rebecca. We've had a lovely time. You and Aden must come to us soon.'

'Yes, of course. Thank you.'

Rebecca waved to her friends then went back into the parlour, tidying a few cushions as she walked restlessly about the room. She had answered Nan's invitation automatically but she was fearful for the future. Aden had never missed one of her dinner parties before. Was this his way of showing her that their marriage was finally over? She thought about it as she walked upstairs and undressed. Perhaps that would be best. A clean break instead of this lingering agony ...

She was not sure what woke her. Some slight sound ... in her room! There it was again. She sat up in alarm as something fell over. Someone was in the room.

She turned up the lamp by her bed and was startled to see Aden lying on the floor just inside the door. For a moment she couldn't imagine what he was doing there. Was something wrong with him? She threw back the covers and jumped out of bed, hurrying to his side.

'Aden,' she said anxiously. 'Are you ill? What's the matter?'

As she knelt beside him she caught the stink of whisky on his breath and was shocked as she realized he must have been drinking heavily. Her sympathy waned, to be replaced with revulsion. He knew how much she disliked overindulgence in strong drink. She touched his shoulder and he jerked, moaning slightly.

'You're drunk.' She sat back on her heels. 'Aden – how could you? How could you?'

He opened his eyes and stared at her. His expression was so strange that she found it disturbing. Was he ill or what? That hint of desperation worried her. It wasn't Aden looking at her from his eyes; it was someone else, a man she didn't know – a man on the brink of despair.

'Only a lil' bit,' he muttered thickly. 'Just enough to get me through.'

'You're a fool,' she said, more sharply than she had intended, and rose to her feet. 'Drinking is a sign of weakness, Aden. I thought you had more sense – more guts.'

He had pulled himself up to an unsteady but upright position using the post of her brass bed, which gleamed dully in the light from the oil lamp. He stood leering at her, an aggressive, bitter expression twisting his face. She felt his anger and frustration and something more, an underlying desperation that she didn't understand. What was wrong with him? What was she missing?

'But you don't know me,' he muttered. 'Always let you down, haven't I? Never quite good enough, never what you wanted.'

'Don't be ridiculous ...' She began, but the words died on her lips as he moved towards her. Something in his manner frightened her. This wasn't the man she had married ... the man she loved. 'Aden ...'

She was frightened of the person who looked at her from his eyes. This was what strong drink did to men, turning them from likeable human beings into mindless devils: it was the reason she tried so hard to help the women who were too often their victims.

How many times had she heard those words on the lips of the women who came to the mission? 'It was the drink in him, missus. He's a good man really – but the drink takes him bad. It ain't him, not really.'

'No, Aden,' she whispered, backing away as he lurched unsteadily towards her. 'Don't ... please don't.'

It was in his eyes – those terrible, staring, desperate eyes.

'Always him you wanted. Never me. Never me!' His hands shot out, grabbing hold of her upper arms, his fingers burying themselves deep in her flesh like steel vices, bruising her, hurting her. 'Was it ever me in your mind when you moaned and sighed beneath me?' He shook her like a rag doll. 'Tell me, Rebecca. Tell me!'

He was so tall and strong and powerful – so angry. 'Of course it was you,' she whispered hoarsely. 'Stop this, Aden. Don't be a fool. Don't do this. Go to bed and we'll talk in ...'

She meant to say that they would sort it all out in the morning but the pressure of his grip intensified as he pushed her back against the bed and she fell on to it; it was so sudden and unexpected that it seemed to trigger something in Aden's brain. She saw a flash of pain or anger in his eyes, then, before she knew what he meant to do, he was on top of her, his hands reaching beneath her nightgown, forcing her legs apart. She knew what he was going to do and she struggled but was trapped by the overpowering weight of his body.

'No, Aden,' she cried. 'No. Not like this. Please, not like this ...'

It was doubtful that he even heard her. He seemed to have lost all sense of reality and was intent on plundering her body, punishing her ... exacting revenge for all the years when he believed she had withheld her love. He acted without thought or feeling, perhaps without truly knowing what he was doing. Yet she made a last protest, hoping to penetrate the mist of anger and alcohol in his brain.

'Don't, Aden. If you ever cared for me ... if you ever loved me, don't do this. Please ...'

It was a waste of breath. His first savage thrust made her cry out with pain. Not once in all the years of their marriage had he ever taken his pleasure without thought of pleasuring her. She had always been ready for him so that he slid into her moistness with a silken ease but now she was as dry and tight as a virgin and he hurt her. He hurt her badly.

There was no point in fighting him. His strength was far superior to hers and he had her pinned across the bed so that she was trapped beneath his bulk, unable to move. Besides, she could not scream with her innocent children lying asleep in their beds at the end of the hall. She could not let them hear her. All she could do was to lie there and let him have his way.

The physical pain was as nothing compared to the mental anguish she suffered as he thrust and moaned above her. How he must hate her to do this! If he had cared or even felt some respect for her he would surely never have behaved so badly. She had longed for him to come to her so many nights and now ... this humiliation.

When he had finished he slumped across her as if all the life had gone out of him. For a moment or two she lay still, then she pushed him away and he rolled to one side, lying on his stomach with his face buried in the pillows. She thought he was asleep but after another minute or so he made a choking sound in his throat.

'Forgive me, Rebecca.' The words were muffled, hardly audible. 'I'm sorry. I never meant ... I was out of my mind ... I'm sorry ...'

'You were drunk,' she said coldly. She felt numb with shock, unable to think clearly. 'I can't forgive you. I never shall but it doesn't matter. It makes no difference.'

She turned on her side, her back to him, holding back the slow, painful tears that burned against her eyelids. She wouldn't let him see her cry. She could feel the weight of his body beside her on the bed and she knew when he moved, when he left the bed and stood there hesitating, looking down at her as she hid her face from him.

'Believe me,' he said in an odd, strangled tone, 'I'm sorry ... for everything.'

She lay with her face in shadow as he walked to the door and went out, her cheeks wet with the tears that would not be stopped.

'Aden ... Oh, Aden,' she whispered into her pillows as the door closed behind him. 'How could you? How could you?'

He had shown his utter contempt for her by using her in that way. She was angry but more than anything else she was hurt. This one act seemed to show that there was nothing left of the love he had once felt for her. Nothing of the Aden who had treated her as if she were something precious ... something to be revered and adored.

'Aden ... Aden ...' She had thought that nothing could hurt

more than when he'd told her he was going to another woman but now she knew she was wrong.

She wept for a while, then slept fitfully. When she woke she was restless, torn by conflicting emotions and the memory of that terrible look in Aden's eyes.

Why had he got drunk in the first place? What had prompted him to come to her room? Had he meant to hurt and humiliate her because of their quarrel earlier? Had it been premeditated or ...?

Her thoughts were confused. Aden had never been a violent man, nor had she ever known him to be vindictive. Had she pushed him too far? If his act had been merely the result of his unaccustomed drinking ... perhaps it was not quite the callous brutality she had thought but something more human. Not that it made it any better but perhaps it was understandable ... even forgivable?

Was she like one of those women she had pitied – the women who allowed themselves to be used and then made excuses for their husbands? Surely not! Drunkenness revolted her: it always had. Philip Braithewaite's attack on her all those years ago at Celia's party had ensured that she would forever find such behaviour abhorrent. Her work for the Temperance movement was rooted in her disgust for the evils of intoxication – and yet she might be able to forgive Aden this once.

She had believed that he no longer found her attractive, but if his act had not been one of revenge ... a tiny seed of hope stirred inside her. If he had been driven to force by desperation ... because he wanted her ...

Had she misunderstood all this time? Her heart jerked painfully. Was Aden as lonely and miserable as she had been? Was there still something between them despite all the quarrels and the bitterness?

23

She ought to hate him but she didn't. Her thoughts went round and round in her head, tormenting her. She could smell the musk of his body on her pillows and it set up a nostalgic longing in her – a sadness she could not fully explain even to herself.

'Aden ... Aden ...'

A part of her still felt hurt and humiliated by what he had done. Rape was a vile and wicked act, even, or perhaps particularly, when it happened in the marriage bed. Yet she could understand why a man might be driven to such a desperate act: if he believed his wife had never loved him, that she had always wanted another man. If Aden had hurt her, then she had also inflicted pain, perhaps more than she had ever known or suspected.

'Rebecca Sawle, you're such a fool!'

These misunderstandings had gone on for far too long! She could lie there in her bed and feel sorry for herself or she could do something about it. She could go to Aden and demand an explanation – as she ought to have done months ago.

Pride had made her accept the situation. She had stood by and let him go to his mistress. But pride made a poor bedfellow. She was tired of sleeping alone. She wanted her husband back. The knowledge flooded through her like a strong, clear light. No matter what Aden had done, no matter what he was, she still wanted him ... still loved him.

Flinging back the covers she slipped on her dressing gown and glanced at herself in the long, cheval mirror. Her figure was too heavy for her own liking and she had never been a beauty, but perhaps Aden still found her attractive. Why else should he come to her room?

This was not the time for hesitation or doubts. She had wasted too much time already. She must follow her instincts now while she could muster the courage. Aden's behaviour had broken the ice, bringing down the barriers they had erected between them. It was now or never.

Her pulses were fluttering like nervous butterflies as she walked the few, short steps down the hall to his room. It was cold and her bare feet felt as if they were freezing but she hadn't stopped to find her slippers. Outside his door she paused, her courage faltering. Supposing she was wrong? Supposing he had simply wanted revenge?

'Don't be a coward,' she whispered softly to herself. 'Better to know the truth than torture yourself wondering and regretting.'

She opened the door and went in, her heart beating very fast. What if he was still angry ... what if he laughed at her?

'Aden ... are you asleep? I want to talk to you.'

It took her a moment or two to adjust to the semi-darkness and a few more to realize that he was not in his bed. The covers were still smooth and unrumpled, so he had not gone to his room after he left her. Was he sleeping it off downstairs or in one of the children's rooms?

She opened their doors carefully, not wanting to wake them. Jay and Fanny were sleeping soundly, their faces flushed and pink. Richie was at boarding school and his room was empty, as were the guest rooms. Where could Aden be? She was aware of a creeping coldness as she went downstairs, still hoping to find him curled up on a sofa but beginning to suspect otherwise.

She looked everywhere but there was no sign of him. It was a quarter to three in the morning and he was not in the house. Had he gone to her – that woman? She felt a swift, scything anger at the thought. If he could do that then there really was nothing left of their marriage. But had he?

She had not heard anything, no sound of wheels rattling on the road outside. She opened the back door, stepping out on to the stone flags and feeling the bitter chill strike through her. A pony was snickering in the paddock – but was it one of the children's pets or the beautiful, high-stepping creature Aden kept to pull the smart rig he drove when he went into town?

It was too dark to see and she had no desire to investigate at this hour of the morning.

'Damn you, Aden Sawle,' she muttered as she went back to her bed. 'If you've gone to her, I hope you land in a ditch and break your neck!'

Aden did not come in for his breakfast the next morning.

Rebecca was upset because it seemed to prove that he had gone to her – that woman in Chatteris – though if he had he must have walked for his pony and trap had not been taken. He might have decided to walk to sober himself up, of course. It wasn't that far. She could do it herself if she had a mind to.

She brooded over his absence for hours, alternating between anger and frustration.

'You can damned well stay there as far as I'm concerned!' she said aloud, and thumped the pastry she was making when he still hadn't arrived by noon. 'If you dare to come slinking back with the smell of her on you, I'll kill you.'

'Is something the matter, Mrs Sawle?'

Molly came into the kitchen carrying a darning mushroom and a pile of working socks which she was about to mend. She looked startled when she saw the way Rebecca was thumping the pastry, as well she might; the reason Rebecca still made her own pastry was that she prided herself on her light touch. The jam tarts she was making were going to be as hard as iron.

'No, nothing is wrong,' she said, and slammed the oven door, causing the skewer rack to wobble and then fall over. 'I'm going out, Molly – and if Mr Sawle wants to know when I'll be back, you have no idea.'

How dare Aden do this? How dare he? She was seething with anger.

Molly stared after her as she marched from the room. Rebecca wasn't sure what she meant to do as she put on her hat and coat. Perhaps she started out to visit Nan but her feet had a mind of their own and she was taking the lane behind the lovely old church of Saint Mary's to Five Winds before she realized where she was going.

May Harris was hanging out washing when she arrived. Her daughter Sorrel was playing ball against the wall of the cottage. She stopped to stare as Rebecca walked towards her, tipping her head to one side, her eyes bright and curious.

'Is your father about, Sorrel?'

'He's behind the barn, I think. Shall I fetch him for you?' She glanced at Rebecca's shoes. 'It's muddy in the yard.'

At that moment there was something about the child that reminded Rebecca of Ruth Perry ... something in the eyes or way of speaking.

'I'm aware of that,' she said, more sharply than she'd intended. 'I can find my own way, thank you.'

Sorrel flushed, then ran off to her mother as Rebecca set out in the direction of the barn. The mud squelched over her shoes and she frowned in annoyance, knowing that she was wrong to have refused the child's offer of help: Sorrel couldn't help it if she had a look of her aunt about her.

Sid Harris was talking to one of the labourers when she saw him. They were examining a pair of wooden hames, used over the horse collars to hold the trace chains, which appeared to have broken.

'Mrs Sawle.' Sid tried to hide his surprise at seeing her but was not very successful. 'Morning.' He touched his cap, an anxious expression in his eyes. 'Bit warmer today.'

'Yes, I suppose it is. I hadn't noticed.'

Sid coughed nervously and hitched up his trousers. He was a large man with a weather-roughened complexion and a big belly which overhung his belt, but she had always found him pleasant to speak to – and he was Aden's closest friend.

'I have a message for my husband,' Rebecca said. 'Have you any idea where I could find him?'

Sid lifted his worn checked cap and scratched beneath it; his light brown hair was thinning and his scalp looked pink and shiny.

'Can't say as I do.' He hesitated, seeming uneasy. 'I was wanting a word with him myself.'

Rebecca sensed there was something on his mind. 'What's the matter?' she said. Sid hesitated; he was clearly bothered and it seemed he wanted to say something, then he shook his head, obviously deciding against it. She pressed him again, asking, 'Are you sure there's nothing I can do?'

He cleared his throat, still uncomfortable. 'It was just something I needed to talk to Aden about,' he said. 'But you might ask him to come round when you see him – if you wouldn't mind?'

'Of course I will.'

She nodded and walked back across the yard, keeping her skirt clear of the mud. May was at the door of the dairy. She waved, looking curious and hopeful, as if expecting Rebecca to stop.

'Anything I can do for you?'

'No, nothing – except send me round some butter this afternoon if you will.'

May had a cream fleeter in her hand and was obviously about to start making the butter; it was hard work and needed patience, as the churn handle took a lot of turning.

'Shall I see you at the church hall this weekend – for the bazaar?'

'Yes, I expect so.'

Rebecca nodded and walked on. She was in no mood for gossip that particular morning.

Her anger was slowly building. She would certainly have something to say to Aden when he did come home!

Rebecca was too restless to go straight home and decided she would pay Nan a visit after all. As she passed Sarah's old cottage she stopped to watch the thatcher at work. He was repairing the roof, laying bundles of straw at a slant and pegging down the spars across it, then laying more straw so that the spars were hidden: when it was finished it would be a smooth slope of gold.

The cottage had been left empty for some time but Rebecca could see that an extension had been built on at the back and Aden had commissioned a whole new roof instead of patching it as he usually did. She wondered why he had gone to so much trouble, then put it out of her mind as she walked on past: there were more urgent matters needing her attention.

Nan was busy making griddle cakes when she arrived and there was a delicious smell of oats browning. She took one look at Rebecca's face and put the kettle on the hob.

'I won't ask,' she said, 'but nothing can be that bad, Rebecca.'

'I think Aden has left me for someone else.'

Nan looked horrified and Rebecca felt a flicker of wry amusement. Nan was so secure in her marriage. Her husband was a quiet, bookish man, devoted to her and his work in the parish. He would not even think of being unfaithful to her.

'Surely not?'

'He has had someone for a while now. You must have heard the gossip, Nan?'

'I never listen to gossip, you know that – especially about my friends.' Her eyes were soft with sympathy. 'You must be mistaken, Rebecca. Aden wouldn't leave you and the children. Even if …' She stopped, not wanting to say the words. 'Well, you know.'

'We had a terrible row last night. He thinks I've never loved him.'

'But you do, don't you?' Nan's smooth brow wrinkled with concentration. She was the mother of two healthy boys but as thin as a rake, always cheerful and full of energy. 'I've always thought Aden was very fond of you.'

'That might have been true once,' Rebecca said on a sigh, 'but not any longer.'

'You still care for him, though? You didn't ask him to leave?'

'No – but it was an awful quarrel.'

Rebecca would not tell her all the sordid details. It would shock her and she might think badly of Aden. Rebecca was not prepared to expose him to public scorn, no matter what he had done.

'These things happen now and then – even in this house.' Nan screwed up her nose as Rebecca's face reflected disbelief. 'Oh, I assure you, we have our moments. Come on, have a cup of tea.' She poured the fragrant liquid into a dainty cup and looked at Rebecca. 'Are you sure you're not making too much out of this?'

'No, I'm not sure. I'm not sure of anything.'

'Drink that.' She pushed the cup of hot, strong, sweet tea in front of Rebecca. 'I would put something stronger in it but I know how you feel about alcohol.'

Rebecca drew a shaky breath. 'That's just it – Aden was drunk last night. I've never known him to come home in that condition before. We'd had words earlier and he stormed out – that's why he wasn't there for dinner – and he must have gone off to get drunk.'

'That's a good sign – I think.' Nan looked apologetic as Rebecca's head jerked up. 'Aden doesn't often drink, you say?'

'He likes the odd whisky or a couple of beers, but I've never known him to go too far before.'

'Well then ...' A naughty chuckle escaped Nan. 'It sounds to me as though you lit a fire under him. I think you're worrying over nothing, Rebecca. He'll come back when he's ready. The point is, will you let him come?' She hesitated, then gave Rebecca a straight look. 'I mean – without making him crawl?'

If anyone else had said such a thing Rebecca would have been mortally offended but Nan was her closest friend and she accepted the implied rebuke without anger.

'I shan't do that,' she said. 'I might have once but ... I'm wiser now. I've learned the hard way. I want him back, Nan – there, I've said it. Do you think I'm a fool?'

'I would if you didn't want him.' Nan's teasing expression made Rebecca laugh. 'That's better. We all need to laugh at ourselves sometimes.'

'Why have you never told me this before?'

'Would I dare?' Their eyes met in perfect understanding. 'He'll come back,' Nan said. 'He would be a fool not to – and I've never thought of Aden as a fool.'

Nan had made Rebecca feel much better. Surely she was right? Aden would not leave his children without a word. Even if he had no feeling for Rebecca, he loved them – and his land. He could not walk away from his land. He would come home soon.

She waited all that day, feeling nervous and on edge as the afternoon wore on and then it was evening. Where was he? Surely he wasn't afraid to come home?

She listened to every sound … for his footsteps in the hall, on the stairs … hoping and praying. When she was too tired to sit up any longer she went to bed and slept but was awake soon after dawn.

The house felt empty and she knew even before she looked that Aden had not come home. He had never spent the night with his mistress before, never stayed away this long. A sense of dread began to mount inside her. Was this the end of their marriage at last? Aden had said they would stay together for the sake of the children but now it seemed that he had changed his mind. He had walked out on them, left without a word. She was torn between anger and grief.

At breakfast that morning Jay seemed restless and anxious, and at last he asked her where Aden was.

'I haven't seen Father,' he said, cramming a piece of toast and marmalade into his mouth and spitting crumbs. 'Where is he?'

'Don't talk with your mouth full, Jay. It is very bad manners.'

He swallowed hastily. 'He promised me a new cricket bat. I've been selected for the school team but I need a new bat.'

'Your father had to go somewhere,' Rebecca replied, patting her mouth with a spotless, white napkin and refusing to meet his eyes. 'There's no hurry, is there? You won't need the bat for a few weeks yet.'

'He promised.' Jay's scowl reminded her of Aden and her heart caught. 'Besides, Father never goes away. You do …' His eyes were accusing. 'But he doesn't.'

'Well, he has this time.'

'Father promised me a new perambulator for my doll,' Fanny said, her face bright with anticipation. 'When Jay has his bat. Where is he? I want him …' Her eyes filled with easy tears.

'I've told you both. Your father is away.'

'But where?' Fanny's mouth set stubbornly. She was used to having too much of her own way. Rebecca had spoiled her. 'Why won't you tell us?'

'Because it isn't your business, either of you. If your father isn't home by next weekend I'll buy you that bat, Jay. Now go to your Sunday school classes – and look after your sister. I don't want those Harris boys pulling her hair again. And make sure you both come straight home afterwards.'

All the village children enjoyed attending Nan's Sunday school classes because she was always thinking up special treats for them, like magic lantern shows and outings to the seaside in summer. Fanny had recently started to attend and Rebecca had insisted that Jay should walk with her, which caused long faces on both of them but especially Jay, who liked to be with his own friends.

Jay gave her a mutinous look but left the table without another word. Fanny planted a sticky kiss on her mother's cheek, then scrambled after him. Rebecca heard her shouting to him to wait as they grabbed their coats from the hallstand, then Molly's mildly scolding tones as they flew through the kitchen. She was very fond of them both and Rebecca often thought Molly ought to have children of her own, though she knew it was unlikely she would ever marry.

Molly was not the marrying kind and perhaps she had more sense than the rest of them!

She gave Rebecca an odd look as she came to clear the table. 'Have you finished, Mrs Sawle?'

'Yes, Molly. You can clear now.' Rebecca pushed back her chair, realizing that Molly would have to be told something. 'Aden has gone away for a few days. I'm not sure when he will be back – it's business.'

Molly's cheeks flushed as she looked down at the table, clattering the cups and plates on to her tray. 'Oh … yes, Mrs Sawle.'

She knew Rebecca was lying, of course, but for as long as neither of them said anything out of place she would accept it. Eventually she would have to know the truth, as would the children – but not just yet.

'Only …' Molly seemed uneasy. 'Sid Harris was here earlier. He said he wanted to see Mr Sawle urgently.'

'Did he?' Rebecca recalled Sid's worried manner the previous day. 'He didn't say why?'

'No, just that it was important.'

'Very well. I'll go round and see him myself later.'

What could be important enough to bring Sid to the house on a Sunday morning? He had had something on his mind the previous day, Rebecca had sensed it, but he hadn't wanted to tell her. Well, now he would have to.

'What do you mean – there's no money to pay the men?' Rebecca stared at Sid as he coughed nervously and hitched up his trousers. He was so uneasy that it set her nerves on edge. 'Surely Aden always pays them on Friday night? This is only Sunday …'

'I'm talking about last week's money, Mrs Sawle. They haven't been paid for last week. Aden said he would be here on Friday as usual but he didn't come. I didn't like to mention it yesterday when you were here. I wouldn't have said anything today if you hadn't insisted …'

'You mean, no one has been paid this week? Not even you?'

'I don't mind for myself,' Sid said and looked uncomfortable. 'But it means hardship for some. I've paid a few bob out myself to help, but I can't manage to pay all that's owing.'

'Nor should you have to,' Rebecca said, feeling a surge of annoyance. 'I can't imagine what Aden was thinking of – to go away without paying the wages. How much do you need?'

'Thirty pounds for the men …'

'And for yourself – for reimbursement?'

'Another ten – but that can wait.'

'You shall have it now,' Rebecca said. 'Please send your eldest boy to the house straight away.'

'I'd best come myself, Mrs Sawle. The lad might lose it. Not that he's careless, mind, but it's a lot of money and I'd rather see to it myself.'

'As you wish. I'm going home now and I shall pay you myself. You will see that everyone gets their money – even though it is a Sunday?'

It was wrong to think of doing business on the Lord's day, of course, and she was upset that it should be necessary – but that was Aden's fault. He always went to Chatteris once a week without fail to fetch the men's wages from the bank. She could not understand what had happened.

Suddenly she remembered how their quarrel had started. Aden had been furious over that donation to the new hostel. He had demanded that she ask for the money to be returned and she had refused. Very properly, she had thought at the time.

Two thousand pounds was a large sum of money but not beyond their means ... or so she had thought. They always seemed to have plenty of spare money. Once when she'd asked at the bank they'd had four or five thousand pounds just sitting there doing nothing. Of course that must have been two or three years ago but the money had been there when she'd inquired at the bank a few days before making the donation. And she had certainly mentioned her intention to Aden some months previously, though he hadn't taken much notice and she hadn't been precise about the sum she needed. It wasn't until just recently that she had known for sure how much it would be.

Had Aden bought more land? Was that why money was short at the moment? Sometimes he bought impulsively and for a while he might need to borrow – if that were the case the money she had taken might have made things difficult for him temporarily. But surely not to the extent of his being unable to pay the wages!

She felt a quiver of unease. The bank would surely advance Aden forty pounds even if he was a little overdrawn – wouldn't they? He sometimes took risks, she knew that, but he had never once suggested that she should be careful because money was tight.

It was very odd and it worried her. Thank goodness she had some money in her dressing-table drawer.

She was able to pay Sid Harris from that.

'Aden must have forgotten,' she said as she saw the relief in his face. 'I'm very sorry about this. If it should happen again, please come to me at once.'

'Thank you, Mrs Sawle. I expect it was like you said. Aden must have had something on his mind; it's not like him to forget. Always most particular about the wages, he's been.'

'Yes – as he should be,' Rebecca said. 'Please apologize for the delay, won't you?'

'I'll do that, Mrs Sawle.' He tipped his cap and went off, leaving her to stare at the table in front of her.

She still had thirty pounds in her drawer upstairs. Enough to pay for her own needs for a while but not enough for next week's wages ...

But surely Aden would come home before then? Even if he wanted to end their marriage he could not simply abandon the farm and all his men; they depended on him for the very food they put in their mouths. No, he would never shirk his responsibilities ... even if he had problems. Problems she had never even suspected until now.

Was he in some sort of trouble over money? He had given her no hint of it ... but then, he had kept secrets from her before this. Secrets ... how many secrets had her husband kept from her over the years?

Why hadn't he told her if he was in difficulty? She could have helped him to sort out his problems if he'd only ... but he had always gone his own way, hiding the truth from her, keeping his secrets.

Secrets had a way of coming out and when they did they so often led to tragedy.

24

The gipsies had camped at the edge of a wood overnight, their waggons separated from each other by little clumps of trees, the horses tethered at intervals along the narrow, muddy track to graze where they could. Lorenzo's waggon was some distance away from the others, in a little clearing further into the woods, a spot chosen by Shima because it was near to a small stream. He had taken their horses down to the shallow edge to drink before finding somewhere for them to graze. Tarina had gone looking for more firewood after having brought in enough to start their fire; she stopped to talk to the youth, who was often the only one to have a kind word for her.

Sadie was skinning a rabbit for the stew pot; it was the first meat they had tasted in days and it was a poor dab of a thing she had caught in her own trap. Lorenzo had contributed neither food nor money to their living for some weeks now. He complained constantly of a pain in his guts and she could see him wasting away before her eyes; she knew it could only be a matter of time now and sometimes when he was in a foul temper she wished him dead.

She could hear him moving about in the van, cursing and knocking into things. He had been drunk the night before – so drunk that when he'd stumbled into their van and fallen on the floor she'd let him lie in his own vomit. He would likely be in rare mood this morning and she would be best out of his way.

'Sadie!' He came to the top of the steps and roared her name before she had time to escape. 'Damn you, woman! Get yourself round here, you skinny bitch, or I'll give you the hiding of your life.'

'Now what's eating you?' she muttered and moved towards him reluctantly. 'I've work to do if we're to eat today, and it's no thanks to you that there's meat in the pot.'

'What's this then?' Lorenzo's bloodshot eyes glowed like hot coals as he thrust a small leather pouch under her nose. 'Know what's in here, do you? Know where I found it?'

Sadie went cold all over. She knew what was in the pouch and where he had found it.

'That's mine,' she muttered defensively. 'You've no right to touch it.'

'No right? No right!' Lorenzo gave a shout of anger and lunged at her, catching her wrist before she could move out of his way. His fingers dug into her flesh, twisting viciously until she cried out in pain. 'Where did you get the money – twenty gold pieces! You've had money all the time and yet you never ceased to complain that there was none coming in. And what do these words mean?' He waved the paper under her nose.

It was a mercy that he had never learned to read. She raised her head, facing him defiantly.

'It's nothing – just the name of someone I once knew, that's all …'

Lorenzo screwed the useless scrap of paper into a ball and pushed it against her mouth. Sadie struggled, trying to twist away from him, but he grabbed her by the throat and forced her to open her lips, thrusting the paper inside.

'Now eat it,' he said. 'Eat it, you bitch, or I'll break your neck.'

His hand tightened about her throat. She chewed and then swallowed and he thrust her away so that she fell on her knees in the mud before him. He kicked out at her and she screamed in pain as his heavy boot struck her ribs.

'Now tell me the truth,' he said. 'What was on that bit of paper – and where did the money come from?'

'It was my mother's … she got it from a …'

'Liar!' Lorenzo aimed another kick at her. 'If you don't tell me, I'll kick it out of you …'

'Stop it!' The voice came from behind them. 'Leave her alone. Leave her alone.'

Leyan suddenly flew at his father from behind. Because the attack came as a complete surprise Lorenzo was caught off balance and fell to the ground where he lay for a moment, clutching at his stomach and groaning while Leyan stared at him in terror. He was twelve years old, still small and slight for his age – and he had been beaten so often by this man that he whimpered in his dreams and wet himself night after night. He had acted impulsively, out of fear for his mother, and his courage vanished the instant Lorenzo was down.

Sadie was on her feet first. She jerked her head at Leyan, gesturing to him to get out of the way as his father struggled to stand upright, his boots slipping and sliding in the thick mud, hands still clutching at himself.

'I'll kill that brat ...' he swore and spat on the ground; his spittle was stained with crimson. 'I'll kill that bastard ...'

'No!' Sadie raised her head and looked into his eyes. She was angry and her anger overwhelmed the fear. 'Leyan is your son – your only son.' Lorenzo stared at her in bewilderment and she laughed, throwing back her head and mocking him. 'You may well stare, you fool! That gorgio woman blinded you, Lorenzo. Her son was not yours. She lied to you ... yes, lied to you. When she died she confessed the name of her lover and I wrote it down so that I should not forget. The twenty gold pieces were hers. She hid them from you and I found them when I burnt her clothes.'

Lorenzo gave a terrible cry, like a wild animal caught in a trap, and sprang at her, knocking her to the ground. 'Liar ... liar ...' he cried in a strangled voice. 'Liar ... Shima is mine ...'

Sadie struggled desperately. The ground was soaked after a heavy rain the night before; she could feel the damp soaking into her clothes and the mud against her hair and face, but her overriding feeling was one of fatality. She knew that one of them would die now – it was his life or hers. The knife she had used for skinning the rabbit was still in her hand and she struck him in the side. He gave a great howl of pain and jerked away from her. Sadie rolled from under him and crawled on her hands and knees until she was out of his reach, then got to her feet and looked for another weapon. She reached for a thick, round stick Tarina had brought in for the fire and stood holding it ready as Lorenzo dragged himself to his feet.

He had pulled the knife from his side and she could see blood seeping through his shirt, but the wound was only flesh deep. Now he would kill her.

'You skinny bitch,' he muttered. 'Tell me you lied or I'll kill you ...'

'She didn't lie,' Leyan cried. 'I know who Shima's father is!'

'No …' Sadie cried as Lorenzo rounded on the child like a mad bull. She raised her stick and rushed at him, hitting him on the back, and then as he turned to defend himself, in the stomach. 'He's your son, you fool! Your only …'

She was suddenly silent as Lorenzo doubled up in agony and the crimson froth started to bubble from his mouth. He sank to his knees in front of her then slumped forward, twitching and jerking as the blood ran out of his mouth. And then all at once he lay still.

Sadie knelt beside him, heaving at him, turning him over. His eyes were wide and staring, the blood still trickling from the corner of his mouth.

'He's dead,' she whispered. 'Dead … Lorenzo …'

She moaned, running her hands over his face, smearing his flesh with the blood, mixing it with the mud and filth and then rocking back and forth on her heels. He had once been so strong and handsome … such a fine lover.

'Come away, Sadie,' a new voice said behind her and she felt hands on her shoulders, lifting her up. 'It's a mercy. He's been in pain for months now.'

Sadie whirled round on the lad who had helped her, anger and hatred in her dark eyes. 'It was your fault,' she screamed. 'Your fault. Your mother lied to him … she cheated him of the fortune that should have been his.'

'Sadie?' Shima stared at her. He had come on them at the last moment and knew nothing of what had been said, what had caused the tragedy. 'What are you saying?'

Sadie saw the bag of gold coins lying on the ground where Lorenzo had dropped them. She shook the coins into her hand then threw them at Shima, striking him in the face.

'Blood money … blood money …'

He touched his cheek and felt the blood where a coin had cut him. 'What are you talking about? My mother lied …'

'You were not Lorenzo's son,' Sadie cried. She flew at him in a sudden frenzy, hitting him about the face and head with her stick. 'Murderer … murderer … you killed him. It was because of you …'

Shima put up his hands to ward her off. He was nearly fourteen and capable of defending himself if he had tried but he was bewildered, stunned by his father's death and her anger.

'Sadie … tell me?'

She had worn herself out with her fury. She drew back, panting for breath, old and ugly in her grief. 'The money belonged to your mother,' she said at last. 'Take it and go – you are not one of us. You have never been one of us.'

'Where should I go?' Shima glanced at the gold coins lying at his feet, then at the body of the man he had believed was his father. 'What about Lorenzo?'

'Leave him to us,' Sadie muttered. 'He is ours.'

'But where ... where should I go?'

'Go to Mepal,' Sadie said. 'Speak to Aden Sawle. Ask him for the truth.'

Shima stared at his father for a moment more, then he turned away, leaving the gold coins scattered on the ground, walking and then running as the grief began to tear at his heart. He heard Tarina cry out to him to stop but didn't look round as the tears began to roll down his cheeks.

25

Rebecca stopped to talk as she saw Nan outside the church. She had been to evening service and it was a cold, wet night.

'Have you heard from Aden?' Nan asked, looking anxious as Rebecca shook her head. 'He's sure to be in touch soon but if he isn't ... you don't think he might be ill?'

'I don't know. I suppose it's possible.'

'Perhaps we should make inquiries?'

'Aden would hate it if he came back and found everyone was gossiping about his disappearance.' Rebecca was almost sure she knew where he was but didn't want to admit it, even to her friend.

'I think he's just sulking,' she said. 'He was in such a mood.' Still, he must have been very disturbed to have gone off and forgotten about paying his men.

'Just as you like. I'm sure he'll come back anyway,' Nan said, and kissed her cheek. 'Now, there's something else I've been meaning to talk to you about, Rebecca. I think we should try to encourage a programme of immunisation against smallpox in the village. The children first, of course, then their mothers – and we might even persuade some of the men to join in.'

'Yes, that sounds like a good idea,' Rebecca said, but without much enthusiasm. 'We'll talk about it again another day.'

'Yes, of course. You can't think about it now, Rebecca. It was silly of me to raise the subject.'

'It's just that it isn't like Aden to behave like this.'

Nan nodded and pressed her hand to show that she understood and they parted. Rebecca's pace increased as she reached her home. Perhaps Aden would have come home while she had been

246

at church … perhaps he would be waiting for her and they could sort it all out …

When the following Thursday dawned and Aden still had not come home Rebecca knew she had to do something. The men's wages were due again the next day and this time she could not pay them. Besides, she was beginning to worry. Supposing something had happened to him?

'I need to go into Chatteris,' she said to Sid Harris when she went round to the farm later that morning. 'Could you spare one of the men to drive me in, please?'

'Of course, Mrs Sawle. I'll take you myself. We need a few bits and pieces for the yard. I can order them from the iron-monger's while we're there.'

'Thank you.' She smiled apologetically. 'Aden talked once of buying an automobile. I might have learned to drive that myself, but I've never been able to handle the horses – not even Aden's pony.'

One of the oddest things about this whole affair was that Aden had not taken the pony and trap with him. Had he walked to Chatteris that night?

He had been behaving very oddly. It wasn't like him to get drunk, nor to stay away, particularly without letting anyone know where he was. Supposing Nan was right and he was ill? A chill of fear went through her. He might be lying in a ditch somewhere … but no, he would have been found before this.

She brought her attention back to what Sid was saying.

'Someone can always take you – but if ever you wanted to learn how to drive the trap, I'd teach you.'

She smiled and shook her head. Aden had offered to teach her long ago but she had refused, because she couldn't conquer her silly fear of horses. She had thought she might like to drive the motor car he'd talked of but somehow it had never come to anything.

'Begging your pardon, Mrs Sawle.' Sid gave her a sheepish look as he helped her up into the trap. 'But do you think Aden will be away long? Only there's decisions to be made concerning the land …'

'I intend to find out what the situation is today,' she replied. The fear that Aden might be ill had subsided; she was sure that he was with his mistress. 'You will please drive me to the bank first – and then there is another call I must make.'

Sid gave her a startled glance but kept his thoughts to himself. Whether or not he had guessed what was in her mind, he had decided it was not his place to comment, and perhaps that was best. She would have found it embarrassing to discuss the matter, though she was determined to go through with her visit to ... that woman.

It was early-April now and the weather was bright but cold, a chill wind nipping at their noses as they drove along the flat country road with its fields of rich, dark soil on either side. Neither of them spoke much and Rebecca was free to look about her and remember.

When they arrived at the bank Sid helped her down, asked when he should return and drove off up the main street. She stood outside the bank for a moment, straightening her hat, half-afraid of what she would learn when she went in, then she pushed open the door and smiled as a gentleman coming out held it for her.

She approached the counter, asked for the manager and was requested to wait; it was about five minutes before he came to the door and invited her into his office. It was a large room, dark but furnished with impressive bookcases and a leather-topped partners desk which held a neat blotter, an inkstand and a file of papers. His manner was as polite and respectful as ever but so grave that she knew she had been right to come.

They talked for a few moments about the inclement weather, then he asked her how her charity work was progressing and mentioned an incident involving Mrs Emmeline Pankhurst, who was the leading light of the suffrage movement.

'Most distressing, Mrs Sawle ... most distressing.'

'It's a sign of the times, I'm afraid,' she said as he tutted and shook his head. 'I agree with her principles, though not always her methods. But I've called to see you on business, Mr Simpson.'

'I'm glad you called, Mrs Sawle,' he said, holding a chair for her before himself sitting down behind the desk. 'I asked Mr Sawle to come in this week for a little chat but ...' He spread his hands in a resigned manner. 'Of course there isn't much we can do but perhaps something can be salvaged.'

'What do you mean?' Her spine tingled as she saw his expression. He looked so severe! Things must be worse than she had imagined. 'Is something wrong, Mr Simpson? Are we overdrawn by much?'

'You mean you don't know?' He looked stunned. 'Mr Sawle hasn't told you?'

'Told me what?' She breathed deeply. 'Please tell me the worst, sir. My husband is away and I need money ...'

'How much?'

'Forty pounds for this week's wages for a start.'

'I'm sorry, Mrs Sawle, that may not be possible. When you drew out the two thousand pounds Mr Sawle had promised against his debts, I was forced to call a halt. Your debts have been mounting up for the past two years – since that disastrous potato harvest and a personal loss your husband incurred for ...' He glanced at his ledger. 'Three thousand pounds, I believe ...' He looked directly at her. 'I dare not advance another penny unless you can assure me that ...'

'What?' Rebecca was stunned, disbelieving. 'I had no idea. We have always had large credit balances to our account.'

'Indeed, that was once the case,' he agreed. 'But not for some time. Two thousand pounds was paid in recently from the sale of a property I believe – but you took that out yourself.'

'Yes, but ...' She struggled to come to terms with what he was saying. 'You mean it has all gone? All the money?' He nodded gravely and she twisted her gloves in her hands. 'Where did it go? Has Aden been buying more land?'

'I wish that were the case. I should be only too pleased to give you an extension of your credit if it could be secured against land that was not already mortgaged. Believe me, this situation gives me no pleasure. You and Mr Sawle have been good customers. If he had listened to my advice ...'

Rebecca was beginning to feel very uneasy. 'I think you should tell me exactly how we stand, sir.'

He was silent for a moment, then sighed heavily. 'A great deal of your land is mortgaged, Mrs Sawle. You will need to meet the repayments next month or my superiors will force me to call in the loans. That was why I impressed on Mr Sawle that he must do something, and of course he did, but ... well, let me see ...'

'How much do we owe?'

He glanced down at his desk, shuffled some papers. 'As far as I can see ... eighteen thousand, three hundred and two pounds. You will need to make a payment of at least a thousand pounds next month.'

'That's impossible!' She stared at him in disbelief. 'Aden

would have had to mortgage almost everything ... the farms, land ... everything.'

'Yes, I imagine so.' He shook his head and sighed over the ledgers. 'I did warn him he was getting in rather deep but he said I was worrying for nothing. He was going to sell something to tide him over ... a property, I think ... but the money was withdrawn recently. By you, I believe?'

'Yes ... Yes, I did.' The colour drained from her face. What had she done? This crisis was all her fault. No wonder Aden had been so angry! 'But where did all the money go?'

'Some of it into a business partnership that failed, I think, but mostly shares ... not blue chip, I'm afraid. Risky ventures I couldn't approve of.'

'Shares? Aden has been buying shares?'

'You didn't know? In a South American emerald mine, I believe, and various others. Your husband has always been keen on new ideas, anything that might make money fast. He told me that he had been lucky a few times – but his luck seems to have deserted him of late.'

'How could he?' Rebecca was suddenly angry. Perhaps she had precipitated this particular crisis but Aden had been playing with fire for some time. 'To risk everything without telling me!' She stood up, scraping back her chair. 'Is there nothing left? Nothing at all?'

'Your house.' There was another grave look accompanied by a deep sigh. 'That is in your name and cannot be touched – Mr Sawle was always most particular about that – and some small parcels of land. Enough if they were sold to cover your debts for a few months, but in the end ...' He spread his hands. 'I think you would be well advised to cut your losses now, before it is too late.'

'Are you telling me that I am penniless?'

'You must consult your lawyer, Mrs Sawle. There may be other deeds I know nothing of. Perhaps Mr Sawle still has shares he can sell. Solid, blue chip shares that will be worth the price he paid. I did advise him to stick to them but he said there was no profit in safety.'

'I see.' Rebecca pulled on her gloves. She was struggling to hide the emotions churning inside her. 'Thank you for your help, sir. I must speak to my husband about all this. How long do we have before we must make our decision?'

'Another month.' He gave her a sickly smile. 'I'm sure Mr Sawle will sort everything out. He has always met his payments in the past.'

'We shall be in touch before settlement day,' Rebecca said. 'Good morning, sir.'

She went outside into the chill of a cool spring day feeling shattered. Clouds had blown up suddenly and the sky was overcast, almost as black as the mood that had descended on her. They had lost everything. Aden had lost it all ... all they had worked so hard to build up ... thrown it all away. And he hadn't told her. Not one word. He had let her go on spending money as if they had plenty of it. Why? Why hadn't he said something?

It explained his rage over that donation she had made. Two thousand pounds! It was a huge sum of money but she hadn't realized how important it was to Aden. She had unwittingly brought it all to a head. If only he had told her the truth! She would never have been so lavish with their money if she had guessed he was in trouble.

It was his damned pride again. Hers too. If she had tried to break down the barriers between them sooner she might have discovered what was going on ... but she had let things drift because she was hurt.

No longer! First she was going to see their lawyers and then that woman. Aden was coming home if she had to drag him by the scruff of his neck!

'Are you sure there's nothing else?' Rebecca stared at Stuart Monroe in disbelief. She had been sure he would tell her things were not as bad as the bank manager had said. 'Just the house and Sarah's cottage?'

'A few tied cottages, not worth much, one or two small pieces of land – but you'll need to sell them to meet your immediate debts. All the rest is mortgaged, I'm afraid.'

'What about the shares?'

'He didn't lodge them with us, Mrs Sawle. I've been through everything and this is all I could find.' He looked as stunned as she felt. 'Mr Ward dealt with your husband's affairs until his retirement last month. I had no idea of the situation. If I had ...' He faltered, looking upset. 'I'm afraid the trust fund is already in place. There's no way I can get the money back for you. I'm very sorry.'

251

'That was entirely my own fault. I should have consulted Aden but I had no idea ...' She paused, wanting to get it all clear in her mind. 'So I own my house and the cottage, and Aden is – or will be – bankrupt if he doesn't meet this payment?'

'That's about what it amounts to, so far as I can see. Of course, if he has shares he may be able to raise something.'

'Mr Simpson seems to think most of them are worthless.'

'I'm very sorry, Mrs Sawle. This is such a shock for you.'

'Yes, it is. I'm not sure what we should do. We have a month to meet our payments ...'

'You must speak to Mr Sawle when he returns. He may have made plans – arrangements that we know nothing about. He may have other assets he did not wish to disclose to the bank.'

'Yes, of course. Thank you for your time.' She stood up, pretending to a calm she did not feel. 'I shall be in touch when I know more.'

'If I can be of assistance ... in any way at all.' He hurried to open the door for her. 'Don't hesitate to call on me, Mrs Sawle, professionally ... or as a friend.'

'Thank you.' She gave him her hand. 'I believe I shall be needing you in both capacities, Mr Monroe.'

'I shall be here,' he promised, his eyes conveying far more than was proper in the circumstances.

She managed a faint smile and went out of his office. For a moment she stared unseeingly about her. What were they going to do? How could they pay the men? How could they carry on without money? She felt so lost ... so alone.

Sid Harris was waiting for her. One glance at his face told her that there was more bad news.

'You may as well tell me,' she said. 'Or can I guess? They wouldn't serve you at the iron-monger's until we settle their bill – is that it?'

'You know then? I didn't want to worry you but ...' He kicked at a stone moodily and wouldn't look at her, obviously feeling all this was a betrayal of Aden.

'How much?'

'Fifty pounds, three shillings and sixpence three-farthings.'

The precise amount made her smile despite herself. 'They will have to wait their turn, I'm afraid, or do you need something urgently?'

'It will keep.' He looked gloomy. 'It's bad, isn't it? I've suspected something was on Aden's mind recently but he never said. Never let on he was worried, but he must have been. Aden's not one to owe folk if he can help it.'

'I've certainly never thought so,' Rebecca said grimly as he helped her into the carriage. 'I think it's about time we asked him, don't you?'

26

Rebecca sat staring at the building for a few seconds after Sid had brought the horses to a stop. So this was the house Aden had bought for his mistress! She took stock of the sturdy, very new brick walls, the smart front door and the pretty lace curtains at the windows, her expression becoming grimmer. It wasn't on the list of properties Aden had mortgaged so presumably the deeds were in that woman's name. What else had he given her? How much more of his money had been spent on his fancy woman?

Sid helped her down. Rebecca could see by his face that he was very uneasy about this but she was too angry to care about his feelings just now. She lifted the black cast-iron knocker, bringing it down sharply three times.

Aden had given a house like this to a woman he had known only a short time – when they were in danger of losing everything! How could he be so foolhardy? Yet it was typical of the man, of his pride and his arrogance. It must have cost him almost as much as Rebecca had given to her charity – but he had demanded that she should ask for her money back!

It was a moment or two before the woman came to the door, and when she did she looked flustered; her hands were covered in flour as if she had been baking. She was wiping them on a pink-spotted apron, not really looking at Rebecca.

'Yes,' she said. 'Can I ...' Her voice died away as she suddenly saw who her visitor was.

She was older and plainer than Rebecca had imagined – older than Rebecca by several years. In her mind Rebecca had seen her as young and beautiful – a modern-day Salome, wanton and pagan. But she was just an ordinary housewife, straight-haired and thin with a pale, almost sallow complexion and faded blue eyes.

Rebecca felt a shaft of pain. Why? Why did Aden prefer this woman to her? Somehow it hurt that she wasn't beautiful. She might have been able to understand if he had chosen a pretty woman for his mistress.

'I would like to see Aden, please.' She glared at the other woman, wanting her to understand how angry she was, wanting her to suffer as she had made Rebecca suffer, night after night, knowing that her husband was with her, lying in her bed. 'I think you know who I am, don't you?'

Her face went red and then white. She was terribly embarrassed and Rebecca felt an unworthy sense of pleasure in witnessing her discomfort. It served her right for stealing another woman's husband!

'Yes ... I know,' she whispered in a shamed voice. 'He isn't here. I haven't seen him ...'

'I don't believe you. Aden hasn't been near his home or the farm for nearly a week. I know he's here and I demand to speak to him.'

The woman licked her lips nervously, her eyes dropping before Rebecca's furious gaze. 'I knew he was ... worried about something but ... really, I haven't seen him for almost a month ...'

Aden hadn't been to her for nearly a month! Was she lying? Rebecca studied her with narrowed eyes. She was tempted to sweep past her into the house, to see for herself.

'You are welcome to look for yourself, if you wish?' She stepped back as if to invite Rebecca in. 'I give you my word, he isn't here. He hasn't been here for weeks.'

'I have no wish to enter your house,' Rebecca replied coldly. 'Since you have given me your word I shall believe you. If Aden should come here, please tell him that it is vitally important he comes home at once. Vitally important!'

'Yes, of course ...' Her hand moved towards Rebecca as if in supplication, then fell to her side. 'I – I know you must hate me.'

Rebecca's look speared her with contempt. 'You will never know how much. You took what was not yours.'

'No ...' Her lips were almost bloodless. 'He was never mine, not really ... it was just for comfort ...'

Her eyes seemed to beg for forgiveness but Rebecca was in no mood to ease her conscience. She had broken the laws of morality and society; she could not expect to be so easily forgiven by the woman she had wronged.

Rebecca turned away from her, her back ramrod straight as she walked to where Sid was standing waiting for her. He helped her into the carriage and she sat staring straight ahead, refusing to glance back at the other woman, though in her heart she had begun to feel some sympathy for her.

Sid respected her silence and neither of them spoke until they were halfway home.

'What will you do now?' he asked at last. 'It isn't like him to go off and leave trouble for others. Not like him at all ... without a word.'

Rebecca shivered as the chill wind struck deep into her bones. The day seemed hostile, dark and overcast – like her own state of mind. What was she going to do without Aden's support? He had always been there, a rock to cling to, even when they were estranged. She had always known that he was there if she needed him.

She knew that she might well have died after her father was murdered if it had not been for Aden. There had been a terrible darkness in her mind ... an emptiness inside her that made her feel life was not worth living. He had shown her the way. How could she go on without him now?

'I was so sure he would be with her.' The words were forced out of her, each one a drop of blood from her heart.

'Maybe she was lying?'

'No.' Rebecca shook her head. Whatever she was, Aden's mistress was not a liar. 'I don't think so, Sid. She was too shocked, too upset to lie.'

'Then where has he got to?'

'I don't know. I just don't know ...'

She had a horrible sinking sensation in her stomach. Until this moment she had been angry with Aden for going to her ... Beth Jones. She could admit the woman had a name now. He hadn't been near her in weeks. Something told Rebecca he hadn't been with her that often at all.

'He was never really mine ...' Her admission had eased some of the ache inside Rebecca. 'It was only for comfort ...' The comfort he had been denied in his own home?

Aden, where are you? For a moment she thought she had spoken the words aloud, then realized they were a cry from her heart.

Why had he disappeared that night? If he had not gone to his mistress ... The anger and frustration Rebecca had felt was beginning to give way to a new sensation, a creeping fear that made her go cold all over.

Sid was right. Aden wasn't the sort to run from trouble. He must have been worried sick over his debts but he wouldn't have walked out and left her to cope alone – or would he? He had been desperate when he came to her room that night. She had seen such a terrible look in his eyes. He had been crying out for help but she hadn't understood; she had turned away from him – refusing to listen even when he begged for forgiveness. She couldn't be sure what Aden might do. She wasn't sure she knew him at all, not really. Not the part of him that he had kept hidden all these years.

She had known that he sometimes took risks – but to gamble recklessly! That was what his dealings in high-risk shares amounted to when she thought about it. Had he gambled in other ways, too? She had always known that he could be impulsive, that he enjoyed dealing, buying and selling, but to mortgage everything ... what had he been thinking of? All those years of hard work gone for nothing.

'Maybe he's had an accident,' Sid said, and she turned to look at him, a trickle of fear running down her spine. 'Maybe he's had a bang on his head and don't know who he is.'

'We must make inquiries at the hospitals,' she said. 'I'll get in touch with Mr Monroe. He will know what to do. Yes, I'll ask him to help me find Aden.'

Rebecca had been restless all afternoon. The events of the past few days kept going round and round in her head until she thought she would go mad. She could not bear to stay in the house for another minute!

She walked through the village, across the bridge and down to the river. The water looked sluggish and brown. She stood at the edge for a while, watching a fussy little moorhen darting in and out of the reed beds. Once she had contemplated ending her own life in that water but today such thoughts were far from her mind. No matter what happened she could not run away from her responsibilities. She had her children to think of, and she loved them – loved them so much that she would do whatever was necessary to protect them.

She walked across the meadows to the brow of the small hill, looking down across the fields, both arable and pasture. Cows and horses grazed peacefully in the shelter of scrawny hedges, and above her a blackbird warbled his last song of the day, as if defying the onset of night.

In the distance she could see smoke coming from the direction of Five Winds, though the cottage itself was hidden from her view by trees. Five Winds ... where he had taken her as a young bride – where the happiest, most fulfilling years of her life had been spent.

It was almost dusk and the light was dying, gradually taking the familiar sights from her view, enveloping the land in a blanket of darkness. Where was Aden? Why had he left her? Her soul cried out to him, silently begging him to return. She needed him, needed him so much that the thought of life without him was almost more than she could bear ... but life must go on. For the sake of their children if not for her own.

What was it Aden had once said to her? Ah, yes, she remembered now ... *'This land we hold ... always remember, Rebecca. Whatever happens, hold to this land ...'*

She hadn't understood him then, but she did now. The land was something to cling to ... something to hold on to when all else was gone. It was a sacred trust, to be passed on to their children and perhaps to generations in the future. It must not slip through their hands through careless stewardship.

Rebecca would keep the faith even if Aden did not. Somehow ... somehow she would hold on to this land that meant so much to him. And perhaps ... perhaps that act of faith would bring him back to her.

Rebecca took the children to Ely that Saturday and bought them the presents their father had promised them; then they had tea at The Lamb Hotel, which was situated at the corner of the High Street, just a few yards away from the beautiful old cathedral that had for centuries past towered over the small market town. Perhaps it was extravagant of her to spend the money in the circumstances but it might be a long time before she could do it again. Besides, she did not want the children to feel that their father had let them down.

In future they might have to face hardship, so let them enjoy the luxury of being spoiled one more time.

Rebecca knew that they must make severe economies. She had

already decided that she would sell the elegant carriage and pair of beautifully matched bays Aden had bought her as an anniversary gift two years before, though for the moment she would not sell his pony and trap. It would be a wrench to part with her comfortable carriage but she did not really need it. It was surprising how little she really needed when she thought about it – and the things that meant most were not to be bought with coin or notes, though of course money had its place.

Stuart Monroe had advanced her enough to pay the men's wages for a couple of weeks, and she took some bits and pieces of jewellery that had once belonged to her mother into a shop near the marketplace and sold it. There was nothing very valuable but the few pounds it raised would keep the house running until she could decide what to do next. Aden had often promised her diamonds but she had always told him to put the money into the land. Now she wished that she had not been so dismissive of his offers.

While they were in Ely she made inquiries at the hospital, which had once been the workhouse and was still thought of in those terms. The matron was polite but unable to help: no one fitting the description of Aden had been brought into her wards. Rebecca's visit to the police station was just as fruitless. They told her that people often went off for a few days and assured her that her husband would probably turn up of his own accord when he was ready.

She thanked them for their trouble, feeling relieved that he was not confined to either a cell or a hospital bed, but it didn't ease her anxiety. Surely a man could not simply disappear?

He must be somewhere. And if he was not in trouble or ill ... perhaps he had simply abandoned them all? It was a bitter thought and one that caused her some restless nights.

The children were beginning to ask for explanations. Aden had always been there, a steady, dependable rock for them to cling to, and they were suspicious when she gave them vague excuses – but what could she tell them when she knew so little herself? Fanny had taken to bursting into tears for no reason and Jay looked at his mother with sullen eyes, obviously blaming her for his father's absence. She knew that it would not be long before she was forced to tell him the truth – but what *was* the truth?

Each day when she woke from a fitful sleep she hoped that Aden would have returned during the night, but he did not come, nor did he send a message to reassure her. She continued to wait and worry throughout two long weeks while Stuart Monroe made discreet inquiries in the neighbouring villages.

At the end of that time he came to see her at home, apologizing because he had not been able to trace her husband.

'It is good news that Mr Sawle has not been found lying unconscious at the side of the road,' he said gravely. 'I think we can rule out an accident – or worse.'

It was raining hard. Rebecca could hear it drumming against the window panes, spattering and hissing on the roof. The nights were still cold even though spring was supposed to be on its way. Supposing Aden was lying hurt in a ditch somewhere? Supposing he had been attacked and robbed, left for dead … supposing he could not remember who he was or where he lived? The thought brought such a swift, sharp pain that she pressed a hand against her breast.

'If he had been found we should at least know if …' She drew a shaky breath. 'It's the uncertainty …'

'Yes, of course. It is most distressing for you.' Stuart touched her hand, his eyes warm with sympathy. 'We shall keep on searching. Do not despair. Meanwhile, I'm afraid that we must speak of other matters. The debt to your bank will not wait.'

'That is why I asked you to call,' she said, and drew a deep breath. 'We have no hope of paying all we owe, Mr Monroe. They will have to foreclose … sell most of the land they hold as security to pay off our debts. There is sufficient equity left to do that, isn't there?'

'Yes, of course. I have been going into the matter more thoroughly, Mrs Sawle, and I believe that some of the land may fetch considerably more than was borrowed on it. There will be costs, naturally, but I believe you may have something left over.' He paused thoughtfully. 'Do you not think it might be better to sell one of those small parcels of land first? We might be able to raise enough to meet the settlement and hold on to the rest for a time.'

'I doubt if Aden could ever pay the whole amount, even if he were here to see to things himself.' She lifted her head, meeting the lawyer's eyes. 'I have made my decision. I believe that I own this house and that it cannot be touched by the bank?'

'Yes, but …'

'I want to sell it as quickly as possible and pay off the debt on Five Winds. Could you arrange that for me, please? All the land in Chatteris Fen must be sold to repay the bank, but I want to keep as

much of the land in Mepal as I can. I shall rely on you to negoti-
ate with Mr Simpson.'

'Keep Five Winds?' He looked puzzled. 'You mean the buildings and ...'

'All of it – the cottage, the original fields that were in Aden's
family for generations, that's what I mean. I think there must be
around sixty acres. We might save the land behind Sarah's
cottage, too. I think that is no more than five acres but good
pasture land.'

'Five acres – yes, more or less. It wouldn't fetch much at the
moment anyway. But I'm not sure I understand you, Mrs Sawle.
You want to sell your home?'

'You think I should keep this house? My children need food and
clothes, Mr Monroe. I cannot afford to live here so we shall go back
to Five Winds. I've already spoken to Mr Harris and he has agreed
to move back into Sarah's old cottage for the time being, though it
is hardly large enough for his family despite the extension. They
have two sons and a daughter a few months younger than Fanny –
but the cottage is all I can offer them for the moment.'

Stuart Monroe nodded. His eyes wandered round the parlour,
assessing the furniture, taking in the richness of the silk drapes
and expensive carpets, the sheen of mellow wood and the glitter
of silver. The trappings of wealth Rebecca had collected so carefully over the years to impress Celia and other friends.

'If we sell everything of value it should fetch enough to buy the
farm and the stock, shouldn't it?'

'I would imagine so – but you can't want to part with all your
beautiful things?' He was shocked and concerned. 'They must
mean so much to you ...'

'Land is more important to a farmer. Aden taught me that if
nothing else.'

Was her voice tinged with bitterness? She hoped not. If Aden
had stuck to buying land none of this need have happened. She
did not know when he had begun to gamble, to deal in shares and
outside businesses that he did not properly understand, but she
would not judge him too harshly yet.

'We can live on the farm,' she explained. 'The house must go. I
should be grateful if you would handle the sale for me. Perhaps
the contents should be sent to a London auction house? I believe
some of the pictures may fetch a few hundred pounds. I was very
careful about what I bought.'

261

'You have a good eye,' he said, and nodded. 'I shall be happy to do whatever I can for you, of course.' There was such warmth, such admiration for her in his eyes, that she felt her cheeks go pink. 'You are a brave woman, Mrs Sawle – but are you sure you can manage the farm? Supposing ...' He stopped as he saw the expression on her face. 'I speak only as a friend concerned for your welfare.'

'Aden will come back,' she said with a calmness she did not feel. 'And he must have something to come back to – something to give him a purpose in life.'

'Yes, I see. May I say he is a fortunate man, Mrs Sawle? Not many women would have been so understanding in the circumstances.'

Rebecca turned to gaze out of the window, hiding her smile. He was young, single, and full of ideals. How little he knew of the pain men and women could inflict on each other within the sanctuary of marriage. Aden had hurt her many times but she had hurt him, too ... perhaps more than she'd realized. A turn of the head, a careless look, a withdrawal of affection ... all those things could hurt so much.

'Marriage is not a fairytale ending,' she said, 'but a journey of discovery.' She turned to the lawyer with a smile. 'It has stopped raining. I believe we shall have a pleasant afternoon after all.'

'April showers.' Stuart's eyes were intent on her face. 'You're so strong ... so fine.'

'Nonsense! I'm making the best of things, that's all.'

'Of course, of course.' He adjusted his silk cravat. 'What will you do about the men Mr Sawle employed? You can't keep them all on.'

'No, I'm afraid I can't afford to keep most of them. I've had a word with Mr Harris about that and he is advising me who should go first. If there is enough money when we've settled everything, I shall pay an extra two weeks wages to all those we are forced to turn off.'

'You are always so generous.' Stuart was still doubtful but he had stopped objecting. Rebecca's mind was made up and it would be useless to argue.

'I am sure something can be managed,' he said. 'We have several farmers as clients. I'll ask round, see if anyone needs labourers.'

'That would be kind. I think Aden will feel worst about any hardship caused to his people by all this.'

'He may have his own plans, of course.'

'Then he will tell me about them when he returns. In the meantime I must do as I think best. The house and its contents belong to me: I can do as I wish with them – and I have decided to sell. I shall pay off whatever Aden owes on Five Winds and the property will revert to us.'

Stuart Monroe sighed and shrugged, giving up the struggle. He clearly knew when he was beaten. Rebecca smiled as he took the hand she offered.

'You know best, dear lady. You may rely on me to fight your corner in this. I shall get the best price possible for the house – and I shall see that the bank does not take advantage of your situation.'

Rebecca smiled and saw him to the front door. She knew that he believed she was making a mistake. She could have moved into Sarah's cottage and invested the money raised from her various assets – which might have brought her in two or three hundred a year: enough to live on if they were careful – but what would Aden have done then? Somehow she could not see him working for a master.

No, she must save the land. She must hold on to Five Winds at all costs.

When Aden came home he must have something worthwhile to come back for. And he must come home. He must because she could not bear it if he didn't.

27

'Move back to the farm?' Richie looked at her incredulously. 'What on earth are you saying, Mother? I've already asked a friend to stay here in the summer hols.'

'He will be welcome to stay at the farm. We can put an extra bed in your room.'

'Ask Chillingbury to stay at the farm – sleep in my room?' Richie was horrified, his thin lips drawn back in a sneer of contempt. 'You do realize his father is Sir Edmund Chillingbury? He's filthy rich and a magistrate.'

'Your friend might enjoy the novelty of staying on a farm.'

Rebecca was filled with dismay as she looked at her son. Was this what she had done by indulging his whims so often – by spoiling him because she couldn't love him as much as she ought? He had become a snob at that fancy school of his. His attitude reminded her of herself when she'd first returned home after that year in Switzerland – but she had been too careful of her father's feelings to voice her doubts. Richie had no such qualms.

'You had better invite him this summer if you want him to visit, Richie. I'm not sure how much longer you will be able to stay at that school. The fees are more than a hundred guineas a year and …'

'Not stay there?' His incredulity turned to hostility. 'That's not fair. Why are you doing this to me, Mother? You've never cared about me and now you're trying to ruin my life.'

'Don't sulk, Richie, and don't say foolish things. You are my son and I love you. If I can find the money, you can stay at school but …'

'I hate you!' he cried. 'This is all your fault. You've driven

Father away with your nagging. If he was here none of this would be happening.'

Rebecca felt a surge of anger. 'I've had enough of your rudeness, Richie. You will go to your room and stay there until supper – and then you will apologize or go to bed hungry.'

'I don't care. I hate you! And I shan't apologize.' He rushed from the room, slamming the door behind him.

There was silence after he had gone, then Jay looked at her with anxious eyes. He had been so quiet that Rebecca had almost forgotten he was there.

'He shouldn't have said that to you. I'll make him come down and apologize.'

'No, leave him,' she said and sighed. 'He's upset because he may have to leave his school. It isn't fair to him, not when he's made friends ...'

Jay was silent for a moment. 'Shall we have to sell the ponies?' he asked at last.

'No, things aren't that bad.' She smiled at him. He was beginning to look more like his father as he got older, even though he had her colouring. 'There won't be much money for luxuries for a while – but I promise you, we shan't sell the ponies.'

Fanny was standing near the parlour door, a rag doll hanging limply from her hand. She was watching and listening but didn't say anything. She was still too young to understand what it all meant. As long as she had her pretty clothes and her dolls, Rebecca doubted that she would mind where she lived; at least she hoped not. It was going to be difficult enough without more tears and tantrums.

There would be gossip in the village, of course. People would find it fascinating for a while, and some of them might gloat over the Sawles' downfall, but they would all have to put up with it – until something else happened to divert the gossips' attention.

Jay was studying her, a serious, thoughtful expression in his eyes. 'When is Father coming home, Mama? Why did he go off and leave us? Was it because he lost all the money?'

'I don't know the answer to any of those questions. If I did, I would tell you.'

'It's his fault that we've got to move, isn't it?'

'Not entirely. He invested a lot of money unwisely, but anyone can do that. He didn't mean it to happen, Jay. And I've spent a lot of money, too. We've all had exactly what we wanted – so perhaps we're all a little bit to blame.'

Jay nodded, then, with a wisdom beyond his years, said, 'You're different, Mama. You're not getting cross or upset but taking it all on your shoulders – is it because of what's happening?'

Rebecca reached out and ruffled his mop of unruly hair. 'Yes, perhaps it is,' she said, feeling a pang of love for him. 'I've never had to fend for myself before. Your father always did everything for me. He spoiled me as much as I've spoiled my children. Don't blame him too much, Jay. Don't hold it against him when he comes back.'

'Will he come?' There was such intensity, such longing in his young face, that it hurt her.

'Oh, yes,' she said. 'I'm sure of it. When he's ready.'

'Supposing he can't? Supposing he's ...'

The wind whistled and howled in the trees; the sound made Rebecca feel cold all over but she hid her unease as she considered her answer. 'We're not going to think about that, Jay, because if we did none of us could bear it. We shan't give up hope. You and I, darling. We've got to be strong for the sake of the others. We'll go on hoping and we'll pray – won't we?'

He nodded but there were tears in his eyes.

Where are you, Aden? Damn you! Where are you? What are you doing to this child you love? Come home. The money doesn't matter. We need you!

'Is Molly coming with us?'

Jay's question broke into her thoughts. The words had been only in her mind, of course, but if Aden were alive – if he still felt anything for them – he must have heard them. For a moment she had felt his presence so strongly that it was almost as if he were in the room with them. She had a sudden overwhelming certainty that he was alive ... that he was thinking of them.

She blinked and looked at her son. 'Of course Molly is coming. We couldn't manage without her, now could we?' He shook his head, a faint flicker of a smile on his face. 'Run along, Jay. You'll have to look after the ponies in future, which means feeding as well as exercise. Mr Harris won't be able to send one of the men to do it for you. We shall all have to do our share from now on.'

'I'll help him when I get home from school with any chores in the yard. I promise, Mama.' Jay looked excited at the prospect. All he wanted from life was to leave school the moment he was able and work on the land with his father.

With his father, Aden! With his father.

'We'll see,' Rebecca said with a smile. 'Now, I have to help Molly with the packing. We've been lucky. Mr Monroe was able to find an immediate buyer for the house. Everything is arranged with the bank. We'll own Five Winds and be out of debt but we have to leave by the end of next week. Most of the expensive stuff is going to the saleroom tomorrow – oh, and if there's anything you don't want, clothes that don't fit or anything else, you might put them out, darling. I'm going to give all that sort of thing to the mission.'

Jay promised he would and ran off. Fanny gave her a long, tearful look and ran after him. Perhaps she was feeling all this more than Rebecca had thought. She would have to talk to her later, try to make her understand that it wasn't so terrible.

Fanny was growing up fast; several of her dresses were too small for her and Rebecca had decided to sort them all out before the move. There was no point in taking things they didn't want; they had collected so much in the good years that it was going to be hard enough to squeeze everything in as it was.

Molly was already hard at work packing when Rebecca went into the large front parlour. She had half a dozen large tea chests, a mountain of fresh dry straw and a pile of old newspapers heaped around her. She had been crying and her nose was red.

'All your lovely things,' she said, and sniffed when she saw Rebecca. 'Your silver tea and coffee service – and you were so proud of it!'

'Less work for you,' Rebecca said. 'We'll manage with one of the china ones, Molly. I think the tea tastes better out of them anyway.'

Molly gave a little sob and Rebecca handed her a clean handkerchief. It wasn't surprising that she was upset; she had grown used to having her own little sitting-room and bedroom. Now she was going to sleep at her mother's house and come in every day as she had at the beginning. When Rebecca had first told her she might not be able to afford to pay her to come every day, Molly had burst into tears and offered to work for nothing but her keep.

'It isn't going to be that bad, Molly,' Rebecca had assured her with a smile. 'My lawyer got us a very good price for the house and he thinks things are not as bad as we feared. Some of the land is worth almost twice as much as was borrowed against it so we shan't be poor – just not quite as rich as we were.'

'You'll have no debts, Mrs Sawle,' Stuart Monroe had told her.

'The carpets and curtains are not included in the price, of course, and when the silver, furniture and pictures are sold you should have several hundred pounds left over. Enough to keep you going until the harvest comes in.'

'I've decided to sell some more jewellery as well,' she replied. 'There is a pearl necklace my father gave me when I was eighteen and … this brooch.' She opened the velvet box to show him. 'I believe it may be quite valuable.'

'That is beautiful,' he exclaimed, taking it out to hold it in the palm of his hand. 'The painting is exquisite … mother and child. It looks as if it might be Italian – and those diamonds are of wonderful quality.'

'It was given to me by a wealthy friend some years ago. I have never worn it.'

'Surely you cannot wish to part with such a treasure? As I've already said, you will have several hundred pounds to spare after the sale, perhaps more.'

'I intend to put this money into a trust fund for Richie, to pay for his schooling for the next few years. I believe that is more important than holding on to a brooch I shall have little occasion to wear.'

'But it must mean so much to you. Perhaps we could reach an arrangement – a loan to be repaid over so many years?'

'I prefer not to owe money. No, thank you, Mr Monroe. I have decided to sell the brooch.'

'Very well, if you wish.'

He had taken it reluctantly. Rebecca was surprised to discover that it had cost her not one tear to part with it. She was too busy to look backwards. Only the future mattered to her now. She was determined to hold on to her land, to provide a secure home for her children – and for Aden if he came back to them.

Rebecca stood in the kitchen at Five Winds and looked out at the yard. It felt a little strange to be back in her old home after several years but it was a good feeling. She could hear the children running about upstairs, their voices raised as they argued over where to put their things; they would settle it between them in time. What she wanted most at this moment was a cup of tea.

'Hello.' May Harris popped her head round the door. 'I came to see if there was anything I could do to help?'

'Come in,' Rebecca said with a smile. 'I was just about to make a cup of tea.' She filled the kettle and put it on the hob. 'There's nothing but the unpacking to do, thanks to you, May. You left it all so beautifully clean. Molly has nothing to do but hang the curtains and make up our beds.'

There was of course a mountain of unpacking, but that was best done a little at a time.

'Well, I like things to be nice,' May said, and looked pleased. 'If you're sure I can't help?'

'You must have loads to do yourself,' Rebecca said, 'but stay and have a cup of tea with me. I want to talk to you about the dairy. I thought we might build a new one behind your cottage. You're so good at butter and cheese making and it would be more convenient for you.'

'Yes, it would,' May agreed and took the tray from Rebecca, setting it with blue and white cups. 'But what would Mr Sawle say? The dairy has always been here.'

'Well, we'll think about it,' Rebecca said, carrying the pot to the table. 'Will you ask Sorrel to come over later, please? I've sorted out some of Fanny's dresses and …' She paused as she saw May's face. 'Have I said something to upset you?'

'It's that daughter of mine,' May said apologetically. 'She won't come, Rebecca – and she won't wear the dresses if I take them for her.'

'Oh. They were so pretty, I thought …'

'And she ought to be grateful,' May said. 'Many a girl would go down on her knees and thank the Lord for them; they're good things, better than I can afford to give her. It was my sister's fault. She told her they were too fussy and that she would look better in something plainer; she made her a new dress and now Sorrel won't wear anything else. Ruth is teaching her to sew and she loves it so …' May sighed. 'It's such a waste.'

'Oh, they won't be wasted,' Rebecca said, a touch of annoyance in her tone. Ruth Perry again! And Sorrel was very like her in her ways, it seemed. 'I'll give them to the mission.'

'I hope I haven't offended you?'

May looked upset and Rebecca shook her head. 'No, of course you haven't. It wouldn't be fair to force Sorrel to wear them if she doesn't want to – and there are plenty of little girls who will be glad of them.'

'And so was Sorrel – until Ruth put her oar in!'

'Well …' Rebecca shrugged. 'That's probably my fault. She has never forgiven me …'

'Then it's about time she did – and I've told her so, don't think I haven't!'

'It doesn't matter,' Rebecca said. 'Now about that dairy, May. What I was thinking …'

'Let me help you with that, Mrs Sawle,' Sid Harris said as she struggled to tip a pail of milk into the churn. 'You look worn out.'

'Thank you, but I can manage. You have quite enough to do as it is.'

Rebecca's back was aching, which was hardly surprising in the circumstances. She had been up before first light, trying to get the cottage sorted out before the children came down; there was so much extra china and glass that she wasn't sure where to put it all. As soon as Molly arrived Rebecca had joined Sid in the yard, leaving Molly to see to their breakfasts. She would have hers later, when the early chores were done, just as Aden always had.

Sid had spent the first half an hour teaching her how to milk a cow in the semi-darkness of the sheds. He had been difficult to persuade but, like others before him, had finally accepted that once Rebecca made up her mind to something there was no moving her.

'I should have learned years ago,' she said to him, 'but Aden was always determined I shouldn't have to work in the yard – but now I want to. It will give you more time for your other work.'

'Well … if you're sure,' he'd said reluctantly. 'Press your head into her side like this. Rub your hands to warm them, then stroke the teats, coax it out of her. She'll give more that way. And leave Dora to me – she's a kicker.'

Rebecca's hands shook as she attempted to imitate his practised performance. The cow she had chosen was a gentle, patient creature; she turned her head as if to see who the clumsy new milkmaid was, discovered she was harmless, looked bored and went back to chewing the hay Sid had spread for her.

'Good … that's good,' he encouraged her. 'Take your time, Mrs Sawle. Easy does it. You're doing very well.'

He looked and sounded as surprised as she felt. She had expected to be nervous of the cows but discovered that she rather liked their solidness and the warm, musky smell of their bodies as it mingled with the scents of fresh hay and the sweet, creamy milk. She experienced a surge of triumph as she finished her first cow, emptied her pail and moved on to the next. She could do it. She could keep this place running until Aden came home.

But when would he come? She prayed it would be soon. She needed him; needed to know he was still alive ... but until then she could manage.

Elation kept her going and gradually her confidence increased. By the time she had milked ten cows, however, she was beginning to feel the strain in her back. For years she had done little real physical work and it was bound to be hard to start, but she was determined to win through.

'I'll drive them back to the top pasture,' Sid said when the milking was done. 'Then I'll do the mucking out when I get back.'

'No – you see to the horses. I can manage here.' The cows were for the most part mild, obliging creatures but she was still nervous of the horses. It was foolish, she knew, but she couldn't seem to conquer her irrational fear, though she knew it all stemmed from the morning of the storm, when she had been terrified that Richie would be killed by the stallion.

Sid hesitated, looking at her for a moment before he spoke. 'Aden wouldn't take kindly to your doing that sort of work, Mrs Sawle. It's not right for a lady.'

'Aden isn't here.' She straightened up, smothering a sigh. 'Until he is, we must manage the best we can. I can't afford to employ another yard man – and you can't do everything.'

'I suppose you're right,' he agreed doubtfully. 'But I wish you'd leave the heavy work to me, Mrs Sawle.'

'Don't you think it's about time you called me Rebecca?'

'I'm not sure.' He hitched his trousers a little higher. 'It wouldn't be fitting, ma'am.'

'Mrs Sawle then,' she said. 'Please, Sid – not ma'am. I really couldn't put up with that.'

He went off with a nod and she thought how lucky she was to have such a loyal friend. Of course he had always been Aden's friend; he had stood by her while others ... but she wouldn't think about that. So far she had managed to ignore all the gossip; it wouldn't last forever. Besides, she had more important things to concern her now.

She stood watching as Sid began to drive the cows through the yard towards the pasture where they would graze daily until they were moved on to the washes they had hired for the summer.

The top field had been ploughed and spread with manure the previous autumn. Sid had told her that it had wintered well and strong winds in the last weeks of March had broken the soil down, leaving it ready for cultivation.

'We'll have a fine tilth if the weather stays dry for a couple of days.' He had discussed it with her earlier that morning. 'Aden always lets the land rest after cultivating so if it doesn't rain we'll be drawing the ridges on Saturday. May and my boys will be there to give a hand with setting the potatoes. We've kept two of our best skilled men on, as you know, but we'll need all the casual labour we can get.'

'I shall be there, Sid.'

'It's hard work, Mrs Sawle,' he warned. 'Hard, back breaking labour.'

'So I've been told – but it has to be done. Jay and Richie can help too.'

There would be complaints from her eldest son but Jay would do his bit with a will. He had wanted to stay off school and help with the milking but she'd made him go that morning as usual. Richie had a longer holiday than the others because he was at boarding school but he hadn't offered to help.

He was going to help with planting the potatoes, though. Rebecca had made up her mind to that.

In the meantime she had the cowsheds to muck out and a pile of unpacking waiting for her in the house ...

Rebecca sat before her dressing mirror, brushing her hair. It was still as thick and long as it had always been and glowed red in the light of her lamp.

Her back ached from the unaccustomed labour but she felt remarkably well – better than she had for a long time. If only ... if only he ...

She got up and walked over to the window, looking out across the fields to the dark sheen of the river in the distance. Where was Aden? Why didn't he come home?

She had tried to recapture that feeling of communication with him but it had never come again. She wrapped her warm dressing gown tighter around her, realizing that she had lost weight. All the worry and work had made those extra pounds fall away, and a good thing too. She had become soft and plump over the years, but things would be different now.

'Aden ...' she whispered. 'Come home ... come home. We need you. I need you ... Damn you, Aden! Come back to us ... please, please, my love. Come back to us soon ...'

28

Rebecca left the village shop and began to walk home, her basket on her arm. She knew that the woman who worked behind the counter and her two customers would start gossiping the moment she left; she had seen the odd looks they had given her ... pitying looks. Well, let them get on with it. She wasn't to be pitied. She didn't need sympathy from anyone.

It was spring at last, the weather fine and warm, the trees beginning to look so pretty with all the blossom coming out. She stopped to look at the tulips and gillyflowers under her parlour windows, smiling to herself as she went into the kitchen. May Harris had kept her little garden well.

'There was a man here earlier,' Molly said, turning from the sink with a half-peeled potato in her hand. 'He asked for Mr Sawle and when I told him he wasn't here, demanded to see you.'

'Demanded?' Something in Molly's tone warned Rebecca that her hackles were up. 'You didn't like him much, did you? What kind of a man was he?'

'No, I didn't like him one little bit – that's why I told him you'd gone into town and wouldn't be back for hours.' Molly wrinkled her nose in disapproval. 'He was dressed like a gentleman but he didn't act much like one.'

Molly's morals were very strong and Rebecca trusted her instincts. If she didn't approve of the stranger he probably wasn't someone Rebecca wanted to meet.

'Did he say what he wanted?' Molly shook her head, turning back to the sink. 'Didn't he give his name?'

'No – he said only that he would be back to see you or Mr Sawle. He was very angry about something – quite rude, he was.'

'I see. Well, next time let me deal with him.'

Rebecca felt a prickle of apprehension at the base of her neck. Who was this mysterious man – and why was he so angry that he had been rude to Molly? If it was a matter of money he would surely have gone to their lawyers?

She was suddenly certain that the visit had something to do with Aden's disappearance and her skin crawled with apprehension. Where was he? Why had he stayed away all these weeks?

And what did their unpleasant visitor want of him?

Rebecca had never worked so hard in her life! Not even when she and Aden were first married and she had struggled to turn the cottage into a home.

Every bone in her body ached as she ran the water for a bath and sank into it. What a luxury a bathroom was! She had never really appreciated how lucky they were to have one before. If she'd had to cart water upstairs for a bath she would have died. Her eyes felt gritty and she had blisters on her hands; at that moment she could cheerfully have lain down and given up the ghost.

'Stop feeling sorry for yourself, Rebecca Sawle,' she scolded herself as she undressed. Some women had to work like this all their lives. She had been spoiled until now.

She stepped into the water, lay back and closed her eyes, sighing with relief as she let her thoughts drift back over the day.

It had still been dark when she'd helped Sid with the milking that morning. Because the weather had been so good they had decided to make a start with setting the potatoes, and the waggons had been sent on to the top field at first light.

Their two skilled men had begun preparing the ridger and drawing out the first rows the previous day and the field was ready for planting. Sid's eldest son's job was to follow the ridger with the horse and cart to place out the bags of seed potato for the rest of them to set in the rich but heavy clay soil.

'Keep them about a foot apart,' Sid told her. 'That's a bit close, Mrs Sawle – like this, see. Otherwise we shan't get the hoes between them when they come through, and they'll grow together too soon.'

His wife and her sons were already at work, obviously accustomed to getting their hands dirty. May had her hair tucked under a red cotton handkerchief; her dress was pulled up to mid-calf and looped over her hips with a cord to keep it out of her way. Rebecca hadn't realized what a hindrance a dress could be when working on the land and took note for the future.

Even though the soil was fairly dry it was still sticky and heavy, clinging to her boots and the hem of her gown, making it difficult to walk. It clogged under her fingernails and the sharp, fruity smell of it filled her nostrils. After the first few rows she could hardly straighten up. She envied Jay his agility as he scrambled along the rows like a little monkey, obviously enjoying himself. As far as her youngest son was concerned this was far better than school.

Richie was making heavy weather of it, doing less than half the work Jay managed, perhaps because he was resentful. He hadn't stopped sulking ever since she'd told him he would have to work in the fields with the rest of them until he returned to school.

'If you want to stay on at that school, you'll have to help when you're home,' she had told him. 'I'm sorry but that's the way it has to be from now on – at least until things are sorted out. We have got to be careful with money, Richie … for the time being anyway.'

He had given her a long, sullen stare, obviously blaming her for their trouble but realizing that there was no getting out of it. He had shown quite clearly that he resented being forced to labour in the fields but in the end he had done his share, albeit grudgingly.

Sid's boys were excellent workers and Rebecca had decided to ask their father if they could come to the yard at weekends to help out. She couldn't pay them much at the moment but they might be glad of a few shillings of their own.

Everyone had worked steadily the whole day, stopping only for short breaks to eat and drink, then she and Sid had come back to do the milking, leaving the others to clear up the baskets and see to the horses.

By the time the milking was finished it was almost dark and Rebecca was so weary she could hardly see straight. She felt guilty because she had left it to Sid to water and feed the stock – but he had insisted.

'You've done more than your share,' he'd told her with a smile. 'Aden would have been proud of you today.'

She nodded, too weary to argue or even answer.

Molly was still out in the dairy serving late customers with milk and cream. There would probably be quite a lot left over

276

because they were so late with the milking; that meant Rebecca would need to make cheeses in the morning. She could not afford to waste anything now, not even half a churn of sour milk – and she couldn't expect May to work on a Sunday.

Her eyelids felt heavy as she relaxed in the warm water. She closed them, feeling that she could sleep forever.

'Mrs Sawle. Mrs Sawle!'

Molly's voice raised her from the depths and she sat up in alarm as she heard the urgency in it.

'Yes, Molly, what is it?' she called, reaching for a towel and rubbing herself down hastily. 'I'll be out in a moment ...' She frowned as she heard Molly gasp and then the sound of a door banging. 'What's going on out there?'

She wrapped the towel around herself as the bathroom door suddenly burst open. For a moment she could only stare, her mouth open like a fish out of water, gasping for air. Aden was standing there in the doorway and he looked angry – so angry that he could not contain himself.

'Damn you, Rebecca!' he yelled at her. 'I know you hate me but I never thought you would stab me in the back like this.'

'W-what do you mean?' She clutched the towel to her as she stepped out of the bath. 'I don't know what you're talking about.'

Her thoughts were whirling in confusion, too fast and furious for her to make sense of anything – except that he was there ... alive! She felt a swift surge of elation but it faded as she gazed into his furious face. He was so angry – so bitter!

Her feeling of joy was replaced by one of resentment. He had been gone for more than a month, simply disappeared with no thought for anyone; now he was back without a word of explanation and accusing her of – what? His attitude stung her into retaliation.

'Where on earth have you been?' she demanded. 'How could you go off like that? Without a word to anyone! Don't you realize everyone has been worried sick? Why did you do it, Aden?'

'I had my reasons,' he said, and for a moment she thought she saw guilt or shame in his eyes, then the anger flashed back. 'Damn it, Rebecca! After what happened I knew it was over between us. I knew you hated me – but I never imagined you could be this spiteful.'

She walked past him into the bedroom. Her knees were turning to pulp and she felt weak. There was no sign of Molly. She had obviously tried to stop him coming up and whatever he had said to her had made her run back to the safety of the kitchen – which Rebecca could understand. The expression on his face was one of intense fury: he looked capable of anything.

'What are you talking about?' Her heart quailed and she longed for the old Aden. She had hoped things would be better when he came back – but this man was so cold and unreachable. 'What have I done to make you so angry?'

'You can ask that?' For a moment the air seemed to crackle around him and she thought he was about to lose control and hit her, but his hands only clenched at his sides. 'Why did you do it, Rebecca? Why did you sell the house – everything?'

'You should know the answer to that,' she replied, keeping her voice steady despite the mad pounding of her heart. 'You're the one who mortgaged everything we owned.'

'Not the house. That was yours. I made sure of that. Always.'

'Yes.' She gazed at him, trying to read his mind, but he was blocking her out, his eyes distant – veiled. 'What use is a big house if there's nothing else left? How did you expect me to pay the men?'

He was silent for a long, tense moment. 'I thought you would manage somehow for a few weeks. I expected you to have more faith in me. I know our marriage is over on a personal level but …'

'We still owe the bank almost fifteen thousand pounds, Aden, even after selling the house and paying off the debt on Five Winds itself. What else could I have done?'

'You could have waited … discussed it with me.'

'I didn't know where you were – or even if you were still alive. The payment was due this week …'

'And I shall pay it. I've come back to pay it in full.'

'How can you?' She stared at him in disbelief.

'With this.'

She watched as he put his hand into his coat pocket. He pulled out a handful of crumpled five-pound notes and tossed them on to the bed. More notes and a fistful of gold sovereigns followed; the money came tumbling out of every pocket, wads of crisp, pristine notes, several pieces of expensive jewellery and a large white document tied with a red ribbon.

'Where did you get all this?' She felt a chill of fear. 'What have you done, Aden?'

His mouth curved in a smile of mockery. 'I haven't robbed a bank, if that's what's worrying you.'

'But where ...' She gazed up at him uncertainly. 'How ... how could you get all this?'

'There's enough money to meet this quarter's payment and more.' He picked up the document. 'When I've sold this we'll be able to pay off nearly half the debt.'

'What is it?' Again she felt that cold sensation at the base of her spine – a premonition of some dreadful consequence of whatever it was he had done to get this money.

'The deeds to a small estate,' he said. 'And a rather large old house – a bit ramshackle but worth at least five or six thousand pounds with its land.'

'Aden! Where did you get all this?'

He gave her a long, cool look, then smiled oddly. 'I won it playing poker with some gentlemen ... at least they call themselves that but most of them are the scum of the earth! Don't waste your pity on them, Rebecca. They would have none for you nor yet their victims. Many a poor devil has taken his own life after playing with that little crowd.'

His words sent shivers running through her. She was aware of a nagging fear deep inside her but all she could do was stare at him in horror.

'Gambling!'

When she had first learned of his losses from buying and selling shares she had wondered if he ever gambled in other ways – now she had her answer and it was quite shocking. Her husband a gambler – and mixing with men who sounded dangerous! What else was there hidden in his past that she did not know about? She was beginning to wonder if she had ever really known him at all.

'Don't look so horrified,' he said, a mixture of amusement and triumph in his eyes. 'I may have made a few mistakes along the way but I was always lucky at cards ... my luck deserted me for a while but now it has come back. I've recovered everything I've ever lost at the tables and more.'

'Gambling is a fool's game!' The words were out before she could stop them.

'And you think me a fool, of course.' He nodded, his mouth drawing into a thin, hard line. 'Yes, you've made that clear often enough in the past. Well, you've done your best to ruin me but I'll survive – I'll survive despite you.'

How could he think that she would deliberately set out to ruin him? She had tried to save Five Winds for him! She had acted swiftly because she had been afraid he might lose everything if she delayed – but he believed she had meant to humiliate and ruin him. She was hurt that he could think such a thing of her and as usual she struck out in her pain.

'How long have you been gambling?' she demanded. 'When did it start?'

'I've always been lucky at cards.' He frowned at her. 'I suppose it really began when you went to France that time ... I was lonely in the evenings so I started going to Chatteris.'

'But you haven't been there this time?'

'Not at first, no.'

That meant he had been there recently ... to his mistress? Rebecca felt pain and then anger.

'And what else haven't you told me, Aden? You might as well tell me everything now ... are there any other secrets I should know?'

He hesitated, then nodded. 'There's one. You might as well hear the worst of me. When I found Frank that day ... there was a cashbox on the side with a hoard of gold coins he'd hidden from his accountants. He always hated paying his taxes. I took it and ...'

'That's where the money came from for my bride clothes!'

He had told her it was his father's nest egg, that he'd found it hidden in the loft ... but he had lied. Rebecca's face went white. She had suspected something at the time but hadn't bothered to ask. She had been proud of his ambition. Now she was wondering just what kind of a man he was; she had sensed a ruthlessness in him but had never known just what he was capable of. She wasn't sure how she felt about this new Aden.

He nodded, his eyes narrowing. 'I took a risk on no one knowing it was missing and got away with it. Marrying you was the biggest gamble of my life – but my luck ran out with you, didn't it?'

Her mouth was so dry she couldn't answer. He was staring at her so strangely, as if waiting – but for what? What did he want her to say?

'You made your own choices,' she said at last.

'Yes, I suppose I have,' he agreed. 'And I'll live with them – but you had a hand in them, Rebecca. I'm not sure how much I can salvage from all this but I'll do my best. I'll save what I can and then we'll see.'

'What do you mean I had a hand in it? I knew nothing of your gambling.' She gave him a straight look. 'You're not going to keep those deeds are you?'

'Why not? I won them fairly. Everyone knows a gambling debt must be honoured. I've always paid mine – including the three thousand I lost to Hauxton after we quarrelled and you went away to stay with Celia.'

She felt angry because he was blaming her. 'I didn't tell you to gamble,' she said. 'What about the man who lost those deeds ... his family ... his wife and children?'

'Hauxton should have thought about that before he put the deeds on the table. One thing I never did was put up your house as security, no matter how desperate I was. And I have been desperate, Rebecca. It wasn't just the gambling – a lot of things went wrong all at once. Besides, he's rich enough to stand it.'

'That doesn't make it right, Aden. You should give them back – the deeds at least. Gambling is wrong.'

'He would have taken everything from me. He hates me – has for years. I've seen him scoop a pot of ten thousand pounds without blinking. I need those deeds, Rebecca. With the money they fetch I can pay the bank enough to see us right.'

'But it's morally wrong, Aden. Can't you see that?'

'To hell with morality,' he said, his expression hard and unyielding, reminding her of this new facet of his character – a side of him she had never seen before. 'You care too much for what people think. If you hadn't given all that money away this wouldn't have been necessary. I did what I had to do to stop myself going under – and you played your part in that.'

'You blame me!' She was indignant. 'It wasn't me who mortgaged the land.'

'No, I'm not blaming you. You had the right to the money if you wanted it. I just wish you had told me what you meant to do so that I could have made other arrangements for the mortgage payments.'

'Perhaps if you'd told me a little more of what was happening ...' They glared at each other furiously, both aggrieved by the other's failure to understand. 'I tried to tell you what I wanted to do but you weren't listening to me.'

A pulse beat visibly in his throat. 'No, I don't suppose I was. I've had other things on my mind.'

He turned towards the door. She felt a start of alarm. Where was he going?

'Are you leaving?'

He stopped, turning back to face her with a wry grimace on his face. 'Don't worry, Rebecca. I shan't go off again. I've learned my lesson. Next time I might come back and find you've sold Five Winds and spirited yourself and the children off somewhere. I'll have lost my family, not just my house and the land.'

He seemed to be saying it was all her fault and his attitude made her hit out again. 'It was my house, remember?'

'Yes,' he said quietly, his eyes moving over her in a way that set her nerves jangling. 'You should get dressed or you might catch a chill.'

She suddenly realized that she was still wearing nothing but a damp towel. The bright colour washed into her cheeks and she clutched her flimsy covering more tightly.

Aden's eyes flickered with some unreadable emotion. 'That's one thing I am sorry about,' he said in a harsh, controlled tone. 'You needn't worry, Rebecca. It won't happen again. I give you my word.'

She stood watching as he went out and closed the door behind him. Tears stung her eyes but she refused to let them fall in case he came back and saw them. She wouldn't let him see her cry! His cold, harsh manner had made his feelings towards her quite clear.

She had been a fool to go on hoping. It was useless to go on longing for things to be as they once had been, to cling to the faint possibility of a reconciliation.

She dressed and went down for supper. Molly was just about to go home and there was no sign of Aden or the children.

'I fed them and put them to bed,' the maid told her. 'They were worn out, poor lambs. Besides, I thought they were best out of the way.' The look in her eyes warned Rebecca of what was coming. 'He's back then.'

Molly had always been on her side. She was clearly outraged at Aden's sudden reappearance with no word of warning – and no apology.

'It seems we've been worrying for nothing,' Rebecca said. 'Apparently we aren't ruined after all.'

Molly sniffed to show her disgust. 'No thanks to him,' she muttered. 'Well, I'll be off then. You'll be wanting me in the morning as usual?'

'Of course.' Rebecca smiled inwardly, amused by her expression. She seemed to have taken Aden's behaviour as a personal affront. 'I really couldn't manage without you, Molly dear.'

She perked up a little at that and went off. Somehow Molly's outrage had made Rebecca feel better about things. Perhaps Aden was right in a way – perhaps she should have trusted him more, waited a little longer before she sold the house. And yet the funny thing was that she felt happier at the farm than she had for years.

Why was that?

She moved about the kitchen, setting the table for supper and singing softly to herself. No matter how angry Aden's attitude had made her she couldn't help this feeling of relief, this burgeoning joy inside her. He was alive! He was home again. Somehow that was all that really mattered.

Molly had left a simple supper of soup and fresh bread. Rebecca laid two places then turned to the stove to serve her own supper, almost dropping the heavy pan as Aden spoke from behind her.

'If that place is for me, I shan't be needing it.'

She turned to face him, her heart jerking. He was staring at her so strangely.

'I thought you might be hungry?'

'I ate earlier. I'm going out now and I may be late. I wanted to tell you so that you didn't think I had disappeared again.'

'You're going out? Straight away?'

'I've things to sort out,' he said. 'People to see – explanations to make. Since you've put the land up for sale we might as well let some of it go but I can get a better price privately than the bank will.'

'Do you have to go this evening? I thought we might talk after supper.'

'Did you?' He looked surprised – as if he thought there was nothing to talk about.

'Don't you think you owe me the courtesy of an explanation? At least tell me where you've been and why you didn't let us know?'

'Ah.' He nodded in understanding. 'If you want me to grovel I'm afraid I don't feel much inclined to do it at the moment, Rebecca. My business is urgent. It won't wait. So, if you'll excuse me …'

'I suppose you're going to her!' The bitter words slipped out before she could stop them.

'Yes, I may call on Beth,' he said in a dangerously soft tone. 'She will have heard gossip. It is only fair to put her mind at rest – let her know I'm alive.'

'Go on then,' Rebecca said, and turned away. 'It makes no difference to me what you do.'

'Of course not.'

She curled her nails into her hands to stop herself screaming. Damn him! How could he do this to her? How could he go to that woman on the very night he had come home?

'Aden …' She turned as the door closed behind him, wanting to call him back but unable to say the words. What was the use? 'Aden … oh, Aden,' she whispered. 'Why … why?'

But she knew the answer.

29

Rebecca went to bed but did not sleep, tossing restlessly on the pillow as she lay for hours, listening for Aden to come home, but he had not returned to the house when she finally succumbed. Her last, rather hazy thoughts were to wonder if he would come at all – and if it was worth keeping up this pretence of a marriage any longer?

When she woke again the sun was shining in at the window. She could hear the cows lowing and the tinkle of bells in the yard. The milking! She must have overslept and she would be late for the milking. Throwing back the bedcovers, she jumped out of bed and began to dress hastily, then she remembered. Aden had come back. She would not be needed in the yard unless ... Had he returned from his visit to Chatteris?

She went to the window and looked out, her heart skipping a beat as she saw that he was there in the yard talking to Sid and his eldest son. She had forgotten that Sid had promised to bring the lad that morning. As she watched she saw two of their former employees come from the direction of the barn. Aden had obviously lost no time in taking more of his men back on. He must have been busy the previous evening, talking to people, sorting things out – just as he'd said when she'd accused him of going to his mistress.

Sid was laughing at something Aden had said to him and somehow that made Rebecca angry; they both looked relaxed, as if nothing had happened – as if Aden had never been away. It was like the return of the prodigal son! All a huge joke. She could imagine the grins and sly remarks amongst the men. After all those days and nights of worrying herself sick, to say nothing of the blisters on her hands!

'Just like a woman to panic,' they would all be saying. 'She should have waited for you to come back. We all knew you wouldn't let us down.'

But it hadn't been like that. Sid had been as worried as she had. They had none of them known if Aden would ever come back.

The feeling of overwhelming relief that he was safe had begun to fade and she was aware of a growing resentment. How dare he simply walk straight in and take over just as though nothing had happened? How dare he accuse her of trying to ruin him and then go off without giving her a chance to justify her actions? It was the money from the house that had saved Five Winds. He thought himself so clever because he'd won all that money at cards – but supposing he'd lost? They would have had nothing left if he had been the one to lay the deeds of his house on the table. It was just another instance of his arrogance that he should breeze in like a conquering hero.

By the time she was ready to go downstairs Rebecca had worked herself up into a temper. She was determined to have it out with Aden that morning whether he liked it or not.

He entered the kitchen at almost the same moment as she did. Immediately she sensed a change in his mood. The harsh, grave lines about his mouth had disappeared and he was whistling cheerfully, looking very much like the man she had married more than thirteen years before.

'It seems as though we'll have a settled period in the weather,' he said. 'I've been up to the top field. You've made a good job of the setting, Rebecca. I thought we should need another week or so before we got on that field but I was wrong.'

'I had very little to do with it,' she replied, her heart missing a beat as he looked at her with approval. This was the old Aden and she had missed him so much. 'You have Sid to thank for keeping this place going while you were away.'

'He did his share,' Aden agreed. 'But he couldn't have done it without you. He told me so.' There was an odd, rueful look in his eyes. 'Told me a lot of things. I hadn't realized quite how things stood. I may have been a bit hasty yesterday ...'

Was he apologizing for the unjust accusations he'd flung at her the previous evening? If so she was in no mood to listen.

'You accused me of deliberately trying to ruin you.' She lifted her head, meeting his gaze defiantly. 'Perhaps I acted in haste – but I did what I thought was best for the family in the circumstances.'

'Yes.' Aden nodded, looking thoughtful. 'I see that now. What I'm puzzled over is why ...'

He paused, glancing over his shoulder as the back door opened and Molly came in. She was carrying a jug of frothy milk and looking upset and uneasy.

'There's a ... person asking for Mr Sawle,' she said, and threw him a look of such contempt that he was startled.

'Who is it, Molly?' Rebecca asked, thinking of the man who had been so rude to her a few days earlier. Somehow she was sure they hadn't seen the last of their mysterious visitor and felt suddenly cold, as if a shadow had moved across the sun.

Molly set the jug down, hesitating before speaking. 'It's that gipsy lad,' she said at last. 'I would have sent him off, Mrs Sawle, but I think he's in some sort of trouble and ...'

'Do you mean Shima?' Rebecca asked, but she already knew the answer. Molly's face had given her away. She obviously suspected the boy was Aden's illegitimate son, though she would never say so outright.

'Shima is here – asking for me?' Aden was surprised but also concerned. He swore softly as Molly nodded. 'What makes you think he's in trouble?'

'His face is all bruised, as if he has been beaten ... and he looks half-starved to me.' Molly was upset, torn between her loyalty to Rebecca and her sympathy for a young lad in distress.

'I shall have to see him, Rebecca. He wouldn't have come here unless he was desperate.'

'Of course you must see him,' she said stiffly, and turned away.

Her emotions were in turmoil and she wasn't sure how she felt about anything at that moment. Earlier, for just one brief second, Aden's expression had made her heart leap like a giddy girl's and she had thought that perhaps there was still some hope for them – but Molly's news had shocked them both, reminding them of all the bitterness that lay between them.

'I'm sorry, Mrs Sawle,' Molly said after Aden had gone out. 'But I didn't know what to do. I couldn't just send him away – not in that state.'

'You did the right thing,' Rebecca replied stiffly. 'I'll leave you to see to things down here. I've some jobs upstairs I want to get on with.'

What she needed was a little time to herself to think things through.

*

287

Rebecca was in the kitchen when Jay came in that afternoon after school. She took one look at his bleeding face and gave a cry of alarm.

'What on earth have you been doing?' She grabbed him, holding him so that she could look at the bruises and cuts. 'Oh, Jay – you haven't been fighting again?'

'I had to,' he said, pulling away from her as she tried to wipe the blood from his mouth with her handkerchief. 'They were bullying Sorrel, pulling her hair. I tried to stop them and they turned on me – all three of them.' He grinned at her. 'But I licked them and they ran off like the cowards they were. I had to protect Sorrel.'

'Oh, that girl!' Rebecca frowned. 'It would be over her, of course.'

'Sorrel's all right. I like her.' Jay stared at her oddly. 'You're not going to get all cross again now that Father has come home, are you?'

Rebecca knew that both Jay and Fanny had greeted Aden with hugs and kisses earlier; they were happy to have him home again – as she was in her heart.

'No, I'm not going to get cross,' she said, and ruffled his hair. 'You were right to stand up for your friend. Run along now, darling. Have you see Richie anywhere?'

Jay hesitated. It was obvious he knew more than he was prepared to say. 'I think he was in with the ponies ...' He broke off as the back door opened and his elder brother came in. 'I promised I'd help Sid.' Jay went out before she could change her mind and stop him.

Rebecca saw the sullen look in Richie's eyes. 'What's wrong?' she asked. 'What has upset you?'

'Are you really going to let that gipsy stay here?'

'Your father says it's just for a while,' Rebecca said, keeping her voice light and emotionless. 'Besides, it won't make any difference to you – you'll be going back to school soon.'

He threw her a look of incredulity mixed with contempt. 'I'll never be able to ask any of my friends here if that bastard ...'

'Be quiet!' she said sharply. 'I won't have you using such language in the house.'

'That's what he is, isn't it?' Richie's mouth curved into a sneer. 'Father's son by a barmaid.'

'Stop it! That's enough,' cried Rebecca. 'I will not allow you to talk to me this way, Richie.'

'Ted Harris told me ages ago,' he went on. 'Don't pretend you don't know. You and Father quarrelled over it – that's why he found himself a fancy woman. If you had any pride you would have left him, especially after he went off last time ... but you're going to let him walk back in as though nothing had happened, aren't you?'

Richie's words stung her. He was so bitter and deliberately trying to hurt her.

'This is your father's home,' Rebecca said quietly. 'He has every right to come back if he chooses.'

'Thank goodness I'm going back to school tomorrow,' he said. 'I don't think I shall bother to come home next holidays. I can stay with friends.'

'You must do as you wish – but remember, this is your home and you will always be welcome, Richie. Both your father and I love you.'

He shot her a look of disbelief and walked off, up to his own room. She knew he would shut himself in and spend the rest of his stay reading, coming down only when he was hungry.

What had they done to their son? His bitterness had upset her. Had he learned this hardness, this coldness, from them? Wasn't it true that children were what their parents made them? She had been bitter and angry when she'd discovered that Shima was Aden's son; she had refused to listen or try to understand – so how could she blame Richie for his attitude now?

She couldn't, of course. She could only feel regret and guilt for the pain he was suffering.

Aden would have to talk to him before he went back to school. He must find a way of explaining ... of reaching his son.

Richie was different from Fanny and Jay, more vulnerable. Somehow they must show him that they loved him ... help him to fight the battle raging inside him.

'I'm sorry,' Aden said when she told him after supper that evening. 'I didn't realize Richie felt that way.' He hesitated, then met her eyes across the table. 'I know you must feel much as he does but I couldn't send him away, Rebecca. Lorenzo died some weeks ago and Shima has walked all the way here ... from somewhere down in the south of the country. Sadie attacked him and told him he wasn't one of them. He has bruises all over him, and he's so thin ...'

'You don't have to explain,' she said. 'You have every right to let him stay here.'

'He won't get under your feet,' Aden went on. 'I've told him he can sleep in the hayloft for now – and it's only until he's had a rest, decided for himself what he wants to do next.'

'You must do what you think right.' Rebecca knew she sounded stiff and awkward but was finding this difficult. It wasn't that she wanted Aden to send the lad away, just that her emotions were a tangle of hurt pride and uncertainty. 'But you will speak to Richie before he leaves? I've tried to reach him but he just shuts me out.'

'I'll drive him to the station myself. Don't worry, Rebecca. He's growing up and finding out it isn't as easy as being a child. He'll sort himself out in time.'

'Perhaps you're right.' Their eyes met once more and she longed to reach out to him, to tell him that she wanted an end to all the arguments and the anger – but the words wouldn't come. 'I think I'll go up now. Good night, Aden.'

Molly had told her that he'd slept on the sofa the previous night, and since neither he nor Rebecca had mentioned the subject, she assumed he was intending to do the same thing again.

His eyes seemed to hold an appeal for understanding and she was forced to look away in confusion. What was he asking?

'Good night, Rebecca.'

She turned away, feeling foolish. He wasn't asking anything; it was all in her mind.

She spent another restless night. When she went down to the kitchen the next morning she saw Molly outside talking to the knife grinder. He was a man of about sixty with grizzled grey hair and a lined, weather-beaten face, and had been travelling the roads for as long as anyone could remember. This particular morning he had pushed his little barrow into the yard and set the grinding stone in motion. He nodded as Rebecca went out but kept his eyes on the job. He was in his way a skilled craftsman and they had used him often in the past, keeping all their broken tools and blunt knives for his next visit.

There was of course a blacksmith in the village. Aden used him when the farm tools needed repairing, but Molly and Rebecca liked the tinker, perhaps because he brought the news from the neighbouring villages.

Rebecca had decided to pick mushrooms in the bottom field. Hawthorn clustered the hedges in veils of white blossom like a bride's coronet, and pink-tinged clouds skittered flirtatiously across the sky, promising a pleasant day.

The horses were at the far end of the field when she entered it but two of them came galloping across as they saw her, obviously thinking that she had come to feed them. Her pulses raced; she wasn't quite as nervous of them as she had been but still hadn't entirely conquered her fear and she was back through the gate before the first horse reached her.

'They won't hurt you, missus.'

She swung round at the sound of the boy's voice.

It was the gipsy lad. He must be nearly fourteen but he looked older, almost a young man, growing out of his ragged breeches and wearing a threadbare coat that had obviously belonged to an older man.

'Shima.' She felt a flicker of the old pain as she looked at him and saw her husband's eyes staring back at her. 'You startled me.'

'I ain't doin' no harm, missus.' Something in her manner must have made him uneasy. 'Mr Sawle knows I'm here. I ain't thievin', if that's what you was thinking.'

The bruises on his face had turned yellow and were beginning to heal, but Rebecca knew he must have been savagely beaten.

'Who hit you?'

'Lorenzo did some of it … Sadie had a go at me when she sent me off … it ain't nothin', missus. I've had worse many a time.'

'Sadie?' Rebecca tried to remember what Aden had told her. 'She's your step-mother, isn't she?'

'Yes … she don't want me around no more.' There was a flicker of something that might have been grief in his dark eyes. 'Lorenzo … died … and Sadie told me to come here.'

'Did she say why?'

He shook his head, avoiding her eyes for a moment, almost as if he was afraid to reveal his thoughts.

Sadie must know the secret of his birth. Had Dotty told her? That was something they would never know.

Rebecca looked at the youth, feeling the pull of those eyes. He was so much like her husband that it was painful to look at him.

'I can work, missus. Don't want nuffing but a place to sleep and a bite to eat.' Shima shuffled his worn boots on the ground, his hands tucked into his trouser pockets defensively. It made the ridiculous trousers shrink further to reveal a glimpse of bare ankles. He didn't even have a pair of socks and somehow that touched Rebecca more than all the rest.

He was Aden's son. His son by another woman! That would always hurt but she couldn't find it in her heart to resent him any more. He was after all only a few months older than Richie. Still a child despite his size and his air of bravado.

'Here – you can pick some mushrooms for me.' She handed him her basket, watching as he went into the field and patted the horses, before sending them off so that she could follow him. 'You're very good with horses. You like them, don't you?'

His face lit up in an eager grin. 'Yes, missus.'

'We need help,' Rebecca said. 'You should ask Mr Sawle if he will let you look after the horses – water them, feed them, groom them, take them to the blacksmith when they need shoeing. And help the horsekeeper with the tackle. Can you do all that?'

'Easy. Ain't a horse born I can't handle, missus.'

His cheeky grin made her smile despite herself. 'Indeed,' she said. 'Well, we shall see. One thing …'

'Yes, missus?'

'If you want to work here you will call me "Mrs Sawle". Do you understand?'

'Yes, mis … Mrs Sawle.'

'I'll find you some clean clothes and you can put yourself under the pump. Molly will give you soap and towels. Cleanliness is next to godliness, Shima. Remember that, please.' She pointed to a plump mushroom. 'Don't miss that one. You did hear what I said about washing, didn't you?'

'Yes, Mrs Sawle.'

'Aden fed you yesterday – are you hungry now?' He nodded vigorously and grinned again. Rebecca drew a deep breath; there would be no going back on her decision once it was made but she might as well do the thing properly now she had started. 'In future you can come to the kitchen for your meals – but wash your hands and face first. And scrape your boots outside the door. Molly will be very cross if you tramp mud all over her clean floor.'

'Yes, Mrs Sawle.'

He stood there grinning as Rebecca left him and walked back to the kitchen, wondering what had got into her. Had she actually told Dotty's son that he could go on living and working at Five Winds?

Well, it was done now. It wouldn't always be easy but she knew it was something she'd had to do – perhaps the only thing she could do if she wanted to put an end to all the bitterness.

30

Rebecca stood waving as Aden drove out of the yard with Richie beside him. Before he left, her son had kissed her cheek and apologized sheepishly for his behaviour the previous day.

'I'm sorry I was stupid,' he said. 'Of course I'll come home this summer.'

She smiled and hugged him, then glanced up at Aden. He must have said something special to work this minor miracle.

'Take care of yourself, Richie,' said Rebecca as he climbed up into the trap. 'Try to remember that I do love you. I always have – even if I didn't always show it.'

Aden shot her an odd look but said nothing, merely giving the reins a little shake to get the pony going. Rebecca felt the sting of tears in her eyes but blinked them away.

She was behaving like a lovesick girl – and she had work to do!

She came out of the dairy later that afternoon to find she had a visitor. Stuart Monroe was talking to Molly at the kitchen door. He turned to look at her as she walked towards them, seeming surprised. She was immediately aware of her dishevelled appearance and put up her hand to tidy her hair.

'I'm sorry if I've kept you waiting,' she apologized, feeling awkward. 'If I'd known you were coming I would have been decently dressed.'

'You look … perfect,' he said, his eyes moving over her with approval. 'A charming dairymaid.'

'Not by choice,' she replied, and found herself blushing. 'Believe me, Mr Monroe, there's nothing romantic about getting up at the crack of dawn to milk cows. I am more than happy to relinquish the chore now that we are getting back to normal.'

'Ah, yes, I'd heard that Mr Sawle was home. I hope he is quite well?' His manner and tone showed clearly that he did not approve of the way Aden had behaved.

'Quite well, thank you. Won't you come in? I'm sure Molly has the kettle on. Perhaps you would wait while I change – unless you are in a hurry?'

'I have time. You look charming, but if you wish to change …' He gave a slight shrug of the shoulders.

He was as always dressed very correctly in a dark frock-coat, plain black waistcoat and a white shirt with a starched collar; his fair hair was slicked down with a light oil that smelt faintly of perfume and he wore a gold watch and fob tucked into the waistcoat pocket. His shoes were black and well polished. Aden always wore brown boots, unless it was for a special occasion. Black shoes were too smart for country wear and not practical for a farmyard. Mr Monroe had collected a little mud on his, which he had not thought to scrape off, and Molly looked darkly at the trail across her clean floor.

Rebecca left him to her housekeeper's care and hurried upstairs. She knew that she must look untidy and she would feel better for a quick wash and a clean gown – but she did not want to keep her visitor longer than necessary.

Molly had given him tea and left him alone in the parlour. He stood up as Rebecca came to join him, waiting until she sat down on a little button-back chair by the fire before taking a seat on the sofa.

'I am pleased to say I have good news for you, Mrs Sawle.'

'Everything is settled then?'

'Yes, and I think you will be satisfied with the results. You will have fifteen hundred pounds when the accounts have all been settled. It isn't a great deal when one considers what you have lost but …'

'It is more than I had hoped for,' she said. 'I can't thank you enough for all you have done. This will at least enable me to keep Richie at school for several years.'

'The brooch fetched five hundred guineas,' he went on, his eyes not quite meeting hers for some reason. 'It was as I had thought in the Italian School but unfortunately not as old as I'd imagined – a copy of a much older, very valuable piece, I'm afraid. I had hoped it might fetch three times what it did.'

'I am quite content,' she assured him. 'Now, let me be quite certain, Mr Monroe. We have no more debts, at the bank or anywhere else – apart from the mortgages on the land, of course?'

'You can rest easy in your mind, Mrs Sawle. All your bills are settled. When all the land and property is sold you may find there is a small sum left over but I'm afraid that much of it may well be swallowed up by various charges. But this fifteen hundred pounds is all yours. I've seen to that personally.'

'I shall ask you to invest it in a trust fund for Richie's fees,' she said. 'But we may not have to sell all the land after all. It seems that Aden was able to raise some of the money he needs.'

'Indeed? That was fortunate.' Rebecca saw that he was less than pleased at the news, as if he had hoped for something very different. 'However, I find it is always best to live within one's means. I trust that you will never find yourself in a similar situation again.' He gathered his papers. 'And now I really must be on my way. I have another appointment.'

'You were kind to come out of your way.' She held her hand out to him and he hesitated then took it, holding it more tightly than was necessary, his eyes a little too bright, too admiring.

'It was a pleasure, Mrs Sawle. If I can ever be of service to you again ...' He raised her hand to his lips, kissing it fervently. 'You know – you must know how I feel about you? About the disgraceful way you have been treated in all this ...'

She tried to remove her hand but he held on to it. 'Please ... please, Mr Monroe ...'

'You must know,' he said hoarsely. 'You must know I care for ... would feel myself privileged to care for you always.' There was a hint of desperation in his eyes and she thought he was about to reach out for her, to take her into his arms. 'Rebecca ...'

At that moment the door opened and Aden walked in. Stuart Monroe looked like a startled rabbit and dropped her hand as if he had been stung. His manner was so guilty that Aden could not fail to be aware of it. His brows lowered as he looked at them, obviously suspecting the worst.

'Mr Monroe,' he said. 'I was going to call on you later this week. I have some business to discuss with you.' Aden looked at Rebecca with narrowed eyes. 'You didn't mention that Mr Monroe was coming, did you?'

'I – I didn't know.' There was anger in Aden's eyes ... jealousy.

'Mrs Sawle asked me to handle the sale of her property for her,'

Mr Monroe said awkwardly. 'I came to tell her that the transaction had been successfully completed.'

There was a heavy silence as they looked at one other with dislike, then Rebecca said, 'I'll walk to the gate with you, sir.'

'Yes, thank you. I must get on.'

They went out into the yard, walking as far as the gate in silence, then Stuart Monroe cleared his throat.

He was embarrassed and Rebecca spoke first. 'It was so kind of you to come – and with such good news.'

'Forgive me,' he muttered in a choked voice. 'Just now ... that was unforgivable ... unprofessional.'

'And flattering,' she said. 'What a very nice automobile you have, Mr Monroe. It was extremely good of you to come.'

He looked relieved, then nodded, accepting her decision to let the incident pass. She stood back and watched as he swung the starting handle then jumped into the motor car and drove away. The noise of the engine disturbed the stillness of the soft spring morning, scattering a flock of sparrows and scaring the life out of the farm cat.

Walking back to the house Rebecca smiled to herself. Fifteen hundred pounds! She need not worry about Richie's education in future.

'What are you looking so pleased about?'

The accusation in Aden's voice wiped the smile from her face. He was standing in the parlour doorway, glaring at her suspiciously.

'Why didn't you tell me Monroe was coming? Or perhaps that's why you wanted me to take Richie to the station – so that I was conveniently out of the way?'

'I had no idea he was coming today.'

'Of course not.' His voice was laced with sarcasm, stinging her to a sharp retort.

'If you'd had more time to talk to me, I would have told you about Mr Monroe's offering to help me. We have fifteen hundred pounds left from the sale of the furniture, Aden. Enough to pay Richie's fees for as long as he's at school and more.'

'Where did that come from? It's more than the silver was worth.' His eyes were bright with suspicion. 'We don't need charity.'

'It isn't charity. I sold some jewellery.'

'What jewellery? You would never let me give you anything worthwhile.'

'The brooch Celia gave me.'

'You mean the brooch Victor gave you?' His lips had gone white with temper.

'It was from both of them.'

He was so angry, so suspicious! She saw his fists clench, as though he wanted to strike her.

'I won't take his money.'

'It's for Richie, not you. Don't be such a fool, Aden. Victor is dead. You can't be jealous of him now – it was all so long ago.'

'I wasn't thinking of ...'

He broke off as there was a knock at the door and then Shima came in. He was wearing a pair of Aden's trousers that Rebecca had cut down for him and a jacket Aden hadn't been able to get into for years; he was also much cleaner than he had been when he arrived and had on some knitted socks to keep his feet warm. The change in his appearance was remarkable; he now looked more like his father than ever – a typical farmer's son in his working clothes.

'Sid sent me,' he said, cheerfully oblivious to the expression on Aden's face. 'The mare's about to pop her foal if ...' He suddenly noticed Aden's frown and faltered. 'It was Mrs Sawle I wanted to see, sir.'

'I asked him to let me know when the foal was about to be born,' Rebecca said. 'I'm busy at the moment, Shima. Go back to Sid, please.'

'You come and see the foal born,' he urged. 'You won't never be afeared of horses no more, missus ... Mrs Sawle.'

'Yes, I shall – in a moment. Run along now.'

There was silence after he had gone, then Aden raised his brows at her. 'Did you give him those clothes?'

'Of course. His own were disgusting rags.'

'And you suggested that he should ask me about working with the horses?'

'It seems he likes them.'

The expression in his eyes was so intense that she could not meet them. 'Why, Rebecca? Why did you do that?'

'He's your son, Aden.' Her heart was behaving so oddly that she could scarcely breathe. 'Excuse me, I must go or the mare will have her foal and I shan't be there to see it ...'

As she made a hurried escape she thought she heard Aden laugh but wasn't sure. It might have been a snort of disgust. He had been very angry until Shima came in.

There was no time to think about it in the musky warmth of the stable. Shima put a finger to his lips as she crept in to watch the tiny miracle unfold. She had arrived just in time to see the mare snort and roll her eyes as the birth sac came out of her with a little whoosh.

'Steady lass,' Shima crooned and stroked her neck. 'Tha's a clever lass ... steady now ... 'tis done ... 'tis done.'

Between them Sid and Shima did all that was necessary for the mare and then she took over, licking away the membrane until the foal was clean, its body hair standing up in little tufts as it lay helplessly against its mother.

The minutes ticked by but Rebecca did not notice the passing of time. It was a wonderful moment, something she felt privileged to share ... the bonding of mare and foal. Somewhere deep inside her she felt the ache of loss. She had never held her little Celia in her arms, never seen her face or kissed her.

'She'll make him stand now,' Shima whispered. 'Watch this, missus.'

'What is it?' she asked. 'A filly or ...'

'A colt, missus,' he said and grinned. 'See, she'll make it stand now.'

They watched as the foal was made to stand; its struggle to make those gawky legs straighten and hold steady was both comical and moving. Several times it fell, but then, finally, it was steady enough to stand and nuzzle at the mare's full teats.

'She'll suckle him now,' whispered Shima. 'Watch this, missus.'

The mare nudged at the foal with her nose, encouraging it to suckle at her teats. Rebecca watched in fascination as the creamy milk spread over its mouth and it swallowed greedily.

'He'll do now,' Sid said with satisfaction. 'He's a right pretty little thing and all.'

'Well, I must get on,' Rebecca said, her throat tight with emotion. 'I can't stand here all day ...'

She walked from the stable before the tears could fall. The day had flown away and Molly would have the dinner ready soon. What with Stuart Monroe's visit and the excitement of the foal being born, she was way behind with her chores.

When she went into the kitchen there was no sign of Aden. He had obviously gone out again and with the children due home from school at any moment the chance for a private talk had gone.

*

It was the next morning when Aden came into the kitchen dressed in his best tweed suit; his boots were highly polished, his collar starched and there was a clean handkerchief tucked into his top pocket.

'Where are you going?'

'I've business in Chatteris.'

'In Chatteris?' Her heart sank. He must be going to see her. 'I see ...'

She turned away, not wanting him to notice the pain in her eyes, but he caught her wrist, his fingers digging into her flesh as he held her.

'Don't look like that, Rebecca. It isn't what you think.'

'Isn't it?' She gazed up at him accusingly. 'You are going to her, aren't you?'

'That's over. It was over when I bought her the house – that was my reason for giving it to her. I did call on her the other evening but only as a courtesy.'

Rebecca stood as if turned to stone. He was telling her that his affair had been finished even before he went away ... before he came to her room that night. She wanted so much to believe him, but how could she when he had lied to her so many times?

His grip tightened, making her gasp. 'Please let go. You're hurting me.'

'I'm sorry if I've hurt you.' He eased his grip but did not let her go. 'Sorry for so many things.'

'Aden ...' She gazed up at him, her eyes bright with tears. 'Do you have to go?'

'Trust me, Rebecca. Please. Just this once. I have things to settle but then ...' She gazed up at him, trying to read his mind but failing. His eyes were so dark ... full of a deep emotion she could not ... dare not believe. 'You must believe me, it's over with Beth.'

Her head went up on a surge of pride. 'I'm not asking you to love me, Aden, but don't shame me like that, not again. Don't hurt me ...'

'Did it hurt you, Rebecca? Really hurt?'

The soft, gentle tone of his voice almost overcame her. 'Of course it hurt,' she said. 'You must have known that.'

'I thought ... but it seems I was wrong.'

'What did you think?'

He looked grim but would not answer as he let go of her wrist.

'I've things to do, Rebecca. Things to put right. We'll talk this evening, when I come back.'

She turned away as he went out. What kind of things? she wanted to ask but didn't. She could only pray that he meant it when he said his affair was over.

Aden was thoughtful as he drove the pony at a spanking pace along the straight, narrow road. He had been out of his mind with grief and shame when he'd left the house that night ... suffering from such a deep, searing shame that he had not cared whether he lived or died. He could never hope for forgiveness for what he had done to Rebecca ... nor could he forgive himself. If she were to have a child as a result of his selfish act ... if she died giving birth to a child she could not want ...

He could recall little of the first few days after he left her lying there with her face hidden in the pillows. He remembered getting on a train in the morning ... then walking round the streets of a city ... he couldn't remember where. He'd had a hip flask of whisky with him and had bought more when he needed it.

His first real memory of those lost days was when he found himself sitting on a park bench staring at a young woman walking with her children ... and then he had wept bitter, painful, healing tears.

He'd been too ashamed to go home at once, even though he knew he would have to eventually; he would have to face Rebecca and the consequences of his folly sometime, but not yet, not until he'd sorted out his thoughts – come to terms with his guilt.

For the first time in days he'd felt hungry and aware of himself. He'd gone to a public baths, had a shave, bought a new shirt and had his clothes pressed, then looked for somewhere to stay for the night. As he'd walked into the smoking room of a small private hotel he'd seen the men playing cards. He'd been about to turn away when one of them called out to him and Aden realized he knew him slightly – they had played poker together once at Joshua Hauxton's house.

'Sit in with us,' he was invited. 'We're playing for a mere five guineas a hand.'

Aden felt in his pocket and took out a handful of coins ... money he'd won that last night in Chatteris before he'd gone home and ... But he couldn't think about that, not yet.

300

He'd been reluctant to play but something – some deep instinct – carried him forward and he'd sat down with the men, most of them strangers to him.

'Maybe just a couple of hands,' he'd said. 'I don't have much cash with me at the moment.'

Three hours later he had risen from the table with five hundred pounds in his pocket. Five hundred pounds ... it was enough to see him through for a few weeks.

'You must come and stay with me,' one of the men was saying. 'We're going down to Newmarket. Do you fancy your chances, Sawle? I've got a nag running.'

'Never been much of a one for racing.' Aden had been on the verge of refusing, then realized it was what he needed. A place to stay, time to think about what he was going to do. 'But I suppose I should give you a chance to get your money back, Orpington.'

Aden brought his thoughts back to the present as he drove into Chatteris. He had business to settle, then he was going to have to face up to it at last. He'd been putting it off for days but it was time to speak out – to see how things stood. He couldn't blame Rebecca if she didn't want anything to do with him, but he'd had such a strange feeling ... It must have been a week or so earlier: it had been as if she were in the room with him ... begging him to come home to her and the children.

The feeling had been so strong that he had really believed she wanted him back. But now, after seeing her with Stuart Monroe, he wasn't so sure. Monroe was educuated, successful, the kind of man she ought to have married in the first place.

31

Rebecca watered the aspidistra in the parlour; its leaves had begun to hang limply and it looked sad, and neglected. She sighed, then plumped up some cushions and straightened the anti-macassars on the sofa; she had spent the morning polishing and tidying but still felt restless and was pleased when Molly told her that Nan was coming through the yard.

'I'm so glad to see you,' she said, and kissed her friend. 'Come and have a cup of tea. I was just about to make one.'

'It's time you started to come to the meetings at the church hall again,' Nan said as she sat down. 'I know you've had your hands full with the move and everything, but now that Aden is home ...'

'I'm not needed in the yard now,' Rebecca agreed. 'Though they may want a hand when the haymaking starts; it all depends whether we get settled weather or not.' She laughed as Nan pulled a face. 'I suppose I could lend a hand with the summer fête.'

'We need you,' said her friend, 'and I'm not just saying that. You organize everything so much more efficiently than anyone else.'

'Are you implying that I'm just the tiniest bit autocratic?' Rebecca looked at her with affection. Nan was wearing a green-striped gown and a jaunty straw boater with a matching ribbon – and she didn't look old enough to be the mother of two strapping sons.

Nan chuckled mischievously. 'Would I dare? Let's just say you have a talent for leadership, something that has been sadly lacking these past few weeks. Everyone will be glad to see you back, Rebecca. Besides, no one can make seed cake like you, and you know how partial I am to a slice of that – or even two. Please say you will come?'

Rebecca stood up and moved about the room restlessly. She fiddled with the cluster of photograph frames on the top of the piano as she studied the pictures: Aden in his best suit looking very stern; Fanny in a pretty dress with her frilly pantaloons showing; the boys looking unusually scrubbed and tidy for the occasion – and Rebecca herself in a formal pose with her hair scraped back in a tight knot and a frown on her face. All the photographs had been taken in the parlour of the big house. On the mantelpiece was a set of much earlier pictures, taken soon after her first child was born: Aden in his working clothes, looking young and eager, Rebecca in a pale summer gown with her hair escaping in fine wisps about her face and Richie in her arms.

The pictures told the story of her life more vividly than any words. She felt she was at a crossroads – she could choose one path or the other. She knew there had been gossip in the village. Aden had risen high and there were always those who were glad to see a man fall, as if by becoming successful he had done something wrong and deserved to be brought down. But she wouldn't let that worry her too much. She hadn't let the scandal of her father's murder drive her away and nor would the loss of a few hundred acres of land and a big house.

She turned to Nan. 'I'll help when I can but the land comes first,' she said, and Nan had to be content with that.

After she had gone Rebecca opened the letter which had arrived earlier that afternoon. It was from Celia and she had delayed opening it, because she had a good idea of what was in it.

'My dearest Rebecca,' she had written. 'It seems ages since we've seen each other. Your letter was waiting for me when I returned from my last trip to Geneva and I'm sorry to hear your distressing news, but I'm sure Aden will soon sort everything out when he comes home. He has always seemed such a strong man to me, not like my poor Victor. I was hoping that you and Fanny might come to stay with me for a few weeks this summer …'

Rebecca folded the letter and put it on the dresser, tucking it behind the large soup tureen. She would answer it later. Celia could come to them if she wanted to see them. Rebecca would be too busy for visiting.

She turned, glancing out of the window as she heard the rattle of wheels and Aden brought the trap into the yard.

Shima ran to greet him and they stood talking for a moment or two before the lad led the pony away and Aden walked towards the house. Rebecca went to the stove, busying herself with the pots, keeping her back towards him as he came in.

'That smells delicious,' he said. 'I'm starving.'

'It's steak and kidney pudding,' she said, without turning round. 'Do you want a cup of tea now or …'

'Leave all that for a moment. Please, Rebecca. Come and sit down. I want to talk to you.'

The serious tone of his voice made her heart jerk with fright. She went to sit at the table, folding her hands in her lap to stop them shaking. Was he about to tell her that he wanted their marriage legally ended?

'Don't look like that,' he said in a husky voice. 'I know things haven't been right between us but I want to try and sort it out – if you'll let me?'

'I'm listening …'

'I know I've hurt you,' he said. 'I know I haven't done right by you – and I know I have no reason to expect anything from you.'

'We hurt each other, Aden.'

'Yes, that's true. Please believe me, Rebecca. This isn't easy …'

'I'm still listening.'

'I want to make it up to you if I can. It will take time to get everything back …'

'All I want is for things to be as they were when we got married.'

'Do you mean that?' He looked at her so intently that she dropped her gaze. 'Please look at me, Rebecca. Let me see your eyes. You've always had lovely eyes – so honest and brave. I always knew when you were hiding something.'

She brought her eyes up to meet his. 'The big house doesn't matter,' she said. 'The children matter … you matter. I couldn't stand living the way we were before you left. It wasn't a marriage at all. If you continue to see her …'

'I swear I won't,' he said swiftly. 'That's over, Rebecca. I bought Beth the house to finish it decently. It only began because … I knew you didn't want me.'

'I was angry after I first saw Shima. Angry and hurt – and I was carrying Celia.' Her voice caught on a sob. 'You know what I'm like when I'm pregnant – not fit to be with. I can't help it, Aden. I just feel so wretched for months and …' She sighed deeply. 'I know we argued but …'

'That was a part of it, but not all. The doctor told me there must be no more children, and when you wouldn't see me afterwards ...'

'Wouldn't see you?' She stared at him blankly, then nodded. 'Oh, yes, I remember. I was so tired, Aden, and they had just told me I could never have ...' She suddenly realized what he had said a moment or so earlier. 'I can't have children anymore. It's not that I mustn't – it's impossible. Something they did when they took poor little Celia away.'

'Are you sure?' He looked puzzled, uncertain. 'I thought they were telling me we had to stop ... I was in such a state. I thought you were dying, that it was my fault ... that you hated me.'

'I've never hated you, Aden. Even when you hurt me by going to her. I may have said it in the heat of the moment, but I never meant it.'

'Didn't you? You certainly convinced me.'

Her heart caught as she saw the pain in his eyes.

'I didn't mean any of the bad things, Aden. I said them because I was hurting so terribly inside. I sent you away but I regretted it. I wanted you back. I've missed you and I want us to be as we were – if that isn't asking for the impossible?'

'We can try,' he said. 'See how it goes, take things easy for a while.'

He was being cautious. She wanted him to sweep her up in his arms and carry her upstairs as he would have done once, but perhaps he was right. Perhaps it was best to go slowly. At least they were talking, listening to each other.

'Yes, that's best,' she agreed.

'This is the reason I went to Chatteris.' He laid a bundle of documents on the table. 'Beth was keeping them for me. I took them out of the bank when things started to go wrong and I realized they might have to foreclose on us.'

'That was my fault. I should have asked you. I shouldn't have taken all that money without telling you, discussing it ...'

'I might have staved it off for a while if you hadn't drawn that money,' Aden said, 'but you had every right to it – and the trouble was coming anyway. I'd been a fool, dabbling in things I didn't know enough about. I should have stuck to the land. I've learned my lesson the hard way. Once these shares are sold I'll never buy another.'

'I thought they were worthless? That's what they told me at the bank.'

'Some are, or nearly.' Aden tossed several bundles to one side. 'Those might as well go on the fire, that's all they're good for.'

'Keep them in case. Remember Sarah's shares.'

Aden looked rueful. 'You might as well know the whole truth. Sarah's shares were worth less than a hundred pounds – I bought that land in Sutton with the gold I found in Frank's kitchen. I hadn't been able to bring myself to spend it, but it took all I could scrape up to build the house and I'd promised to buy the land …'

'Oh, Aden.' She'd suspected that some of Frank's money had been used for the house and was glad that now it had gone. 'Well, at least you've told me. No more lies, Aden, please. No matter what happens … no more lies.'

'I give you my word.' He looked thoughtful. 'I suppose it was Sarah's shares that started me off. I thought it was an easy way to make money and I was lucky a few times, made a lot of gains fast – then I made some mistakes. I should have cut my losses but I couldn't seem to stop. I kept thinking I had to get it all back for you … that perhaps things would be right again if I could just …'

'It doesn't matter, Aden. None of it matters. We'll start again.'

'I'll get you another house somehow.'

'All we need is this house – and the land. We have to hold the land, Aden, for our children.'

'I think we can raise something like a thousand – perhaps twelve hundred pounds from these,' he said, handing her three bundles of documents tied up with red ribbon. 'You take them, Rebecca. Give them to Monroe. Let him invest the money for you.'

'No. You sell them. Use the money to buy back some of our land.'

'I let you down before.' He sounded so unsure, so unlike himself.

'But you won't next time.' She shook her head as she heard voices at the door. 'Leave it for now, Aden. The children are home.'

'Rebecca … won't you take these?'

'No. You sell them. Buy back our land, Aden. Buy it for all of us.'

She left him to gather up the papers as the back door opened and Fanny came flying in, closely followed by Jay and then Shima, who had stopped to scrape his boots at the door.

She glanced over her shoulder at Aden and smiled. He nodded as if he understood.

*

It was not until after supper, when the children had gone to bed and Molly had left, that Aden gave her the small box. She recognized it at once and looked at him in bewilderment.

'This is my brooch but ...'

'I was able to buy it back for you.'

'But why? Why did you do that, Aden?'

'Because I wanted you to have it. It is something special – something you treasure.'

'The money was for Richie's schooling.'

'I can pay for my son's school fees,' he said harshly. 'Everything is being sorted out, Rebecca. I got a good price for some of the land, better than I'd hoped – and I've sold those deeds I won at the card table. The money has already been paid in at the bank to settle the mortgages on the land we want to keep. We shall still have enough to bring in a decent living, though we shan't be as rich as we were. I can't get the house back for you, not yet – but I'll build you another one day.'

'I don't want one, Aden. I'm happy here. Honestly, It doesn't matter.'

'It matters to me.'

She realized that he was still suffering from hurt pride and decided not to press things for the moment. 'Thank you for the brooch. You were lucky to get it back.'

'Monroe had bought it himself.'

'Why should he do that?' She stared at him in surprise.

'Perhaps he intended it as a gift for someone – perhaps you, Rebecca. You must know that he's in love with you?'

'Infatuation,' she said. 'That's all it is, Aden. He'll soon get over it.'

'Perhaps,' he said, shrugged and turned away. 'Excuse me, I must go. I have some business to attend to.'

'More business?' She couldn't help the accusing note in her voice. 'This evening?'

'You just can't trust me, can you?' His mouth drew into a thin line. 'Don't bother to wait up for me, Rebecca. I shall probably be late.'

She was silent as he got up from the table and went out. Why must they always quarrel? Why was it so impossible to forget and forgive?

She went slowly upstairs, undressing by the light of her lamp then taking the pins from her hair, letting it fall about her

307

shoulders. She picked up her brush and began to stroke it through her hair, her face pale in the reflected glow from the mirror.

Why must Aden go out again this evening? She had hoped that they were beginning to sort things out, to understand each other, but now … and yet he had sworn his affair was over. He had begged her to trust him and she must try. If they were ever to be happy again, she must learn to trust him.

She heard a cry from one of the children's rooms – it was Fanny, calling for her. Dropping her brush on the dressing table, she picked up her lamp and hurried down the passage. Fanny was sitting up in bed, tears rolling down her cheeks. Rebecca set down the lamp and went to her.

'What's wrong, darling? Did you have a bad dream?'

Fanny nodded tearfully. 'A bad man was coming to get me,' she said. 'Don't let him get me, Mama. The Bogey Man eats little girls.'

'Not my little girl,' Rebecca said, and took her into her arms, inhaling the sweet, warm, fresh smell of her as she rocked her back and forth until the tears dried. 'Hush, my darling. Hush now. It was only a dream.'

'Don't leave me, Mama.'

'I'll stay with you until you sleep,' Rebecca promised, tucking her back into bed and stroking her soft hair back from her forehead. 'There's no such thing as a Bogey Man, darling.'

'Sorrel says there is … her aunt told her about him.'

'Then Sorrel is wrong and so is her aunt.' Rebecca frowned. That girl again! First Jay fighting over her and now Fanny having nightmares – she was as bad as her aunt! 'Go to sleep, darling. Mama is here.'

Fanny stared at her with huge grey eyes. 'Father won't go away again, will he?'

'No, my dearest.' Rebecca bent to kiss her. 'I promise you, your father won't go away again.'

32

When the storm broke it was sudden and unexpected, waking her with a start. Rebecca lay for a moment, shivering and wondering where she was, then she remembered.

She sat up in bed and listened for any sounds from downstairs. Had Aden come home? Was he asleep on the sofa in the parlour?

She threw back the blanket and swung her legs over the side of the bed, knowing that she would not sleep. The wind was howling outside, sounding almost evil as it tore through the trees, and she had an uneasy feeling that something was wrong – she was as bad as Fanny with her dreams of the Bogey Man! It was only the storm; storms always made her nervous, even if it was just a few rolls of thunder.

It was no use! She would never rest, not while her thoughts continued to go round and round like the ceaseless churning of a water mill. Why had Aden bought back that brooch? Was his affair really over – and was there still a chance for them?

She wanted more than a loveless pretence for the sake of the children!

This mental torment could not continue. She must talk to Aden. No matter how difficult, how painful, they must settle things between them.

She pulled on her dressing robe and crept downstairs, pausing for a moment to peep in at Jay and Fanny, both of whom were sleeping peacefully.

The curtains had not been closed in the parlour and there was enough light to show her that the sofa was empty, though a blanket and pillows told her that he had been resting there for a while.

'Aden,' she whispered. 'Where are you?'

'Here.' His voice came to her from the kitchen. 'Did I wake you?'

'No,' she replied as she walked through. 'It was the storm; they always make me restless.'

'Yes, I know. I was about to put the kettle on – will you join me?'

'I wanted to talk. We have to talk, Aden.'

'It *was* business this evening,' he said. 'Please believe me, Rebecca. I went to see Joshua Hauxton, to have something out with him – but he wasn't at home.'

'He's the man you won those deeds from, isn't he?'

'Yes. I've sold them back to the man who rightfully owns them … Joshua's cousin Keith. He was cheated out of them in a card game months ago.'

'Cheated?' She strained to see Aden's face in the half-light. 'Are you sure?'

'Quite certain. I knew Joshua had cheated several times in the past but I couldn't see how. When I was away I met someone called Toby Orpington; he told me that he had caught Hauxton cheating and how to spot it. After I left him and some other friends I'd been staying with in Newmarket, I came back to Chatteris. Hauxton had cheated me and I was determined to win it all back from him. That was the reason I accepted those deeds as his stake. I wouldn't take a man's home and his living away from him, Rebecca. I'm not that much of a rogue. Surely you know me better than that?'

'Oh, Aden …' She felt an overwhelming sense of relief. This was the man she knew and loved – sometimes reckless, a little arrogant but basically decent. 'I'm so glad.'

'Keith and I have been friends for a long time. He was desperate, Rebecca, on the verge of suicide. When I had the chance to get that estate back, I knew he would pay me what he could – not what it was worth, of course, but enough to help me out of trouble. We've helped each other and both of us have learned our lesson. Neither of us will be playing with Joshua and his cronies again.'

'I should have known,' she said, taking a step towards him. 'Forgive me, Aden. Forgive me for not trusting you more. I've learned something too …'

'Rebecca …' he said, and there was a husky throb of emotion in

310

his voice. 'I'm the one who should be asking for forgiveness.' His hand reached out to her. 'Can you forgive me? I swear ...'

What was that strange glow outside in the yard? She moved away from him as something caught her eye. There it was again ... a flickering light.

'Aden!' she cried. 'I think the barn is on fire. Look – out there!' She rushed to the window. The barn was well and truly alight but there was another light flickering near the haystack. 'I think someone is out there ...'

'It's probably Shima ... My God!'

They stared at each other in dismay.

'Shima! Shima sleeps in the hayloft ...'

Aden was already wrestling with the back door latch. The wind tore at the door as he opened it, almost snatching it from his grasp. Rebecca's feet were bare but she did not even notice as she followed him outside, the wind catching at her, whipping through her thin robe as she shouted the youth's name.

'Shima! Shima!' she cried. One side of the old thatched barn was blazing furiously. She thought it must have been struck by lightning and so far the flames seemed to be confined to one small area where the bolt had hit. 'Oh God! Wake up, child. Shima ...'

'Get back inside, Rebecca,' Aden shouted. 'It's catching fast. That thing is like a tinderbox – the whole damned barn will go up at any minute.'

'We've got to get him.' She was close to hysteria. 'We should never have let him sleep there ...' She would never forgive herself if anything happened to the boy. He was Aden's son ... his son!

Aden didn't answer her as he raced towards the barn. Thunder cracked overhead and she could hear the mare's sharp whinney of fear from the stables. Aden was wrestling with the barn door ... he was inside now but flames were racing along the top of the roof and part of it looked as if it might come crashing down at any moment.

'Shima ... Shima ...' she screamed again – and then the stable door opened and a shadow came hurtling through the darkness towards her. Shima had been in with the mare and foal. He was safe but Aden ... 'Aden! Aden, he's safe ...' called Rebecca and ran towards the barn. 'Aden ... Aden, come back. Shima's here. He's safe ...'

'I'm here, Mr Sawle,' Shima added his cries to hers, then slipped past her into the barn. The smoke was thick, black and choking. It was difficult to see anything but Shima had found the ladder to the loft by instinct and went swarming up it.

'Shima – no!' she screamed despairingly as he disappeared from her view. 'Come back! Aden! Damn you! Come back both of you!'

The smoke forced her out into the night air. She picked up a bucket, dipped it in the rain barrel and started throwing water at the barn door in a vain attempt to stop the spread of the fire. It was beginning to drizzle with rain now but not enough to do any good. Where were they? She screamed their names over and over again but the wind just whipped her words away and she knew they could not hear her. Then she saw them both come staggering out of the barn, clinging to each other so that she wasn't sure who was supporting who; they were coughing and spluttering, gasping for air.

Relieved that they were safe, Rebecca threw her bucket of water over the barn and went back to the rain barrel for more. The blaze had spread across the whole of the roof and there was a hellish crack, a terrific burst of flame that shot several feet into the air, sending up a stream of hot, smouldering splinters.

'Oh, no!' Rebecca cried. 'The stables ... the mare ...'

Suddenly she was running for the stables, her bucket abandoned on the ground. All she could think of was the mare and her foal trapped inside those old buildings. If the wind carried a spark to the thatch ... She had the door open and was inside before she had even thought about what she was doing. She heard the mare snort and sensed her terror as she unlatched the door of her stall.

'Come on then, lass,' she said. 'Out you come, Rosie. You and the little one. Into the field where you'll be safe.' Rebecca could see the mare now. She was trembling with fear and reluctant to leave the warmth of the stable, but the colt nuzzled at Rebecca's hand trustingly. She grabbed hold of the tuffty mane at the back of his neck and urged him forward. He went willingly enough, driven by the sense of adventure common to all young things. 'Come on, Rosie,' she coaxed the mare. 'Look at your baby. He's not frightened. Come on, lass ... come on then ... easy does it.'

The mare snorted again, obviously alarmed by the smell of burning, but following behind them. Rebecca opened the gate to the first field and led the colt through, then gave it a little push; it set off at a run and the mare went after it. Rebecca sighed with relief, turning back to fasten the gate bolts; she screamed as someone suddenly grabbed her from behind.

312

'Be quiet,' a man's voice muttered close to her ear. 'Or it will be the worse for you.'

'Who are you?' Rebecca tried to look round but his arm was across her throat and she could hardly move.

'The man your husband robbed of a fortune.'

Rebecca's eyes swivelled towards the barn. It was engulfed by flames but she couldn't see either Aden or Shima.

'Where are they?' she asked, gasping for breath as his arm tightened across her throat. 'If you've harmed them …'

He had one arm across her neck, the other holding her arm twisted behind her. She gave a cry of pain as he yanked on it, deliberately hurting her.

'The barn was just to show him I mean business,' he growled. 'I want what belongs to me – and you're going to help me get it. If he wants you back in one piece, he'll have to pay up.'

'You fired the barn?' Rebecca had thought it was a lightning strike but as she looked at the man's profile and saw the hard, cruel set of his jaw, she knew that he had done it out of revenge. She was so angry that it lent her a new strength and she struggled violently, screaming for all she was worth. 'Aden … Aden … help me!'

Hauxton gave a jerk across her throat, cutting off her air supply so that she began to choke and gasp for air. 'Be quiet, you bitch, or I'll make you sorry! You and that cheating husband of yours.'

'Aden isn't a cheat. He won those deeds fairly – and you can't have them. He sold them to your cousin …'

Her words enraged him. He jerked at her viciously but in that same moment Rebecca bit his hand and he gave a howl of pain, releasing his hold around her neck, though retaining his grip on her arm. She swung round, struggling desperately to get free, and saw the glitter of an insane hatred in his eyes. The next moment he had grabbed her by the throat and started to shake her as if she were a rag doll.

'Then I'll have my revenge on you!'

Rebecca knew she was about to die. Hauxton had lost all sense of reason. He was obsessed with hatred – of his cousin or Aden. Perhaps both. And she was to be the sacrifice. If he could not make Aden pay one way, he would exact another kind of revenge.

His hands were crushing her windpipe. Her strong desire to survive gave her the strength to fight him for a few seconds but she was losing the contest, the breath being slowly driven from her body. Then she was suddenly aware of a rushing force and his hands were torn away from her. She was free. She stood reeling and gasping for air as the fight began between Aden and his enemy.

The sky was streaked with red and orange, and behind the two men, as they struggled and fought, the barn was a ball of raging flame. It meant that she was able to see every moment of their fierce encounter.

They were both big men, powerful men, equally matched in strength and temperament – and both driven by a terrible anger. She sensed that this clash had been building for a long time ... had been inevitable.

Shima was watching from the kitchen doorway and she shouted to him to get help but the words came out only as a rasping whisper.

'Fetch Sid Harris! Go on, Shima – get someone quickly.'

He understood her gestures if he did not hear her, darting out of the house and across the yard. Rebecca stood where she was, transfixed by fear, watching as the fight seemed to go on and on endlessly. She was alarmed as she saw Aden stumble and go down, then Hauxton flung himself on top of him and she screamed. The two men rolled over and over on the ground, punching, kicking, pounding at each other in a frenzy of hatred and bitter anger.

All at once Rebecca came to herself. How could she stop this? What could she do to help Aden?

She looked round for a weapon and noticed a spade lying against a pile of rubble. As she darted forward to snatch it up she saw that the men were on their feet again. Without considering what she was doing, she grabbed the handle of the spade, lifting it in the air as she ran towards them.

Hauxton's fist exploded into Aden's face as she reached them, sending him reeling back. She yelled with fury and struck at Hauxton's back with the spade. The blow glanced off his shoulder, rocking him for a moment but not felling him; he whirled on her with a shout of rage, grabbing for the spade. Rebecca hung on and they struggled for a moment but he was too strong and wrested it from her, then turned as Aden came back at him and the flat heel of the metal spade went crashing down on Aden's skull. He staggered backwards for several paces then slumped to the ground.

'Aden ... Aden ...' she cried shrilly. 'You've killed him! You devil, I'll see you hang for this!'

For a moment Hauxton stood there staring at her, his mouth opening in a strange, bewildered gasp as if he found it difficult to breathe. Then there was a terrific cracking sound and suddenly she saw the whole side of the barn beginning to fall, tumbling towards them in a mass of smouldering flame and smoke. She turned and ran to where Aden had fallen, grabbing his shoulders and pulling at him desperately, dragging him back, away from that wall of death. He was too heavy for her to move more than a foot or so but they were just far enough away to escape the shower of burning rubble as it fell with an almighty crash, knocking the stunned Hauxton to the ground and crushing him beneath it.

Rebecca screamed wildly. It was a terrifying nightmare ... like the cauldron of Hell. She bent over Aden, running her hands over his face and head. There was blood seeping from the wound at his temple and she was sure he was dead. Tears streamed down her cheeks as she stroked his face, then bent to kiss his eyelids and his lips. His blood was all over her – on her hands, her night clothes and her lips.

'Aden ... Aden,' she cried. 'Don't be dead, my darling. Don't die, don't leave me. I can't bear it if you leave me. I love you. I love you so much ... so much ...' She was weeping, sobbing wildly as she begged him not to leave her, over and over again.

Then she felt hands on her shoulders and looked up fearfully. Had Hauxton managed to escape that deadly inferno after all?

'It's all right,' Sid Harris said gently, lifting her to her feet. 'We'll get him inside. It's all right, Rebecca. Your friends are here now. You're safe ... it's all over ... it's all over.'

'He tried to kill me and Aden saved me,' she sobbed. 'He saved me ... now he's dead. I love him ... I love him so much. I can't bear it ... I can't ...'

'It's all right, missus.' Shima's voice made her look down, to see him bending over Aden. 'He ain't dead, missus. His eyes are opening.'

Aden's eyelids flickered and he moaned. Rebecca flung herself down beside him, taking his hand, pressing it to her cheek as he opened his eyes and looked at her.

'Aden ... thank God!' Tears were streaming down her cheeks. She didn't care. Nothing mattered to her now except that he was alive. 'I love you, Aden. I love you ...'

'Rebecca ... are you all right?' Aden shook his head and sat up in sudden awareness. 'There's blood all over you ...'

'It's your blood,' she said, and gave a choking laugh. 'I thought he had killed you.'

'Not quite.' He clung to her arm as he pulled himself upright, put a hand to his head and felt the blood. 'Where is Hauxton?'

'Under that.' She glanced at the pile of smouldering rubble and shuddered. 'He didn't move, didn't try to save himself – just stood there as if he were rooted in the ground.'

Aden drew a ragged breath, then put his arm around her shoulders. 'He brought it on himself – but I wouldn't have had that happen if I could have prevented it.'

'I know.' She gazed up at him. 'You have your faults, Aden, but you're a good man – a decent man. He said you'd cheated him at the card table but I told him you would never do that. It was when I told him you had sold the estate to his cousin that he tried to kill me.'

'He hated Keith,' Aden said. 'More than he hated me, if that's possible.' His face was pale in the eerie light. 'He must have lost all sense of reason to do this.'

'Come inside,' Rebecca urged. 'Let me bathe your head.'

'Yes, you take him into the house,' Sid said. 'We'll see to this now. Don't worry, Rebecca. The fire has started to die down. You've lost the barn but with any luck it won't spread. The rain is dampening it down.'

She had hardly noticed the rain, but now she realized it was pouring down. They were all getting soaked through.

Aden leaned on her as she helped him inside. He sat down at the kitchen table, looking white and shaken.

'That poor devil ...'

'He must have died almost at once,' she said. 'They'll do what they can but he can't have lived through it.'

Aden nodded. 'It was a terrible way to die, Rebecca. No one deserves that.'

'No.' She turned to look at Shima who was watching them anxiously. 'Go upstairs to the airing cupboard at the top of the landing, please. Bring me a clean sheet – and get some towels for yourself. You're soaked to the skin.'

'You're wetter than me, missus.'

'I suppose I am. You can bring me some towels too, please – and just peep in at the children, Shima. Fanny had a nightmare earlier and I don't want her getting upset again. If they're awake

316

they had better come down and see that everything is all right for themselves.'

Rebecca poured warm water into a bowl and carried it to the table. When Shima came back with the sheets and towels she tore off some strips to bathe Aden's wound. He winced as she wiped away the blood.

'It's a nasty cut,' she said. 'I'll bind it up for now, but you should see the doctor tomorrow.'

'Fanny was asleep,' Shima said. 'But Jay is awake. I'll go up and see if he's coming down, shall I?'

'We'll all have a hot drink,' Rebecca said, 'then you can sleep in Richie's room, Shima. You might find something of his to fit you until we can dry your own clothes.'

He nodded and went out. Rebecca finished cleaning the wound, then wrapped a clean bandage around Aden's head.

'That should hold it until the morning,' she said. 'Does it hurt very much?'

'Enough.' He pulled a face. 'I can bear it.' The intensity of his expression made her heart jerk. 'Rebecca ... just now ...'

'You should tell Shima,' she said, to cover her nervousness. 'He ought to know he's your son. You should tell him before someone else does. Has he said anything to you?'

Aden shook his head, obviously reluctant – perhaps even afraid of Shima's condemnation. 'I think he knows in his heart. He told me earlier today that he was going away. He has a friend who owns a circus and wants to join him.'

'You can't let him do that. He's only a child. You should tell him to stay here with us.'

'I can't force him to stay if he doesn't want to,' Aden replied softly. 'Anymore than I can force you to be my wife if you don't want to.' His eyes met hers, compelling her to look at him. 'Is there any hope for us?'

'Aden ...' She could feel the foolish tears smarting. 'Aden ... I love you. Just now when I thought you were dead ... I couldn't bear it.'

He stood up and moved towards her, gazing into her eyes for several seconds before reaching out to take her in his arms. A little sob escaped her but then his lips were on hers and he was kissing her – kissing her with such passion and sweetness that she clung to him, her hands going up around his neck, her fingers threading through his hair and encountering the bandage.

317

'Your poor head,' she murmured as his mouth released hers for a moment. 'My dearest love …'

'Am I your love?' He gazed down at her, the question in his eyes. 'Truly, Rebecca?'

'I was such a fool, Aden. I wanted Celia's life and so I thought I was in love with her husband – but he wasn't the man for me. He wasn't half the man you are.'

'I was so jealous of him. It tore me apart.'

'I'm sorry. Sorry I hurt you. If I could go back and start again I would … from the first moment I saw you looking up at me from the yard at The Cottrel Arms.'

'I knew it was you I loved even then,' he said, a smile beginning deep down inside him. 'I wanted you even when I went with Dotty. I was a fool to go with her in the first place. And I should have told you about her – begged you to forgive me that day instead of lying. I was afraid of losing you … and once the lies were begun it was impossible …'

'Oh, Aden …' She caught her breath on a sob. 'I was such a foolish girl. I didn't know how lucky I was until it was too late.'

'I thought you hated me – when you wouldn't see me after our little Celia died. And I knew you must never have another child …'

She touched her fingers to his lips, repeating herself so that there should be no misunderstandings between them. 'I cannot have another child, Aden. You were upset and confused at the time and did not hear what the doctors said to you. Losing Celia was terrible but when it was over I felt such relief, to know that I could be a proper wife to you without fear of conceiving – but then you didn't want me. You told me there was someone else.'

'It was for your sake,' he said throatily. 'I wanted to end it finally so that you would never let me near you again … so that I could not endanger your life …'

'Did you love me that much?' she asked, and drew an aching breath as she saw the answer in his eyes. 'And I broke my heart because you were with her … night after night.'

'No,' he said and, touched her cheek. 'Only when I was desperate … when I couldn't have stopped myself coming to you … but it was always you I wanted. Always you I loved.'

'What fools we've been.'

'I was the fool, not you.' His look was tender, as loving as it had always been. 'I'm sorry we lost the house, Rebecca, but I'll get it back for you.'

'I don't want it. No, I mean it, Aden. I'm happier here than I was in the big house. And I like to be busy – to be a working farmer's wife. All I want is for us to be as we were when we first married – and for our children to be safe and happy.'

'Are you sure?'

'I should have known that first day when I saw you,' she said as she went to the sink to empty the bloody water. 'I was a silly, spoiled girl, Aden. Now I know what I want – it's to be here with you and our children, to watch them growing, to hold on to our land … let it nourish and heal our spirits. To grow old together, with love and laughter.'

'Rebecca,' he whispered. He stood up and held out his arms. 'My brave, beautiful, wonderful Rebecca. We'll have all of it. I promise you – we'll have it all … love, laughter and tears … but it will all be good, because we're together.'

They had known bitterness and pain but that was in the past. She knew it would not always be easy; they were both stubborn and proud, both capable of making terrible mistakes, and sometimes they would quarrel … but it would not matter because they loved each other. Their love was stronger because of all they had suffered.

'Yes, we'll have it all … everything that really matters,' she said, and then she turned and walked towards him, meeting him halfway.